NORTH KOREA
DECEPTION

★ BOOK 1 IN THE DECEPTION SERIES ★

RICHARD LYNTTON

MALCHIK MEDIA

www.richardlynttonbooks.com

Published by Malchik Media

ISBNs: 978-1-7354905-0-2 (paperback)
        978-1-7354905-1-9 (hardback)
        978-1-7354905-3-3 (audiobook)
        978-1-7354905-8-8 (ebook)

Library of Congress Control Number: 2020919982

Second publication/printing.

Cover and map design by Jae Song
Interior design by Gary A. Rosenberg • thebookcouple.com
Editing by Candace Johnson • Change It Up Editing, Inc.

Thanks in advance for reading

NORTH KOREA DECEPTION

The audio book is available here:
**https://www.audible.com/pd/
North-Korea-Deception-Audiobook/B08WDWVFZQ**

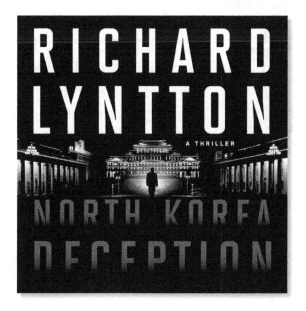

Get your FREE chapters of

HYDE PARK DECEPTION

BOOK 2 IN THE DECEPTION SERIES

Available NOW! CLICK on this BookFunnel link:
https://dl.bookfunnel.com/jjhh5hgelt

HYDE PARK DECEPTION

BOOK 2 IN THE DECEPTION SERIES

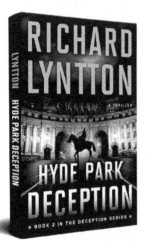

Buy NOW!
https://www.amazon.com/gp/
product/B08R7RMJQ6

Visit https://richardlynttonbooks
.com/contact for more information
and to join our FREE Reader
Regiment newsletter (click the
black *JOIN NOW* button).

Follow this link for THE DECEPTION SERIES book trailer:
https://www.youtube.com/watch?v=OUnIz_M63Nk

For Michelle Wenitsky
Lovely, amazing, *and* talented

Honi soit qui mal y pense
Evil to him who evils thinks

—Motto of The Life Guards,
Household Cavalry, British Army

Moscow

Nizhny Novgorod

Yekaterinburg

Kazan

Omsk

Krasnoy

KAZAKHSTAN

© Vemaps.com

Harbin

Changchun

CHINA

RUSSIA

Vladivostok

Chongjin

NORTH
KOREA

SEA OF JAPAN

Pyongyang

Seoul

SOUTH
KOREA

N

JAPAN

© Vamaps.com

AREA OF DETAIL

RUSSIA
РОССИЯ

CHINA
中国

Vladivostok

Tumen River

Chongjin

NORTH
KOREA
북한

SEA OF JAPAN

0   50   100

DISTANCE IN MILES

CHAPTER ONE

Khabarovsk, Russian Far East

The battered Trabant taxi faded to a speck of blue. Jack Steele's boots pounded the compact snow. He scanned the unfamiliar horizon and made his way down from the road to the frozen Amur River, scattered with white chunks of ice and snow. Its surface seemed solid enough. The river was one mile wide at this point, but Jack Steele's destination was much closer.

"Zdrazvyute!" he called. *Hello!*

No reply, though three fur-clad figures stood just thirty yards away. One of them, hopefully, was his contact, Natasha Klimova. Beyond the group, the ice plateau stretched away toward distant mountains inside China. Cloudless sky. Sun on the descent. North Korea was just a few hours south, and China lay twenty miles to the west.

The fur *shapka* of the woman he thought was Natasha had crept down over her eyes, but her doll-like face was still clearly visible. Even at a distance, she was as *kraseevaya*, striking, as the crusty old babushka at the hotel had described. Perhaps it was the contrast of mink fur against her milky skin, or perhaps it was simply that it was three months to the day since he'd seen his wife. He'd left London on a six-month assignment to Russia, but already it seemed like six years.

Odd that Natasha Klimova wasn't alone. On the telephone, it was Natasha who had insisted on meeting him in person and alone. She'd said it was a matter of life and death concerning two UN officials who had gone missing. Perhaps she didn't trust

1

foreigners? Most Russians didn't—the legacy from a century of communism and its authoritarian masters. Still, the frozen river seemed an inappropriate place to talk after flying all that way—seven time zones—for the interview.

He'd have to get her away from this group, sit her down over a Turkish coffee, or something stronger—this was Russia, after all. Take off all the fur, get comfortable, and extract her story.

Steele's slender silhouette and slightly darker complexion than the average Caucasian was a contrast to the heavier, pale locals who usually frequented the river. He crunched across the ice toward the small group.

"Zdrazvyute!" he called again.

Still no response from Natasha or the other two. They were clad from head to toe in fur and *veniki*—the Russian winter boot made of felt and insulated with rubber—and they were huddled together. Their attention focused on a hole in the ice directly in front of them. The smallest figure—possibly a young boy—appeared to be fishing.

The boy cast a line, then tripped and stumbled headfirst into the large hole. The old man, also carrying a fishing rod, lunged forward in an attempt to save the boy. He grasped the edge of the boy's overcoat but lost his footing. He slung his cumbersome wooden fishing rod away to one side, stretching out his now-free arm to maintain balance. Drenched in a thick fur coat and *shapka*, he resembled a crazed prehistoric caveman as he called on God. "Bozhe moi! Bozhe moi!"

Natasha started forward and plucked the old man back from the edge, but the boy was already in trouble in the water.

His arms flapped like a deranged duckling caught in chicken wire. It was clear he couldn't swim. The disturbingly calm look on his face flicked the adrenaline switch in Steele, who then began to sprint across the ice as he mentally calculated the seconds needed to lose his jacket, jump in, and save the child before both of them perished under the thick layer of ice.

"Move! Out of the way!"

Natasha and the old man stood aside.

Steele yanked off his jacket and boots, held his breath, and plunged into the ice hole feet first.

Every muscle tensed involuntarily. The shock of freezing water made him retch. He inhaled and exhaled to calm the convulsions and then submerged. Seconds later, numb to any sensation, he tried to get his bearings. His clothes ballooned, forcing him upward. *Wrong direction.* He struggled to force himself down and sink below the surface.

Three feet underwater, Steele wrestled one arm around the boy's torso. Spinning him, he tore off the boy's coat, grabbing his legs and pushing them upward while pumping his own legs like a frog. Kick! Kick! Drowning, given the choice, had always been his least preferred way to die.

The boy was one foot away, twisting, panicking, arms flailing. Someone had thrown in a lifeline—literally a length of fishing line that led back to the outside world. Bubbles dwindled from the mouth of the boy who hopelessly clawed at the fishing twine. Time slow marched.

Dark shadows loomed above the surface. A rescue attempt was underway, Steele presumed. He shoved the boy's feet up to the surface, but flinched suddenly from a sharp blow to his nose from the boy's boot. Steele recoiled. Around him, swirls of blood—his blood—bellowed in slow motion. His arms sliced like wild pistons, trying to stop the boy from sinking further. Bubbles danced from the boy's mouth as he drifted away into the darkness.

Steele was alone. He'd lost sight of the boy. He twisted full circle. It was dark below the ice, and he couldn't decipher where the boy had gone.

Steele kicked frantically and pulled himself upward through the ice water. He scraped in vain at the ice-vault roof, forced to take a huge gulp of freezing water. The pain seared his throat. Completely numb, his fingers bled raw from the ice formed like broken glass on the underside. The cold made him impotent.

Every attempt to move drained what little strength he had left—his adrenaline was nonexistent.

He tried to gauge his position in relation to the point of entry on the ice. *Twenty feet to the hole? Perhaps more?* Even his thoughts were numb. He wanted to swim, but his arms made zero progress, circling like wheels on a paddle steamer. Like the boy he'd tried to save, now he was and sinking and drifting away.

He could make out distorted human shapes moving around above him on the ice. A man shouted ... or was it a woman's voice? He couldn't tell. *God help me ...* On the verge of blacking out, he heard a voice inside said, *For fuck sakes, fight, damn you!* Whipping his head left and right, he made one last attempt to grasp the fishing line. The bubbles from his lungs skipped away. He looked back into the black depths of the Amur River. The boy was nowhere to be seen.

Steele felt a ripple and a splash in front of his face. An object had been thrown into the water. He kicked, and kicked again, stretching both arms toward daylight, fingers splayed, tendons stretched.

Contact.

The fisherman's line, thin as horsehair, brushed the back of his hand. The attached piece of wood spiraled toward him. He pawed at it; a kitten unable to hold its prey. His brain gave the command to grasp the wood but somehow misfired. The winter current and ruthless temperature were about to claim their prize. *No!*

Then his hand touched the line. He wrapped it three or four times around his hands and wrists, the weight of his body causing the line to cut deep into his flesh. His limbs were too numb to feel the pain or notice the blood. Tensing every muscle, he used what strength he had left to pull. *God help me. I want to live.*

He was moving now. Upward. Chips of ice nudged his cheeks; he felt the skin stretched taut from the cold. He reached up. Suddenly, warm hands gripped and pulled him upward and out of the water.

A rush of cold air lashed his hands and face as he broke the surface of the river. He saw a perfect blue sky. The air was paradise.

Safe, on his stomach on the ice, he drank his first breath for more than a minute that felt like an hour. *Thank you, God. Thank you!*

He was looking straight at the sun creeping toward the horizon. It hurt, but the piercing sunset was a tonic. He exhaled, smiled, rested on his elbows. A passing cloud blocked the light.

He looked around. No sign of Natasha.

Steele was shivering and exhausted. Someone began wrapping him in a woolen blanket. *Make me warm. Wrap tighter, damn it.* He had to stop hypothermia. *Tense, flex, tense, flex. Keep the circulation pumping.* A lesson learned on the escape-and-evasion survival course his regiment had sent him on a few weeks after his passing-out parade at the Royal Military Academy Sandhurst.

A few yards away, a faded green police Jeep idled. Its exterior blue light did a lazy pirouette. Every few seconds, the icy wind changed direction and whipped the Jeep's fumes toward him, making him nauseous. Two disheveled policemen in thick, blue greatcoats stood over him, both staring and frowning. Through the legs of one of them, Steele could make out tiny dots in the distance—presumably locals—trudging home across the ice, some pulling sleds. But no sign of the boy he had tried to rescue or the woman he had come to meet. *What the hell is going on?*

"What is your name?" The first policeman spoke in English with a heavy Russian accent.

Steele looked up, squinting, catching his breath. "Pozhalsta …" *Please…*

"What—is—yourrr—name?" The second policeman had a heavier accent than the first. He knelt down and rolled Steele over onto his back. "Kak vas a vute? Your name?"

Steele swallowed and tried to lift his head. "Steele … my name is Jack Steele."

"You'll survive." The first policeman nodded. "Eto ohn. Samai glavnoi. Nasha babushka dorogaya pravda skazala." *It's him. That's the main thing. The babushka was right.*

The policemen bent down to heave Steele's sodden frame up by his arms and drag him to the Jeep. *A setup? Damn it!* Someone inside opened the rear door. They bundled him into the back of the fur-insolated vehicle.

"Lucy in the Sky with Diamonds" blared from two small speakers mounted on brackets above the back seat. A heavy-set man sat in the back. He had fair hair and a very short US Marine-style haircut. His half-moon face was wide, and he had a pasty complexion like a peasant from the Russian steppe. The smell of his expensive leather coat said otherwise.

"Back to base?" the first policeman asked. He unfastened the brass buttons on his bulky greatcoat and settled behind the steering wheel, waiting patiently.

"Na vokzal." replied the man. *To the railway station.* "Nu poy-exali!" *Just drive.*

The Jeep sped off across the ice, slipping and sliding as it made a huge effort to accelerate up onto the road.

Jack Steele said another silent prayer: *Thank you God, but what the hell?*

CHAPTER TWO

The man sitting next to Steele in the back of the Jeep spoke English with a thick accent and dubious grammar. "My name is Ryzhakov, Igor Pavlovich, police chief of Vladivostok and Primorsky Kraj." Thin strands of saliva stretched across the side of his mouth.

They drove toward the center of Khabarovsk, the last city foreigners were allowed to visit before entering forbidden or closed territory to the East. The two policemen sat in front, and "Lucy In the Sky with Diamonds" continued to snap and crackle through the cheap speakers. The driver occasionally grappled with the steering wheel, then cursed the slippery road conditions and himself for not fitting the snow chains correctly. "Bled darog," he muttered. *Damn this road.*

"Ostarozhna!" said Ryzhakov. *Be careful.* "And kill the music. I want to talk to our guest."

The second policeman leaned forward and pressed the eject button on the battered tape player. Rocking horse people were silenced before they could eat marshmallow pies.

Ryzhakov sat cocooned in a knee-length leather coat that matched his black European synthetic snow boots. Expensive ones. Instead of the ubiquitous Russian *shapka,* a black woolen ski hat hugged his oversized head. "I ask you some questions, Mr. BBC, yes?"

Steele nodded. A feigned smile crossed his lips. "Jack Steele." *Arsehole. But, by all accounts, an important one.* He extended his numb-with-cold hand. "Ochin priyatna." *A pleasure.* "I'm worried about the boy. Is he okay?"

Ryzhakov turned away and eyed the white landscape.

Steele squirmed uncomfortably in a seat covered with blue synthetic fur. *Funky seats. But at least the heater's blasting now.*

He shivered involuntarily. "I don't work for the BBC. I'm a reporter. Print journalist. *London Daily Standard.*" A native Londoner and foreign correspondent for the *London Daily Standard*, he was following a lead. Really, it was more of a hunch. His instincts had raised the possibility that the sudden disappearance of two UN officials in the Russian Far East was more sinister and nefarious than other foreign correspondents in Moscow wanted to believe. He had no intention of trying to explain that to this imbecile police inspector or whoever he was.

The driver cursed again and sounded the horn. The Jeep swerved to avoid a sturdy old babushka, bent double, pulling a sled laden with firewood along the road with no house or dacha in sight. *Berioski*—silver birch forest—decorated the landscape left and right.

Ryzhakov broke the short silence. "Don't worry. Be happy. Ja vsyo znayou. I know everything, Mr. BBC." Ryzhakov spoke in a lyrical mix of Russian and English. "Unfortunately, you will not stay long enough to worry for the boy, or his grandfather. It is better you leave us today." He took out a leather-bound hip flask and offered it to his passenger. "Russian fuel?" He grinned, showering Steele with a vicious slap of cigarette smoke, vodka, and halitosis.

Steele's lips were cold and dry. He moved a little to alleviate the discomfort of his wet clothes. The temperature was rising, thankfully, but he couldn't stop thinking about his narrow escape from drowning. *And the boy? Was he alive or dead?*

Steele took the flask. "Spaciba, Igor Pavlovich." *Thanks.*

"You will be famous one day, Mr. BBC. But not today."

"Izvestni? Kak eto? " *Famous? How?* Steele put his lips around the flask and tasted metal. It didn't matter—anything to warm up his insides. He threw his head back and swallowed hard, relishing the welcome burning sensation in his throat and upper chest. He had often wondered how Russians could consume so much vodka, or the homemade version—*sam-a-gon*—every day, as habitually as the English drank tea. Now he too was hooked on vodka. It had become a crutch for his writing even. His articles were invariably drafted while buzzed on caffeine or alcohol, depending on his location and time of day. Both stimulants had become indispensable tools of his trade. The quantity depended on the time of day and the urgency of the deadline. The further a story was from Moscow, the more vodka he consumed with locals, and the more hungover he felt on the return flight or train journey.

This vodka wasn't as rough as he'd expected. It was smooth. Whatever dislike he'd taken to Ryzhakov, he approved of this Stolichnaya Black Label or equivalent. It was the best vodka rubles—or more likely with this goon, euros and dollars—could buy.

"We are honored to entertain an official guest of Her Majesty's government."

"You think I'm a spy?" Steele scoffed. "I'm a reporter. Print journalist, understand? Newspapers … magazines. Nothing to do with the BBC, the government, or the Queen, for that matter."

This was true now, but eight years earlier, it would have been a lie. He thought about his brother, Peter Steele, also a journalist, who had been murdered because of the story he was working on in Bosnia. *Thinking of you, brother.*

"Of course. Whatever you say." The inspector tipped his head left and right as though weighing his reply.

Steele squeezed the hem of his trousers. Wet and soggy. He needed to get back to his hotel.

"Look—I came here to interview Natasha Klimova."

Natasha's urgent tone on the telephone and the exotic location of the men's disappearance close to the Russian border with China and North Korea to the south had seized Steele's curiosity, not to mention she was the sister of an old girlfriend he had dated many years ago. Just one dynamite snippet of information about the UN officials might be his long-awaited break to score on the UK media map. Maybe even that of the world.

"Who?" asked Ryzhakov.

"Natasha Klimova, the woman at the river. Where is she? Have you arrested *her?*"

"Peace, my friend. No one is arrested. You are paranoid."

Steele flapped his collar to allow some warm air to get down his back. "What happened to the boy?" he asked for the second time.

"It is better you leave us." Ryzhakov gestured to the flask to see if Steele wanted more.

"Thank you." He took another swig. "Are you arresting *me?*"

"Why? Because you robbed an old man and tried to drown his grandson?" He pulled his hat off and stroked his cropped blonde hair with his fingertips.

"That's ridiculous." Steele suddenly noticed two dark hairs protruding from Ryzhakov's right nostril. *Uglier by the second.* "You can't be serious."

"You wish to tell me something, Mr. Steele?"

"I don't understand, Mr. *Ryzh*—"

"*Ry-zha-kov.*" He enunciated each syllable.

"You've got no reason to arrest me. I haven't done anything. The old man on the ice was there when I arrived. With Natasha and the boy. The boy fell into the water, and I tried to rescue him. He was drowning. I almost drowned as well, for crying out loud. You saw me."

"Why does the old man have a fractured jaw? Why is the boy fighting for his life in hospital?"

"What are you talking about?" Steele took a deep breath and said slowly, "I came here to meet Natasha Klimova … I'm on assignment … She contacted me a few days ago with information about a story. We were supposed to meet up at the river. When I arrived, the boy tripped and fell under the ice. I tried to save him."

"Jack. Let me explain you. There have been several attacks

on our citizens for money. We suspect those responsible are not ... *nasha* ... our people. They are outsiders—foreigners. Like you." He took back his hip flask.

"That's absurd. I only arrived this morning. On a flight from Moscow. You can check with the airport."

"These people work in gangs. They have accomplices, bosses. We must investigate all possibilities. How do you say? We do our homework."

"I'm a British journalist, not a spy or thief. Call my office in Moscow." Steele's voice rose. He wanted to hand over a business card, but remembered they were in his backpack along with his cell phone and miscellaneous electronic equipment.

"It's not important. I am releasing you. You are free. This is Putin's Russia!" Ryzhakov squeezed his bottom lip so hard that the slippery pink skin turned pale. "Let us agree, as gentlemen, that it would be best for our relationship that you leave immediately."

"What?"

"This is my order."

The Jeep bumped across another smattering of Khabarovsk potholes, partially filled with snow and ice. *Must be hell without snow.* He steadied himself on the metal frame above his seat.

The buildings had become more elegant now. The presence of grand white stucco, mixed with much plainer, more dilapidated brick structures, was an ever-present contrast between Tsarist and Communist Russia. Even though it was getting dark, bundled-up locals seemed to be doing battle with each other as well as the elements as they made their way along the slippery, snow-covered sidewalks. They shopped for a few bits and pieces before heading home—a loaf of bread, some Kvas from the popular drink stand, unappetizing vegetables or pieces of stringy meat from the butcher.

"You're asking or telling me?" Steele's voice was dull with cold and fatigue, only partially alleviated by the car heater and the alcohol from Ryzhakov's flask.

"I am telling you. Do not waste your valuable time. There is nothing for you in Khabarovsk. I promise." He lay his pudgy hand on his chest, as though the gesture would make him seem trustworthy. "And Vladivostok, as you know, is closed town for foreigners."

"*Was* a closed town. The Cold War finished more than a decade ago." Steele's nostrils flared with indignation.

"People need time to change. They do not like foreigners. Better you do not go to Vladivostok. How you say? 'Nothing personal.'" Ryzhakov glanced at his Rolex, then continued to squeeze his bottom lip. "We take you to the railway station. Rossiya leaves in fifteen minutes."

The Rossiya was the express train back to Moscow. *Wrong destination. Wrong direction.*

"Igor Pavlovich. Na Vokzal? Mozhna?" *To the railway station? Is that right?* Ryzhakov's police driver was trying keep up with the English conversation.

"Da. Davai, davai," Ryzhakov replied. *Yes. Let's go.*

"My stuff?" asked Steele, more irritated than ever. "My bag is at the hotel."

"We have your bag." The inspector reached over into the back and plucked out Steele's backpack.

My camera? A quick squeeze in the bottom told him it was still there. "Thanks. How thoughtful."

Ryzhakov stared out at the streets laden with piles of gray slush. He gently nodded to himself, humming his own made-up words to the Beatles' song playing on the tape machine. "No vorries ... Be xeppy ..."

"If I refuse?" asked Steele.

Ryzhakov flashed a smile, then, with the full force of his clenched fist, punched down his knuckles into Steele's thigh.

He winced. "Bloody hell, mate!" His body tensed with rage, but retaliation would be futile, and would probably land him in a cell.

Ryzhakov slammed his fist down again. "My order, do you understand?"

"OK, OK ... you made your point, Inspector."

★   ★   ★

Their Jeep pulled up outside Khabarovsk railway station shortly before 5:30 pm. The policemen descended from the vehicle. The driver, his faded blue *shapka* perched on the back of his head, manhandled Steele from the back of the vehicle. His partner walked around to assist. One on each side, they escorted the foreigner toward Platform One, where the daily Trans-Siberian Rossiya Express departed for Moscow. Ryzhakov, lighting a cigarette, sauntered after them a few steps behind.

Steele slung his backpack over his right shoulder. He needed to check the battery power on his international cell phone; he had not been able to charge it for a day. Better not to check it now. These brainless policemen might confiscate it. He felt the side pocket in the rear of his backpack. Cell phone unharmed. One small blessing. But there was nothing else for it ... He'd have to leave Khabarovsk. At least for now.

"I hope you find Natasha," he said. "Tell her from me, something came up."

What a colossal waste of time he didn't have. His editor had already balked at his assignment proposal and projected expenses. He needed some results before he could return to Moscow.

Steele climbed the steps of the dingy first-class train car. Each car had its own train guard, the *provodnitza*. His was an old woman who wore a shabby uniform. She greeted him with a smile carefully managed to avoid showing her decaying front teeth. She couldn't do anything about the dark bags under her eyes. Although she looked as though she should have retired long ago, she leaned down the steps and offered to take his bag. "Davai, malchik!" *Give it here, boy.*

He smiled. Most of the old women in Russia called him *malchik*. This reminded him of his Great-Uncle George, a parish priest—or vicar as they called them in England—from Tolleshunt D'Arcy, Maldon, who used the same greeting—"There's my boy!"—which he boomed as young Jack Steele and his mother stepped off the coach from London.

Steele told the *provodnitza* he could manage his own bag, thank you. He pointed to the inspector, and the inspector nodded to the train guard. *No tickets necessary for the foreigner.*

Steele walked along the corridor, picked an empty compartment, threw off his backpack, and collapsed into the seat. Beige hand-embroidered slipcovers were fitted on each headrest with the scarlet Rossiya train insignia. *They'd be stolen in five minutes on British Rail.*

Few passengers were boarding the train, fewer still were in his first-class car. A man, probably Korean, walked past his compartment, conspicuous because he didn't look inside, as if he didn't want to show his face. He was the only other person on the platform who wasn't humping luggage of some description—giant nylon holdalls, cheap plastic suitcases bound with string, or cardboard boxes similarly bound.

Steele glanced out the window at his police escort. Ryzhakov looked like a proud father about to wave good-bye to his children. The police chief took out a packet of cigarettes and glanced at his driver. The policeman driver, who was already smoking, fumbled around, eventually finding a book of matches. He struck a match, offering it to his boss and then his colleague. Three plumes of cigarette smoke swirled above their heads into the open night sky as the train pulled out. *Probably the most important assignment they've had for months.*

Bastards. He hated following orders, being *told* to do something. Sandy, his wife, had once told him that he could never work for anyone but himself. She was amazed he'd been able to handle five years of military discipline. The day he'd left the British Army, he'd promised himself never to listen to anyone who ordered him to do anything ever again. Especially not a jumped-up Russian so-called police chief. The man standing on the platform was a thug. Or worse. No wonder the former Soviet Union was such a disaster. It was great to have studied here, but the thought of living here was utterly depressing.

The train departed Khabarovsk town at twenty minutes to six. Less than a minute to reach the outskirts. The almost-deserted streets flashed by. No streetlamps, just random brush strokes of car headlights, as toy-like Trabants and Skoda's plowed their way through the snow. The cold air accentuated plumes of exhaust spewing from the cars in the fading light.

The streets merged into countryside. He thought of Sandy. He hadn't been able to talk to her in several days since he'd left Moscow on this latest assignment. She'd recently arrived in London and was staying with a girlfriend in Hampstead. He was nervous about his next conversation with her. The six-month assignment had ripped open the seams of their relationship, exposing a fragile core and a variety of problems, mainly to do with money, but perhaps more, too. Three months earlier when he'd first arrived in Moscow, he'd put their first stilted conversation down to jet lag and bad timing. He'd hoped the next one would be better. And the next. But things hadn't improved. Sandy grew distant and disinterested in his tales and descriptions of Moscow. Awkward silences dominated their conversations. *What was she really thinking?* Sandy had changed. Or was it him? What the hell had happened to the Jack-and-Sandy chemistry their friends used to envy?

They had argued about the Moscow assignment—six months in Russia, based in Moscow, with a remit to travel all over the country. This was "his chance," he had promised her. *This was it.* The opportunity he craved to launch his career. *This one's for you, Peter,* he had also promised himself in memory of his brother. When he returned to the UK, he would get a more stable position. Local. One that didn't require too much travel. They would hunt for their dream cottage in the Cotswolds. Wake up every morning next to each other to look out at the velvet-sandpaper Cotswold stone cottages and patchwork quilt of lime-green fields and blobs of sheep.

They had been married less than two years, trying for the last several months before his departure to get pregnant. Without success. Sandy's meticulously monitored temperature charts didn't seem to be working, but they both wanted a family more than anything. He also needed a decent income—and fast. Somehow, he would have to at least match the generous allowance Sandy was used to getting from her father, which stopped abruptly when Blake Danner was told of his daughter's plans to marry Steele.

He banged the window with his fist. No way he could admit to Sandy that Russia had been a waste of time. Their separation had to mean something. He had to get back to Khabarovsk. He had to nail this story. Natasha was the key. He would find her and follow all leads until he found one that lit.

He took out some dry clothes from his backpack and walked along to the WC at the end of the corridor to change. When finished, with the stench of stale urine in his nostrils—Russian trains appeared devoid of much disinfectant—he returned to his compartment, sat down, and slurped the hot sweet tea the *provodnitza* had served. Apart from being the cheapest drink in Russia at thirty kopeks, tea on Russian trains was served fit for a king. Presented in an ornate metal holder on a chased chrome tray with an elegant, lace-edged underlay.

The *provodnitza* waddled into his compartment, bursting his bubble of introspection. "Like it? Want some more?" she demanded in Russian.

"No thanks, babushka."

"Where's your woman?"

"Sorry?"

"Where's your woman?"

Ah yes, "woman" and "wife" were the same word in Russian. "She's a long way away," he replied. "In London."

"London?" The babushka was awestruck. "You're a real Englishman?"

"Yes."

"You speak very good Russian."

"Thanks." He smiled graciously.

"But you shouldn't be on your own. It's no fun all alone. Your wife shouldn't let you go so far all alone."

Steele smiled and nodded in agreement. "I'm on business."

"Business? No business here. Not in Vladivostok Kraj. No fun here, young man."

"Thanks, babushka. Don't worry, I'm not staying. I promise."

"If you need anything, just ask Tatyana Ivanovna." The babushka turned to leave. "And drink your tea while it's hot."

He nursed his glass. Small black flecks floated near the top of his tea, but it didn't matter. It was hot, and he was thankful.

The warmth of the beverage spread through his exhausted body. He used the white napkin on the tea tray to dab and clean up the cuts on his hands. For the first time since plunging into the icy water, he felt his circulation coming back, pumping through his body. Then he thought of Natasha.

He had been suspicious of Natasha's telephone call out of the blue. How had she found him? After some compliments about his articles, she explained that she was the sister of Katya Klimova, his former Russian girlfriend from St. Petersburg. Katya had been his Russian language tutor during a one-year undergraduate study program he had taken a decade before. Natasha said she had read one of his Bosnia articles on the internet and also his more recent articles about the inefficient distribution of humanitarian aid in rural Russia. She had important and unprecedented information, she had said. It would mean the most sensational news story of his career. *How many times have I heard that?*

Natasha was the key to his story. He was certain of it. Why else would the police chief eject him? He would find her, whoever she was, wherever she was. She had information about the missing UN officials. No one had investigated the story because there wasn't much to go on—no witnesses and no leads. Local police hadn't even opened a case file. Relations between UN investigators and Vladivostok police seemed nonexistent. Having made the acquaintance of Police Chief Ryzhakov, he understood why.

Damn, he was exhausted. He'd close his eyes for a minute. Then he would call Sandy.

CHAPTER THREE

A few minutes later, the train lurched forward. *Must have dozed off.* Steele was glad to be woken, albeit abruptly. Peering through the sleet-spattered window into the evening murkiness, he observed the blurred zigzag of electric light bulbs above him, their pattern in the window's reflection reminding him of the overnight train journey across Europe he'd enjoyed with Sandy two years before.

They had set off on their first official adventure. The honeymoon. They were passionately in love, free, together at last. Tucked up in a couchette traveling across Europe on the Orient Express, they were far away from Sandy's interfering father, Blake Danner, a successful hedge fund manager.

If he'd had his way, they would never have married. Danner had not only stopped Sandy's allowance, but he'd even threatened to disinherit his daughter if she married "that British guy." She was his only child, and *he* knew what was best for her. Nothing against Englishmen per se, but Steele was neither a doctor, lawyer, wealthy nor American. It followed he was not the right man for the job. *The right man for the job.* He had actually said that.

They married anyway. A small, private affair with a dozen friends that took place at St. John's picturesque, cream-colored church on Downshire Hill, Hampstead. Danner had not been invited. Jack's mother was the only blood relative in attendance. Because he had fallen out with his brother before the murder, Jack would never know if Peter would have accepted the wedding invitation.

The newlyweds made love three times on the train that night and many more times over the next few days. The Orient Express to Vienna was luxurious. Crisp, white bed linen, silver napkin holders, room service in the first-class compartment at the press of a button, English breakfast cooked to perfection, designer hand cream on every basin, and the smoothest ride of any passenger train in Europe, if not the world. And, of course, the scenery—French farmland scattered with human-sized sculptures of twirled hay too perfect to be real, and picture-postcard Austrian chalets at the feet of snow-capped mountains good enough to eat.

She had knighted him Sir Jack, her tour guide extraordinaire, and teased that she couldn't believe she'd fallen for a guy who unrepentantly sported white tennis sneakers and black socks at the same time. They visited the *Wien Staatsoper*, the *Prater Stern* Ferris wheel, and the Spanish Riding School. The ubiquitous smell of horses in the heart of Vienna's cobblestone *gasse* reminded him of his days serving as a Queen's Life Guard subaltern before the Sarajevo debacle that changed his life and his career forever. He had always obeyed other peoples' rules, regulations, and recommendations, and allowed himself to be influenced by their judgments. *The trouble is, Dicky, as an Army superior once said, "You're not as bright as you think you are."* He had followed his intellect, not his heart. He had been stationed at Hyde Park Barracks in Knightsbridge, London, escorting Her Majesty and a steady stream of foreign leaders through streets of central London on state visits as well as the daily Changing of the Queen's Life Guard at Whitehall.

In Vienna, the couple goaded each other through giant portions of Wiener schnitzel and devoured enough *Sacher torte* to last a lifetime. He developed a taste for the perfect cappuccino. In the finest cafés, coffee was served on a silver tray with a dollop of *Schlagobers*—whipped cream—and a highly polished teaspoon laid across a glass of water next to a delicately wrapped Austrian biscuit, or cookie, as Sandy would say. They gave each café marks out of ten for coffee presentation and awarded an imaginary prize to the grumpiest-looking waiter. They had the best time together.

But after the honeymoon, living in Philadelphia, it had been impossible to erase Blake Danner's shadow. There were visa complications because they had married in the UK, and Sandy's father had used his influence and connections to force them apart, even sabotaged his son-in-law's attempts to secure a work permit and the magic Social Security number that in the USA was even more important than a passport. Steele was convinced that Danner had a contact at the IRS, because despite the entitlement that came with marriage to a US citizen, his temporary green card never arrived. After two years of administrative obstacles and setbacks, which they were still working on, the couple had decided to move to London. Sandy was now visiting her girlfriend, Christine, while Steele was on assignment in Russia. Officially, she was also flat hunting for their new London apartment.

★   ★   ★

The Rossiya express train was a far cry from the Orient Express. Ornate fixtures and curtains gave an inviting first impression, but the seats were grubby, and the WC stank like the inside of a septic tank. At least this was a free ride thanks to a few nods and handshakes, and a few rubles had been slipped to the *provodnitza*.

The train finally began to pick up speed. It sliced through the sub-zero Russian steppe like an Olympic speed skater. Steele shivered, thankful at last to be warm again.

Steele checked his backpack for contents. Miraculously, everything was still in place. He took out his cell phone, scrolled down to "A1 SANDY," and hit the talk button.

"It's me." He raised his voice to compensate for the time lag. "Hello?"

"Jack? Is that you?" replied Sandy.

Her greeting was disappointing. Her tone was lackluster. He had prepared himself for friction. Her words on recent calls had been hesitant, verging on hostile, but he tried hard not to come across the same way.

"How are you?" he asked, standing for a moment to close the sliding door of his compartment.

"Fine. You?"

"I tried to save someone's life today. And someone saved mine. That's about it."

Silence.

Finally, she said, "What did you say?"

"It's a long story." He spoke louder. "I'm leaving Khabarovsk."

"Where?"

"Near Vladivostok."

"Can you hear me?"

"*Kha-bar-ovsk*. Russian Far East. Vladivostok ..."

"Sounds like another planet."

"It's not Vienna, that's for sure." He was grasping at the past ... something, anything to find that spark from the old days with a laugh-a-minute and a joke for every occasion.

"Jack. I've been thinking. I need to tell you ..." She paused.

Here it comes. She wants to finish this. He feared the worst and hated the physical and emotional distance between them. But what was the alternative? He wanted to provide for Sandy. Apart from commanding tanks—being a "trained killer, retired" he used to joke—foreign news journalism was the only thing he knew. "Go ahead. I'm listening. No, wait. Hang on ..."

The door had opened, and the *provodnitza* shuffled in again, a tray of tea in one hand. She lost her balance momentarily as the train jolted, but quickly found her feet. Not a drop spilled. Steele waved her off. "Ne nada." *No need.*

She ignored him, insisting that he must take the tea. "Nada, nada. Obyazatelno nada." He gave in. *Futile to argue with a Russian babushka.*

She set the tray down. He kept the phone clutched to one ear while he fished a five-ruble note from his pocket and put it on her tray. Anything to get her out, even if it was ten times the price of the tea. A mini reward to a Russian worker would hardly compensate for a lifetime of pitiful paychecks. She smiled gratefully, revealing her yellow teeth, then left.

Sandy's voice called him back to the cell phone. "Jack? You there?"

"I'm here."

"Look. There's no point in wasting time. I mean, this is both our lives, right?"

"Yes," he replied. His stomach tensed; he was starting to feel sick.

"Jack. This isn't going to work. I mean, us. It's not going to work, OK?"

He didn't reply, just thought about the three years they had been together.

"Jack?"

"I'm here."

"Jack. I had a miscarriage. I was pregnant." She laughed faintly. "It finally happened."

"Miscarriage?"

"It wasn't meant to be." Sandy's voice trembled.

"You had a miscarriage?" He put down the glass of tea and sat forward on the edge of his seat. "When? What happened?"

"Last Friday."

"Why didn't you tell me?"

"There was no point. It's over."

"For crying out loud," Steele said, "Sandy—"

"Jack, listen … I've been thinking about what we should do." Steele snorted at her practicality. "What?"

"I needed you, Jack, and you weren't here," she continued. "But even if you were, it wouldn't make any difference. It's over."

"Sa—Sandy," he stuttered. "You're not making sense."

"I can't stand it any longer. Not saying anything, I mean. We both deserve the best, right?"

"That's why I'm here. So we can be together eventually. That was the plan, wasn't it? That was *our* plan. You agreed."

"But when is soon, Jack? We got married two years ago, and we're still broke. Nothing's going to change that. I need more. I can't stand it anymore."

"Who do you think I'm doing this for?" His heart was thumping. He took a deep breath and exhaled sharply. "Look, just tell me. Are you all right?"

"Yes, I'm fine."

"Sandy, I love you. Tell me you don't love me. You'll never hear from me again." Steele cringed at his choice of words. It sounded like a line from a bloody soap opera. *Lord, it probably is a line from a soap opera.*

"I don't know anymore," she said.

"I'll be home soon."

"I don't want to wait. I'm sick of waiting."

"Have you met someone?"

"No. I want to be free. It's not how I imagined."

He wanted her to say it—*I don't love you,* or, *It's over, Jack*—if that's what she really meant. Typically, he was the one who couldn't express himself. She had often made him feel inadequate, unable to communicate, even emotionally inept. But he really did want their relationship to last forever. Absurdly, he had never been able to express how much he loved her.

"Look, I'm depressed," she said. "What d'ya want from me?"

"You're upset. That's normal." He paused. *Be objective. Be positive.* "I want to be with you, but I can't. I'm fifteen hours from you. I'm sorry."

Sandy had no time for apologies. She had made up her mind. "I know. I'm sorry too."

Beeps rang out in his earpiece. The signal was fading.

"I'm losing you. Sandy, I love—" He tapped the volume button on the side of his cell phone in vain. The signal died.

He slapped his cell phone shut, then opened it immediately to redial. Three failed attempts. He massaged his aching neck while going over their conversation—words, subtext, thoughts, hidden meaning, more hidden meaning, thoughts, subtext, words … Around and around in circles.

Once he thought perhaps he'd found his soul mate. In Bosnia. But that hadn't worked out either. He'd almost got himself killed as the first major European war in fifty years ignited.

Restless, ambitious, searching for the perfect career and the perfect partner, he'd blamed his other failed relationships on being raised by a single parent. He and his brother had never known their father. At least if your parents spent the whole time arguing, you knew what you *didn't* want in a relationship. A child with one parent was half a person. Then, finally, with Sandy, he thought he had found his friend and partner for life.

The door opened again. He was starting to lose patience.

"Plenty of hot liquids," the babushka lectured. She proudly described the exotic North Korean tea she offered her passengers. "Chornim!" *Black market!*

He accepted another glass. She remained in front of him in position, knees bent, offering the tray at arm's length. She nodded, signaling with her eyes that he was missing something.

A note was tucked under the sugar bowl. He picked it up.

Jack. Sorry for problems. Come to meet me in dining car.
No time. NATASHA.

No need to track Natasha down after all. She had found *him*.

Hampstead, London

In bohemian Hampstead, Sandy was not as miserable as she had made out during the conversation with Jack. But pangs of guilt gnawed away. She had lied. It was true she had felt terrible. But the cause was a yeast infection she had been nursing for the last few days, one that had lingered even after medication. Her story about the miscarriage was a lie.

She walked down the tree-lined road to her friend's flat, and wondered if she had made a huge mistake. Yes, she felt relieved, having finally told him she wanted to separate. But she didn't expect this feeling of disappointment—the same sinking feeling she had felt when her father stopped her allowance and made her choose between the money and Jack. Why couldn't she feel good about her decisions? Maybe she was wrong?

She had been wanting to tell Jack about the pregnancy for several days. The miscarriage thing was a cheap shot. Dishonest and even despicable? She had lied about the only thing that would bring significance to their relationship—they both wanted children, even if it meant adopting, they had agreed. But things had changed. She wasn't good at being alone, and Jack had been away too long.

She glanced at the small screen on her cell phone and pressed talk to redial. She would explain why she had lied about the miscarriage—because her father had carried out his threat to disinherit her after all, and she couldn't cope with the prospect of being broke. Her father had cut her off completely.

Picking her way across the uneven paving stones in Gayton Crescent, she tried to reach him again. Busy signal every time.

Number Twenty-Seven Gayton Crescent, her friend Christine's flat, was what she would call a basement apartment. Here in London, it was a two-bed garden flat. The black iron gate had squeaky hinges. She made a mental note to oil them for Christine with the can of WD-40 under the sink in the bathroom.

About to descend the steps, she glanced up and down the street for Christine's car. She was due back first thing that morning, but so far hadn't shown up. There was, however, a middle-aged man with black hair, unshaven, and wearing a red tracksuit top sitting in a white Mercedes. Christine's street was one way, and the man was studying a map. *Must be lost.*

She turned the key in the lower Chubb lock and hoped Christine would return soon. She didn't want to be alone when—

Suddenly she was knocked to her knees beneath a crushing weight.

Something, no, someone had landed on top of her. *What the fucking fuck!* Survival instincts ignited. Wrestling a half-turn, she caught a glimpse of the red top, the man from the white Mercedes. She recalled the short black hair and unshaven, chiseled jaw she had seen moments before. She could smell his cigarette breath. The attacker wore leather gloves, which he clamped across her mouth to muffle her attempts to scream. The man squeezed her upper arms with pincer-like precision. Then he enveloped her with his wrestler arms, simultaneously using his powerful hands to swat down her protests.

You are not going to rape me. Anything else I can handle. She felt a surge of power and adrenalin.

Sandy jabbed her right elbow back over her shoulder but missed her target—the bridge of his nose or an eyeball. Next, using her cell-phone antenna as a weapon, she punched rearward, aiming viciously for his face, any part of it. The antenna, though flimsy, made contact with the attacker's eyeball. It was enough to reward her with a split second of opportunity.

She managed to free herself. "Get off me! Get off!! Mother—" She tried to shout as she squeezed through the front door. Then she rammed her back, the full weight of her body, against the door, almost closing it. But something was blocking it—the gloved hand.

She turned and grasped the edge of the door with both hands, making three swift piston movements. With what seemed like enough strength to rip a telephone directory in half, she smashed the edge of the door against the attacker's grasping hand, fitting the end of the safety chain into its slot as the man's other hand pushed through the crack in the door, violently grasping for her face. She bit into his wrist.

She knew her next move. Christine and her neighbor, another young single woman, had made a pact—half-joking, half-serious—that if one of them was ever in trouble, they should escape over the garden wall to the other's back door. A key would be found under the doormat. Christine had left a key, but Sandy had no idea if the neighbor had left hers. She sprinted through the flat and flung open the back door, which lead to a small patio garden, praying she could make it over the wall in time and that the key would be waiting.

CHAPTER FOUR

Khabarovsk Krai, Russia

Steele turned left out of his compartment. The *provodnitza* waved her craggy finger to the right toward the dining car and told him his backpack would be safe. He retrieved his phone just in case and strode toward the end of the compartment, scanning Natasha's note for clues. Finding none, he folded the note and slipped it into his pocket.

Passing from one car to the next, as the train trundled across sub-zero Russia, was like walking into an industrial refrigerator. His hand slid across smooth globules of ice several inches thick that had crept through the gaps from the outside and formed on the metal housings between the cars. He tried to focus, but his mind was racing. A sudden high-pitched screech from the wheel housings set his teeth on edge. The news of Sandy's miscarriage was devastating. Getting pregnant had been their greatest wish. But he had to focus. This story could be the one—the big one. Once he found Natasha, he would flesh out the details of the missing UN officials and file his report. Then he would return to London and save his marriage. Natasha would give him hard evidence—signed, sealed, delivered in a crisp buff envelope? She would hand it over gushingly, grateful he had made the trip across Russia just to meet her. If this was the best-case scenario, what might be the worst?

He reached the dining car and entered. The lone passenger seated at the other end was almost certainly Natasha Klimova.

Apart from the waitress and a cook behind the counter, they were alone. The smell of boiled frankfurters reminded him that he hadn't eaten for hours. *Tough shit*. He had work to do.

The train suddenly picked up speed. He steadied himself on the headrests as he moved down the aisle between the tables, all the while studying the woman in front of him. Yes, it was her. Now he recognized Natasha's striking face from the brief encounter at the Amur River. She ate purple-pink borsch, delicately spooning the rich broth with one hand and nibbling a hunk of bread with the other.

"Natasha?" He stopped a few feet away.

"Privjet, Jack. How are you?" She said hello and switched easily to English, inviting him to join her. "Sit down, please." Her voice was soft and slightly husky, like that of a confirmed smoker, but her youthful complexion said otherwise.

He noted her petite hands with long fingers and unmanicured nails, an anathema in Sandy's world. Natasha wore a pale blue cardigan with delicate white flowers stitched on the bottom of the sleeves and collar. Her mink coat lay folded next to her, but she wore her tall *shapka*—the hat was also mink—while she ate. "Hungry?" she said, pointing to the battered menu.

He slid into the seat opposite. "Natasha—if that's your name—what's going on? How did you find me?" He spoke in a false whisper, casually glancing over his shoulder.

"I need to tell you something," she said, folding her napkin. "You are journalist. You know my sister. I have best story you will ever write. Understand me?"

"Not exactly. In fact, I have no clue." Steele frowned. "Tell me—"

"Don't worry, Jack. Be calm." She smiled, reassuringly. Her teeth were surprisingly white for a Russian. They complimented her perfect face, but he was already becoming skeptical about her willingness to tell him anything useful.

"I almost drowned today, and then they arrested me. I have a wife, and I'd like to see her again. Understand me?"

"You are very English. I understand why my sister fell in love with you."

"That was a long time ago. You said Katya has nothing to do with this."

"Correct. I invite you because you are competent journalist. My sister said you are intelligent and sensitive Englishman." Natasha stared intently at him, then ate a spoonful of borsch.

"Thanks."

"But we have no time."

The middle-aged waitress wearing too much mascara and lipstick arrived to clear away Natasha's empty bowl. He waited for her to retreat.

"What happened to the boy? What about the UN officials? You said you had information for me. That's why I'm here, remember?"

"Maybe they are not UN?"

"What do you mean?"

"I don't know, Jack. Anything is possible here. I explain everything. Please listen to me carefully. We are in danger."

"*We* are in danger?"

"Someone is trying to kill me. They don't want me to talk to you." She frowned, and the corners of her mouth tensed up.

Now that he was closer to her, the lines around her eyes and mouth told him she was older than he had suspected.

"Wait," she said, taking out a small black box from her pocket. It was the size of a matchbox. She switched it on and looked at her watch. "I have plan."

"What is that?"

"I planted a microphone in your compartment."

"How?"

"Train guard is my new friend." She leaned closer to him. "For protection."

"Whose protection?"

"Our protection. I knew you would come."

She glanced down at the small device, cupping her hands

around it. She focused on the LED lights flashing from red to green.

Clear reception.

A second later, they both heard short, sharp bursts of static interference from the tiny speaker followed by a loud bang. Then muffled shouting. He recognized the voice but couldn't place it. At first. Then he realized—the *provodnitza*.

"Ne nada! Ne nada!" He heard her screams through the tiny speaker. *No! Please!*

"Jack, we go now." Natasha sprang up from the table, throwing down a ten-ruble note for the waitress. "They will find us. Let's go."

"No." He too slid out of his seat, but instead of following her, he hurtled down the dining car in the opposite direction toward the old babushka two cars away.

"They will kill you," Natasha said, catching up with him then tugging at his arm. "Are you crazy?"

"Kill me? Who will kill me? Why?"

"They will kill you if they find us together."

"So, get lost." He tried to shake her loose, but she hung on.

"It's too late, Jack. It's a trick. Listen to me."

"Stay here," he ordered. "I'll take care of it." He kept moving.

"They will kill you."

The train was slowing down, chugging through the outskirts of Smidovich, the next small town seventy miles west of Khabarovsk. Steele reached the end of the car where he had left his backpack and glanced out of the window to monitor the speed of the train. If necessary, he could jump. And Natasha? Impossible to say. Either way, he would open the door manually from the inside.

He cautiously pulled open the heavy sliding door and craned his head around the corner of the end of the car to survey the scene. Broken glass glistened on the floor-runner next to his compartment. The *provodnitza* was on her knees. Her Rossiya Express *shapka* lay on the floor. Strands of gray hair hung down each side of her face. She was rocking back and forth, crying and wailing like a little girl, tightly clasping her hands and staring up into Steele's compartment. For a moment, he thought she was looking up to pray. Then he realized someone was next to her, inside the compartment.

A shadow flickered across her face. She shivered involuntarily. A trickle of blood painted a red line down the side of her cheek.

"Jack," whispered Natasha from behind him, "We must escape ... Please." Again, she tugged at his arm.

"Wait. Someone's in there." There must be a rational explanation, he thought. No one had any reason to harm the old *provodnitza* ... There must be enough male crewmembers on board to overpower a petty thief. A police patrol at the next station could make the arrest.

"Babushka!" he shouted, immediately regretting his outburst.

The attacker seized the initiative. He came out of the compartment pistol in hand. The man pointed it at him, but before he could pull the trigger, the babushka lunged at the man's leg, digging her fingernails deep into the flesh of his calf. The gunman fired at Steele but missed.

Steele had been under fire in Bosnia and the first Gulf War, but never at such close quarters. He recalled the horrifying image of his brother in the Chelsea flat several years ago. Now, relieved the first bullet had missed, he braced himself for a second bullet he knew could not be far behind. Like the first one, the second sounded like a harmless firecracker. Far from it. The *provodnitza* fell back into Steele's compartment. The back of her head was probably ripped open.

Steele's turn to seize the initiative.

"Go!" he screamed, pushing Natasha through the sliding door.

The gunman kicked aside the *provodnitza's* body and took aim. Too late.

They were halfway through into the next car. Steele glanced out the window as they sprinted down the train. A station came into view; passengers on the platform shuffled forward, preparing to board.

★　　★　　★

The shooter looked down at the *provodnitza* and spat. She was still moving, but he made no attempt to save her. She would be dead shortly. At least as far as the foreigner was concerned. He pulled off his mask and wiped the sweat from his nose. He tucked the pistol into his belt and sat down on a seat inside the compartment. "Otlichna!" he said. *Excellent!*

"Ne za shto," she replied. *You're welcome.*

He handed her two one-hundred-ruble notes.

CHAPTER FIVE

Steele's senses were on steroids. Not quite eyes in the back of his head, but close. He grabbed Natasha and pulled her along with him, sprinting now into the next train car. The sound of the heavy wooden and metal door slamming was as loud as the last shot fired. Outside on the Smidovich station platform, a sea of fur coats greeted them like a scene from *March of the Penguins.* Passengers carrying suitcases, bags, and boxes shuffled forward as the Rossiya Express pulled into the station. Unsure if the gunman was following, Steele continued in the same direction until they reached the end of the next car.

"Jack … No police!" said Natasha.

"Fine with me," he replied. He wanted to get off the train as quickly as possible, but he also did not want to lose Natasha again.

The train's brakes screeched as it prepared to stop. He opened the window and put his arm out to open the door. The faded, white-painted safety line sped past below him.

"Come on! Davai!" He kept hold of her hand, and they jumped before the train had come to a full and complete stop.

Steele heard the *click* and felt the bolt of pain shooting up his leg the moment he landed. *My bloody ankle!* He'd heard the same noise and felt the same shooting pain jumping from a second-floor apartment on the front line in war-ravaged Sarajevo years before.

Natasha turned to him.

"It's okay," he said. "I'll be fine." *Bullcrap!* But he had to put his full weight on her as they maneuvered their way down the platform. She lowered her head and surged along the platform struggling to hook his arm around her shoulder. *Tougher than she looks.*

The pain was bearable; for now, it was the least of his worries. Two Russian policemen scurried up the platform straight toward them. Natasha squeezed him closer as they tried to melt into the sea of fur coats and hats.

"What happened?" One of the policemen had seen them fall. "Are you hurt, comrades?"

"Vsyo normalno," she replied. *We're fine.* She continued in Russian, "Comrade policeman, there's a madman on the train. He shot the *provodnitza*. Please, you have to catch him."

The policeman checked Steele's bent-over body and for a split second became suspicious. But her words were a call to arms. "Don't worry, woman. We'll get him." He ran off with his partner toward the front of the train.

Steele and Natasha hobbled down the platform. It was the closest, physically, Steele had come to her. She wore Coco Channel—passé he thought, but one of his favorites nevertheless. He glanced down at her cheek as they advanced, and observed the youthful texture of her skin and the neatness of her small ears. His mother used to say small ears were a sign of great intelligence.

A young boy pushed through the crowd toward them. They were almost at the main exit by the time he reached them. The boy threw himself at Natasha. Wait, not just *any* boy. *The* boy! It was the one he had failed to rescue.

★   ★   ★

They exited the station and made for a line of taxis.

"Spaciba," the boy said, staring at Steele. *Thank you.*

"Don't mention it." Steele turned to Natasha but saved his questions. No time.

Natasha ignored the main line of taxis and stopped at a

battered Trabant. Steele recognized it—the one he had taken to the river. The same driver sat inside. Seeing them, the driver reached over and opened the door.

"Pu-kha!" the boy said. *See you!* He ran back across the street, narrowly avoiding an ambulance arriving at the scene.

"Good lad," Steele said to Natasha. "I'm glad he made it."

"He's a good swimmer."

Steele's eyes widened. "Must be."

"Three times Vladivostok Kraj Junior Champion." She pulled open the door of the taxi and got into the front seat. Steele got in the back.

"Poyexali," said Natasha. *Let's go.*

The driver frowned. "Kuda ta?" *Where?*

"Na dachu. Gdye ne opasna." *To the dacha, where it's safe.*

CHAPTER SIX

The taxi sped through the outskirts of a near-deserted Smidovich. They passed gray apartment blocks, identical to the ones in Khabarovsk. Soviet architects had left their unremarkable stamp all over the former Soviet Union. In the murky evening shadows, freshly washed laundry flapped in the icy breeze on apartment balconies. Many of them were protected with cagelike metal bars. People saw fit to guard even a child's bicycle on a third- or fourth-floor balcony in these parts.

The taxi skidded as the wheels lashed inefficiently into the mud and slush. Steele made himself comfortable. He had no idea where they were going and no choice but to enjoy the ride and give his hosts the benefit of the doubt. The smell of worn leather seats and the manual choke reminded him of his first automobile—a Morris Minor 1000; he had paid three hundred pounds for it on his nineteenth birthday. That seemed like a century ago in another world.

He took out his cell phone, flipped it open, and checked the screen. He wanted to talk to Sandy again. Now wasn't the time, but he had to make her see sense, convince her she was making a big mistake. His cell had international access, but there was no signal. Sod's law. The conversation with Sandy and now this gunman ... his brain felt as though it would implode. *Steady... One crisis at a time.*

A few minutes later, they were traveling through the desolate winter countryside, spotted with lone, single-story dachas, then silver birch woods, then more silver birch woods, then flat, open fields so barren that nothing, he suspected, could ever grow there.

"I need to make a call."

"Not now," Natasha replied. "No signal."

"I'll try anyway."

"Please."

"My wife's ill."

Would this driver object? Who was in charge here? The man sitting in front had a full head of jet-black hair, late forties. The man kept his eyes on the road, swerving to avoid dirt mounds, ice patches, and potholes.

Steele took out his cell phone and scrolled down to Sandy. After a few seconds, he was both relieved and surprised to hear the purring of a British telephone. Three rings later, there was a loud crackle, then silence.

"Hello," he said. "Sandy?"

"Jack?" It was Sandy's voice, almost as if she was expecting his call. "Jack, is that you? I'm—"

Jack heard distress in her voice. He regretted his negative thoughts on the train an hour before. He recalled how beautiful Sandy was, why he had not taken his eyes off her the first time they had met. His flashback was interrupted by a man's voice with a foreign accent on the other end of the phone too muffled and brief to make any sense from it. *What in God's name?*

"Who is this?" he demanded. He sat up straight. His stomach tightened. Sandy had been alone the last time he spoke to her. But now the connection faded. Either the man had hung up or the signal was as unreliable as Natasha had warned.

He hit the redial option several times in quick succession. No luck. *Damn it.*

As he waited in vain for her to call him back, he stared through his mud-spattered window, mesmerized by how many minutes, miles, hours, and time zones he was from his wife and the place he called home.

He did not share the incident with his fellow passengers.

Who to tell? Who to call? He put his hand to his face and squeezed his cheeks in frustration. The voice in London had sounded Russian, perhaps? He couldn't be sure. *Was this somehow all connected? Nightmare.* His mind careened from one horrific image of Sandy to another. Robbed? Beaten to a pulp or worse? Perhaps she had simply dropped her cell phone in the London street? *A passerby had picked it up.* That was one explanation. Plausible. But he was sure he'd heard her voice. Perhaps she'd dropped her phone in The Coffee Cup, the Hampstead café she was sure to be visiting at this hour.

"Where are we going?"

"Yes, Jack. Do not worry the whole time."

He continued to talk to Natasha in a mix of Russian and English. "Spaciba." *Thank you.* "Very reassuring."

She glanced at him like a schoolteacher addressing her pupil. She had elegant cheekbones and a perfectly symmetrical face, which gave the initial impression that she was a young beauty in her twenties—*krasavitza,* the Russians said. But her piercing blue eyes with dark shadows etched underneath, possessed a suffering and fatigue beyond her years.

She touched his arm. She was gentle, sensual even, but not intentionally so. Her expression revealed nothing. "Soon, Jack. I will explain. Please, be calm."

Twenty-five minutes later, the Trabant turned off the main road and drove down a track leading into the heart of a stately silver birch forest. The Trabant negotiated another bend, then slid askew to a complete stop. All around, trees were laden with cushions of snow, their branches dipping politely under the weight. A branch snapped overhead as the car pulled up, showering their windscreen.

"*Confetti!*" guffawed the driver.

Before them, a lone dacha stood invitingly among the slim, silver trees. A neat curl of smoke meandered from the chimney. If this were a fairy tale, Steele thought, it would have been the witch's house in *Hansel and Gretel.* The ornately carved window shutters reminded him of the children's picture book his mother had read to him a thousand times.

The driver cut the engine and slid the choke lever back into the dash board.

Jack's ankle throbbed. They had arrived, but God only knew where. There was a soothing moment of stillness before anyone spoke.

"Please. This is Viktor," Natasha said. Viktor turned to face them. He had dark brown eyes, gaunt cheeks, black stubble, and a distinguished, chiseled jaw. "Viktor will drive us to Vladivostok tomorrow. We will all work together."

Vladivostok? They were at least three or four hours from Vladivostok by his reckoning. And what kind of work was she talking about? He didn't want work. He wanted a bloody story.

"Delighted to meet you, Viktor," he said. Viktor looked like a famous Italian opera singer whose name Steele had forgotten. They shook hands. "Sorry, no change …" He held up two empty hands.

For a moment, Viktor looked nonplussed. Then he smiled, getting the joke. "Ah, no tip!" He spoke English after all. "Welcome to FSB dacha number forty-one, Mister Jack." He revealed two gold caps on his front teeth and punctuated the end of his sentences by nodding and smiling more than was necessary. Like many Russians, Viktor had two facades—one for Russians, and a more enthusiastic one for foreigners.

"FSB?" Steele, of course, knew the meaning of FSB, but was this really one of their safe houses?

"Old KGB," Viktor replied.

"I know. I just wasn't expecting to be on assignment with them."

FSB was Russia's newer security agency. It had replaced the archaic and infamous KGB, and helped the maverick Russian leader, Vladimir Putin, rule with an iron fist. Steele had written several articles on media censorship in Russia but had to tread a fine line between telling it like it was and maintaining his journalist work-visa status. It was a delicate balance.

Viktor opened his door and heaved his heavy frame out of the taxi. His somewhat lumbering movements reminded Steele of a large bear. "Please," continued Viktor, "I help you." He held out his large cushioned hand, pulling the foreigner up and out of the vehicle.

Steele hopped on his uninjured leg. He was furious with himself for landing awkwardly on his ankle at Smidovich station. He cursed, praying it would heal quickly. The British Army instructors on his survival course all those years ago would have teased him mercilessly. *No pain, no gain, sir!*

The group made its way into the dacha.

The front door opened directly onto a sitting room with a fireplace that led to a small, basic kitchen. The dacha was furnished like a hunting lodge—wooden table and chairs, timber frames, walls covered with wildlife trophies, and threadbare Persian rugs that covered dusty floorboards. The comforting smell of cinders lingered. Again, it reminded him of Uncle George's vicarage in Tolleshunt D'Arcy.

Twelve hours earlier, Steele had been sipping cappuccino at the Samovar, a trendy café in central Moscow. This was his preferred location to type up stories on his twelve-inch laptop, and he could use the internet connection to catch up on emails. Now, he was in the middle of nowhere. What began as a sense of excitement and a challenge had turned into an acute sense of dread. *Was it madness to come this far alone?* Being at this dacha made him nervous. His mind kept going back to the wailing babushka. *She was wearing a gold chain with a locket. I wonder if there was a photo inside.* His insides churned at that thought. He gulped. She was dead. An innocent life was snuffed out because of his desire to get a sensational scoop. Were it not for her, that first bullet might have reached its target. Him. He squeezed his eyes, a headache pounding the side of his head. He thought back to her serving him tea, trying to make him comfortable, and his heart sank further. *It's my fault. I'm responsible for her death. I don't deserve to survive when she hasn't.*

★　★　★

Natasha returned from one of the bedrooms. She handed him a pile of clean clothes, including a thick, gray seaman's turtleneck. Then she stepped outside to fill a large metal basin with fresh snow. She returned and peeled off his socks with the efficiency and care of a nurse. She placed his ankle into the basin, scooping and patting the snow around it to ease the swelling. "The ice box is frozen up. Snow will help you," she said, smiling for the first time since he had met her.

"Spaciba." He studied her eyes for truth or fiction. Her actions appeared genuine.

"Bolna tibye?" *Is it painful?*

"It'll be fine."

Viktor had been rummaging around in one of the kitchen cupboards. He found a small tin and rattled it. "Aspirina?"

"Ne nada, spaciba," Steele replied. *No thanks.*

"Kak xochesh." *As you like.* "You prefer this?" Viktor reached into the noisy, cream-colored refrigerator and produced a bottle of clear liquid with no label. "I brought this for us. Forty-five percent proof."

"Maybe later." Steele tried to sound enthusiastic. He found it amusing. *Forty-five percent proof* was the answer to everyone's *problema* in Russia. If Americans obsessed over making mega-bucks, and the British complained incessantly about the weather, Russians loved to sluice down their problema with vodka. The stereotype had a ring of truth. The plight of the Russians, he mused, was that with so many problema in their turbulent history, they didn't know what to do without problema.

Viktor scraped a chair across the floor and sat down. Natasha served the men a hunk of fresh bread, dried meat, processed cheese she had found in the fridge, and some hot tea—very sweet, no milk.

They ate in silence.

Both men demolished their doorstop sandwiches. Then

Viktor picked up three shot glasses in one hand and retrieved the bottle of vodka with the other. "Nu davai!" *Come on then!* He filled the glasses.

Steele smiled. "Look, I'm grateful for the hospitality and all, but I'm not here for a party. Would it be too much to ask what the bloody hell is going on?"

He picked up his glass and downed the vodka. He loved the infectious, ice-cold bite hitting the back of his throat, making life seem more bearable in difficult situations. Even when he had served in Bosnia, the locals would conjure up a bottle of *slivovica* to ease tensions in the direst circumstances. Every swallow was worth the inevitable destruction of brain cells. *Jesus, I've been in Russia too long.*

"You are safe with us," Natasha said. "I invited you here to help us, and to make big story for you and your newspaper."

"I thought you'd never offer. Great, I'm listening." He took another piece of dried meat and began to gnaw, at the same time holding out his glass for a refill. *What the hell ...*

Natasha got up and placed more wood on the fire. "I met my husband seven years ago. It was dusk. I took a shortcut through a park overlooking the port."

"Vladivostok," Viktor added. Apparently, he'd heard the story.

"Three sailors blocked my path. I thought they were harmless ... you know, *piani,* drunk. They joked around—then one of them began touching and stroking me ... my face. He ran his fingers through my hair. Then he slapped my face, gently at first. Second and third time much harder. Suddenly he dragged me into bushes.

"He took off his belt and lashed my thighs with the brass buckle—military. He ripped my shirt open."

Steele gnawed his inside cheek. He felt awkward. She seemed to be working herself up and reliving this for his benefit.

"They forced me to undress—under the trees. It was freezing. The second sailor took out a knife and lay the point against my chest." She placed her palm on her heart. "The first one wanted to perform his '*fantasma*' with me. I smelled his sour breath when he pulled me down on top of him on a bench next to some grass. I did not care anymore. I spit in his eye. He raised his hand to beat me. I looked behind his eyes. He wanted to kill me—" Natasha wiped away a tear.

Steele listened sympathetically but couldn't help thinking that her tears had dried up a fraction too early in the arc of her story.

"Then a stranger arrived. A powerful man. He changed my life."

"How?"

"He took the sailor's head in both hands and smashed it onto a wall. I heard his teeth break. He was banging until he crushed the man's skull."

"That's terrible. I'm sorry," said Steele, unable to come up with something more appropriate.

"When the second sailor tried to save his friend, this stranger grabbed the switchblade and slashed his throat. He threw the sailor headfirst over the wall to his death. The third sailor ran for his life. The stranger wiped the blade on his sleeve and snapped the knife closed. Then he laughed out loud."

Steele's cheek muscles tensed, forcing a smile. "Nice guy."

Natasha looked up. "I married this man."

"What?"

"Na zdoroviya!" *Cheers!* She had finished her story, another tear running down her cheek.

"Where is he now?" Steele asked. "Is he still a maniac?"

Natasha nodded. "He is sick," she said. "He thinks of money. He thinks of sex. He thinks of power. I am his slave. But I do not blame him."

"You don't?"

"He had a cruel experience as a child. That's not—"

"My heart bleeds." He doubted her generosity. Or was it naïvety? "You're still together? You can't leave him?"

"Impossible. He is a very important man. I can never leave him—alive. He would find me. In this country or any other if I run away." Natasha stopped.

"What?"

"Not important."

"Natasha, what's going on?"

"I have a son. You know him."

"The boy? He's your son?" Steele leaned forward.

"Yes."

"I thought he was dead until we reached the station. Why didn't you tell me?"

"Sorry."

"What's his name?"

Natasha looked as though she was about to give away a state secret. "His name is Bova."

"Why didn't you tell me sooner?" Steele sat up straight shaking his head. *What is this? Alice in Wonderland?*

"It's safer like this."

"Where is he now?"

"With his grandfather. I cannot trust my husband."

"He threatens his son?"

"Bova is not his son. I only met my husband seven years ago. Bova is twelve."

"You think Bova's in danger?"

"If I leave my husband, I'm afraid for my son."

"How can you live like that?"

"My soul is still mine. For the moment."

Natasha was either incredibly vulnerable or a fantastic actress. None of this made any sense. He said, "Natasha, what happened to you is terrible. But if you don't tell me why you brought me here, I'm going to walk out the door."

"My husband is a murderer. Now he's terrorist. No one can stop him except—"

She stared at Steele until he understood.

"Me?" he asked slowly. He was beginning to think he'd made

a huge mistake. A sensational scoop was one thing, thwarting a terrorist campaign quite another. "I'm a journalist with a note-pad and pencil. And the killer on the train stole that."

"I will help you."

"Is anyone else on your side?"

"UN wants to deliver economic aid package for Vladivostok Kraj, North Korea, and China. This will bring us wealth and prosperity. There is great potential in this area—many natural resources. I believe in this plan."

"I know. I've written about that. It makes sense."

"If my husband stays here, this is not possible."

"He has that much power?"

"UN will not work with corrupt authorities."

Steele smirked. "Are you sure?" Honest question.

Her eyes sparkled as she thought about the future. "We have been waiting many years. Korean Peninsula and China also."

"North Koreans? Why would anyone help them?"

"They are not as bad as you think."

"Really?"

"That is why the UN officials came … to research needs of all parties in this region. To make things equal."

"The UN officials are here? You've seen them?"

"They were here, and then they disappeared."

"Why would anyone kill them?"

"My husband does not want UN to destroy his empire."

"He killed them?"

"I don't know."

"And you called me?"

"I will give you the more evidence. You will see."

"You're out of your mind." He resisted the temptation to shout.

"I trust you."

"So?"

"You can help us."

"You want me to stalk your husband until his next murder?"

"Worse than murder."

"Of course."

"UN has millions of dollars at stake for our territory. Many lives are at stake."

"What's he going to do?"

"If I tell you, you might leave and never return. If you stay, you will write your story. This is the only way we can stop him. He is a terrorist."

"Write an exclusive on your husband's terror campaign—the insider's perspective?" Steele was almost laughing now. The idea was absurd.

"You'll see. Tomorrow. We go to Vladivostok in the morning," Natasha said. "You will come with us."

"Do I have a choice?"

"It's up to you. We can leave you at the station in Khabarovsk and you can return to your life of mediocrity."

Steele sat for a few moments in silence. "I'll sleep on it." He took a deep breath and exhaled slowly, shaking his head in disbelief.

"How is your foot?" she asked. She leaned forward and put her hand on his ankle. Her skin was smooth. Her touch was gentle; even the temperature of her hand was perfect. The sensation gave him goose bumps. Natasha was beautiful. *Stop it.* Sandy, his wife, was beautiful, too.

"It's fine," he said, looking at her. "Not the first time it's happened—bloody annoying. My fault."

The shape of Natasha's face was enchanting, like the old master portrait on the cover of his ancient Penguin edition of *The Cherry Orchard*. The vodka was working now. His world was becoming surreal. If he had had a magic wand, he would have made Viktor disappear. He and Natasha would make love in front of the fire. He forgot the rest of his life. It was a pleasant feeling. Then he remembered. Sandy. His wife. He felt sleepy. Natasha. The name alone excited him …

By the light of the tired electric lamp and the dwindling fire, she gently placed her hand on his swollen ankle. "Quiet now," she said. "You can sleep."

His eyes crinkled. "Spaciba." Surrender to the situation, he told himself. Sleep.

His eyelids closed.

He dreamt that he and Natasha were getting married in Smol'nyy Sobor, a landmark cathedral in St. Petersburg, Russia. Its architecture was a colorful mélange of ornate cornicing that looked like icing sugar layered on a grand turquoise façade. Naked, they took each other in front of the guests, who enjoyed the spectacle, laughing, gesticulating, and gyrating to their sensual entanglement. His brother was waving. A military band clad in scarlet and navy-blue uniforms pumped out the first movement of Tchaikovsky's Symphony No. 6. Hundreds of well-wishers waved American, British, and Russian flags. Somewhere in his subconscious, a voice told Steele he was dreaming, but the same voice told him to enjoy it anyway.

★　　★　　★

Natasha waited for Steele to fall asleep. She nodded to Viktor as she got up and placed a copper fireguard around the fireplace. Then she went into one of the bedrooms, opened a cupboard, and picked up a telephone next to a satellite receiver. She dialed a local number.

"Allo?" she said sotto voce.

"Da?" It was her husband. "Slushayou tibya." *Go ahead.*

"Vsyo normalno. Ohn speet." *Everything's OK. He's asleep.* "He believes everything I told him."

"Xorosho," replied the man. *Good.* "Do zavtra." *See you tomorrow.*

CHAPTER SEVEN

Sofiyskaya Embankment, Moscow

In the main building known as "the sanctuary" of the British Embassy in Moscow, Simon Anderson sat at his desk—standard civil service issue. Flimsy panels and vinyl surfaces covered in decades of dings and scratches characterized its lack of sophistication. His desk had always been a nagging bone of contention. *Piece of shit.* Was it really too much to expect H. M. Government to provide a decent desk? *Goddamnit! It's the little things ...*

Old friends and colleagues, making a packet in the city, would ridicule the conditions he'd put up with over the years if they knew the truth. Anderson, however, was unaware that many of them laughed at him for entirely different reasons and had done so for many years irrespective of his desk or administrative insecurities. But their opinions wouldn't have made any difference. He didn't care what people thought of him, and he wasn't a civil servant—albeit a very special one—for the money.

British Council staff were not allowed access to the gloomy, oak-paneled inner sanctum of the main building in the embassy compound. But Anderson was no regular staff. His work at the British Council was a cover, and he could hardly give out a business card that said:

Simon Anderson, Director MI6, Russia

He picked up the secure telephone to London. The Kremlin's golden domes were etched onto a cloudless blue sky out the window in front of him. His office boasted a stunning vista. Nibbling at a fleck of hard skin on the tip of his index finger, he waited for London by surfing the satellite news channels—Sky News, CNN, BBC World.

"We're ready," he said finally, pressing the mute button on the TV remote.

"About time too. We've been waiting all morning," replied the voice.

"My apologies," replied Anderson.

"My secretary accused me of forgetting you people are three hours ahead."

"I had to make some calls. Three languages involved, you understand—last-minute kinks. Translators needed a kick. That sort of thing."

"Anything else we should know?"

"No." Anderson frowned. He detested the pompous tone of his superior, nothing more than a jumped-up desk wallah who had never stepped foot outside of London SW1.

"I've got something for you."

"Fire away."

"Some plonker from Fleet Street is causing trouble on a train near Vladivostok."

"British?" Anderson sounded bored, even to himself.

"Apparently."

"First I've heard of it."

"That's why I'm here. Covering your arse, dear boy."

"Thanks. Is he a threat?"

"I've no idea. That's your job. Worst-case scenario, we abort with a few red faces. The last thing we need is a loose cannon poking around screwing everything up for everyone else."

"I agree." Anderson did not agree—over his dead body would he abort. *Not in this lifetime or the next.* All the effort, all the work. He'd gone out on a limb and would not return without his reward. And his reward was just the beginning.

"No need to start World War III just yet." His tone was jovial.

"If you say so."

"What?"

"Nothing, sir."

"Let me make myself perfectly clear. Any doubts, we abort. Is that understood?"

"Yes. What's his name?"

"Jack Steele."

"Do we know him?"

"I sent you articles with his photograph. *London Daily Standard*. He's been in Moscow for them since September."

Anderson tapped swiftly at his laptop to retrieve the secure e-mail.

The voice continued, "Look into it. Any concerns, get back to me. If I don't hear from you, I'll assume we're on for tomorrow. Heard back from the Yanks?"

"Don't worry, they'll approve. They need this as much as we do."

"Hope you're right."

Anderson studied the small photo-attachment at the top of the article. "I'll follow up on Steele. Make sure there's nothing to worry about."

"Do that. Anything else?"

"No."

Anderson hated his superior's Yorkshire lilt. His mother had always frowned upon regional accents, and this prejudice had rubbed off on him. A grammar school boy, he had practiced for hours in front of the mirror to erase all trace of his London accent. His mentor, a kindly, blue-blooded, conservative-with-a-small-and-large-C-neighbor, had told him the only thing missing to get him to the top was the true British accent. *Oxford English.* Once acquired, Anderson joined the civil service, passed all selection boards with flying colors, and was fast-tracked into the Secret Intelligence Service known as MI6. His "accent" work had paid off with bells and whistles on.

Anderson hung up and clicked his jaw from side to side—an

annoying habit numerous old girlfriends could never persuade him to kick. He continued to monitor the latest CNN headlines on screen.

"Damn it! Who the hell is Jack Steele?" he muttered.

He closed all the windows on his desktop except for Steele's article. The piece on trade and development in underdeveloped parts of rural Russia made for interesting reading. He noted Steele's observations that under Vladimir Putin certain areas of the Russian Far East were verging on lawlessness, although no specific allegations were made against specific people—or solutions offered. But the journalist seemed surprisingly well-informed given the short amount of time he'd been on assignment in Russia. That made Anderson nervous.

With support and cooperation from the US and Russia virtually guaranteed, he was one day away from the most outrageously ambitious—and potentially explosive—piece of foreign policy decision-making since the Cold War. Now some smart-arse journalist was threatening to screw things up. Jack Steele, whoever he was, would regret being in the wrong place at the wrong time.

★   ★   ★

Against his better judgement, Steele decided to find out what this potential bombshell was all about. If even half of it was true, Natasha's story was a blockbuster. And perhaps, just perhaps, the success of a blockbuster scoop might help restore Sandy's trust and confidence in him. *Go with the flow … at least for now.*

Steele, Natasha, and Viktor departed the dacha in the same taxi at 4:30 am. Almost immediately, Steele willed himself to get more sleep. Whatever was coming, he would need to be on top form. One thing he had learned in the British Army was to get your head down whenever possible. Today he could bail at any time, decide what to do later, even if it meant getting arrested in Vladivostok. In the meantime, not even the stomach-churning potholes of the Russian countryside could disturb him.

Three hours later, he woke with a start. The Trabant sailed through a red light in early-morning Vladivostok. No other cars around. The cloudless sky presented a vibrant red-fading-to-yellow morning hue. The trees and forests had long been left behind. They chugged past giant, black-silhouetted cranes and ships' towers etched against the crisp morning canvas. Thick steel arms crept slowly across the skyline like mechanical monsters waking from a deep sleep.

"Congratulations!" said Viktor. "You slept like Queen Titania! Welcome to Vladivostok."

"Is it still a 'closed' city?"

"Officially, no. After perestroika, no more closed cities."

"So I'm not breaking the law?"

"Some foreigners are here. We watch them closely. We must."

The taxi drove past a shipyard in the port section, then deeper into a jungle of sprawling city suburbs—concrete squares, rectangles, and straight lines, more generic housing like every other town in Russia. It was a bleak-looking part of the world.

They pulled up outside a small movie theater opposite a five-story apartment building. Steele could hear dogs barking in various directions. "Anyone for Harry Potter?" he asked quietly. Seeing the title of the movie in Russian, he smiled and was amazed and impressed J. K. Rowling had come so far. He had taken her out on a date when they were students together at Exeter University, but she had declined a second round.

"Where are we?" He rubbed his eyes.

Natasha looked behind to see if they had a tail. All clear.

"Viktor will take care for you," she said, climbing out of the Trabant. "I will return soon."

Viktor exited the car and handed Natasha a set of keys for a black Mercedes parked across the street.

"Wait!" Steele protested, following them out of the taxi. "You expect me to just sit here and wait?"

"You have no choice," Natasha said.

"Natasha, I'm a journalist. You can't—"

"Jack. Be calm. Viktor will attend to you. Go make your calls. You have satellite in the apartment. Call Moscow. Call London. Talk to your wife."

Natasha started the Mercedes and drove away, leaving the two men standing on the sidewalk.

They entered the dimly lit lobby with a flickering fluorescent light. A strong smell of disinfectant reminded Steele of inner London council flats—*the projects,* as Sandy would say.

They took the elevator to the third floor. Halfway along the corridor, Viktor stopped and unlocked the door to an apartment. He shuffled inside and set the bags down on the highly polished wooden floor. "Kak doma," he said. *Just like home.*

Compared with the building's common parts, the apartment was clean and tidy. A living room next to a small kitchen was cluttered with tacky, highly polished furniture and Russian dolls—*matroshki*—the ones that got smaller and smaller as you fitted them inside each other. A glass cabinet with mirrored shelves contained vulgar porcelain figurines and chintzy souvenirs from various parts of the former Soviet Union. Steele also noticed an electric samovar in the kitchen and an antique chrome samovar in the living room. Russia was an eclectic mix of the exquisite and the tasteless.

"Another safe house?" he asked.

"Pocket money for the owner," Viktor replied. "In my country, every little helps."

"Where's the telephone? I need to call London."

"Satellite is in the bedroom." Viktor pointed down a short corridor with a poster of Guns N' Roses taped askew on the wall. "But you must wait for battery to charge ..."

"What?" *The last straw—*

"Shutka!" *I'm joking.* Viktor's grin became a chuckle, revealing his gold-capped front teeth top and bottom.

"Very funny." Steele flashed a plastic smile. Then he walked down the corridor and entered the bedroom. He knew the conversation would be taped, but he didn't care. He had to speak to Sandy. If not, then at least his editor. Someone needed to know where he was, and someone needed to find his wife.

He unclipped the telephone receiver from its base.

As he dialed, he heard a series of beeps and clicks. He tried Sandy's number three times, but it was busy every time. After three more attempts, he replaced the receiver and called his newspaper.

As he dialed, he noticed the bedroom windows were covered with cardboard and newspaper. He could see the building opposite through a small gap in the tape. Nothing out of the ordinary. At first. Then he noticed movement directly opposite—a child sweeping a net curtain to one side. A moment later, the small figure disappeared back into the dark shadows of the apartment. He thought it looked like Bova.

"London Daily Standard," a young woman's voice sang with a cheery tone and a London accent trying to sound professional by overenunciating her consonants. "How may I direct your call?"

He'd finally made contact with the outside world. *Thank the Christ.* He exhaled and then requested to be connected to Tim Henshaw, his editor. After sharing salutations, Steele recounted the story so far, including his efforts to contact Sandy and her sudden vanishing act.

"What do you mean—abducted?" Henshaw was the foreign editor at the *London Daily Standard.* "Jack, can you hear me?"

"Yes, go ahead." The line to London was breaking up.

"Did you say, *abducted*?"

"I don't know, Tim. I spoke to Sandy last night. I called again today. A man's voice answered. Sounded Russian … possibly. Doesn't make any sense."

"Except that you're in Russia."

"I know, but—"

"Is she having an affair?" guffawed Henshaw.

His staff had learned to tolerate his frequently insensitive sense of humor, but the comment only served to annoy Steele.

"She's not having an affair. As a matter of fact, she had a miscarriage."

"Sorry, Jack. I didn't know. Not helpful," said Henshaw. "Have you called the police? Shall I call the police?"

"No. I wanted to talk to you first. I can't get hold of her …"

"You think it's connected to the story?"

"I don't know."

"Do you think she's in danger?"

"I said I don't know. All I know is that I can't get hold of her and I'm worried."

"I'll send someone around to the flat. What's the address?"

Steele recited the Hampstead address with postcode.

"Got it. I'm on it."

"Thanks, Tim. Much appreciated."

"Sure you don't want me to call the boys in blue? Be on the safe side?"

"No police. Not yet."

"I understand."

"See if you can find her first. If not, we'll send in the cavalry."

"How do I get hold of you? Your mobile's not working. Tried it earlier."

"I'll call you."

"Understood." Henshaw paused. "Jack …"

"Yes?"

"Let's be careful out there?"

"Ay, ay, Captain."

Steele smiled as he put the telephone back on the cradle. He walked over to the window. No sign of the boy. He looked into the street below. A child was playing in the snow. Bundled up in bright red snow gear complete with a hat with ear flaps, he couldn't tell if it was a boy or girl. He smiled at the tenacity of the child who was determined to stand on top of a trashcan covered in snow and perform a delicate balancing act. The child jumped off into the pile of snow, arms outstretched, giggling merrily—do-it-yourself thrills.

At that moment, Steele wondered if he would ever watch his own child or children playing in the snow. Time was passing. He was getting on, as they say. What the hell was he doing here so far away from home? More importantly, so far away from her. Sandy was right. She needed him, and he wasn't there. He should have been with her, not on a wild-goose-chase story on the other side of the world.

Too late now.

★   ★   ★

The lemon morning sky was fading to its daytime blue. It was a crisp, cold morning, and the icicles had no intention of melting. Natasha drove into Vladivostok town center and parked on *Okeanskiy Prospekt,* the main street. She always used the same parking space outside the Hotel Stalingrad. Few foreigners or Russians had official business there. Few foreigners or Russians owned the make and model of vehicle allowed to park there.

She entered the hotel, nodding to the doorman whom she knew by sight. The hotel lobby would not have looked out of place in the movie *Casablanca.* Marble columns and ornate white stucco arches decorated the reception area. Miniature fake palm trees complimented a fountain with water gushing from the mouth of a bronze bear. Unlike most Western hotels, there was no piped-in music.

Her boots clicked across the black and white slabs of marble tile, a feature many of the VIP guests had admired over the years. Regardless of its five-star status, less than a dozen guests were staying at the hotel during these winter months. Natasha stepped out of the elevator on the third floor. She could smell the wood polish spray used by chambermaids minutes before and thought about her mother who used to clean at this hotel many years ago. Her pace slowed as she approached room number thirty-seven. She took a deep breath and quietly recited a short prayer as she turned the doorknob and entered without knocking.

Inspector Igor Ryzhakov, Natasha's husband, stood on the far side of the room wearing a white tank top and green paisley silk boxer shorts. He stroked his closely cropped hair and rubbed his eyes when she entered. Although he had an official government apartment, he preferred the hotel. His luxury suite cost virtually nothing. The hotel owner, an ex-Communist party member who knew how to play the game in these parts, had wisely decided to accommodate the police chief and sanctioned a drastically reduced rate.

Pruning and admiring his well-defined torso in front of a full-length mirror, Ryzhakov picked up a thirty-pound dumbbell and completed one last set of arm curls before resting. His brown eyes lit up when he saw her. But the glazed look he sported told her he had been drinking, or perhaps it was just a hangover?

"Privjet, Natashinka!" *Hello, my little Natasha!*

"Privjet …" she replied without emotion.

He rubbed his face with both hands. "Opoxmalitza nada." *Hair of the dog.*

She made no comment.

"Ny-ka?" *What's going on?*

She fell silent and tossed her mink coat onto the leather armchair. Then she walked toward the French windows made more elegant by the ornate wrought-iron balustrade outside that overlooked the main street. A tram rumbled past causing the glasses on the coffee table to jingle against one another. Outside, sparks spewed from the electric tram cables overhead.

He beckoned to her with his eyes. Closer, they said.

She approached obediently.

"First, business. Can we trust him?" he asked in Russian, scratching his ear in an excessive vibrating motion.

"Yes, I think so."

"He will obey orders? Are you certain?" He inspected the tip of his finger.

"Yes."

They stared at each other. She knew he trusted no one completely—*not even my own mother*, he often said.

"Excellent. Our plan is good. Afterward we will kill him if he cannot help us."

"As you wish. Less complicated."

"That's right. Less complicated."

"Perhaps it will not be necessary," she said, unbuttoning her blouse. "Let me take care of everything."

"We will see." His mind was already on other, more immediate needs.

"Promise me," she said.

"No promises, my dear."

Natasha paused, then swallowed. Memories flooded black. They always did. Every time she made love—no, had sex with him—she felt nauseous. She remembered the sailor lashing at her legs with his belt and his rank breath. The metal buckle etched with the Soviet military star had left a scar on her thigh. Igor or the sailors. She could never decide who was worse.

Reliving the nightmare that began the nightmare, she performed her duty. She consented with her mouth and body but never with heart or soul. As she mentally prepared to pleasure him, she thought about killing Ryzhakov then and there. Simple enough. Take the pistol from the drawer by the bed, use a pillow to muffle the sound, and shoot him. No one would hear a thing. There were few guests staying at the hotel anyway.

"Let me kill him," she said, "if this is necessary."

★　　★　　★

"Kill the foreigner?" Ryzhakov wasn't convinced.

Then she inserted her middle finger into his mouth, and

using his saliva, traced it in a circle around his lips. "Let me kill him ... for you."

"Perhaps." Becoming aroused, he sucked on her middle finger, repeating the action on her lips then sliding it back and forth into her mouth. He cradled both hands around her head and kissed her with his bulbous tongue. He drooled like a teething baby. Then he lowered her head and smelled her hair, his hands remained clasped as if trying to protect her.

He inhaled long and deep, kissing her forehead, gently, slowly, lowering her face to his loins where he yearned for her. He reached for the television remote and switched off the news. *Too fucking distracting. Need to concentrate.* He picked up a glass of water and guzzled as she toiled. He drank too quickly so that the contents spilled down the smooth pectorals he admired daily in the mirror. He plucked them often to keep his thick chest hair at bay. He guzzled again, and water spilled onto Natasha's face so that she flinched in the middle of the sex act. He forced her head back to work.

★　　★　　★

Another tram rumbled by.

She promised herself this was the last time she would obediently perform. She would find a way out ... for her sake and for her son.

CHAPTER EIGHT

Hampstead, London

Sandy sat on the bed in the guest bedroom of the garden flat where the man had imprisoned her. Christine's neighbor had not left a key after all. Although Sandy had struggled to get away over the wall in the garden, the man had clamped his hand over her mouth and dragged her back inside. *What the fuck? What the fuck does the asshole want from me?*

She rubbed her cheek where he had indiscriminately lashed out with the back of his hand. Raising her body temperature, the force of the blow filled her with rage and an overwhelming desire for payback. Sandy's father, Blake Danner, had taught her to fight for just causes, to stick up for herself intellectually, and, where possible, physically. She had always admired Danner's girlfriend, Anna—her feisty independence and ability to defend herself. Anna had practiced the ancient art of Jiujitsu. Now Sandy wished she had, too.

Furious, she wanted to beat her captor's head to a pulp. But she knew she would lose. Sandy had never been attacked or abducted before. The closest she had come to a real fight was in high school.

Breathe rhythmically. Calm down, think straight. She sifted through motives for the abduction. Money? Mistaken identity? Jack Steele?

The breathing helped. She had been attacked, thumped in the face, and imprisoned. Yet, after monitoring her breath for a few minutes, she centered herself. She recalled one of her husband's war stories—a British soldier abducted by Bosnian Serbs in Sarajevo had been beaten one minute and offered a flask of tea and some fruit the next. She remembered what he had told himself—*calmly active, and actively calm at all times. Breathe. Breathe. Breathe. When in danger, control the breath. Detach from the outcome.* She understood the wisdom but found it hard to detach herself from this particular outcome. It was happening to her.

"Hey! Excuse me!" she yelled. "I need the bathroom!"

The bedroom was situated at the rear of the apartment. There were bars on a window that looked onto the small patio. No sign of neighbors on either side. Christine's building was deserted, and the flat above was empty and for sale. No one would hear if she tried to shout her way out. And even if someone did hear her, it would take just seconds for the thug to silence her.

At least he hadn't gagged her. Having watched all those movies where victims were gagged, or even worse had a handkerchief stuffed into their mouths, she was grateful for one small mercy.

"Hey!" she shouted. "I need the goddamn bathroom!"

The door opened.

He said nothing. Dark, swarthy, tall, and lean—if she was honest, she found him attractive. Could have been a track athlete of some kind. Mid-thirties, probably. He'd added a beat-up brown leather jacket over the red top, jeans, and dirty white sneakers. He gestured politely for her to go across the corridor to the bathroom.

"Thanks." She moved slowly, maintaining eye contact in case he tried anything. He allowed her to enter the bathroom, and she locked the door.

She could hear him moving around outside. She wondered if he was listening to her in there. She shivered—the thought made her nauseous. When she had finished, she leaned down and quietly retrieved the can of oil lubricant from the sink unit, tucking it into her back pocket and concealing it with her T-shirt.

She swallowed nervously and then opened the door and gave a fake smile, thanking him, as she returned across the hallway to the bedroom.

Should she flirt with him? Use her voluptuous charm that people used to compliment her on? She had to get out of this mess somehow. *Whatever it takes, motherfucker!* Her life did not appear to be in danger. Yet. But that might change at any moment.

As she approached the bedroom, she glanced over the man's shoulder into the living room. Through the net curtains, she could see the top of the cars parked along the street. Suddenly, a lone figure appeared on the sidewalk from the right. She considered screaming. Then she heard the sound of the metal gate creaking at the top of the stairs.

Someone was about to descend the stairs.

Her captor also heard the gate opening. He looked at Sandy. He read her thoughts, or so it seemed. He probably wished he'd gagged her after all. She lunged at him, sinking her nails into his cheek and drawing blood. From her back pocket, she produced the can of WD40 and pressed hard on the nozzle, forcing the spray lubricant into his eyes. *So what if it blinds him for life?* The man bent double, trying to wipe the oil from his eyes but making it worse in the process. Simultaneously, his body tensed as his right arm flailed in all directions to ward off her attack.

This was her moment, and she was ready. She prayed the person coming down the steps could help her—a mailman, a delivery man, even a wrong address—anyone strong enough to overpower this guy and allow her to escape.

She bolted for the front door; confident her ordeal was almost over. Too confident. Thinking she would beat him to the door, she failed to make a sound or do anything to warn the person outside. As soon as she reached the front door, she felt a thud on the back of her head.

She could feel herself being dragged back into the living room as the visitor reached the bottom of the steps. *I'm losing consciousness.* A searing pain melted down through her head and spine. The last thing she saw before she passed out was a face peering through the molded circle of glass on the front door. The man was tall, gray, and broad-shouldered. It was her father, Blake Danner.

The doorbell rang. Sandy's world went black.

Vladivostok, Russia

In the FSB safe house apartment in Vladivostok, Steele walked down the corridor and back into the living room where Viktor sat sipping hot tea.

"Chai budish?" Viktor asked. *You want tea?*

"No thanks, I'm fine. Viktor, I'm leaving. Tell Natasha I changed my mind."

"Changed your mind?"

"About the story. Sorry, it's not worth it." He grabbed his jacket and walked toward the front door. He had no idea how he was going to get back to Moscow. No ticket. No money. But he would think of something. He turned the heavy latch anticlockwise.

"Jack, it is better you stay." Viktor stood up and entered the vestibule. "Better for *you.* Understand?"

"Sorry, Viktor. I need a change of scene. I've had enough of twiddling my thumbs. Thanks anyway."

"What about your wife?"

"What about her?"

"Do you love her?"

"Of course."

"Our leader will kill her if you leave. No doubt. Her life means nothing to him."

"We're separating …"

"She's your wife."

Steele tried bluffing. "You think I care about her so much?"

"Yes. Do you love her?"

He froze. The cogs in his head began turning. Viktor's matter-of-fact tone was for real. "Yes."

"I tell you as friend. You leave now and she will die."

Steele turned, not sure whether to leave. "Is she in danger right now, friend?" So this explained the London call cut short at least.

"She is safe."

"If I stay with you?"

"That is my understanding."

Steele closed the front door and returned to the living room. "Viktor, what do you people want from me?" He sat down at the table and looked at the teapot. "I'll have some chai."

"Our leader is very important man."

"He's a thug."

"This thug needs you."

"Me?" Steele scoffed. "Why would you work for a man like that?"

"I owe him. He was generous to me—he saved me from prison for something I did not do. Others were ready to condemn me."

"Fair enough. But I thought Natasha needed me, not her boss?"

"They both need your help?"

"How?"

"I do not know details. My understanding is that you are his insurance."

"For what?"

"He gives her orders. She has a son. If you listen to her, you will see your wife again. Trust me."

Steele took two large gulps of tea. "Tell me something."

"I will try."

"What's so special about this guy? How does he have so much control over everyone?"

"I have known him for many years. He was nothing. Now he is everything. He owns many people. Do as he says, and you will be free. Your story will be on front page of *Times, Washington Post*, and others."

"What are you planning to do? Invade China?"

"Almost."

"I was kidding."

"We are going to North Korea. But we are invited. That's all I know."

"Interesting."

"Be patient."

"Where do you fit in, Viktor? You don't strike me as a murdering bastard."

"No one is murdering anyone."

"Are you sure?"

"Life is complicated in our country. It is not black-and-white, as you say. Gray, like weather. Unfortunately, I owe too much to Igor."

"You use the FSB as cover for crime?"

"We are the police. We defeat criminals. Sometimes we are forced to make deals … in the 'interests' of all parties. This is strana chu-des."

"Strana chu-des," Steele repeated. *Wonderland.* "And I'm the Mad Hatter." Strana chu-des, he recalled, was the incongruous comparison of the former Soviet Union with Alice's Wonderland. In a country where there was so little of anything, it was astounding to everyone how much you could achieve with widespread deficiencies and disfunction.

Enough with the philosophy. It was official. Sandy's life was in danger. For now, he had no choice but to follow Viktor's "advice." His insides churned. Viktor's ultimatum had certainly changed everything. Adrenaline throbbed through his mind and body. He had no choice. Now there were *two* gigantic challenges—get the story *and* save his wife. He felt as though he was standing on the edge of a precipice, and there was no turning back.

CHAPTER NINE

Natasha returned to the apartment sooner than Steele had anticipated. He glanced at the American-flag wall clock hanging in the kitchen. It was 8:05 am. Her business, whatever it was, had taken less than two hours.

She gave him a polite smile, but her eyes were elsewhere. "We leave in ten minutes," she said. "I have spoken with my husband."

"Did he mention Sandy?"

"Your wife is safe. You must do as I say, or you will—"

"Never see her again?" Steele glanced at Viktor and back to Natasha. "Viktor already mentioned that. Your orders? Or did your lunatic husband tell you what to say?"

She did not answer.

With Sandy's life in play now, these were orders he couldn't disobey, even if the story itself did make world news.

"Give me something, Natasha. Anything, for God's sake."

"I don't understand."

"Give me a bloody clue. You can't expect me to tag onto your charade without something concrete!"

"If you trust me, you will find your UN officials. Good enough?"

"Not really."

"Jack. Listen—" Natasha shot Viktor a glance. "There is not time for this."

"OK, yes. Good enough." Steele lied. *Nowhere near good enough, but what choice do I have right now?*

Minutes later, they climbed into the black Mercedes sedan,

whose engine had been left running. It was less than a mile to the port. At a deserted quay, an olive-green military launch waited to take them due west across the estuary to mainland Russia. Cutting across the bay to the mainland was the quickest way toward the border with North Korea, which was due south.

The water was choppy, and the vessel lurched from side to side as it bounced on the waves, periodically spraying all those aboard. In the distance, he saw the jagged outline of the mainland. Beyond the coastline, threatening purple mountains beckoned, snow on their peaks like dripping wax.

"Where are we going?" he yelled above the noise of the engine as the wind lashed at his face and hair.

"North Korea," Natasha replied calmly.

"You're kidding?" Steele was flabbergasted. Viktor wasn't exaggerating after all. "You're taking me to North Korea?"

"You are our guest." She looked at her watch, then scanned the coastline.

"Great," he said.

The chipped olive-drab paint and metal-studded walkways of the launch reminded him of a British Army regimental training exercise on a freezing lake in the Welsh mountains years before. But this wasn't Wales, and it was certainly no exercise. No "end ex" in sight.

"I don't have a visa."

Viktor smiled. "You don't need one," he shouted above the wind. "You are our guest. It will take us several hours to arrive. Enjoy the scenery."

The wind whipped the edge of his zipper against his cheek. "What about your husband?" he asked Natasha.

"He will join us."

Steele nodded. "Can't wait."

Ten minutes later, they arrived on the mainland. A small military convoy with drivers stood waiting. They drove three miles inland and reached a barren complex of brick buildings that, at first, looked like an old factory or industrial plant. A fifteen-foot-wide red star hung precariously atop the redbrick chimney. The remainder of the chimney was painted with a mural of a young couple waving a hammer and sickle at one another—presumably some sort of Soviet-era love dance. On closer inspection, Steele concluded this place was probably a disused army barracks.

Two Russian soldiers waved the convoy through the gates of the deserted military base. Viktor directed the driver of their military jeep into a large hangar with a corrugated iron roof. Military personnel scurried around three BTR-60BP armored personnel carriers—APCs. Steele scanned some dozen soldiers making final checks and preparations for what seemed to be imminent departure. Each APC had its name painted on the side under a small animal emblem—a dragon, bear, or snake with a Roman numeral.

In one corner of the hangar, a Russian army sergeant stood behind a long table and issued extra winter clothing and equipment to those in line—fur-lined jackets, backpacks, waterproof boots, food rations, and, more worrying to Jack, Makarov 9mm pistols and AK-47 assault rifles complete with boxes of ammunition.

Steele was freezing. He shuffled along the short line behind Natasha and Viktor. A senior sergeant handed him a quilted cold-weather suit for which he was thankful. Meant for sub-zero temperatures, the loose-fitting jacket-and-trouser suit was insulated and big enough to wear over several other layers. He pulled on the quilted suit as quickly as possible. *Thank God for the quartermaster.* He held out his arms for the rest of the equipment and stuffed it into the issued backpack.

At the next table, he was handed the Makarov 9mm pistol with holster and three boxes of ammunition. "Pozhalsta," said a Russian corporal. *Here you are.*

"Me?" Steele hesitated, glancing at the boxes of ammunition thrust toward him. He turned to Natasha.

"Take it," Natasha said. "Anything can happen in the next twenty-four hours."

He took the pistol and three boxes of ammunition, still hoping to never go back on the symbolic promise he'd made to himself the day he left the British Army—to never again fire a lethal weapon. The promise was a pacifist thing. He'd have to live with himself. He actually felt excitement—the same excitement he'd felt on deployment to Operation Desert Storm in 1991—a cocktail of nervous tension and fear mixed with an unexplainable desire to experience active duty and risk one's life for Queen and country. Churchill once said that every man thought less of himself for not having been a soldier. Steele agreed, but wished he didn't. That thrill of danger, pushing boundaries, was part of his makeup both in the army and now as a foreign correspondent in war zones and other dangerous locations. He wasn't sure if he'd ever shake his appetite for danger and was pretty sure he didn't even want to.

The velvet-textured red star insignia on the uniforms of the non-Russian soldiers intrigued him. *North Korean? Probably.* Like the Russians, they were also proud of their communist red star. Now both Russian and North Korean soldiers were packing up the APCs. Czech-made Kalashnikov AK-47 rifles slung over their shoulder, they meticulously stowed every last piece of equipment. They were focused on their work and made no eye contact with Steele's small VIP group.

He watched Viktor climb into a Jeep and order the driver to take him to the other end of the hangar. Steele observed Viktor shaking hands with a Russian NCO—another senior sergeant type—who was busy placing small metal objects into a selection of secure metal boxes. *Detonators? Explosives of some kind?* Viktor made a cursory check of the NCO's work, and, appearing satisfied, took out a piece of paper from which he punched in a series of codes on an external combination pad on the metal cases. Once the boxes were loaded into his Jeep, Viktor escorted his cargo back to the group in the middle of the hangar. Two

North Korean soldiers snatched and loaded the boxes into the back of the APCs.

Steele's insides began to tingle. Even with a pistol on his belt, he had zero control over his fate—just as it was riding into battle against the Iraqi Republican Guard as a young tank commander in Operation Desert Storm. A dangerous concoction of terror and exhilaration at the same time.

They reached the end of the kit-issue line and inspected their equipment—body armor first. Natasha flung the heavy flak jacket over her head as if putting on a crocheted shawl. The flak jacket contained lead plates front and back. Bracketed by the thick Kevlar collar, her pretty face resembled a Rubens portrait. He was surprised how easily she stood the weight of the protective jacket. No stranger to body armor, he concluded, as she secured the Velcro tapes left and right across her chest.

He followed the same drill.

"Are these guys for real?" he asked. "North Koreans?"

"Yes, North Korean soldiers," she replied. "They will help us with the mission. Without them, it is impossible. We have Russian units too."

Five minutes later, fully loaded with equipment and personnel, three APCs roared out of the old Soviet army barracks. Eight huge wheels on each vehicle pounded into the frozen ground like pneumatic drills. Steele was nervous and acutely curious and suspicious about all the high explosives loaded into their vehicles.

The strong smell of oil and gasoline inside the APC reminded him of his regimental tank park. He wasn't impressed with the driving skills of this fresh-faced Russian driver. Being thrown about in the back of the APC was unpleasant. The BTR-60BP rattled and shook as it hit the smallest bump. Red Army suspension did not compare to British hardware, he thought.

One dim light bulb inefficiently served the passenger area inside the back of the APC. He glanced at Natasha in the pale orange light. Even with sweat on her nose and dirt and grease on her cheeks, she was beautiful.

As he tried not to stare at her, Natasha stared back, and it was more than a casual glance. He sensed they had an emotional connection, but now wasn't the time or place. He looked down at the row of military boots along each side of the vehicle. *Get a grip, for crying out loud!* He would never forgive himself if anything happened to Sandy.

He dug his heals into raised metal ridges on the floor and wedged himself firmly into the seat to steady himself. Two North Korean soldiers riding with them stared straight ahead, avoiding eye contact as if there were no one else in the vehicle. Natasha adjusted her safety straps, and also wriggled in the seat to make herself comfortable.

"Whose vehicles?" Steele raised his voice above the engine.

"Russian-Korean military," replied Natasha.

"Cross-border cooperation?"

"Officially does not exist. But my husband organizes this."

Your husband is a busy fellow.

Khasan, Russia-North Korea Border

One-hundred-and-sixty-miles south of Vladivostok, police chief Igor Ryzhakov eased his foot off the gas pedal and cracked the window. His personal transport, a black bulletproof Range Rover SUV, approached the border checkpoint with North Korea. The Democratic People's Republic of Korea—DPRK—its government preferred to be called. He was alone. The way he liked it.

The Russian sentry—a conscript with ruddy cheeks—took a few steps back from the first vehicle he had seen on duty that day. His black leather boots were not yet broken in. They creaked as he made fresh footprints backward in six inches of fresh snow. He opened the door to the sentry post. "Shas mashina!" *Vehicle!*

The guard commander—a staff sergeant—stood up and walked to the door. Once he had adjusted his belt, he stepped outside into the snow. The approaching vehicle was familiar. "It's him. Let him pass," he ordered in Russian.

The guard commander saluted.

The conscript raised the barrier with one hand until the SUV was clear, then lowered the metal bar. The Range Rover with the distinctive thick, tinted bulletproof windows passed through the checkpoint. It was a familiar sight to the elite Internal Security Border Guards, who manned the border checkpoint. No further action required. The VIP never descended from his vehicle on the Russian side. No documents or ID were shown or checked. None of the sentries had ever snatched more than a glimpse of pale flesh through the three inches of open window. Protocol successfully ignored.

Ryzhakov acknowledged the sergeant's salute—a swift, karate-style movement to the middle of the chest, both hands gripping his rifle. The Russian wasn't *voyenni,* not military personnel. But the distinction between military and police in this part of Russia had become increasingly blurred.

The tarmac road became a dirt track. The Range Rover lurched from side to side as it crunched down on the frozen soil across no man's land. Thanks to the bulletproofing and the reinforced side protection, it weighed and cost more than twice as much as a normal SUV. He could afford it.

Freezing air rushed through the open window. Ryzhakov inhaled it along with his own cigarette smoke, exhaled, and coughed up loose phlegm. He spat and closed the window, at the same time squinting into the distance to see if his contact had arrived on time.

Fifty meters on the other side of the Russian checkpoint, he crossed a wooden bridge over the Tumen River. A North Korean military Jeep stood idling. You had to admire North Koreans. Contrary to popular opinion—make that Western opinion—Ryzhakov admired the ruthless discipline and efficiency of their regime, even if he had personal reasons for loathing them. He could do business with these people for now. Revenge later. At the same time, he wanted to do business with the West, deftly playing one against the other to his own ends.

Ryzhakov pulled up to the Jeep and waited.

Open fields spread into surrounding countryside away from the border to the south. On DPRK territory to his left were desolate farm buildings. He wondered if anyone lived there. He had never seen any sign of life. The small group of buildings reminded him of his home village thirty miles outside of Vladivostok. In that bleak setting he had been told of his father's brutal murder thirty years before by the North Korean regime.

A Russian policeman had come to the Ryzhakov family dacha, ordering the youngest member of the family to wait outside on the porch. On hearing the news a few moments later, his mother had wailed for what seemed like an eternity. He had peeped through the window and saw his mother slumped on the floor, shaking. When the policeman left, he told the young Ryzhakov, "For your mother's sake and for the Russian people, you must be strong. One day you will take revenge for your father. His memory and his reputation will guide you."

The young Ryzhakov understood the part about being strong for his mother, but he couldn't fathom how his actions or behavior might affect the entire Russian people. Years later, his mother had told him the truth about his father's death. That was when he finally understood what he had to do.

The fading daylight descending no man's land played tricks on his vision. Dark shadows appeared to change shape like morphing figures or ghosts. The snow glowed a dark shade of violet, and the snowy fields resembled a wild moonscape.

A North Korean man with black hair got out of the other Jeep and approached the Range Rover. "Greetings, comrade!" His Russian was poor, barely understandable. He was dressed in a mixture of brown and green fatigues and wore a military cap with a small red metal star above the peak. He pulled the fur collar of his parka up on both sides with the hand that wasn't carrying a black vinyl attaché case. Ryzhakov rolled down the window. The man carrying the case placed it on the Range Rover's wing mirror, balancing it like a tray of drinks.

"Privjet!" *Hi.* Ryzhakov twisted his upper body so he could snap open the case's two metal clasps. His nostrils puffed with pleasure. "Shall I count?" he asked jovially. He already knew the answer.

"It would be impolite not to count, comrade," replied the man.

Both chuckled. Two columns of breath rose above the black SUV and evaporated into the oily twilight sky.

"Of course, I must not be impolite." Ryzhakov scanned the wads of one hundred-dollar bills and grunted. It took him a moment to find the map tucked inside the lid of the attaché case. The words neatly scribed in pencil along the edge read:

YONGBUK—$$$ LOCKY LOCATION $$$

Ryzhakov appreciated the humor (and the typo), but not as much as the fact that he was being paid obscene money for this enterprise. The key location at Yongbuk had been marked on the map. That was all he needed. He began counting and ruffling through the stacks of bills to be sure each was as it should be. He knew he would reach two million dollars, and he did. Easy money. Particularly since he would be paid another two million from Western sources for exactly the same task. Idiots. All of them. They distrusted each other and trusted him. For the moment, at least.

"All correct," he said. "Thank you, comrade."

"You have everything."

Ryzhakov took the attaché case, closed his window, put the automatic gear lever in reverse, and pressed play on his CD player—"She's Got a Ticket to Ride" began. As he made his three-point turn, Ryzhakov skillfully avoided two landmines lying a few feet apart from each other on the road. He hit the accelerator. It always gave him a thrill to negotiate his way over stray landmines with the precision of an Olympic carriage driver. Prince Philip, his hero, had put the sport on the map.

Ryzhakov was excited. "Bled!" he muttered his favorite curse. *Fuck. A useful day*, he thought. Once he had executed the task, he would collect the second half of his "prize" money. He was expecting an unofficial delivery by official UN courier—the most convenient way for Western governments to deliver illegal payments nowadays. No wires, no internet transfers, no paperwork, no secret bank accounts in Switzerland. It was post-9/11, and cash was king. A man with a briefcase was the cleanest and least traceable way of doing business.

He hummed along to "She's Got a Ticket to Ride" and wondered if Natasha had completed her task as he commanded.

Khasan, Russia

Thirty minutes later, Natasha's convoy reached the border crossing at Khansan. The convoy drove straight through the Russian checkpoint and across the Tumen River. Thirty yards from the North Korean side, a sentry left his post and walked into the middle of the road. With his foot, he slid three anti-tank mines out of the way. Once the convoy had passed by, he slid them gently back into position.

Then the convoy halted. A North Korean soldier opened the rear door of Steele's APC and gave a cursory glance inside. The convoy, apparently, had official clearance, so the inspection was a formality. The door was slammed shut.

"That was easy," said Steele.

"Just the beginning," she replied.

"How long?" He pointed to his watch.

"Soon."

He gave up deluding himself that his press card might save him in an emergency. His presence here would implicate him in whatever was about to take place.

A few minutes later, he leaned toward Natasha. "I hope this is worth it. When can we—"

His question was drowned out by the noise of a helicopter above them and slightly to the rear. They were being tracked. Natasha stood up to lock the hatch. She gave Viktor the thumbs down.

"Problema?" he asked.

"Da!"

He acknowledged, gesturing for her to sit.

The APC engine exploded into a roar of cylinder horsepower once the driver realized what was happening. His foot smashed down on the accelerator pedal. Steele was thrown forward, his protective helmet crashing against the soldier next to him. The *rat-tat-tat-tat-tat* of machine gun fire pummeled the side of their APC. Up ahead, the other two vehicles were also under attack. The North Korean soldier next to Steele stood to secure the rear hatch but was hit by the pinging ricochet of a stray bullet. As the wounded man stumbled back to his seat, the rear hatch worked its way open, providing a clear view of the sky and the attacking mechanical birds.

North Korea near the Russian Border

Two helicopter gunships fired simultaneously at the convoy. Their mission, it seemed, was to destroy Dragon I, Bear III, and Snake III. Automatic fire rained down, a shower of scorching lava. Steele was thankful for the lead plates in his flak jacket— one of them might just save his life—again. For a second, he flashed back to his mission in Bosnia several years before.

The BTR-60BP slowed, clunking through several gears. Violently swerving again to the left and right, Steele thought he might be sick as the vehicle veered from side to side. The engine noise was deafening. Bullets pelted the APC's metal skin as though the entire North Korean army had launched an assault. Steele felt the blood drain from his face. He felt light-headed and put his head between his legs to stop himself from passing out. *Pansy!*

The driver observed that the lead APC was in trouble. He hesitated, lifting his foot off the gas pedal.

"NYET!" shouted Viktor. *NO!* He peered down into the driver's compartment. "We must keep going!" He motioned violently, his arm like a piston slicing back and forth. "Ravno! Ravno!" *Go straight!*

"Ponyatna! Ponyatna!" The teenage driver's acne-covered face grimaced and sweated with fear. He waved his hand to acknowledge the command.

All three APCs were now speeding at sixty miles an hour on a narrow mountain road with a hundred-foot drop on one side. Pockmarked with bullet holes, the APCs reached the edge of a forest. Firing ceased as the convoy disappeared into a wooded section of the road.

Steele craned his neck right, trying to see past Viktor's head into the driver's compartment and what lay ahead. The wounded Korean soldier on his left was bleeding heavily through his camouflage jacket. Steele instinctively felt in his breast pocket, the place where all British Army soldiers carried field dressings.

Wrong country. Wrong uniform. Wrong army. Breast pocket empty.

Natasha pulled a dressing out and handed it to Steele, who applied pressure to the soldier's gurgling chest wound. Death closes in swiftly on a heavily bleeding man. He had seen enough to know when it was worth trying to save a man's life, and when it was a lost cause. This was a lost cause.

Nonetheless, he made an attempt. *Poor bastard. At least we can give him some hope.* The soldier's face was blank. Steele maintained pressure on the wound, and the soldier made eye contact for the first time. He smiled in resignation. *Minutes before lights out.*

Viktor shook his head and made the slit sign across his neck. *Thanks for nothing, Viktor.*

Things were not looking good for anyone inside Dragon I. But Steele wasn't ready to die. Too many hopes and desires, wisdom he hadn't gained, peace and tranquility he had never enjoyed. *Stop. Enough with the philosophy. Death not an option.*

The APCs tore into open terrain and were immediately under fire again. He heard the sound of pinging metal. Turning to his right, he saw Natasha bent over. She'd been hit.

"Natasha!" He let go of the soldier and swiveled round in the close confines to give first aid.

"It's OK," she said. "Just my shoulder."

Steele examined the wound and held his foul-weather mitt against it to stop the bleeding. With the other hand, he retrieved a fresh dressing from Natasha's pocket. "Flesh wound, I think," he confirmed. "You'll make it."

★   ★   ★

Again, Steele glanced up ahead through the driver's compartment. The lead vehicle took a direct hit. Veering to one side and flipping several times, it crashed through the metal safety barrier on the side of the road and disappeared down a ravine. Clipping the first vehicle, the second vehicle crashed headfirst into a large boulder on the side of the road and burst into flames.

Steele's APC headed straight toward the fireball.

"Ravno! RAVNO! Viktor commanded the driver. *GO STRAIGHT!*

The driver turned toward them keeping his eyes on the road. "We don't make it!" Sweat poured down his face.

Steele grabbed Natasha and pulled her close to him. It was instinctive. She winced as he pressed against her shoulder, but she did not protest. She gripped his forearm. He wanted to protect her.

"We'll make it!" he said, pulling her closer.

He was surprised by his own optimism. Or was it delusion?

"I'm sorry, Jack!" she said. "It's my fault."

What is she talking about? "It's okay. We're going to make it!"

He switched focus to the obstacle ahead. Dragon I narrowly missed a steep incline to the right. It was impossible to see beyond the smoke and flames. Behind them, heavy machine gun fire continued from the helicopter. Viktor slapped the driver's helmet. "Bistree! Bistree!" *Faster! Faster!*

They disappeared into the fireball, clipping the second vehicle but missing a potentially catastrophic collision by inches. They shot through the cloud of smoke like a high-velocity rifle bullet.

Clear. Dragon I is safe. But for how long?

One hundred yards ahead was a T72 Main Battle Tank, its barrel pointing directly at them. Their driver slammed his foot on the brakes. Steele glimpsed a pinprick of red light shining at them—the T72 was target "lasing" them. The T72 main armament laser locked on to Steele's APC.

It could fire at any moment.

CHAPTER TEN

Steele stopped breathing. He stared at the perfect black hole of death. The T72 tank, barrel quivering as it made final adjustments, was about to fire. He had never seen a live tank round fired from this angle—directly *at* him. He had often imagined what it would look like from the enemy position, and now he was about to find out.

He swallowed. No saliva. His throat was dry.

Suddenly, the tank readjusted—upward. It searched for a target high above. Then it fired, its huge hulk rocking gently back and forth like a mother holding her infant.

Steele exhaled.

The blood-orange flash of the projectile was followed by the sizzling *whiz-bang* over their heads. The helicopter flying high and to the rear exploded in a violent thunder ball. Jagged chunks of metal showered earthward, reminding Steele of his boyhood tantrum when he had thrown his kaleidoscope against a brick wall and watched it smash to pieces.

Then the tank fired another round in quick succession. The second helicopter went spiraling into the forest like a slain pterodactyl. Another frenzied explosion ripped across the snowy landscape as the bird crashed.

Dragon I came to a halt several feet in front of the T72 tank. The engine's hot metal pipes creaked and hissed. Then stillness, as if the overworked engine was catching its breath.

Someone outside fumbled with the handle on the rear door. Steele's army background kicked in. He removed the Makarov 9mm pistol from his holster and chambered a round. He looked at Viktor, who flicked off his safety catch and then nodded at Steele to do the same.

I'm out of practice.

The door swung open. Daylight gushed into the APC's dark metal hulk. Steele shielded his face and squinted, his eyes growing accustom to daylight.

The silhouetted hulk of a man flanked by three burly soldiers stood outside. They were dressed in blue and gray camouflage with black leather belts studded with ammunition.

The man smiled, almost laughing. It was Igor Ryzhakov.

"You are pleased to see me?" he said to Steele. He held out both arms. "Unfortunately, we had mopping-up operations to perform. I hope all personnel are unharmed."

"Naxal!" hissed Natasha. *Arsehole.* "You are sick. Are you insane? You almost killed us."

"Unwelcome visitors … confusion among our North Korean partners. The dangers of heroic deeds." He shrugged his shoulders and turned down the corners of his mouth in mock concern.

Steele was flabbergasted. Ryzhakov—Natasha's husband— was responsible and now seemingly in charge of all of this? *God help us.*

She stumbled out of the vehicle, pale and sweating, clutching her shoulder. She leaned forward and without warning vomited over Ryzhakov's boots. One of his men laughed. Ryzhakov silenced him with a look and then scolded Natasha, "Suxha!" *Bitch!* He struck her face with the back of his hand. She remained upright and defiant.

Viktor clambered down from the transporter. *He wouldn't dare to physically intervene,* thought Steele. He watched as Viktor held up both hands trying to defuse the situation. "Pozhalysta, ribyata! Davajte!" *Please, everyone. Come on, now.*

Glaring at her husband, Natasha wiped her face with the back of her sleeve. Then she spit in his face. Ryzhakov's bodyguard— a new recruit—howled with laughter again, looking to his colleagues to share the joke. Big mistake. Ryzhakov pulled a pistol from his belt—he wore no holster—and shot him in the forehead as the man looked to his colleagues for help that never came.

"Bastard!" Natasha screamed, still nursing her bruised face. "Sick bastard!"

Ryzhakov had almost broken Natasha's jaw and murdered an innocent young man in the space of twenty seconds. *What's next?* Steele wondered.

Ryzhakov grabbed Natasha's hair with one hand. He wiped the saliva from his chin and paused, except for an involuntary twitching around the eyes. "Suxha!" *Bitch!* Pulling her toward him, he kneed her in the stomach with the finesse of nightclub bouncer.

Steele bolted from the APC and flung himself at Ryzhakov, taking everyone by surprise, including himself. He knocked the Russian to the ground. "Who the fuck—!" he grunted as the two men rolled around on the ground.

No one intervened. The foreigner was harmless, and unarmed. A daily brawl was commonplace in the Russian army. Ryzhakov didn't need any help. He could wrestle any one of his men into submission. His bodyguards reacted to bullets not fists.

Locked in combat like two boys in a schoolyard, Steele and Ryzhakov gasped and huffed for breath, Steele more so than his opponent. Punches were thrown and blocked, but it was more of a wrestling match. Steele managed to get himself on top of Ryzhakov, who was grinning and seemingly having way too much fun. Steele released another punch but was blocked from behind before it landed. Viktor and one of the bodyguards moved in. They pulled Steele up off the ground. "OK, OK," he said, brushing off the dirt and snow. "Are you all right?" he asked, looking at Natasha.

"Of course!" she said, spitting. "Idiot! This was none of your business! I can fight my own battles."

I suppose chivalry hasn't made it this far east. "I won't bother next time," he said, wiping his cheek.

Ryzhakov smiled and said to Steele, "I play with you. All's fair in love and war."

He held out his hand.

"Whatever floats your boat, Igor."

"Floats—"

Lost in translation. "Never mind."

They shook hands.

"Pleasure to meet you again, Mr. Steele. Welcome to Operation Tumen."

Of course, Operation Tumen. Made sense. The Tumen River was over three hundred miles long and separated the boundary between Russia, North Korea and China. Good name for an op.

"The pleasure is mine. I can't wait."

★ ★ ★

Two hours later, the depleted convoy—one APC and two SUVs—snaked through a narrow section of mountain terrain less than twenty miles from the border with Russia. Ryzhakov ordered the vehicles to pull over for a rest stop. A cloud of dust settled as the engines were cut. Steele, Natasha, and Viktor got out of Ryzhakov's SUV to stretch their legs. Ryzhakov's men climbed out of the APC and obeyed his order to dispatch the body of the North Korean soldier unceremoniously over the cliff to an equally unceremonious grave.

The group began to stretch, bend, and admire the view of snowcapped mountains and ravines as if they were weary tourists stepping off their tour bus. Steele approached Ryzhakov, who stood with his toes inching over the edge of the cliff, staring down at an emerald-green lagoon in the valley below.

"Pity about the soldier," Steele said. *This man is a psycho.*

"Accidents happen," replied Ryzhakov calmly.

"Do they?" He took a few steps away from the inspector. *I might just push him over the edge.*

Both men stood silent for a few moments. *So close to the edge. But Natasha can fight for herself.*

"Stunning," Steele said finally, glancing at the emerald lagoon below.

"Too bad we have no time to swim. Work is work."

"I've had enough swimming recently." Steele looked over the edge. It was time to play his game. "Igor, I apologize for my behavior. This whole situation ... it's a shock, you understand? I thought this was a routine assignment." He felt a knot in his stomach; he hated sycophants. He detested bullies, but for now he feigned respect.

"No problem, my friend. How do you say? 'No hard feelings.' You are an English gentleman, I think."

"Not quite, but thanks anyway."

Steele was starting to wonder if the spitting incident with Natasha had been staged for his benefit?—to test him? Ryzhakov was the kind of man who stopped at nothing to achieve his goal. If Ryzhakov's men were watching Sandy in London as Viktor had said, he would not hesitate to harm or even kill her if Steele refused to cooperate.

Remain open to all possibilities. Be calm and flexible. Steele knew that by staying with these people, he too might be implicated in highly dangerous and criminal actions. Quite probably crimes against humanity if what he'd seen so far was any indication. Ryzhakov had executed his own bodyguard for laughing. Christ knows what else he was capable of. He had access to military hardware and personnel, police, and cross-border access. Perhaps he'd even controlled the helicopters and then had them destroyed? From now on, he would control his temper, even if Natasha was assaulted. It was the only way.

Steele said, "Can I ask you something?"

"Please."

"You think this will work?"

"What?"

"Your attack on North Korea?" Steele was probing, trying to provoke a reaction.

"You overestimate us, my friend. We are not going to attack our friends in North Korea. They have invited us."

"Really?" Steele was baffled and intrigued.

"Pravda." *Yes, really*.

"Why do you need me?"

"I do not need you, my friend. But you may be helpful to us under difficult circumstances. We have much work to do. An impartial British journalist will help us."

"Sounds interesting ..."

"Sense of fair play ... cricket ... and all this English bullshit your country is famous for. No?"

He has a point. Steele parried. "Not exactly, Igor ... if I'm honest."

Ryzhakov drew two letters in the dirt with the tip of his boot: "U" and "N."

"UN people from New York want to improve our lives. Some of us do not want this."

"What do you want?" asked Steele.

"It's the same in North Korea. Some want help from UN, and many do not." With a nod and a wave, he ordered one of the soldiers to bring hot drinks from the boiling vessel inside the APC. Ryzhakov slipped off his gloves, rubbed his hands, and turned to Steele. "I am working for those who do not want help from UN. We have a plan for them. A surprise."

"Don't tell me. You've kidnapped the missing UN officials, and are about to hand them over to the North Koreans in exchange for hard currency?"

"British sense of humor. I love this." Ryzhakov chuckled. "Some factions of military may not agree with our plan. But their leaders pay me. I name my price, they pay me, and I work. I like to work."

"Win, win ..." Steele took the cup handed to him by Ryzhakov's man. He sipped. A sweet, exotic vapor told him it was some kind of fruit tea he couldn't place—no milk, too much sugar. "Your line of work sounds more lucrative than mine, Igor."

"Perhaps."

"Who are you fighting?"

"I am fighting for my revenge."

"Revenge?"

"For my father."

"He's dead?"

"For his memory. Legacy has a soul also."

"Explain." Steele hoped he would elaborate on Natasha's comment about her husband having a miserable upbringing.

"The last time I saw my father, he was dead." Ryzhakov paused, as if deciding whether to continue. "Laid out like a bloated fish."

"I'm sorry." *Explains a lot, though.*

"Your father is alive?" asked Ryzhakov.

"I never knew him."

"Then you can't understand. I saw this body. His mouth and jaw were three times normal size. The flesh around his mouth was slit in two places to allow access for the extractions."

Steele thought about sharing the painful memories of seeing his brother in that terrible state but decided against it. He grimaced. "Extractions?"

"Disfigured. They ripped his teeth and gums from his head."

"Who?"

"His face was like rubber, encrusted with blood. Flaps of skin looked like pieces of torn cloth. I will never forget this. Why such mutilation? Humiliation?"

"Yes, why?"

"He was a doctor doing his job—saving the life of a North Korean politician. They asked the Russians for help, and my father volunteered."

"To help the North Koreans?"

"Yes."

"And they murdered him?"

"I never found out what happened and why."

Steele took a moment. Then he said, "So this is payback for your father?"

"The money I am paid for this mission is a small reward for my mother's misery and my father's suffering. And mine. It is just the beginning."

"Of revenge?"

"Yes."

"You're going to attack North Korea?"

"Conservative generals in North Korea are paranoid. They think everyone wants to attack them. There is confusion in government. I will profit from confusion. And so will you."

"Who was in the helicopters?"

"These are hardliners—your friends in America call them 'hawks.' America is not only country with hawks and doves."

"You're helping the doves?"

"I am helping highest bidder."

"Fair enough. So you don't actually care about anyone? Just money?" Steele slurped his tea, wondering if he'd crossed a line.

No reaction.

Steele tried again. "Viktor told me I'm your 'insurance' … What does that mean?"

Ryzhakov smiled. "Of course, I cannot allow you to put *all* the pieces together. Not yet. I can tell you that you will be voice of reason, or should I say voice of Bush House on the battlefield."

"Battlefield?"

"I have studied your articles. You write well, I think. You have strong voice. People will listen to you."

"Thanks. Which battle are we talking about?"

Ryzhakov looked away as though he had suddenly remembered something important. He lost interest in their polite conversation.

"So many questions, so little time," he continued. With two slicing motions Ryzhakov threw the rest of his tea into the snow.

"Davayte ribyata, poyexali!" he shouted to his men. *Come on people, let's move.* He walked back to his vehicle and placed both hands on the warm hood, leaning forward to stretch his calf muscles.

All the while, he watched Steele, who had now crossed to Natasha. She stood at the side of the road also taking in the view.

"Are you OK?" Steele asked her. "Your shoulder?"

"It's nothing. Do not worry yourself for me. Everything is okay." Steele saw Ryzhakov looking at them. "The schedule is good—this is the most important." Natasha lowered her voice to a whisper. "It is better if you do not ask me again. It is better Igor has no reason to become angry."

"One question."

"Please."

"The helicopters. Won't they be hunting the people who shot them down?"

Natasha shook her head. "The helicopters were probably sent by hardliners. We are one step ahead. Everything is under control."

★　　★　　★

As the convoy made its way through the mountains, Viktor studied his map. He announced they had about ten miles to go. "No more stops. Better arrive as soon as possible." Viktor also told Steele that the North Korean escort had been hearing military chatter over the radio net. North Koreans had found the helicopter wrecks.

Steele turned to Ryzhakov. "You said we were invited. Why is Viktor so worried?"

"Chain of command is complicated. Some will try to stop us, whatever the orders. These people are not as well organized as you think. Not like the West."

"Clear as mud." Steele was more confused than ever. Like Ryzhakov, Steele also concluded he should trust no one.

The last time he had felt this confused and perplexed by fragile foreign government hierarchy was during the market massacre attack in Sarajevo, Bosnia. A single mortar shell had killed sixty-eight people in one fell swoop in downtown Sarajevo. His UN sources suspected the Bosnian army might have targeted their own people on the tiny, packed marketplace, but no one could be sure. A senior British officer gave Steele permission to leak the evidence to a well-known BBC TV news correspondent who filed a sensational news report. But Jeremy Tucker, foreign correspondent—*aka fucking bastard*—also revealed his British Army source—Capt. Jack Steele—in exchange for information on his next story. From that moment, Steele became as cynical and distrusting of the human race as Ryzhakov now seemed to be—you could never trust anyone a hundred percent, not even prominent journalists or respected generals.

This was the main experience from Sarajevo that made Steele want to become a freelance journalist—he was consumed by the desire to find truth and to tell the truth first hand as *he* saw it in Bosnia. Not the truth of the UN or Bosnian Muslim or Bosnian Serb authorities, not mass media news organization truth, or truth of international charities, who all tried to manipulate for their own interests. Truth, Steele had learned many years ago, was in fact a very subjective matter. *In the end, it is only your truth that matters.*

Now he sensed he was getting closer and closer to a story that would make world headlines. But first he needed to figure out what his "insurance" role in this Tumen debacle was, and how he could turn it to his advantage.

CHAPTER ELEVEN

Hampstead, London

The first sound Blake Danner heard on regaining consciousness was the familiar ticking of a black London taxi on the street. He tried to recall what had happened at the NW3 garden flat. His head was sore. Someone had smacked him with something very hard—that much he could remember. *Sandy must have been in the apartment. That was highly likely though not certain.* He had seen a blue yoga mat on broken glass outside the front door. That was the last thing he could remember.

He heaved himself up off the floor and listened for signs of life. He made a cursory search of the flat, but it was empty.

He had to find Sandy. He blamed himself for losing touch with her, cutting her off in fact. *I'm a shit dad.* Had he not been such a miserable son-of-a-bitch, Sandy and Jack would not have been moving to London in the first place. He had come after Sandy to change her mind, tell her he was sorry, but now it was too late. *Or maybe it wasn't?* Why was Sandy in trouble? Why? If he had only helped his son-in-law land a job in Philadelphia instead of making sure he didn't, instead of using his clout to block Jack's work visa, Sandy might be safe, and he might not have a huge bump on his head. *Damn it! What an ass!*

It was raining. He clambered up the slippery wooden basement steps to street level, holding onto the black metal railing. At the top, he paused to catch his breath. The light drizzle freshened the early morning air.

After setting down a fare a few houses further down, the black cab began to pull away.

"Taxi!" shouted Danner. Its brakes squealed. White reverse lights illuminated the glazed surface of the tree-lined street. Danner met the taxi and slumped onto the left passenger door. He felt weak.

At first the taxi driver was dubious, but seeing Danner's face close up, he opened the electric window. "You all right, Guv'?" he asked.

"Fine, thanks. Just fine." Danner climbed into the cab, slamming the door behind him. He collapsed into his seat, steadying himself on the thin passenger handrail.

"Where to, Guvnor?"

"Drive around the neighborhood. I'm looking for my daughter. She's blonde, early thirties—looks a bit younger."

"Wish I could say the same." He chuckled, glancing into his rearview mirror to see if Danner had appreciated his quip.

You can quit it with the jokes. Danner saw the driver's eyes checking on him. "Sorry, I've got a sore head." Danner settled in the back seat of the cab and rubbed the back of his head. He could feel a large, painful swelling.

"Right you are. Don't worry, Guv'. If she's still around, we'll find her."

"Thank you. As long as it takes. Just keep driving. Keep the meter running."

The taxi moved off. Danner wished, as he had wished many times before, that he had never started to gamble. *Too late for regrets.* He knew that much. The damage was done.

He had made choices and had to live with the consequences. Sandy's abduction, he told himself, was yet another consequence of his selfish living. Maybe his crazy ex-wife, Anna, was responsible? Who else? Danner was in deep. *God damn it! How could I fuck up so badly?* He owed a lot of people a lot of money. Anna was among them. It was impossible to see a way out. That was one of the reasons he wanted Sandy to marry money and not a poor British journalist.

Damn it! He had to find his daughter before something happened to her that he would never forgive himself for.

Pyongyang, North Korea

In the most prestigious and highly protected quarter of Pyongyang, Colonel Cho Myung-chul, the North Korean President's Chief of Staff, sat watching forbidden satellite TV. He channel-surfed between BBC World and CNN International. He was keeping up to date with world events but had also found it an excellent way to improve his English. It had become a ritual to study the news reports and take notes on the hour every hour duties permitting. A tall, lean, man with black shiny hair slicked back, Colonel Cho Myung-chul was one the few trusted officials in President Kim Jung Ryul's government. He was permitted to watch satellite television, read international newspapers, and surf the internet.

His office also served as his apartment. He rarely left, not even to see his wife and ten-year-old daughter. He loved them deeply and missed them. He had hardly seen his family these past two years. Since he had been appointed chief of staff to the president as well as chief military and political strategist, his country was his second child, his new and most coveted responsibility and priority. His own family came last.

The president, Kim Jung Ryul, often held council in the middle of the night after he had satisfied his insatiable desire for an endless stream of beautiful women eager to accommodate his unusual sexual habits. Each woman in his "private zoo," as he affectionately called it, was required to adopt an animal character albeit sexually. They remained in character for the duration to entertain the president and fulfill his sexual needs and desires. Kim had offered the Colonel unlimited access to the women, and the Colonel had come close to taking up the offer on several occasions—but the black-and-white photograph of his wife and daughter proudly displayed in the middle of his desk served as faithful anchor to his wife and had saved him from temptation when the pressure of work became overwhelming. *All I have left are my principles.*

The colonel leaned across his desk and opened the swivel-tap on the electric tea urn. His attendant had filled it with freshly brewed tea a few minutes earlier. Sometimes, the colonel slept for only two or three hours. Last night was such a night. Kim had urgent domestic and foreign policy issues to resolve. The two men had talked geopolitical strategies until close to dawn.

A knock on his door interrupted his musings.

He did not even have time to respond before it burst open. General Yoon Tae Sung entered the nerve cell of the North Korean political apparatus.

"Enter," said the colonel to make his point, glaring at the general thereafter in silent protest. The general outranked the colonel by several degrees and years of service, but the colonel was Kim's chief advisor and, in his humble opinion, outranked the general by several degrees of brain matter. Both men observed a reluctant respect for each another.

The general was one of a handful of old-guard politicians and military officers who felt it their duty to uphold and safeguard—as they saw it—the communist traditions and the "old" way. The general felt he had earned the right to enter at will, day or night, to speak with the president's advisor.

"We have announced the press conference for today at noon," he said. General Yoon Tae Sung was a short man with gray hair—sixty years old. He strutted rather than walked and found it difficult to keep still even when he was sitting down, which he had now done without being invited to do so. He removed his peaked cap, lavishly decorated with cheap-looking gold braid, and raised his black, bushy eyebrows. "Well?"

"Impossible," the colonel replied. "As you are aware, all press conferences must be requested through the Ministry of

Information on *my* order. Urgent matters of national security are the only exception. Have you told our Dear Leader?" The colonel already knew the answer but was covering protocol just in case.

"He does not necessarily need to know. But I invite you to inform him of the decision as soon as possible."

The colonel was genuinely surprised. He had not reckoned on the old guard moving this quickly—and efficiently. *Ruthless old buzzards.* The old-guard generals had recently conspired to use their country's nuclear threat leverage in the international community's six-party disarmament talks with China, Japan, South Korea, Russia, and America. Meant as both snub and blatant provocation to the international community, they planned to publicly threaten to extract weapons-grade plutonium from fuel rods at Yongbuk, the nuclear reactor facility two hundred miles north of the capital, without Kim's blessing.

Insanity, but nowadays, anything is possible. "What decision?"

"Today, we announce to the world our intention to remove an unspecified number of fuel rods before the end of the week to facilitate plutonium extraction."

"Your audacity will offend our Dear Leader."

"That is why I have come. This is a serious matter, and I wish to keep our Dear Leader informed of our intentions." He smiled obsequiously. "There can be no misunderstanding."

"Informed or forewarned?"

"We have ordered the UN inspectors to leave our country within twenty-four hours. Then we will begin."

"Comrade general, with respect, we must wait until the inspectors leave of their own accord. Forcing them to leave will not serve our strategic interests. We must adhere to our agreement."

"With respect, Colonel, *we* disagree. The process begins after the press conference at noon. My committee is unanimous. We recommend the extractions be completed within forty-eight hours. Preferably—but not necessarily—with our president's blessing. I am counting on you to facilitate our decision."

Facilitate. Cunning little fat lizard. The colonel pictured the gaggle of gray-haired, sullen-faced generals nodding in unison as they sat around their gigantic table in the Ministry of Defense headquarters. He waited patiently to see if the general had finished. Then he said, "Allow me to consult with our leader."

"As you wish. Extraction process begins in three hours. It is time for the world to take us seriously. It is time to live up to our reputation. We are, after all, the infamous *axis of evil.*"

"Thank you, general. I urge you, with respect, to wait for Kim's reply."

The general frowned. "In order for the press conference to coincide with our plans, we must receive his blessing by noon today." Short of bursting into the president's private apartment for an answer, there was nothing more he could do. And he knew this.

With a limp arm, General Yoon Tae Sung feebly saluted, clicked his heels, did an about turn, and strutted to the door. Formality required the colonel to stand up and return the salute.

There was a *clunk* as the guard outside pulled the heavy oak door shut.

Apart from an almost inaudible hum from the television on mute, his office was still and quiet again. The colonel nestled into his leather armchair and turned up the volume. He would think through the important decision with the heightened and melodramatic voice of the CNN anchor man or woman in the background. Today, it was a woman reporting breaking news of a huge explosion in Karachi. Fifty people dead, but the colonel detected an almost undetectable relief in her voice—relief, he guessed, that the victims were not American, and the news was happening on the other side of the world. *I could be wrong …* He reminded himself to listen more often to the more authentic and reliable, in his opinion, BBC World Service radio.

The anchorwoman's voice faded from his immediate awareness. The colonel replayed the conversation he'd just had several times over in his mind to be sure he had played his part and set the trap correctly. Then he smiled and nodded to himself. Everything under control, he thought. *Our Dear Leader will be pleased.*

Chongjin, North Korea

The three-vehicle convoy arrived at the deserted airfield near the small town of Chongjin. There were no guards at the entrance located on a long, straight road ten miles north of the town. You had to lift the barrier yourself. It was abandoned—at least that was the story fed to the locals. Beyond the base loomed an ominous mountain range that meandered westward to China.

The convoy halted outside the aircraft hangar on the far side of the runway. Steele noticed a small team of DPRK guards patrolling the gigantic structure as well as what looked like two small accommodation blocks next door to it. There were no other buildings for miles around.

Steele and the rest of the Russian party got out. Ryzhakov stretched, Viktor yawned, and the bodyguards released long-held flatulence. The second and third SUVs drove straight into the hangar, where soldiers began unloading the equipment.

It was midmorning. Steele watched the sun hiding behind a dense layer of cloud, its fuzzy circle barely filtering through. In Russia, he had missed the audacious, brazen colors of the West. Even the grass, he noted, was greener in England.

He had spent too long in Russia, and North Korea was even more depressing. A different world, he reflected, as he looked at the bleak countryside—so different from the Los Angeles, California beach where he and Sandy had loved to spend time on vacation.

A few months after their wedding, Sandy had taken Jack to watch the sunset during a visit to her Aunt Lexy in Rolling Hills. Steele stood on Redondo Beach holding Sandy close as they watched the giant orange ball sink below the horizon. The beach was so enchanting he decided he might even have his ashes scattered right there. But even then, he recalled looking at his watch, unable to completely appreciate the moment. *Why can't I live in the moment, for God's sake? The sunset? The ocean? Isn't love enough?* He had cursed himself as his thoughts meandered. He wanted to pick up where his brother had been forced to stop far too early. *If I had called him back that morning, Peter might still be alive.* He was determined to make up for it, become a renowned and respected journalist—a Jeremy Bowen, a Kate Adie, a Ted Koppel, or a Dan Rather. He yearned for professional success so hard it was exhausting. And so, even in that idyllic setting watching the sun setting and the tiny shape of an oil tanker sailing across the shimmering horizon, he felt restless and nervous about his relationship with his new wife. *Will she accept me for what I stand for? Have I been honest about goals, fears, hopes, and dreams?* He wanted to see his name on the front page of the *London Daily Standard.*

Now his eyes focused on the Russian and North Korean soldiers slamming down boxes of ammunition taken from what was left of the depleted convoy vehicles. The sun had completely disappeared, replaced by a light drizzle verging on sleet that hung in the air outside the aircraft hangar.

On the tarmac, three propeller-driven aircraft waited patiently—two Yak-18s and one Yak-18T, frequently used in North Korea, China, and Russia for flight training and air transportation. Steele had scored top marks at Sandhurst for aircraft recognition. The unusual thing about the Yakovlev 18T, he recalled, was its multifunction as a trainer, transporter, air ambulance, and aerial photography platform. Notable for its range and aerobatic capability, it could hold a heck of a lot of stuff and go almost anywhere.

As a teenager, he was trained to fly the De Havilland DHC-1 Chipmunk, a single engine trainer aircraft. Students were allowed to take the controls and fly the aircraft. The ex-RAF pilot instructor guided them through a stall turn, a barrel roll, and a loop-the-loop.

Both of these Yak aircraft before him could seat two pilots, but Steele saw just one in each cockpit. Mechanics stood patiently on the ground as the pilots ran through preflight checks.

Aircraft? Jeez, what did Igor have planned now?

Steele studied the scene before him. One of the pilots looked familiar. "Who are those guys?" he asked Natasha.

"Lower your voice. They are pilots—suicide bombers," she replied calmly.

"What?!" He hissed incredulously.

"Serving their country."

"Excuse me?" He frowned again, unable to believe this could be happening around him. "You're joking. Please tell me you're not serious."

"They serve their country."

No joke.

"I heard you. Which country?" He took a few more steps toward the front of the SUV to get a closer look at the pilots.

Natasha followed. "My country. North Koreans volunteered also."

"Are they criminals? Did Igor bust them out of jail?"

"They are educated men. Idealists, perhaps."

"That sounds good. Convenient too."

"Suicide bombers are the most effective tool in today's political struggles. Igor chooses his tools wisely."

"I can see that."

"Killing innocent people is not difficult. Living with your conscience is the difficult part. Igor brainwashed these men. He can live with that."

"Natasha—"

"They believe this is a noble cause. It is politics. Philosophy. Every man needs a philosophy."

"I agree. But this is off-the-charts extreme, don't you think?"

"They hate Western influence and pressure on their lives. They want to give something back."

"Back? With their lives?"

"This is their chance—to do what is right and help Russia and the citizens of this region. Their families will be taken care of."

"Do what, exactly?"

"Smash bubble of inertia that plagues our region." Natasha walked toward the accommodation block, looking back at Steele. "So that it bursts like infected wound."

"You really believe that?"

"It is not up to me. I am responsible for my son. I care only for him."

They entered the one-story building. Steele was hit by the dry heat and stagnant, musty smell. He unzipped his thick winter jacket. "How does helping your crazy husband kill people help your son?"

"It is difficult. No one will die."

"So what are we doing here? Explain?" Steele waited for an answer that never came.

They walked down a long barren corridor.

"This is your room." Natasha pointed to a door slightly ajar as she continued down the corridor. "Wait there for instructions. Rest."

"Poka." *See you.* "And thanks …" *Thanks for nothing.*

But Steele obeyed and entered the barren room.

He sat down on the single bed—a thin mattress on an iron frame. It reminded him of the guardhouse duty officer's bunk at his regiment in the British Army of the Rhine (BAOR), Germany. A neat pile of three green blankets, each with a faded red star stitched into each corner, lay on the end of the bed. There was a plain wooden desk with a single drawer and a small metal basin in one corner.

Steele sat quietly. His mind was spinning. He sifted through the implications and consequences of witnessing and reporting a suicide bombing, not the least of which was the inevitable devastation of innocent lives. This had not been part of his plan nor his deal with Natasha. She hadn't mentioned suicide-bombing missions! But then, it wasn't exactly as though they'd had a written agreement.

He kept mulling over his situation. It was simple, he told himself. *It's your job—observe and report back to the world. It's the job, damn it!* He brushed both hands through his hair and pulled hard. *Observe, assimilate, and report.* His London boss's words rang true.

Steele repeated the phrase several times, but he was unable to convince himself. He stared out of the window toward the aircraft hangar. Relentless activity—soldiers checking aircraft tire pressure, sealing boxes, polishing cockpit windscreens. One of the pilots approached an aircraft. Ten yards from it, he stopped and looked up at the cockpit, held both hands out palms up, and closed his eyes. He was praying. When he had finished, the pilot walked to the accommodation block where Steele had been watching.

He wondered what it would be like never to return home—for something to happen to him that night—to be shot in the head like Ryzhakov's bodyguard or the old babushka. Why should he have any more control over his fate or mortality than them?

The journalist in him desperately wanted to interview the pilot. What was his motivation? Get the sinner's story before he did the damage. *How can the young man commit such a heinous act? Ryzhakov's tentacles spread far and wide. Does he even know who Ryzhakov is?*

Steele pinched his bottom lip and rolled it back on itself into a point. He realized he should be asking these same questions of himself. Why was *he* doing this? Morally, he couldn't allow this secret plot, or whatever it was, to continue. He would have blood on his hands forever. He might end up at the war crimes tribunal in the Hague like some of the players he'd come across in Bosnia. A caring, compassionate man, journalist or no, would prevent the destruction, especially if there were innocent lives at stake.

But how? His options were limited. Probably too late to change anything now without getting a bullet in the head. But if he did nothing, what was the difference between him and the suicide bomber? They both believed in their mission. Steele wanted this story more than anything else in his world—the recognition, the success. He wanted to be present when it happened—it would be like being the only witness to Tiananmen Square, Hiroshima, or 9/11. If people died, it wouldn't be his fault. *Or would it? I can stop this. But ...* It would be a spectacular story, and he would tell the world exactly what had happened, who was responsible. Everyone was depending on him. Someone had to report the truth, however disastrous. He would not let them down, and most importantly, he wouldn't risk doing anything to jeopardize Sandy's safety.

★   ★   ★

Natasha reached the far end of the corridor. She entered a bare office with a chair, table, and a few dusty filing cabinets and a fridge. As Natasha appeared in the doorway, Ryzhakov was screwing the cap back on a bottle of vodka from the icebox.

"Close the door," he snapped.

"Slushayou tibya." *I'm listening.* She closed the door and shuddered involuntarily, reminding her that she did not like being alone with this monster. *Bova. Bova is my son. I will not do anything to endanger him.* She had to stay calm for as long as it would take to execute her plan. "Shto takoy?" *What's wrong?*

"U nas yest dyela. Nada pogovoritz." *We have things to sort out. We must talk.*

"Please."

"I have a little question." Ryzhakov took a hand towel from his leather bag and wiped his face. The broken thermostat in the building had caused the heat to rise and make him sweat profusely. "I need you to be honest with me, my dearest one."

"Kanyeshna," she replied. *Of course.* Natasha hated it when her husband talked with that low, calm voice. She feigned a smile.

"You have feelings for the Englishman?"

Natasha froze. "Shto ti govorish?" said Natasha. *What are you talking about?*

Why is he asking me this? What had she done to give this impression? Maybe he was right? If she was honest, she was attracted to Steele, but romance was the last thing on her mind right now. "Feelings? Of course not," she said.

"Do you *love* him? Our beloved Englishman ..." Igor said mockingly.

"Ti suma sashol." *You're crazy.*

But Ryzhakov wasn't crazy. Nor was he drunk. This time. Natasha felt she was the one who was going crazy. How could he possibly know that Steele had been part of her plan? Perhaps Viktor had said something? No question he had always been a loyal servant. The night at the dacha? Had she been *too* attentive to Steele? Yes, it had been her idea all along to contact Jack Steele. And it wasn't just because he was a competent British journalist.

Natasha took a mental breath, preparing for the performance of a lifetime. She approached Igor and ran her hand across his face and to the back of his shaven head. "Why do you ask me this?" She sounded hurt, crushed even. *So far so good. It is working.*

"*Natashinka*, I am sorry for the pain I have caused you." He sat down and stared at Natasha, lifting his hand to stroke his velvet pad of short hair. "You must tell me."

"Why do you ask now?" Natasha took his hand and placed it between her legs. She began to stroke the top of his head and the side of his cheek.

Ryzhakov opened his mouth, about to speak. His stale breath hit Natasha as she gazed into his eyes midperformance. "I am sorry. I wanted to tell you this for a long time. I thought you were happy with me. I want you to be happy, Natasha."

"Igor, I—"

"You deserve to be happy. I see you look at him. I think he likes you."

"He's married. You are mistaken, I promise."

"I want to finish this mission. Then I want us to be together."

He was testing her, she thought, trying to provoke some kind of reaction.

"Igor Pavlovich, we are together. We will always be together. I owe you everything."

"The truth?" Ryzhakov flattened his palm and again stroked the smooth bristles on top of his head. "I must have the truth." He placed one hand on her face, squeezing both cheeks, then harder still.

His hand tight across her face, the pressure on her cheeks made it hard to speak. "This is the truth. I swear it on my son's life."

Ryzhakov nodded slowly. "OK."

She said, "Igor, tell me about Yongbuk. Are there many people there?" She sat down next to Igor and put her arms around him. The bags under her eyes looked darker than usual.

"You are tired?"

"I am ready …" Natasha gently blew out her flushed cheeks and smiled. She knew this was one of her mannerisms Ryzhakov loved. Despite a day's rough traveling, her breath smelled sweet. "Tell me, Igor. You have to trust me. I have to instruct our personnel."

"There are five thousand criminals in Yongbuk. Maybe more." His tone was blasé.

Natasha remained still. Her eyes welled, but she held back tears. *There weren't supposed to be any people involved let alone five thousand!*

"You lied to me. You said no one would be hurt. Just military weapons and hardware."

"The prisoners are not important. Small mental adjustment, that's all." He smiled.

"What about the nuclear reactor?"

"It's true. This is also our target." He shrugged.

"You said no killing."

"What's the difference? They are North Korean peasants." Igor leaned back in his seat and grimaced.

"They are innocent. You know they will perish." Natasha stood up shaking her head and pulling her hair in frustration. It was impossible to disguise her horror.

Igor wrinkled his nose. "Most will be sleeping," he continued. "They will never know. We attack tonight."

CHAPTER TWELVE

Sofiyskaya Embankment, Moscow

D ay or night, Simon Anderson's office boasted one of the most exotic views in British Embassy global real estate— so much so that the Kremlin had already begun moves to claim the rental property back for themselves. The golden domes of the Kremlin and the colorful, vibrant mosaic-chippings and swirls of St. Basil's Cathedral on Red Square were truly remarkable landmarks. Conceived and designed by Postnik Yakovlev, Ivan the Terrible ordered the architect to be blinded once St. Basil's Cathedral was built to prevent it being copied. Poor sod. Still, at least the bugger will always be remembered.

Anderson swallowed the final drop of espresso served in the inappropriately large government-issue teacup—the least of Anderson's worries. The six-party talks concerning North and South Korea, China, Japan, Russia, and the United States were falling apart … a stalemate, any observer might reasonably deduce. The US ambassador was about to arrive. Anderson desperately needed American support for his audacious plan. Not materially or financially, but strategically and symbolically. His superiors in London insisted on the American blessing, and his master plan would be worthless without it. Once the Americans were on board and Jack Steele, the renegade journalist, had been removed from the picture, Anderson could finally call London with the green light.

At 3:45 am, Edward Warrior, US ambassador to Moscow, entered Anderson's office and offered a firm handshake. Warrior was tall, broad-shouldered with a good head of straw-colored hair and a freckled face to match. In his late fifties, he could have been mistaken for a retired tennis pro. Apart from briefly attending the Queen's birthday cocktail party in the British Embassy grounds last June, this was the first time Warrior had stepped foot inside the compound since his arrival in Moscow two years before. "Sorry it took me so long," he began. "Crossed wires. Better late than never, right?"

"Absolutely, Ambassador."

"Where's Sir Brian?"

"Running late. Should be back any moment."

"Roger that. Let's get on with it, shall we?" He sat down.

Anderson loosened his tie and swallowed. "Ambassador Warrior—"

"Cut the British bullshit. Call me Edward, for God's sakes. You know me well enough, don't ya?"

"Sir … Edward … The situation is very serious. I've been analyzing North Korea's claims and counterclaims concerning the reactor over the last few weeks."

"Yongbuk? Five Megawatt? I thought it was shut down."

"Correct. They closed it down last October. The very latest intelligence, however, suggests the reactor's fuel rods are ready to be extracted again."

"Plutonium?"

"That's my understanding."

"Dangerous games."

"Quite. Their press releases and public announcements make out Pyongyang has no idea what's going on."

"Tell me something new." Warrior shifted in the squeaky leather armchair.

"If I may Ambassador … Edward …" Anderson smiled nervously. "This foreign policy debacle continues to spiral out of control. Our hopes of a denuclearized Korean Peninsular are fading fast."

"I agree."

"For the second time in six months, North Korea is about to announce the removal of fuel rods from its nuclear reactor in order to extract weapons-grade plutonium—"

"Press conference?"

"Yes."

"You think they mean it?"

"At best, a blatantly aggressive act of provocation that demands a response; at worst, preparation for hostilities in earnest."

"You think they'll attack?"

"Very possible."

"Nothing positive from the Kaesong border summit?"

"No luck." Anderson shook his head. "And, as you know, their requests for food aid and fertilizer have been rejected by the US State Department."

"It's a mess. What do your people suggest?"

"To be frank, the British government was dismayed that your hawks and doves could only agree to disagree about your role in the future of North Korea ..."

Warrior slowly finished for him, "...which is why we've handed over to the IAEA."

"And the IAEA has warned us categorically that DPRK possesses enough weapons-grade plutonium for five or six nuclear weapons from this harvest of fuel rods alone." Anderson leaned back. "And that's the stuff we know about."

"Agreed. But at least—"

"I'm sure you read yesterday's IAEA statement." Anderson picked up a copy of *The Times* and quoted a section he had ringed with a black marker pen: "There is only really so much we can do. It is up to the International Community to take the next step."

"I read the original report. So what are you suggesting?"

"The North Koreans have their own brand of hawks and doves."

"Says who?"

"Friends and comrades." Anderson raised one eyebrow.

"Russians?"

"Not quite—North Korean ambassador, actually."

"Cozy."

"Ultraconservative elements within the North Korean apparatus plan to use the nuclear capability as a diplomatic bargaining chip against their own."

"Their own?"

"Kim Jong-ryul *and* the international community."

"Smart move."

"Quite."

"And you think you can change that scenario?" asked Warrior.

Anderson unclasped his hands and stretched them toward Warrior, as if extending the hand of a half-century of bilateral friendship and brotherhood. "I have come up with a simple—ingeniously so—plan to rid North Korea of its internal political problems."

"Really?" Warrior seemed amused. He cocked his head to one side. "Well fuck me sideways. I can't wait ..."

"The destruction of their nuclear capability."

Anderson did not move.

"That's it?" Warrior sat forward. "You have my full attention."

"Kim is furious about the *axis of evil* label. Resents the pariah status like a mad dog. Totally unwarranted and unprovoked—in his opinion."

"I get that."

"After discreet communications with the North Korean embassy, I was informed they desire a more immediate and finite approach to their domestic conundrums."

"They want our help?"

"Pyongyang has been seeking a fresh start—a way out of the current impasse."

"What do you have in mind?"

"Simple. Eradicate the political pressure on the new guard leadership from the ultraconservative old guard by destroying their main point of leverage …"

Warrior raised his eyebrows, waiting pensively as if he was about to take a shit, Anderson thought.

Anderson delivered. "The nuclear reactor at Yongbuk."

Now it was Anderson's turn to wait. In fact, he held his breath.

Four weeks to the day since he had conceived the idea. He had the experience, drive, ambition, expertise, contacts, local knowledge, and, most importantly, authority, to pull it off. He prided himself on thinking outside the box. He would rid the west of the *axis of evil's* nuclear blackmail by taking action that no country had dared to consider. Absurdly simple, really. All great ideas usually were. He had conspired with the North Koreans to blow up their own nuclear reactor. But he needed the Americans too. All Warrior had to do was say yes.

"This is insane. Are you completely nuts, Anderson?" asked Warrior.

Anderson had expected as much. He placed his palms together, prayerlike. "Foreign terrorists will carry out the attack. They will be invisible because they've been hired by the North Koreans with our support. They can never be blamed or caught because there's no one to catch them. It's an inside job, so to speak."

Warrior grimaced again slowly piecing it all together. "What does the Dear Leader get out of it?"

"First, he gains support from his people because they've suffered a 'brutal and unprovoked terrorist attack.' Second, and this is the key, the old guard currently screwing things up for their president will lose their favorite bargaining chip."

"Insane," Warrior repeated. "But interesting …" He tapped his fingers lightly on the arm of his chair. "I love it, goddamnit! One thing that bothers me …"

"What's that?"

"When things sound too good to be true, they usually are."

"I agree. But not this time." Anderson smiled, the steely expression in his eyes contrasting the jubilance of his smile. "Edward, once we get rid of their capacity to threaten us with nuclear, we can concentrate on other crucial matters—political, diplomatic, economic. The North Korean people will enjoy a unified government, which is what we all want too."

"I like it. At best, outrageously provocative and dangerous. At worst, it could start World War III in the Asia-Pacific." Warrior spoke slowly, weighing up the advantages and disadvantages. "What does Sir Brian think? Where is he by the way?"

"I'm sure he'll be here any moment now. *Think?* It was *his* idea," Anderson lied. And he knew Sir Brian would not arrive in time for this meeting. Such details would be forgotten once the plan gained momentum. The end justifies the means. He had even typed the slogan on his screensaver.

Warrior exhaled, nodding affirmatively. "It would solve a shitload of fuckin' headaches, that's for sure. But if it goes wrong—"

"It won't."

Warrior exhaled. "Your ass, my British buddy."

"Is that a yes?"

Warrior remained perfectly still. Slowly, he leaned forward and held out his large freckled hand. "Yes, sir. What do you need?"

"Nothing." Anderson could barely contain himself. He wondered how Warrior could have such dry palms at a moment like this. "Nothing at all. You won't regret it."

Warrior stood up. He looked at his watch. "Alright if I hit the sack now? Only four hours to breakfast."

"Be my guest. Not sure where Sir Brian got to. I'll be sure to update him. He'll be delighted to hear you're on board."

"We'll talk tomorrow." Warrior heaved himself up, gathered his papers, and left.

★　　★　　★

Anderson was buzzing. He had been tormented for years by thwarted ambition, a chronic lack of achievement and promotion, as he saw it. He was thinking so hard he started when the telephone rang.

Moments later, he was engaged in a heated debate with London—his superior's haughty accent reminding him of his intense dislike of the British upper-class obsession with private boarding school education. He loosened his tie and pressed the earpiece firmly to his ear to make sure he didn't miss anything.

Finally he said, "But, sir—"

"I'm sorry," the voice insisted, "Operation Tumen has been compromised."

"There's absolutely no reason—"

"Two words—Jack Steele."

"I'm onto him. He'll be taken care of."

"Too risky. He's a bloody British journalist, for God's sake. He's a fucking Brit. Abort."

Silence.

Anderson stood up and said, "But sir—"

"*Abort.*"

Anderson refused to admit defeat. Just minutes before, he had managed to convince the Americans to cooperate. He had worked too hard for this—for the entire plan to be swept from under him. He ground his teeth, nostrils flaring.

"This is absurd," he said firmly. "Steele is one civilian. We can eliminate him."

"*Eliminate?* This isn't the bloody CIA, Simon!"

"But the Americans—"

"You *must* abort. We have our reputation. British sense of fair play and all that British bullshit. Don't you see that?"

Think, damn it, *think!* Anderson took out his paisley handkerchief, mopped his sweating brow, and wiped a nasal drip tickling the tip of his nose. "Everything? The entire operation?" Anderson still couldn't believe what he was hearing.

"How many times must I repeat myself?"

"We may never have another opportunity—" Anderson saw his desire for diplomatic stardom, promotion, and one day perhaps even parliament flying away over the Kremlin domes.

"Nature of the beast, my dear fellow. Gems of diplomacy are like the twenty-four bus to Pimlico. Always another one not far behind."

"But we've spent—"

"Yes, precisely—a small fortune. Pity you couldn't have cottoned onto Steele a bit sooner and saved Her Majesty's coffers some."

"I'm doing my best, sir. I had no idea—"

"Frankly, Anderson, we'll think twice about your 'ideas' in future. Let me know when you can confirm the abort." The man hung up.

He was sitting, but Anderson's legs turned to jelly and his brain to porridge.

He knew that London's latest bombshell meant twenty years of service down the drain. He imagined being passed over at the next civil service promotion board; years of sucking up and kowtowing to these public school chinless wonders for nothing. *Fucking imbeciles!* Getting rid of Kim Jung Ryul's ultraconservative cronies to promote a new era of détente on the Korean Peninsula would be doing everyone a favor for Pete's sake. It was a stroke of diplomatic genius, nothing less. Couldn't this toffee-nosed twat see that?

Even if he could reach Ryzhakov, it was probably too late. London had cut their decision too fine. *Abort Operation Tumen? Over my dead body, damn it.*

He opened his cell phone and dialed a Moscow number. The Ministry of Defense.

"Colonel Chenyenko, please … it's urgent," he said in Russian.

After a couple of loud clicks, a voice said, "Comrade Simon, this is an honor and a pleasure."

You could always count on a Russian for a cunning blend of enthusiasm and protocol—just before they stab you in the back. "The feeling is mutual, Colonel."

"Please. What is on your mind?"

"I need a favor, Colonel."

"A favor?"

"Yes. A bloody big one."

"This is former Soviet Union. We like it big!" The voice bellowed at his own quip. "I am listening, Comrade Simon."

North Korea

Steele opened his eyes and got up off his steel-framed bed. He'd been dozing for twenty minutes or so. He needed to stretch his legs.

After checking the safety catch on his Makarov pistol was definitely on, he opened the door and walked out into the empty corridor. He could hear a television not far away and wondered if it had satellite. Feeling totally cut off from the outside world, five minutes of CNN would help. Under the circumstances, any kind of news was an elixir of knowledge, comfort, and security.

Inside another room a few doors down, Steele could hear a muffled sobbing. Someone, a man, was crying. Drawn to the whimpering, Steele peered through the crack in the door. He saw one of the suicide bomber pilots. The young man was lying on his bed, staring at the ceiling, crying like a child. Tears ran down his face.

Steele recalled a similar image of his friend and fellow tank commander, Charlie Meadows, sitting and sobbing on his army-issue camp bed in the British Army desert basecamp at the outset of the first Gulf War. They had both graduated from the Royal Military Academy Sandhurst, followed almost immediately (after two weeks leave) by tank commander training at the Royal Armored Corps depot in Dorset on the south coast. They became fully trained battle tank subalterns and commanders but with no combat experience. Their training had been cut short, graduation cancelled, and the enthusiastic young subalterns had been ordered to join their regiments prematurely. Operation Desert Storm was calling for their leadership, training, and boots on the ground—or to be precise, boots in a tank. Steele and Charlie Meadows had sat in the desert, each with a twelve-man troop under their command, waiting to be called forward into battle. *Daunting yet exhilarating.* Charlie's troop had been chosen to spearhead the Brigade counterattack against the Iraqi Republican Guard. In other words, Charlie's tank would be one of the first into battle—*cannon fodder* they joked until it was you who became the fodder. The young subaltern had been devastated. He was crying simply because he did not want to die. The reality of an army officer's job—trained killers—had finally sunk in.

The expression on the suicide bomber's face reminded Steele of his friend Charlie more than a decade before. Both Charlie and the young pilot had become the instrument of someone else's cause. Charlie had been killed in action. Steele had an acute feeling this young man would suffer a similar fate.

He wanted to comfort the distraught young Korean. He put his hand on the door handle, about to enter, but stopped himself. He spoke no Korean. Counseling suicide bombers was not his job. For a moment, he wrestled with his conscience—journalist versus human. His job, he told himself, was to tell the story. Then a more sinister thought: *I don't want him to change his mind.* Without this maniac, there would be no story, no glory or professional accolade for Steele. He had invested too much to lose the story now. Like it or not, good or bad, he too was playing his part.

"Jack ..." Natasha surprised him. She was walking toward him.

Steele turned, almost slipping on the wooden floor. "You

frightened the shit out of me. You have an unnerving habit of appearing out of thin air."

Natasha nodded toward the lone suicide bomber's room. "His brother was the one shot in the chest."

"That's why he's crying."

"Yes."

"Poor sod. I'm sorry."

"Yes. Come with me now." Her tone was deadly serious.

He followed as Natasha rounded a bend in the direction of the hut's farthest wing away from the aircraft hangar. "What is it?" he whispered, scuttling along on Natasha's heels. "Where are we going?" He could not help thinking about what happened to them the last time he followed Natasha—on the train.

She led him through an empty room with a couple of metal lockers. Also inside the room was a fire exit leading to the outside—the sign over the door was in Russian and Korean. Clear evidence of military cross-border cooperation between Russia and North Korea? *What other explanation is there?*

They stepped out into the icy temperature, and their freezing breath instantly shrouded their faces in two clouds of mist expanding like a bubble as they exhaled. They walked across to the by-now-deserted aircraft hangar. Natasha got into one of the Jeeps and turned the ignition key. The engine spluttered into action, choking as most old military vehicles do. Then she leaned over to the back seat and retrieved a spare winter jacket with a fur-lined collar and handed it to Steele. She was already dressed for a journey. Steele hoped she had not decided to back out of her part in all this. He had come too far to give up. He wanted his story with or without her.

"There are people next to the Yongbuk reactor," Natasha said as she put the Jeep into gear. "Many innocent people in danger." She revved the engine a couple of times and plunged her foot to the floor. Within seconds, they were speeding across the ice rink-like runway. Steele was impressed with her driving.

"People? What people?"

"They will die if Igor continues."

"How many?"

"Several thousand."

"Damn it, Natasha. What you're talking about?"

She handed him a map. "This village is not marked on our maps—only nuclear facility."

"How do you know?"

"I know when my husband is lying."

"Wait," said Steele. "There are two targets?"

"No." Natasha hesitated. "Yes—in fact. Igor was supposed to destroy the reactor only. No civilians, he promised. I said I would help him if there were no civilians."

"Who are they?"

"I don't know. North Korean peasants. Prisoners. They will die like innocents from *pogrom*."

"How many exactly?"

"Five thousand, perhaps."

Steele paused, taking in the enormity of what Natasha told him. "*Shit.* Are you sure?" His eyes widened.

"Yes," she replied.

"And you want to back out?"

"It's not too late."

"What are you going to do? What are *we* going to do?"

"Stop the aircraft."

"Igor will kill both of us if we screw up his mission." Steele studied her face.

"We'll escape."

"What about your boy? I thought you said Igor will harm him …"

"He is safe. There is an arrangement with his grandfather if I do not return."

"I thought Yongbuk was an empty shell. UN inspectors gave the all clear."

"Believe nothing unless you see with your own eyes. You should know that as journalist."

"There's nothing there. Why does he want to destroy it?"

"Do not always believe CNN."

"It was BBC actually. The UN declared it safe. Empty and safe."

"This is North Korea. No one knows the truth." Natasha pulled her fur hood over her head as they hurtled across the airfield.

"Does anyone anywhere know the truth?" Steele shouted over the engine. "Where are we going?"

"There are two Yongbuk targets." Natasha raised her voice to compete with the engine. "North Koreans have a nuclear reactor in Yongbuk and the other location close by is a detention center for those who refuse to denounce God."

"God?" Did she say God? Steele glanced behind to see if they were being followed. "What can we do?"

"I don't know yet. If we do nothing, can you live with your conscience?"

"You forced me into this. I'm just the reporter. But I'm listening."

"I was following orders. You chose to be here."

Steele took a moment. "Fair enough." This wasn't exactly his choice, but just by being there, he was implicated—guilty even. He exhaled. "Can you live with *your* conscience if anything happens to me or my wife because I trusted you—because you're Katya's sister."

"Katya is not my sister."

Steele almost choked. "What?"

"Strana chu-des." *Wonderland.* "Sorry, I needed you."

"Nothing surprises me anymore. I should have guessed."

"You will be famous anyway."

"Fame's not much good to me if we're running away from the story and I never see my wife again. And we both die."

"You said she wants to finish your relationship?"

"No, I didn't. I never told you that."

Steele paused. He recalled the transmitter in the train.

Natasha must have been listening to every word of his conversation with Sandy. "It's personal. None of your business."

"Your wife. She is Igor's insurance. I have no control."

Steele eyed Natasha. "What *do* you have control over?"

"Listen to me. They prepare fuel rods today. Igor plans to destroy the reactor tomorrow. And five thousand people will die. Maybe more. No one even knows about these people."

Steele shook his head. He was beginning to grasp the enormity of the situation. His mind began to race—his breathing shortened. This was something the British or American governments or the UN should be dealing with—not him, on his own, with the unpredictable wife of a maniac. He grimaced, nervously scraping at his chin, glancing rearward to see if anyone was following them. In the distance, two Jeeps were gaining on them from the right flank. He stared at Natasha, searching her eyes to see if he could trust anything she said. *I'm the only Westerner in the entire world who knows what the fuck is going on here. Or am I?* His breathing quickened. His chest tightened.

A short burst of semiautomatic fire rang out.

Natasha braked and swerved, throwing Steele forward. He raised both arms to stop himself from hitting the windscreen. After gunning it at breakneck speed across the airfield, Natasha halted the Jeep, its engine hissing.

Two Jeeps arrived from the flank. A third vehicle—Ryzhakov's black Range Rover—pulled up a few yards from them. Steele looked at Natasha. In the light from the headlamps that reflected off the glistening runway, he could see her eyes watering.

Ryzhakov got out of his vehicle and walked toward them. He extended his arms to Natasha. "So this is how you repay me?" he snarled. His otherwise pasty complexion was distinctly flushed and verging on red.

Steele's entire body was exploding with adrenalin. He was ready to burst.

★   ★   ★

Steele and Natasha stood in the aircraft hangar surrounded by Russian and DPRK armed guards. Ryzhakov approached Natasha and squeezed her face again so that her teeth protruded like a rabbit. Enraged, she spit in his face.

"Natasha!" Steele exclaimed. *My God, he's going to shoot both of us.*

"Bastard, I will kill you!" she said, flinging herself at Ryzhakov. He knocked her to the ground as if swatting a fly.

"Da nyet, dorogaya. Ja tibya ubyu, i on," Ryzhakov said. *But no, my dear. I will kill both of you.*

"She meant no harm, Igor," Steele pleaded. "I can explain. This was my idea. I got confused. I shouldn't be here."

"No need to explain, my friend. My wife has betrayed me. Her son will be disappointed."

"Leave my son in peace."

"He will have peace. No worry. But before this, I have task for you both. Very dangerous, but I am sure you will both appreciate importance."

Sofiyskaya Embankment, Moscow

The perspiring British diplomat tapped the pane of his Palm Pilot and scrolled down to Ryzhakov's direct cell phone number. Again. He had been trying to contact him all night.

Ryzhakov finally answered. "Mr. Anderson?"

"Ryzhakov? Where the hell have you been?"

"I receive your message."

"Listen very carefully. I have put a great deal of trust in you—"

"Everything is under control. Relax—"

"I am in charge, damn you! You must be available at all times. That means you answer when I call." Anderson's lips tightened; his nostrils widened. He hated the idea of aborting. "Listen. There's been a slight change of plan—"

"No worry, Mister Anderson. I want to tell you that everything is under control."

"Listen to me. You are—"

The line went dead.

Anderson ran the tips of his fingers nervously through the strands of Brylcreamed hair that had slipped down over his forehead. He looked into his empty cup, and, with his highly polished teaspoon, played with the coffee-soaked sugar cube. He scraped up the sugar and swallowed.

CHAPTER THIRTEEN

North Korea

"You betray me? I gave you your life back, and this is my reward?" snapped Ryzhakov, breath enveloping him in the cold night air inside the aircraft hangar. He looked out at the two twin-engine aircraft that had taxied into position outside on his order. "You want to escape? Please." He extended his hand toward the aircraft and sneered at Natasha.

The older pilot walked with Viktor from the hut and climbed into the front seat of his cockpit. He made no eye contact with anyone on the ground, silent as he clambered aboard to adjust the seat harness and make final preparations for takeoff. He gave the headset a cursory glance and donned his headgear. After a series of preflight checks, he gave the ground crew two thumbs up.

"These men will die for their beliefs," Ryzhakov said as he turned to Steele. "You will join them because you have none."

"I don't know what Natasha told you, but—"

"Enough." Ryzhakov motioned for Steele to climb into the first aircraft.

"Parachute?" Steele muttered under his breath. *No one said it was going to be easy, sirs!*

"We shall see if Natasha obeys orders now. You will not fly alone, Mr. Steele." Ryzhakov nodded to one of his men. The soldier jabbed Steele in the ribs with the butt of his AK-47 rifle. A second soldier began to bind Natasha's wrists with a length of thin rope.

The first soldier manhandled Steele aboard the Yak-18T.

Is this the end? Ceremonious for sure. Steele thought of cappuccinos in Vienna with Sandy. "I know it's a cliché," he had once said, "but we have our whole lives ahead of us. Prost! Na zdoroviya! À la tienne!" He'd toasted her in three languages.

Climbing into the aircraft, Steele contemplated death for the second time in a week. It was becoming a habit. In the Bosnia conflict, he had extricated himself from firefights, shelling, sniper fire, and kidnapping attempts. He had narrowly escaped an attempt on his life after witnessing a murder at his regiment's ceremonial mounted unit in London, and he had almost been executed by the infamous Bosnian Serb war criminal General Ratko Mladic. But on a freezing morning deep inside North Korea, Steele could not imagine how much worse things could possibly be. Forced to take part in a suicide-bombing mission— albeit against his will—was an abhorrent and unacceptable way to die.

The aircraft was packed with explosives. The load itself wasn't going to be dropped on the target—the aircraft itself was the bomb. There were two aircraft, presumably one for each target. Both were suicide missions.

Steele watched the younger pilot mount the second aircraft. From his seat behind the older pilot, he looked down at the group of hostile armed spectators.

Ryzhakov leaned forward and spoke softly to Natasha. "You can go with him now. You will leave your son forever."

Hands tied, Natasha lunged forward on the attack but was powerless to do any damage. "Your father would be sick to see the animal his son became. Thank God he died before he could know."

Ryzhakov held Natasha's arm and escorted her toward Steele's aircraft. "You want to die, my beautiful one? Please …" He pushed Natasha up onto the wing and forced her to climb inside. The soldier strapped her in and tied her hands to the frame of the aircraft.

Steele glared at Viktor, praying for intervention. *Bloody coward.*

Viktor had appeared reasonable. Now he avoided eye contact. He had the power to reverse this scenario—save all of them if he wanted to.

Failure not an option. Death not an option. There was still time. Viktor was close to Natasha. Why would he let Igor send Natasha to her death? Steele's stomach tightened.

Steele stared at the back of the pilot's head inches in front of him. The man's collar was spotless, not a drop of grease or sweat. This stranger controlled whether Steele and Natasha lived or died.

"You have a family," said Steele in Russian. "They want you to live. They need you. You don't have to do this."

No response.

Natasha tugged in vain at the rope attaching her hands to the seat; in front, the pilot remained emotionless and silent. Then he raised his arm and began to slide the canopy shut—

"Minutka!" yelled Ryzhakov. *Wait.* He climbed up onto the wing. Taking Natasha's head in both hands, he kissed her, forcing his tongue deep into her mouth. "May your soul live forever, my dearest one."

"You make me vomit. Sobaka!" Natasha spluttered. *Dog.*

"Thirty miles to your destination. Fifteen minutes to get to know each other intimately. Plenty of time to think of a way out." Ryzhakov laughed. "Let me give you a clue—there *is* no way out." He cocked his head in feigned sympathy.

Ryzhakov jumped down off the aircraft, taking out his cell phone and turning back to smile at Steele. He held the end of the antenna and dangled the cell phone from side to side in a *tick-tock* motion. He shouted, "Excuse me, I have to make a call … to London. I give Sandy your love."

Steele began to tremble with anger but still refused to admit defeat.

The pilot flipped some switches, pressed some buttons, and

slid the Perspex canopy forward with a clunk and secured it for takeoff.

★ ★ ★

The aircraft ascended into the clear winter sky. Scrunched up in this small aircraft reminded Steele of the Air Experience Flying (AEF) he did as a high school Royal Air Force cadet. If Steele could make this pilot vanish, take the controls, perhaps he could get them out of this mess, land the aircraft even?

There must be a way out, he repeated to himself like a yoga mantra—*calmly active and actively calm*—there *must* be a way out.

Two thousand feet above North Korea, between the gentle rumble of the aircraft and the faint hiss of the outside air finding its way through tiny cracks in the cockpit, Steele felt a strange kind of peace. For the first time in a seemingly never-ending assault course across life's pitfalls, he finally felt he had caught up with life. Or maybe it was the reverse? An unexpected wave of calm washed over him as he slowly exhaled. He had always imagined that being about to die would be more traumatic. But there was nothing he could do. His lack of options even faintly amused him.

"Why are you smiling?" Natasha asked, nudging him with her elbow. Her wrists were still bound tightly. "What is funny?"

Steele gnawed at the inside of his cheek so that he could taste blood. "I don't know, Natasha. My insides are eating me up. I want to throw up. I feel pathetic. But it's okay. I'm okay with this somehow."

"I don't understand."

"Never mind." *Natasha's not giving up. Shame on me.*

"We must persuade him." Natasha glanced at the pilot. Russian? Korean? They didn't even know which language he spoke.

"You speak Korean?" His words were drowned out as the aircraft's engine surged, banked to the right as it climbed, then straightened out with an unexpected surge in power, the noise drowning out Steele's question.

"Korean?" Natasha had to shout now even though she was right next to him.

"Do you speak Korean?" repeated Steele.

"No," she replied. Amid the pungent aircraft smells of oil and metal, he could still smell Natasha. Pure desire, nervous tension, or was he falling for this woman after all? The condemned man's last request, he thought wryly. Or perhaps *desire* was more accuate?

The pilot turned his head for a moment but still said nothing.

The noise of the engine receded to a soothing purr as the aircraft became level again, but even if the pilot could understand them, their voices could probably not be heard in the front of the cockpit. One mile ahead, Steele caught sight of the other aircraft. His heart sank. *Safety in numbers* not! Two suicide bombers were more likely to succeed—go through with the plan—than one. Even if he and Natasha could communicate with this pilot, Steele suspected their chances of getting out alive were slim to none.

Ten minutes to target, tops.

The engine's hum was now even more subdued. Jack and Natasha reluctantly settled—albeit uncomfortably—into the journey. It was freezing cold. The physical discomfort made them concentrate more intently on their conversation. Talking to each other was the only thing they had left.

"Jack, why did you join military?"

"Wait, I need to think." *No time for chitchat.*

She insisted. "I want to know." Her expression seemed habitually somber.

"I'll tell you some other time. I promise."

"Your father was a soldier?"

"The opposite. He was a peacenik—a conscientious objector. Didn't believe in the military, or the right of any government to assert its power and laws on its citizens."

"This sounds like my husband. Except that Igor thinks he is the state."

Steele smiled. "My father refused to serve his country. Went to prison in London—Wormwood Scrubs. Wore the uniform and all."

"Vormwood?"

"Wormwood Scrubs is the name of a notorious London prison. One of our finest."

"Russian prison is death. They rip out your soul. North Korea is worse. Concentration camps."

"I thought the rumors were an exaggeration?"

"No rumor. Do you believe your government?"

"You mean do I trust them?"

Natasha nodded.

"I joined the army ... it was a knee-jerk reaction to my father's antiestablishment inclinations."

"You had a choice whether to join the army?"

"Yes."

"In our country, it is obligatory."

"I had a choice." Steele looked at the dials on the dashboard trying to see how high they had climbed. He exhaled. "I read in a book recently that we live in a world of duality."

"Duality?"

"Opposites: Good, bad—black and white. If your parents are anarchists, you want to be a fascist. If your father wants you to be a doctor, you become an artist—law of opposites.

"I agree with this." Natasha bent forward to wipe her perspiring forehead with the back of her bound hands. "Is there an alternative?"

"I've no idea. We have ten minutes to our destination."

"Why did you marry?" Natasha pulled at the rope binding her wrists so tightly her skin was turning white. She cursed.

"We wanted a family. We love each other ... I think."

"Think?"

"I know I love Sandy, but I was never sure whether she

loved me. I once heard her talking to a friend on the telephone. She didn't know I was listening. She said: 'I love him in my own way.' After that, I was never sure."

"Always dangerous to listen to other peoples' conversations."

Steele explored Natasha's exquisite features. High cheek bones, small nose and rosebud lips. Even now with deep shadows under her eyes and no makeup, she was *snogshibatelnaya*—a quirky Russian word Steele loved because it literally meant *knock-you-off-your-feet beautiful*.

"Your parents were happy together?" she asked.

"On the surface, yes. But who knows?"

"Don't understand."

"Inside our own mind—that's the only place we know for sure. Even your closest-ever relationship—you'll never know what they're really thinking."

"Why no children? You are both young."

"Almost ... with Sandy." He paused. He wanted to say yes. A few days ago, he could have said it, "We're expecting ..." But Sandy had miscarried. He hadn't been there to support her. Now he didn't know if he would ever see her again.

He knew he should be trying to *do* something, but he had spent his whole life *doing*, and now he just wanted to talk. *Cathartic*, didn't they call it? It was as if his bond with Natasha—the one he had sensed as soon as he heard her voice on the telephone the first time—was now more important than even the suicide mission: "I was almost a father once," he continued. "An ex-girlfriend at college. We argued about whether to have the baby. I wanted it, she didn't. She didn't want it to screw up our lives." He looked out to the clouds. "The baby was stillborn."

"I'm sorry."

Natasha and Steele gazed at each other.

"I'm sorry, Jack ..."

He smiled. "I know." Then he looked at the pilot. Calmly, he asked in English. "What's your name ... Can you help us?" English was the only language they hadn't tried.

★　★　★

The pilot took off his headgear and pulled his headset to one side. "Sure can," he said, turning briefly to face them for the first time.

Steele studied the face and his eyes widened. "I know you."

His American twang cut through the drone of the aircraft. "Mike Sullivan. CIA." He put one hand over his shoulder to shake hands. "I apologize, but I have to watch our man up ahead there. Make sure he sticks to the plan."

"Plan?"

"I've been on your tail for three days."

"You were at the station in Khabarovsk."

"Very observant."

"You walked past my compartment when Igor put me on the train."

"Must be the journalist in you." Sullivan was shouting now as he turned back to talk to his passengers again. "You had me guessing. Wasn't sure which way you two were going. Pity about the babushka," he said, with the stress incorrectly on the second syllable.

"You were there," Steele noted.

"I guess Miss Natasha here was just following orders from her boss?"

Natasha spoke up, "He's not my boss. He's my husband. You understand nothing."

"Whatever, lady … all I know is that because of you and your husband there are a drop load of problems in Washington, London, and Moscow. Way to go!"

"I don't understand." Natasha squirmed in her seat, pulling at the rope biting into her legs.

"Me neither," Steele added. "What the hell is going on?"

Sullivan continued, "Let's just get this baby down safe after I see—"

"*Down?*" Steele exclaimed. "Down where?"

"Get you to safety."

A deafening roar suddenly filled the cockpit.

Steele and Natasha instinctively ducked as if their entire orbit was about to disintegrate.

Sullivan stayed still and focused. The black outline of an unidentified fighter jet roared past them so fast it was impossible to make out its type, color, or markings.

"Who the fuck was that?" Steele asked, "*What* was that?"

"No idea ..." Sullivan replied. "Not part of the plan." He replaced his headset back over his short, dark, curly hair. His voice was calm. "Hello, unknown call sign, this is sierra alpha one, identify yourself, over ..."

Seconds passed. No reply.

He tried again: "Hello, unknown call sign, this is sierra alpha one, identify, over ..."

Still nothing.

Suddenly, a huge explosion ripped the sky open one mile ahead. The other aircraft melted into an orange-red kaleidoscope of death and destruction. As Steele had sensed, the North Korean pilot had perished.

Everyone in the aircraft was forced to shield their eyes, turning their heads away from the blinding light.

"Hate to ruin your day, guys. We could be next."

Sullivan cut the engine and gently lifted the nose of the aircraft until it was above the horizon. Then, jerking the controls forward he took the aircraft into a sharp decent—a stall turn—the quickest way to lose height and send the aircraft plummeting. Steele had studied enough about principals of flight to know that if the dive went too steep, it would be impossible to pull out.

"You think he wants us too?" The aircraft plunged. Steele rammed his palms into the headrest in front, trying to steady himself. He pressed himself against Natasha to prevent her from falling forward out of her loosely fastened harness into the pilot's seat. The rope around her legs was tight, but the soldier had paid no attention to her safety harness.

"Hold on!" commanded Sullivan. "I'm doing my best!" Tightly pursing his lips, he exhaled a sharp steady stream of air.

The jet's black silhouette shot past again, tore into a vertical climb in front of them, twisting as it ascended into the infinite blue. Russian? Korean? Chinese? Steele had no idea.

Neither did Sullivan. "HELLO UNKNOWN CALL SIGN, THIS IS SIERRA ALPHA ONE … IDENTIFY, I REPEAT, IDENTIFY, OVER …" Sullivan's voice was no longer calm.

Again, radio silence.

Hampstead, London

At 3:15 am in North London, Sandy opened her eyes and saw black. She was locked in the trunk of a moving vehicle. A searing pain ran from the crown of her head down through her spine. Her body trembled involuntarily.

She strained her eyes, finally seeing a glimmer of faint red light coming from somewhere close by—probably the brake light? There was a strong smell of gasoline but little air. As she brought her knees up toward her head, she hit a cold metal wall inches from her chest. Over the next bump in the road, her nose smashed against the trunk, the pain almost making her sneeze. She felt a draft on the back of her neck. Then she remembered the last image before she was knocked unconscious—her father. Blake Danner. *Had he seen her? Was he in the car too?*

Sandy tried to move her legs again, but there was no room. *Breathe*, she told herself, *breathe. Calmly active, actively calm, Jack would say.* Now was the moment to practice the yoga techniques she had been mastering for years. *Breathe! Channel the energy through the spine to the point between the eyebrows.* She recalled the words of her yoga teacher in Philadelphia. *Maintain energy, keep the muscles alert and active. Squeeze, flex, hold, and relax. Life is good…* You could do this all day long to keep your muscles alive and well even in a confined space. But if she panicked, it would be over. Small spaces terrified her. If she lost control, she would suffocate. *My choice. I have control.*

She said a prayer for her dad. Had he also been abducted? Injured? But as she prayed, she changed her mind—he didn't deserve it. She did not wish him any harm, but he hadn't exactly been the perfect father. She began to convince herself his presence must be connected to her abduction. *How did he find me? What's my dad doing in London? How could he let this happen to me?*

Sandy berated herself for arguing with Jack and telling lies about the miscarriage. Was she *crazy*? If she ever got out of this alive, she would make it up to him. She needed to see him and tell him the truth. For that matter, she also needed to ask her father *a lot* of questions about her past. The truth. His behavior over the years had made her uneasy and suspicious—for example, numerous sudden and unexplained absences when she was left with Anna. There were strange telephone messages, which no one except her father was allowed to replay.

Her mind was racing. Her heart was pounding. She suddenly came to her senses as the car made another abrupt turn, and again she banged her head on the inside of the trunk.

The car suddenly pulled over and stopped. She heard no one, not even the sound of a door slamming.

No one would hear her kicking the trunk, especially as she was wearing sneakers. It wouldn't help if she kicked them off. She'd break her toes in vain. With these sneakers, she had less than six inches to gain momentum and make some noise. *Zero chance. Waste of time.* She pushed upward with her head seeing if she could sound the alarm with her head. But there was a small rivet right above her.

Unable to wriggle more than a couple of inches, she turned her head trying to find air. She felt dizzy. She craned her neck and pointed her nose like a lost mole in all directions sniffing for air. *Conserve energy and oxygen.*

She felt as though she was suffocating slowly but surely.

CHAPTER FOURTEEN

Somewhere above Yongbuk Region, North Korea

The Yak-18T continued to plummet. Sullivan had intentionally stalled the engine. A pencil scrawl on the horizon, the hostile fighter jet turned slowly in a gigantic loop.

"Looks like a MiG," Sullivan shouted over the wind that syphoned through the cracks in the cockpit. "Can't see a damn—"

Steele lost the end of Sullivan's sentence in the middle of a sudden downward acceleration.

Sullivan rolled the aircraft to the left, spinning on its axis but still heading down.

Anything to gain an extra second, Steele thought, might mean the difference between landing this thing in one piece, smashing them all to smithereens, or being blown apart by the enemy fighter. But then again, Steele wasn't the one flying.

The unidentified aircraft made another pass and pulled away from the target without firing. Sullivan's tactic had paid off. He'd made it look as though the aircraft had lost control and was about to crash. The fighter lost interest at last.

He's cutting it too close. "Pull up!" Steele shouted as North Korean forest rushed toward them. "For Christ's sakes, pull up!"

Sullivan was already using full force to pull up on the controls. But the spin of the aircraft was too strong to be corrected.

Steele watched as the American followed his pilot instincts. He allowed the aircraft to surge downward, now five hundred feet from earth. Then, using both hands and his entire body strength to pull the controls sharply toward him, he made one final attempt to win.

Yes! THANK YOU, GOD!

With each second, little by little, Sullivan gained control of the aircraft, finally pulling out of the dive completely. Recovering, the Yak-18T tipped from side to side, like a fledgling tightrope walker on his maiden walk.

Terrified, Steele and Natasha had forgotten to breathe during the last few moments. They exhaled. The same feeling of relief, Steele recalled, as he'd felt in his stomach on the Big Dipper roller coaster as a boy.

The aircraft clipped the treetops. Steele watched Sullivan checking left and right, his eyes like electronic sensors, as he leveled out to land. In his mind's eye, Steele saw their plane mangled in the forest wasteland. He scolded himself—*think positive, damn it*. A few seconds later, the Yak-18T finally touched down on a strip of farmland with two small buildings at the edge of a forest in the distance.

The enemy fighter jet had disappeared—north, south, east, or west, they'd lost track. The pilot had, apparently, retreated with only half its mission executed—one aircraft of two shot down. "We owe you," Steele said, as the aircraft barreled along the bumpy terrain.

"Don't mention it." Sullivan applied spoiler and pumped the tail rudder from left to right in quick succession to slow the runaway aircraft. "God damn … no brakes. Got to stop her flipping!"

But it was too late. The front undercarriage suddenly hit a ditch, pitched forward, and slammed against a hillock.

Steele and Natasha were loosely strapped to their seats, but Sullivan had not tightened his seat belt securely. The aircraft settled at a forty-five-degree angle, nose in the ground. Sullivan had somehow got tangled in his harness but was also thrown forward, his head hitting the cockpit window.

The tail of the aircraft came to rest a couple of seconds later. Steele and Natasha were suspended in midair like two giant puppets, looking down and held precariously in place by their seat harnesses.

Sullivan lay scrunched up against the cockpit window, awkward, like a half-crushed beetle. He was still breathing, blood trickling down the side of his jaw. On closer inspection, however, Steele assessed the wound was not serious—mild concussion at most. *He'll live.* Icy branches prevented the CIA man from climbing out of his seat.

"Where the hell are we?" Steele asked, craning his neck above the spidery branches.

"North Korea," Sullivan replied, gasping feebly, and attempting to put his hand up to feel a very sore head.

"I guessed that much. How far from the border?"

"We need to hide this aircraft until I can figure out where our friends are."

"Friends?"

"Don't worry. We have friends here." He tried to smile. "No friends—you don't get to play."

"Is that right?"

Steele and Natasha slowly untangled themselves, slid back the sliding roof and clambered out of the cockpit. Without permission, his hands still bound together, Steele reached over and rummaged inside Sullivan's pockets. "Knife?" he said.

"Breast pocket. Top left."

Steele ripped open the Velcro fastener on the pilot's jacket. He took out the Swiss Army Knife, flipped it open, and turned to Natasha to saw through the ropes binding her wrists.

"Anything broken?" Sullivan asked.

"I'll let you know." Steele continued to saw. "You?"

"I'm fine." Sullivan looked Steele right in the eye, but there was a look of distrust. "Forget about Yongbuk. We need to get you guys out of the way."

Forget about Yongbuk? "Why's that?" Steele asked, finally freeing Natasha with a sharp jerk of the knife.

"Thanks," she said, taking the knife and returning the favor.

Sullivan went on. "Get you guys to disappear … for a few days. They'll let us know." He shifted his position but realized he was pinned down by branches and harness.

"Who'll let us know?"

Sullivan raised his brow. "Our masters."

"Forget the masters. I work for myself."

Helping Natasha to her feet, Steele snapped a couple of branches in two with his foot and sat on the wing to work out his next move. He scraped his hair back over the top of his head. "What else do you know about Yongbuk?" he asked.

"You interrogating me?" Sullivan replied.

"Why? Are you working for Igor Ryzhakov?" Steele glanced at Natasha to see her reaction.

Nothing.

"Not your concern for the moment," Sullivan said.

"Wrong answer. It's very much my concern. You know about the civilians?"

"Civilians?"

"Natasha says there are five thousand civilians about to die if this thing happens. Ryzhakov told her about them last night. And this place is not marked on any maps."

Sullivan looked away frowning.

"Do you know about the civilians," Steele repeated. "Yes or no?"

"No, but if there's anyone within ten miles of the reactor, they'd better get their butts outta there …"

Steele began to clear away branches to get at Sullivan's harness. "Why let them take this so far?"

"What do you mean?"

Steele shook his head. "If you're so concerned about stopping the attack, why let it go so far?"

Sullivan frowned. "I'm not concerned. I didn't know—"

"Why not just rescue us sooner and get rid of Ryzhakov once and for all?"

"Hate to disappoint you, buddy, but we have no plans to get rid of him. We invited Ryzhakov to help us." He smiled.

"What?"

"Ryzhakov works for us. We need him."

"Impossible." Steele exhaled.

"He's worth every cent."

Steele snapped another branch and then paused, allowing the intel to sink in. He leaned back and sat on the edge of the fuselage, looking down at Sullivan. "Let me get this straight."

"Sure."

"You work for the CIA?"

"Correct."

"They're responsible for this?"

"Yep." Sullivan's eyes widened with confidence. "It was our idea, along with your compatriots. Came right out of the British Embassy in Moscow."

Steele grimaced, hardly able to fathom what he was hearing. "British Embassy?"

"Yes. Operation Tumen is *our* baby—with a little help from our kid brother Brits—and the Russians."

"Anyone else?"

"The Chinese, as far as I know, have agreed to look the other way. But we couldn't do the air ops without them."

"If the Chinese or Russians didn't destroy the other aircraft, who did?"

"Wasn't part of the plan—whoever it was didn't try very hard anyway."

"What do you mean?" Steele sat erect.

"If they'd wanted to take us out, we wouldn't be sitting here now. Unless we were incredibly lucky. But I don't believe in luck. They were trying to scare us." He tried to move again. "Can you get me out of this?"

"You're making shit up as you go along …"

"No reason to make it up. We're in this together, my British buddy. I need your help more than you think."

This is bollocks. Steele felt as though his brain was about to short-circuit. He glanced at Natasha, wondering how much she did or didn't know. This was fantastic, but not in a good way. It wasn't the story he came to investigate, and if he couldn't get to the target location, there would be no blockbuster headlines either. "And why do we want to kill five thousand innocent civilians?" he asked.

"We don't *want* to. *Collateral*—as Mr. Steinburger says." Sullivan shrugged.

Donald Steinburger, the US Defense Secretary, had a reputation for not caring about civilian casualties—*collateral damage*: he used the phrase nonchalantly, as if talking about the weather.

And there isn't even a bloody war, thought Steele. "You can't just let them die. You can't ignore them," he challenged.

"The White House and your guys in Whitehall have more important concerns—"

"More important than five thousand innocent lives?"

"I guess."

"Like what?"

"Like how to stop the North Koreans blackmailing the West for the hundredth time?"

Steele frowned. "So *we* are blackmailing them instead …with terrorism?"

Sullivan smirked. "Relax, buddy. Call it aggressive foreign policy."

"I'm not your buddy." Steele glanced up at the bleak landscape then looked back at Sullivan.

"Come on, my friend. You're a journalist. You have your agenda, we have ours."

"The US agenda—"

"Whatever it takes to keep the shit out of your own back yard."

"Give or take a few thousand lives?"

"Maybe. Harsh but fair—in the world of the big picture."

"Afghanis, Iraqis ... North Koreans. What's the difference, right?"

"You got it."

"But you can't even take care of wounded veterans back home." Steele was referring to an article he'd read in the *Washington Post* about the near epidemic levels of PTSD in US servicemen returning from Afghanistan.

Sullivan ignored the taunt.

Steele squatted back on one knee. *The British and American governments were about to attack the Yongbuk reactor!* They had hired Ryzhakov to do it. Innocent civilians would be slaughtered. If Sullivan wasn't concerned, then neither would his masters be. But even more troubling, why would the CIA tell a journalist the whole story before the end of the mission? They could never let this story out of the cage. Unless the spy already knew the journalist would never write the story?

"I need more. Humor me," Steele continued. He felt as though he now had two archenemies. It was bad enough playing Russian roulette with Igor Ryzhakov, but he never thought he would have to do battle with his own people.

"Ask away."

Steele glanced at Natasha, who was leaning into the cockpit. She shrugged her shoulders and shook her head. "This is completely crazy."

"Natasha's right." He turned to Sullivan. "Tell me one thing."

"Sure. Just get me out of here, will you? I'm starting to itch like crazy."

"How do you plan to hide us?"

"That's my problem. Now we've crashed, the Agency will launch Plan B. The North Koreans know we're here. It won't take long."

"For what?"

"They'll probably take us in, hold us until this thing is over. Until our people can get to us. Then you can return to Moscow. I'm sure Russian authorities will give you some great quotes when this thing is over." Sullivan tried to heave himself up. "I guess you forgot your camera. This is one for the album."

"It's in my backpack," Steele smiled sarcastically. "I seem to have misplaced it." Steele felt betrayed. "You expect us to wait until this thing is over?"

"Won't take long, I promise."

"I'm suspicious when people make promises they have no control over."

"Two days max."

"We just wait patiently until Ryzhakov destroys the reactor, not to mention five thousand North Korean peasants?"

"Bit dramatic. But yeah, that's the gist."

Steele placed both hands on the fuselage and began drumming. A penetrating wind whipped his cheeks. He scanned the area. *Which direction? No fucking clue.*

Sullivan tugged at his straps. "What are you waiting for, Jack? Get me out of here, pronto!"

"Maybe." Steele continued to weigh up his options.

"Look," said Sullivan, "my job is to make sure you don't get into any more trouble. That's all. You're lucky we didn't just erase you. My orders are usually more … how can I put it? Permanent."

Natasha said, "I don't trust him."

"You think you have a choice, buddy?" Sullivan jabbed his index finger at Steele, his tone both more threatening and desperate at the same time.

"Bloody right, my friend … *buddy.* As you wisely point out, I'm a journalist. I'm expendable. No one gives a shit about me. The good news is I don't take orders from spooks, and I don't sit around waiting for news to beat me to the headlines. I'm here, and you're stuck there. Remember?"

"Trust me—you're in deep shit if you go it alone. This thing is way bigger than both of you and me together."

"I've escaped death three times in two days—enough to last me a lifetime. But guess what? I'll risk it, I think I'm on a roll."

"Cut the ego bullshit. It's nothing personal, OK?"

"Too late, *buddy*. Operation Tumen has already screwed up my health and my marriage. Trust me, I'm taking this *very* personally."

Steele leaned forward and searched Sullivan's pockets, this time inside his jacket.

"Whoa! You're making a big mistake," the CIA agent spluttered, trying to free his arms that had been pinned down by stray branches and the harness.

Steele found diagrams and maps and stuffed them into his own jacket. "I'll make my own decisions. Shouldn't be long before some of your mates find you."

Sullivan wriggled violently, pushing his legs forward to try and stand. He lifted his left forearm through the branches and stretched his fingertips toward the buckle in the middle of his chest. The buckle was out of reach. He could not move more than a couple of inches. "You're making a mistake, Jack."

"One more thing," said Steele, helping Natasha down off the wing, "I hate the word 'buddy.'" He grinned and saluted the American way—short way up and short way down. "So long."

He led Natasha away from the aircraft and out of the undergrowth, ignoring Sullivan's pleas for reason.

Steele picked up the pace even though he had no idea which direction to head for. He could feel his face flush with both anger and frustration. The North Koreans hadn't even attacked anyone, and the West was ready to kill thousands of innocent men, women, and children. *Completely outrageous.* Or, perhaps Natasha was wrong? Perhaps Ryzhakov had fed her false info to test her loyalty, provoke her? Steele's heart was thumping so hard he could feel it through his padded jacket. He was breathing more heavily as the latest news consumed him. He became as excited as he was frustrated. Then proverbial sparks. It dawned on him slowly. *This ... is ... it!* He was the only journalist in the world who knew what Western allies were planning in North Korea. *Allegiance to Queen and country? Next time, perhaps.* This was *his* blockbuster for the taking, and he would make bloody sure he took it.

CHAPTER FIFTEEN

DPRK President Kim Jung Ryul sat stroking a large, gray Persian cat. The creature's spiky fur had an uncanny resemblance to the President's own hairstyle. Although he preferred to think of it as a *coiffure*, the Dear Leader's hair was an unruly mess to the untrained eye. Surrounded by brightly colored satin pillows on a voluptuous peach sofa, he sat in his private apartment that doubled as his operations center. The sofa would have comfortably accommodated at least ten people. And often did—usually beautiful, scantily clad women who in the real world wouldn't have looked at him twice.

The rooms were as lavish as any Beverly Hills mansion, in some ways more so. Everything had been custom made— finishes, lampshades, wallpaper. Pale blue satin drapes with bright yellow sashes flopped around the large windows. The diamond chandelier had half-blue, half-clear crystals that efficiently reflected what little daylight there was inside the room. Kim preferred to keep the shades drawn. He was paranoid about people spying on him—even from government buildings opposite on the other side of the Square of the Rising Sun. The Dear Leader spent most of his spare time watching CNN or old American classic movies—he also loved Lucille Ball and Jack Benny. He was passionate about his English studies, determined to be one step ahead of the interpreters at any given future summit meeting.

Kim's chief of staff stepped forward. "Your Excellency," Colonel Cho Myung-chul began. "General Yoon Tae Sung has ordered the press conference for this afternoon."

"Too early."

"My sentiment also. Unfortunately, the general does not wish to listen to my recommendation, Your Excellency. Or yours ..."

"So be it. Let him have his conference. A few hours will make no difference."

"But we risk getting ahead of ourselves. Timing is everything."

"No matter."

"But the world, the Americans, will perceive this as the boldest act of aggression since our war. They may attack before we launch the Tumen Operation."

"It is my opinion they will not." The Dear Leader combed through his vertically erect slick hair with the tips of his fingers. "It is a risk we must take. Let us keep the general confident in his actions."

The colonel reflected for a few moments and stared at the purring cat. He disagreed with his Dear Leader about the timing, but he also knew that his president was a master strategist; that he had a remarkable knack of manipulating Western powers and, frankly, being right most of the time. "I agree, Comrade Leader." The colonel gathered his papers and stood up to leave—he still had a lot of last-minute details to tie up.

"One more thing," said the Dear Leader.

The colonel pinned his arms to his sides and clicked his heals. "I serve you, Excellency."

"You have devised an ingenious plan. I am indebted to you. I believe it will be a great success."

"Thank you, Excellency. It is my honor to serve you and the exalted citizens of DPRK." He strode confidently toward the door, then did an about turn to face his leader. "Health and prosperity to the Dear Leader!" he barked, again clicking his heels, arms pinned.

★   ★   ★

For twenty minutes, Steele and Natasha crunched their way through the snowy woods in silence. Steele held out his hand occasionally if he thought the terrain was insecure or dangerous. But the truth was Natasha was perfectly capable of taking care of herself. The main goal for now was simply to put distance between them and Sullivan and reach Yongbuk to warn the civilians.

Light snow was falling.

They made their way up a steep incline away from the farm buildings near the crash site and kept going. The frozen landscape and smell of cold, damp undergrowth reminded Steele of all the hours, days, and sometimes weeks—all of them miserable—he'd spent on regimental exercises in his tank on Salisbury Plain and the British Army Training Area Suffield (BATUS), Canada. One day, he had often hoped, he would rediscover his love for nature and the countryside—it was hard to appreciate nature when you were stuck in a dirty, smelly tank for twenty-four hours a day.

Natasha studied the map periodically, and Steele concurred with her navigation. It was impossible to know who to trust, if anyone, and who not to trust—and who, in this myriad of shifting American, British, Russian, and North Korean alliances—was after them.

"Natasha, can I trust you?" Steele asked.

"You must decide. I can't help you decide."

"How did you meet Igor? Tell me the truth?"

Natasha took a few more steps before answering. "It is true we met in Vladivostok. But there were no drunken sailors."

"What then? Can you tell me?"

"Igor invited me for dinner. He noticed me and a girlfriend walking down Okeanskiy Prospekt in Vladivostok. He sent one of his men over to invite me to dine with him. No woman in my position would refuse."

"Why?"

"I was single parent. Igor Ryzhakov is a very wealthy,

powerful man. It would be a good situation for me." She shrugged as they negotiated a fallen tree trunk.

"What happened?"

"He invited me to Aurora Restaurant—most expensive in Vladivostok—afterward we walked through the park toward the port. We sat on a bench. He wanted to kiss me."

"You let him kiss you?"

"Of course. At first, I wanted. I encourage him. But then he forced himself on me. He was licking my face and sucking with much saliva on my neck and arms. It was disgusting."

"I agree."

"I said, no. Unlike the other women. He was shocked. No one says no to Igor Ryzhakov."

"I can believe it."

"Normally he would rape the woman who refuse him." Her nostrils widened.

"What did you do?" They trudged through the snow.

"Nothing. He told me that night he had fallen in love with me."

"But you hated him?"

"I didn't hate him. I thought of my son. We got married a few months later."

★ ★ ★

This latest version of Natasha's story with Igor rang true more than the previous tales. She wanted the best for her son. *What self-respecting mother wouldn't?* Steele was becoming more trusting of her. She was an excellent operative in the field. She might even save his life. Of course, he wished he had more options, or allies, but he didn't.

Natasha had a good sense of direction. After twenty-five minutes, they had covered more than two miles.

"Are you afraid?" Natasha asked.

"Of what?"

"Sullivan works for the American government. And your government. He probably wants to kill you now?"

"I'm not sure. Maybe. Maybe not. But he must have had a reason to save our lives in the first place."

"He didn't. He just moved us away from Ryzhakov. Igor was not going to kill you."

"How can you be so sure?"

"He needs you. He wants everyone to know about Operation Tumen."

"He wants me to write a story saying Britain and America kill five thousand innocent people?"

"Yes. That's what he told me."

"But he's the one about to attack?"

"He's just following orders. They paid him a lot of money—cash."

"But the cash is the icing on the cake?"

"Icing?"

"Money is not his primary motive?"

"I don't know."

Steele paused, then said, "He told me he wants revenge for his father's death."

"Yes. This is true." She took a deep breath and sighed. The bags under her eyes seemed deeper now. "What do you want us to do when we get to the town?"

"We get to Yongbuk and warn those poor bastards!"

Steele suddenly tripped on a tree root. He grabbed Natasha's arm to stay upright, but it was too late. He fell sideways, ripping the side of the same ankle he had injured jumping from the train. *Fuck!* The pain was unbearable. His ankle began to throb, but he continued walking. Or at least, he tried. He needed to rest.

They sat down on the nearest fallen tree.

"Natasha, you brought me here. I'm going to file this bloody story if it kills me."

"If you think that it will kill you, then it will kill you," said Natasha with a deadpan face.

Steele stared at her. He didn't know whether she was serious or joking. He smiled. "I was joking. It's a turn of phrase."

He got up and tried to start walking again, steady at first. Natasha followed. He stepped up onto a fallen tree and was about to step down on the other side. "Tell you what, let's just get to the—"

Clunk! Steele let out a throat-grating shriek of pain as his uninjured foot touched the ground and was immediately consumed by the powerful metal jaws that lay hidden just below the snow and branches. *Fuck! Some kind of animal trap!* His head shot up and back from the sensation that catapulted through his body as though he had stepped into the mouth of some ravenous beast. He wrestled with the urge to rip his leg away from the metal jaws. He hardly dare look down.

Caught like the wild animal it was meant for. Two iron jaws had sunk deep into Steele's lower leg. Blood seeped into the cushioned layers of snow he was standing on. The excruciating pain reminded him of the oral surgeon's needle being jabbed into his gum prior to the extraction of his wisdom teeth.

Steele sharply exhaled. He looked down. The visual shock of seeing his crushed leg increased his breathing tenfold.

Natasha dropped to her knees. She flicked off her hood and scooped away the snow surrounding the vicious metal jaws. She gripped the jagged bars with bare hands, bearing down in vain, to release them. She scanned the area for a stick, a rock, anything to pry open the teeth. The contraption itself was old and rusty but still highly lethal.

Steele cursed. How could he not have seen it? *Idiot.* In his mind's eye, the image of his front-page headline and byline disappeared as fast as the enemy jet had disappeared less than thirty minutes before.

Natasha said, "I'm not strong enough, Jack. Sorry." Going red in the face, she made a third attempt. "I cannot."

Steele leaned forward, and they tried together. *Fail.*

"Bloody hell." He wanted to keep the rest of his body mobile, sit up, use his arms and hands, any kind of physical movement to prove to both of them he would not be defeated. The trap remained clamped around his leg. The searing pain throbbed up Steele's leg and into his torso. Every nerve in his body was on fire. He felt light-headed. He thought he might pass out. What would happen if he didn't get help? If he passed out, he may never wake up. He might die of hypothermia. He maneuvered his upper body downward on the slope to get blood back to his brain.

"Go!" he said. "You must go. Find help. Not Sullivan. We can do this ... We can't be far from the town ... Please go, Natasha!"

She pulled out a spare field dressing, her last, and placed it as close as she could get to the wound. "Five or ten kilometers, I think." Natasha smiled, but her breaths had shortened.

"Go ... Find a car and come back for me."

"I'm not leaving you."

"You must. No choice." Steele winced.

"Sullivan?"

"No ... keep going. Forget him. The snow's covered our tracks. I'll be fine." Steele pushed her away, spitting with frustration, shivering but sweating at the same time. "Natasha, give me one of the maps."

She tucked one of the local maps inside his jacket. "Jack, I promise, I will come back."

Steele smiled and nodded. He clenched his teeth so hard they grated from the pain.

He watched Natasha disappear and then adjusted the dressing to soak up blood surrounding the wound. He took out the Swiss Army Knife to cut off his hood from the jacket. He needed something more to soak up the blood. *Stop the blood flow.* He separated the long strip of fur from the edge of his hood and tied it just below the knee as a tourniquet.

Then he took some slow, deep breaths. He wondered what Sandy was doing right now and if he would ever see her again. Steele's lower leg was going numb. Surprisingly, he was still warm. He squeezed and tensed every muscle in his body to keep the circulation going, a technique taught by British Army instructors on the survival course on Pen y Fan, the highest mountain peak in South Wales. He had to keep the muscles working and blood flowing—for hours if necessary.

The wood offered some shelter from the wind and cold. His goal was simple: stay awake at all costs. If he fell asleep, he would die of hypothermia.

CHAPTER SIXTEEN

Hampstead, London

A church clock struck eight o'clock. British churches kept notoriously dubious time, and to the untrained American ear, their chimes all sounded the same. Sandy knew there was a church close to her flat, but she still had no idea for sure how far she had been transported, and whether, in fact, it was the same church. How long had she been confined—five minutes or five hours? At least she had not suffocated.

She wondered if she had blown her chance to seduce her captor. Clearly, she could not physically overpower him now. And he would probably never let his guard down like that again.

The vehicle was idling. Sandy heard muffled clunks and keys jangling and the sound of a car door closing. Her car. He was coming.

She wriggled onto her back facing upward, her knees pulled tightly to her chest so that her legs were charged like a mousetrap ready to snap. *Ready to fight.* Sandy closed her eyes, pretending to be asleep.

Someone popped the trunk. The Russian?

Morning daylight blinded her for a second. At first, he kept it open just a few inches, probably looking around for passers-by or anything suspicious? Through half-closed eyes, Sandy saw it was same man. She was inches from his leather belt and was able to make out the small embossed head of an eagle on the buckle. He leaned in toward her, his waist inches from her knees, and was about to close the lid once again.

NOW!

Sandy's legs catapulted upward like an exploding piston. The trunk lid smashed into the man's face but ricocheted back down onto Sandy's legs, almost shutting her back inside the trunk but stopped by her knees. The Russian put his hand to his head, disoriented and dazed. She fired again using her piston feet against his abdomen. He bent double, stumbling toward her, almost falling on top of her.

Make hay! Survival instinct took over. She grabbed the man's head with two hands, and with all the strength she could muster, she wrenched and twisted his head and neck, ramming his face onto the metal edge of the trunk. There was a *click* as his mouth slammed into the metal lock—the sweet sound of shattering teeth. She was certain he'd lost some. Blood flowed down his chin. Completely bewildered now, the Russian slumped to his knees, and Sandy seized her chance.

She sat up, flipped her legs over the edge of the trunk, and heaved herself onto the street and to freedom. Using the man's crumpled body as a stepping-stone, she set off across the uneven London paving stones, not sure which way to go. Disoriented, she did not look back to inspect the damage. Sandy was free, and she ran for her life.

Dashing across a side street, she gradually recognized the street she found herself in, one that lead to the High Street. In the distance, Sandy could see people sitting outside *The Coffee Cup* under the awning, her usual routine. She was still in the heart of North London's Hampstead Village with the elegant, quaint shops and boutiques she had often enjoyed just minutes away. She must have been locked in the trunk, unconscious, for several hours.

She felt light-headed but kept going. As Sandy rounded the bend, she saw the High Street a hundred yards away. *Safety?* A London bus accelerated away from her, and the familiar sights and sounds of morning traffic welcomed her—horns, exhaust fumes, and a redfaced cyclist dinging his bell. Tuesday morning rush hour was underway.

A black London taxi chugged slowly past her. She should have taken it, even though she had no money. Suddenly, the taxi stopped and reversed toward her. The passenger door was flung open.

Sandy could not believe her eyes. "Dad?"

At that moment, Sandy forgot the last five tumultuous years of their relationship. For a few seconds she beamed as though her father was picking her up from her first ballet class thirty years ago.

This isn't Hallmark. Move on.

Back to reality. Blake Danner, who Sandy always maintained bore a remarkable resemblance to Joe Biden, approached, but he wasn't smiling. "I've been searching for hours. Get in."

The taxi driver with his full set of wavy white hair despite his age and pale Irish skin, reached out of his window and opened the rear passenger door.

"Everything all right, Guv'nor?" he chirped. "Told ya not to worry. Told ya we'd find her."

Danner slammed the door as he got in behind Sandy. "Everything's fine, thanks." They collapsed onto the back seat, and Danner looked at his daughter. "I'm sorry," he said. "It's all my fault. He might have killed you." He rubbed his forehead and squeezed the bridge of his nose. "Goddamn, I'm a screw up."

Sandy turned toward him, exploring her father's eyes, not knowing whether to laugh or cry. The cab sailed down Fitzjohn's Avenue toward Swiss Cottage. Sandy took some deep breaths. Then the ordeal hit her, and her eyes watered.

Sofiyskaya Embankment, Moscow

Simon Anderson was a past master at the double bluff, but now the stakes had never been higher. As per London's pathetic order, he would report that he had ordered Ryzhakov to abort. When Ryzhakov refused point-blank—what he would tell his superiors after the fact—the Russian Air Force had destroyed one of the suicide bomber aircrafts and forced down the second. Anderson had given explicit orders that only the first aircraft was to be shot down but the second should be allowed to escape.

Thank God the Russians had cooperated. Thank God they had a special "arrangement" in North Korean airspace. Shooting down the aircraft was enough to convince London that Anderson was still doing his job. But it also allowed Ryzhakov to launch his Plan B.

Operation Tumen was alive and well.

Anderson stirred his sixth cup of espresso, four more than usual at this time of day. It was just after ten o'clock in the morning. If the British journalist discovered who was behind this mission, he would broadcast it to the world as soon as he got to a phone. Once the truth was out, media damage control would be a nonstarter. Steele would have to be bribed, blackmailed, but most likely assassinated.

Anderson needed leverage. And fast.

He picked up the telephone. "Department C1 … quickly, please." The secure line tapped through to the head of operations at MI5 in Thames House, Millbank, on the north bank of the River Thames.

"Yes, sir?" the female operator replied. "Secure or routine?"

"Secure."

Anderson flicked open the manila file that had arrived on his desk a few minutes earlier. The pile of photocopied newspaper articles was impressive. Steele had been a busy chap in Russia. On top of the pile was an 8x10 black-and-white photocopied headshot of Jack Steele. He was smiling. Intelligent *and* handsome, Anderson noted. *Lucky bastard.* No one had ever said that about him. He pushed the pile aside and picked up a thick black marker pen. He underlined four sentences on a sheet of paper titled *Personals*:

Name: Sandy Steele [née Danner]

Last known location: as at 17:00hrs local, Monday 6ᵗʰ February

27 Gayton Crescent, Hampstead, London NW3.

Action: Await instructions

Surveillance: LIVE

Waiting to be connected, he circled Sandy's name several times with the pen then underlined her.

"C1. Who am I speaking with?" said the security officer.

"Anderson here, Moscow, P3."

"Good morning, Simon. How are things in miserable Moscow?"

"Miserable. We've had sunnier days."

"Not a cloud in the sky over here. Wonders shall never cease. How can we help today?"

"I need to locate and escort one of our subjects under surveillance."

"Name?"

"According to my latest, either Steele or Danner. First name, Sandy. Danner's her maiden name." He underlined her name again on the file in front of him.

"One moment, old chap," the public school voice said.

"Thanks." Anderson sat back in his chair, picked up Sandy's personal details, and stared blankly at the page until the words became blurred. He would feel much more confident when Sandy Danner—or Sandy Steele, or whatever she called herself—was under his personal supervision in Moscow.

"Are you still there, Simon?"

"Go ahead."

"Found her. Shouldn't be difficult. We'll pick her up as soon as we can. Might take a couple of hours. As long as she's still at Hampstead address."

"Fine. Get her on the next flight to Moscow. And let me know immediately if you have any problems."

"Roger that," the voice confirmed.

Anderson despised fake military phrases used by his superiors in the civil service—their secret vocal handshakes. Anderson was ex-army too. But still he thought the tradition childish and unwarranted.

He pressed the END CALL button on his handset, and then bent down to undo the laces of his black brogues. His feet ached even though he was wearing an expensive pair of Church's handmade shoes from Jermyn Street. A loud knock at the door, which was already ajar, startled him.

"Come in!"

"Sir. You should see this right away." An eager young career diplomat with prematurely balding hair, Hugo Jenkins, hurried across the nondescript carpet to hover at Anderson's desk. He pointed to the television.

"What?" said Anderson as he flicked on the TV. He turned the volume up on CNN International. There was breaking news in Pyongyang—a live press conference. He glanced at his watch. It was early evening in Pyongyang. A North Korean general with black bushy eyebrows spoke in English:

It is with regret that the Democratic People's Republic of Korea must distance itself further from the Western allied powers, in particular the United States of America who seek to humiliate and … alienate us from our rightful place in this imperfect world. We … are a peace-loving nation. We note the persistent, slanderous accusations orchestrated by the United States government and its supporters that we are part of the so-called 'axis of evil.' The DPRK rejects this accusation in the strongest possible terms.

We demand therefore … a full and complete withdrawal within forty-eight hours by the United States of America of its occupying forces from our comrades and neighbor, South Korea. If United States does not comply with our invitation, and we predict that it will not … we reserve the right to retaliate immediately against aggressive acts as a result of the new preemptive policy recently set out by the United States government and her military forces stationed in close proximity to our border. We cannot be held responsible for actions of self-defense along the DPRK border, and furthermore actions upon any military units or positions which DPRK deem a threat to our national security.

Anderson's face changed color from pale pink to red. "They weren't supposed to go public. Bloody idiots! What on earth—" He was lost for words. "They know the Americans won't stand for this."

"Quite, … sir," replied Jenkins. He hovered as if he needed to use the bathroom but dare not leave.

"They honestly think the US is going to buckle because of Iraq and Afghanistan."

"I suppose so, sir."

"Jenkins …"

"Yes, sir."

"Be quiet."

Yongbuk Region, North Korea

Almost five hours after she had left Jack, Natasha picked her way across a raging stream, its rocks slimy and green with moss. She had been lost for at least two of those hours but managed to retrace her steps back to the stream. A few minutes later, she finally reached a road—probably now several miles from Steele's location—and heard the comforting sound of an approaching vehicle. A truck, she suspected. She would only take help from a civilian vehicle—definitely not military. If there were any doubt, she would hide, let it pass, and wait for the next one.

She was tired, cold, wet, and hungry. But she would not give up. The image of her son, Bova, smiling in her mind's eye gave her all the energy and power she needed to keep going. As long as he was safe and well, she had a reason to live.

Natasha crouched by the side of the road and waited. She

thought about the blood seeping from Steele's wound into the snow. How long before he bled to death? How long before he died of hypothermia?

To the right, she saw a flatbed truck with red and white fenders approaching. Harmless, she thought, and stood up. She gently waved the truck down with one hand, not wishing to appear too desperate. The truck downshifted gears and stopped a few yards from her with a hiss and a squeak of brakes. Two men in brown uniforms and brown fur hats with ear flaps jumped down from the back of the vehicle. *Thank God not army.* But on closer scrutiny, she noticed the brown coveralls had yellow insignia on the sleeves. If not military or police, then who? *This doesn't feel right.*

She swept her hair from the front of her face and smiled at the strangers. The warmth of her smile contrasted with the nervousness in her eyes. *Will they notice?* She wondered if they would be prepared to scramble across the frozen forest to help an injured Westerner. *Probably not.*

Both men eyed her suspiciously. Their fur hats perched on the back of their heads, one man was short with black hair and the other had brown hair and was slightly larger. The driver in the cab was too high up to get a good view. She could hear people moving around in the back of the truck.

The men were walking too fast toward her and staring at her too intently to be safe. They were *expecting* to find her! Closer to them, she saw that the men were not surprised to find a young woman in the middle of nowhere.

Thirty seconds later, Natasha understood. The men had been specifically searching for *her.*

They escorted Natasha to the back of the truck and invited her to climb up over the rusty tailgate. Natasha fell onto the floor of the truck with a thud.

Glancing back, she cursed the men. Then she looked up. Lying on the wooden floor on a pile of hemp sacks was Mike Sullivan. Three other Koreans in brown uniform sat next to him staring at Natasha as though they had never seen a non Korean woman before.

"Hi lady!" He turned to the other passengers. Sullivan spoke several words of Korean to the men surrounding him. "I was just telling the Civil Defense guys about you." He smiled but didn't mean it. "We've got a shitload of work to do, you realize. You and your British boyfriend are really screwing things up."

Natasha's heart missed a beat. She thought of Igor, and then she thought of Jack Steele lying in the forest. "He is not my boyfriend."

"Give us all a break," Sullivan demanded. "Where is he?" His tone was harsh, much more so than it had been during the crash landing a few hours earlier. "Just tell us where the fuck he is …"

Sofiyskaya Embankment, Moscow

"We've changed our minds." Anderson's superior was adamant.

To Anderson, it sounded like the whole of London was as equally adamant.

"Because of the press conference?" he asked.

"None of your concern. But basically, yes. Adapt to the situation and all that."

"Have you people any idea just how complex this situation is? You can't just keep changing your mind, sir. I don't have a magic wand."

Righteous indignation. That should do the trick.

"*We* can do what the bloody hell *we* want, my dear boy. And *you* can either obey instructions or pack your bags and get on the next plane home to green and pleasant pastures. Do I make myself perfectly clear?"

"Sir, I have ordered Ryzhakov's aircraft to be blown to smithereens by Russian fighters."

"Was Ryzhakov in the aircraft?"

"No."

"Then he still works for us. The North Koreans want to play rough … we can too. If you have any problems, tell your maverick Russian to name his price for the inconvenience. Execute and complete the task."

"The Russians are bound to take offence. I called in favors."

"Don't worry. You'll be promoted back to Millbank if you pull this one off—room with a view, I promise. It'll be worth a few insults from our dear comrades." The voice coughed a smoker's cough.

"Very well. I'll do my best."

Perfect. Fucking, bloody, perfect! Anderson could hardly contain his glee. The old guard announcement was enough to convince London that the threat from North Korea was serious—enough to revive Operation Tumen. How bloody fickle they all were—sitting in their ivory tower on the River Thames back in London town. *Imbeciles.*

The good news was that he need take no further action. His creation, Operation Tumen, was back on course with full support from London, Washington, and Pyongyang, not to mention Vladivostok.

CHAPTER SEVENTEEN

Yongbuk Region, North Korea

Steele opened his eyes and stared at the wooden rafters above. *Where am I? Country? Day? Week? Year? Assignment?* Slowly, it all came back like a fog clearing in the mid-morning sun. Russian Far East, Natasha, Yongbuk ... Nuclear reactor, innocent people about to die. He tried to get up but couldn't. *Too weak.*

A shaft of daylight penetrated the wooden shutters—he studied the tiny particles of dust floating in the slice of brilliant sunlight. *What happened? Where the bloody hell am I?* He examined the shutters further. No way to open them from the inside, even if he wanted to. The shutters were closed on the outside. He lay still, his eyes scanning the room searching for more clues on his whereabouts.

The space was tidy, though bare. On the wall, an old, faded black-and-white photograph of a young couple on their wedding day hung proudly. Warped and stained, it looked at least fifty years old. No matter where you were in the world, he thought, that bright, optimistic look of a recently married couple—Sunday best clothes, hair perfectly in place, flower-in-buttonhole—was unmistakable. The couple was smiling, revealing teeth that were jagged and decayed. With good teeth, the couple would have been no more than twenty-years-old. But even on their wedding day, these people looked prematurely middle-aged.

Steele became more aware of his surroundings and the heavy

wool blanket covering him. It was stiff and scratchy, perhaps handmade? He was thirsty and sweating profusely. He threw off the blanket and listened intently for sounds elsewhere in the house.

How still his world had become. Given his predicament, the silence was strangely comforting. After the noise of the motor-boat, the armored personnel carrier, the explosions, and the aircraft crash landing, it seemed as if he had now been transported to another planet. He could hear and feel his own heart beating. He had a thousand questions, but no answers.

From the shadows mingled with sunlight outside the shutters, he guessed from the mass of trees that he was still in the woods near where he'd fallen. But there was something else.

Then he remembered. *The pain.* The excruciating pain had gone—vanished.

The last time he'd looked, his shin and the metal teeth ground into it had been like a scene from *Jaws*, no pun intended. But now, under the bandage someone had dressed for him, it was as if the wound had never existed. *No pain. Nothing!?*

This was certainly no hospital. He couldn't have slept for more than a few hours. He rubbed his shin again, pressing and kneading to find the pain. Still no pain.

Then he heard a noise in the next room. He was not alone. He could smell burning wood. The wrought iron stove in his room was cold. It must be coming from the next room. *Natasha? Sullivan?*

Steele sat up then tried to stand. Still weak. Still too ambitious. He crumpled to the floor. Then he crawled on his hands and knees toward the door, kicking a metal container accidentally, which stayed spinning for a few seconds—a metal potty. How long were they expecting him to stay? He reached up and tried the door. It was locked, and there was no key, on this side at any rate.

"Anyone there?" he shouted. He tried again in Russian. "Tam yest kto-to?"

No one answered, but he thought he heard movement. He leaned closer.

"Hello!" He banged on the door, at first politely, then more aggressive. "Anyone in there? Open the door, please!"

Still nothing. But there *was* someone on the other side. He was certain.

A thin band of light crept under the door. He dropped to the floor and scrambled closer, trying to steal a glimpse of who or what lay on the other side. The gap was at least an inch. He could feel a draft on his cheek.

Plucking a splinter from his temple and cursing it at the same time, he got his head closer. Under the door, he saw the flickering flames of an open fire. And something—no someone—was in front of it. Yes, someone was sitting on the floor—motionless, his or her back to Steele. He couldn't see above the pair of knees that sat cross-legged on the floor.

Now he was starting to remember. He had been in the woods … with Natasha. He'd caught his leg in a trap, an animal trap. Natasha had gone to find help. *Where was Natasha? Where was his wound?*

And the story? He had to get away. Immediately. He had to get to Yongbuk. Five thousand innocent peasants were about to be murdered. *Mad Russian renegade hired by Western power blows nuclear reactor to kingdom come!* This was the story! It was spectacular. He was the only Western journalist for hundreds of miles around. This was *his* story. He had endured enough already. So much he had to do. *Now!*

His head started pounding from too much thinking. He was exhausted. Steele slumped to the floor, but just thinking made him tired. That was the least of his problems.

He turned on his side and crawled toward the door, peering under again. The person sat perfectly still. He or she was either sleeping, or meditating perhaps? The person wore some kind of sheepskin waistcoat, or vest, as Sandy would say. Steele was sure now. This person was praying or meditating. *Meditating in the middle of nowhere in North Korea?!*

"Hey!" Steele banged on the door again and shouted, "Hey! Come on! Wake up! I need to get out of here. Look, I'm fine. You can let me go!"

Silence.

Steele backed away and began to search for a tool to use on the windows or door. Absurd ... had he been imprisoned by some old hunter? Peasant? Woodsman? Madman? Perhaps this person had set the trap? Perhaps they had planned to catch him like a wild animal?

He lay back down on the floor, mulling his next move. Out of the corner of one eye, he noticed movement on the other side of the door. A note was pushed under. He stretched out his arm and retrieved the piece of paper. It was written in English in capital letters:

DEAR GOD, LEAD ME FROM IGNORANCE TO WISDOM, FROM RESTLESSNESS TO PEACE, AND FROM DESIRES TO CONTENTMENT.
OM, PEACE, AMEN ...

Om, peace, amen? Excuse me? Steele shook his head, slapped his cheek a couple of times to make himself alert. He must be dreaming. He read it again to make sure he wasn't seeing things. The note was written in pencil with delicate, ornate handwriting. True, it was one of the simplest common-sense prayers he had ever read. But it would take more than God to solve his problems right now. He slapped the piece of paper against his hand, folding it a couple of times for safekeeping. A prayer was the last thing Steele had expected to receive at this juncture. He had nothing against prayer per se, or the church or Buddhism or whatever this person practiced, but obviously there were more pressing matters right now.

"Hey! Listen, my friend. I need to get out of here. I'm a British journalist. My name is Jack Steele." He spoke louder. "I have a job to do, my friend … whoever you are." He slapped the door again, in frustration, but got no response. He looked under the door. Whoever was there had returned to his or her position, still and silent.

Regent's Park, London

The London taxi accelerated around the bend at the northwest corner of Regent's Park Outer Circle. The copper dome of the Regent's Park mosque shone magnificently; no, glinted would be more precise, its seasoned copper panels visible for miles around. The first tourists of the day were rowing on the boating lake, their peals of away-from-it-all laughter floating across the water.

Danner leaned forward and tapped on the driver's glass partition. "Here's fine," he said. "Thank you."

The driver pulled over. He opened his passenger-side window to collect the fare.

"Can you wait for us?" requested Danner. "Family business." He slipped a fifty-pound note through the window. "Will that cover you for now?"

"Right you are, Guv. Name's Tom. Just give us a shout if you change your mind, alright?"

"I promise."

"I'll wait here." The cabbie left the engine running and glanced in his mirror to check his white, wavy hair was in good order. He picked up his *Sun* newspaper, turning immediately to the nude on page three. He held the newspaper up nice and high, almost against the windscreen—a little trick he often used in addition to switching off his marmalade For Hire light.

Danner shut the passenger door behind Sandy. "Let's talk," he said, leading her into the park, just far enough inside to find a wooden bench and a view of the boating lake. He tapped the seat with the palm of his hand for his daughter to join him. Sandy perched reluctantly, surveying the self-confident ducks that had waddled over from a nearby willow tree in search of hopefully rich pickings.

"Dad, what's going on?" She tried to sound in control. "You're scaring me half to death. And that's putting it mildly." So far, he hadn't shown any emotion—surprise? Sympathy? Remorse? Regret? *Nothing. Did he have something to do with her abduction? Please God no!*

"I apologize" he said. "There's a lot to discuss."

"Dad—try the truth for once." She lifted her feet off the ground and hugged her knees to her chest, making herself into a ball. It was something she had done since early childhood when she was upset.

"Look, there's no easy way …" he started, and then paused. "I think I'm being blackmailed."

"*Blackmailed?*" Sandy kicked both legs away and stood up. The ducks gave up their food quest and scattered in a flurry of wings and feathers. "What do you mean, Dad? What did you do?" *Whatever it was, he probably did it.* Sandy turned both palms to the sky searching for answers.

"Honey. There are things you don't know."

"What have you done?"

"It doesn't matter. I'm sorry you had to be involved."

"Dad … *talk* to me."

"I got into some financial difficulties."

"You're kidding? We always had everything we needed."

"An illusion."

"Our life was an illusion?"

"Not exactly. It wasn't always like that."

"How *not exactly*?"

"When your mom and I divorced, I had a lot of pressure and stress—maintaining the house, cars, vacation homes, tuition fees, college fund, your mother's needs—or demands, I should say."

"But you took care of me. You had custody."

"That's right." Danner nodded gently.

"So?"

"I started gambling—blackjack, sometimes poker. I was better at blackjack." Danner gave a wry smile.

"This isn't funny."

"I apologize."

"Where?"

"Atlantic City. 'A place to unwind.' It started at Trump Plaza casino. Then, more recently, the Trump Taj Mahal. I spent so much—they comped me my own suite every visit. Leeches."

"I thought you hated gambling?"

"I do. Because of what it did to me. I'd lock you up if you ever started."

"Thanks, Dad."

"I lost my self-control."

"The one thing you've always lectured me about."

"Yes. That's why I've always been so hard on you."

"Dad, fast forward! What are you telling me? What's going on? It's *me* here … your daughter. But not for much longer, I swear it. If I get up and leave, you'll never see me again." Sandy's cheeks flushed.

"I got into debt."

"How much?"

"Thousands … at first."

"How old was I?"

"You were in junior high, seventh grade. I remember worrying about how much to spend on your thirteenth birthday." Danner sighed. He seemed genuinely embarrassed. "We had that party at the zoo, remember? You loved animals." His eyes watered, and he shook his head.

"Spare me the tears, Dad. Not now." Sandy hovered, not knowing whether to run away or sit down and hug her father. She did neither. She had never seen him like this and wasn't quite sure how to react.

She sat down again. "I didn't know." She put her hand on his shoulder.

"That was the general idea." He grimaced, remembering all the years of deceit. "I did a good job, right?"

Sandy also shook her head and made an exasperated sigh through clenched teeth. She couldn't believe what she was hearing, especially after the last twenty-four hours. Even her own nightmare paled somewhat as she thought about the lie her father had been living all these years. He had been deceiving her for most of her life.

"What happened then?" she asked.

"Short version?"

"Fine, yes."

"I dated rich women."

"What?"

"I found myself a rich wife."

"Anna?"

"Yes. Eventually I found Anna."

"But you weren't married."

"We were."

"How long?"

"A year after we met. Local justice of the peace married us, a friend of mine. No guests. His wife was the witness."

"Did you love Anna?"

He hesitated. "Yes." *Now he was lying.* "It doesn't matter. None of it matters now. You're safe."

"Really?" Sandy looked him straight in the eye and gripped his arm. "I'm abducted, imprisoned, dumped in the trunk of a car and nearly suffocate. You, or Anna, or both of you, had something to do with that, and you say, 'it doesn't matter'?" She glared at him.

"I didn't say that ... I didn't mean that. I don't know." He pressed his thumb and middle finger to the inside corners of his eyes to extinguish the tears. *"Shit!"*

"Bastard!" She turned away in disgust.

"You're right."

She looked over at the boating lake and saw a family of four rowing, laughing as they tried to swap seats as the boat rocked precariously. She wished her parents had never gotten divorced.

She took a deep breath. "How does all this get me kidnapped in the middle of London?" Her lips began to tremble. "The truth," she said slowly. "You owe me the truth."

Danner paused. "Cut a long story short," he went on, "Anna found out I didn't love her and threatened to ruin me. She'd hired a private detective and gathered all the evidence she needed."

"For what?"

"Divorce."

"On what grounds?"

Danner paused. "My indiscretions ..."

"You never loved her? You took all her money, *and* you cheated on her? All those years she took care of me. She treated me like her own daughter."

"I loved her, too, in my own way."

"That's bullshit!" she shouted. Even the ducks glanced back in their direction. "That means absolutely nothing."

"Sandy, listen. Anna loved you like a mother."

"I'm not saying she didn't, Dad. But she wasn't Mom. And she wasn't you. Are you going to tell me what this is about?"

"I'm sorry you had to go through this."

"Go to hell, Dad!"

Sandy jumped up and darted off back toward the park entrance. She still had no idea how her father's impropriety had got her assaulted and abducted, but she didn't care anymore. She just had to get away from him. He was the same old *Mr. Disappointment.*

Sandy reached the gate at Outer Circle and jumped into the waiting cab without looking at the driver. She slammed the door and ordered him to drive.

"You all right, luv?" he asked, deftly folding his newspaper, glancing in his interior mirror, glancing at his exterior mirror, indicating right and pulling out all in under five seconds. "What about your old man?"

"Just go."

"Where to?"

"I don't know."

"If we drive towards Baker Street, we'll avoid traffic outside the congestion zone, see? All right?"

"Fine. Whatever."

The cabby hit the accelerator, narrowly missing another black cab making a U-turn in front of them. "Sorry, mate!" he shouted. "You nearly got me into trouble there, miss."

"Just keep going, please."

"Congestion zone, see. If we're inside Marylebone Road, there's less traffic. Mayor Livingston's brainwave—"

"That's great." Sandy sat back in her seat and pouted her lips, but this time it was the tears that won.

★   ★   ★

The taxi sailed along the west side of Regent's Park Outer Circle. Danner meanwhile had hailed the black cab, which had caused it to make the unexpected U-turn. Danner climbed in and told his driver to follow Sandy's taxi. He also said there was an extra twenty if he didn't lose it.

For the first time in many years, Danner felt the smallest sense of relief because his daughter at last knew something of his duplicitous past. It wasn't much, but it was a start. These were things he wished many times before he'd told her but could not. He understood her anger. He wished he could have found the words to help her to calm down. But he was too slow. Whether or not his bitter separation from Anna was connected to Sandy's abduction, he didn't know yet, but someone was after Sandy, and they might try again at any time.

Yongbuk, North Korea

Ryzhakov's old guard military escort had received word from a senior North Korean general about the location of the foreigners—an American man and a Russian woman. Unfortunately, it appeared that Jack Steele wasn't with them. But now, having located Natasha and having her by his side again, Ryzhakov was confident it wouldn't take long to locate his British insurance policy. By this time, the Englishman would be eager to cooperate. Steele would be convinced Natasha was his ally, even if the two of them had for whatever reason been separated. This had not been part of the plan. No matter. He was confident that he would make up for lost time and execute his mission—on behalf of North Korean *and* Western authorities—within hours.

He relished this thought.

East and West knew he was working for both sides at the same time—it was a "joint venture," you might say. Each side was under the impression, however, that they were paying Ryzhakov the larger sum of money for greater leverage. Both sides, therefore, mistakenly presumed Ryzhakov was under their influence more than the other. He had played them against each other like a Russian balalaika. His bank balance would reap sellout box office rewards.

Ryzhakov entered the dilapidated one-storey building on the main street of Yongbuk—Street of Kim Il-sung. He approached the front desk inside the primitive police station. Next to the counter was a piece of cardboard with the word STOP written by hand on a conventional NO ENTRY sign. *Odd.* He took a cursory glance around the room. Anyone sitting on the one beat-up plastic chair would have been taking a risk it might collapse. The lone chair was next to the filthy, sleet-spattered window looking out onto the main road. His escort had delivered him to the right place, but protocol demanded that he now negotiate a merry dance with local officials.

He approached the desk cautiously, but with confidence.

He reminded himself that although he had the blessing of the North Korean government for his task, he nevertheless needed to negotiate as diplomatically as possible on the local level to ensure his plan succeeded.

Two uniformed policemen sat next to each other behind the counter. Ryzhakov asked to speak to the officer responsible for the foreigners they were holding. Nonplussed, one of the men scurried off through a door to the rear of the building.

Two minutes later, a thin, wiry man with greased-down black hair and very large nostrils arrived wearing the same uniform but with considerably more trappings—badges, shoulders boards with stars, and even metal bars pinned to the top edge of his breast pocket. He shook hands with the visitor.

They communicated in broken English. After overly polite introductions, Ryzhakov was ushered into a small, dimly lit interview room halfway down the first corridor they came to.

The police inspector denied any knowledge of foreigners. Ji Chang-wook said, "Is it possible your information is incorrect?"

"Inspector, I assure you I am not mistaken. You must be aware of General Yoon Tae Sung's reputation. He does not make mistakes."

"Again, please?" the inspector replied, feigning ignorance. "Please repeat the name?"

"General Yoon Tae Sung." Ryzhakov handed him a small white envelope and smiled.

The inspector raised an eyebrow, took off his peaked cap, and wiped his sweaty brow with his hairless forearm. As he opened the unsealed letter on official DPRK notepaper, he gestured for the Russian to take a seat.

"I prefer to stand."

By the time he had finished reading the first few lines, the inspector was smiling. He raised an eyebrow.

"You have many privileges as a Russian citizen in Vladivostok, Comrade Ryzhakov." The inspector studied the letter for a few more seconds. "But you must understand that I am in charge here and that we are poor people ... There was a war, you understand."

Ryzhakov was expecting these shenanigans. His stomach tightened at this peasant police inspector's audacity. Had they been on Russian soil, he would have put a bullet between his eyes. "War? That was fifty years ago, inspector, if I am not mistaken."

Ji Chang-wook tipped his head to one side. "But it was a long, hard war ... we are still suffering. Look around you. We are a wretched country ... poor and backward. Our leaders do not understand how to care for their people. But we stay loyal to our Dear Leader, of course, and we understand the difficulties he faces—"

"Will you cooperate or not?"

"Please allow me to finish." The inspector scraped the chair that was tucked under the table and sat down. "You see, we are not selfish as those in the West. We love our country, and we are prepared to make sacrifices. We live day by day. We are grateful for what we have, and we do not expect anything. Our people are content."

Ryzhakov was prepared for the bribe. "How much?" Things worked this way at home too. He also knew things worked differently on the ground "in the field" so to speak, and bona-fide orders from Pyongyang would not necessarily filter down quickly and efficiently. In this world, there were empires within empires, and yet more mini-empires within those, where law, order, and discipline could never be guaranteed as it could in a Western democracy. The Kremlin hoped to change that. He'd heard several rumors that the GRU had a master plan for future American presidential campaigns, and other European general elections for that matter. But it was always the good old US of A that was a permanent fixture in the Kremlin crosshairs. The Kremlin's attitude toward America, he thought, was verging on schizophrenic. Since perestroika, Russians were desperate to mimic and recreate the Western lifestyle, yet at the same time wanted to destroy it at any and every opportunity! Furthermore, the draconian rule of law in North Korea was not nearly as centralized as Western intelligence thought it was.

"Comrade Ryzhakov, I am not a greedy man. I have a family, four children. You understand?"

Ryzhakov put his hand inside his jacket and fished out a wad of cash—Euros.

"What is this?" Inspector Ji Chang-wook became flustered, as if he was being tricked.

"Don't worry, Inspector. Haven't you heard? Euros are more valuable than dollars these days. Be thankful, Comrade Inspector." He held out the cash.

The inspector took a couple of notes off the top. He carefully inspected a couple of notes, sampling his bribe, stroking it alternatively with his thumb and forefinger as if deciding whether it was good enough to eat. His rigid persona began to relax. The smell of fresh European currency had the desired effect.

The inspector smiled. "Any time you wish to visit Yongbuk, you are welcome."

Poor swine had no idea that he would be dead before the day finished, Ryzhakov thought. He would make sure of it. He wasn't about to hand over 10,000 euros to a North Korean peasant, even though he was an official with some limited authority and power. No, the inspector and his miserable life would be extinguished before the day's end. He would come back for his money.

"Take me to the American and the Russian before I change my mind and you regret your filthy greed." He threw the remainder of the cash at the inspector's feet.

The inspector clicked his fingers. One of his police guards bent down to collect up the notes.

"As you wish," said the inspector. He took the cash and stuffed it into his back pocket. Then he led Ryzhakov out of the room and down a pale blue passageway with flaking paint.

Moments later, Ji Chang-wook reached the end of the corridor and, without knocking, entered a small room with no windows. Sullivan and Natasha sat opposite each other, shackled to a table by means of a a metal ring bolted down to each end.

Sullivan looked up. "I knew you'd make it," he said, "It's not true what they say about the Russians."

"What is that? I am curious."

"I'll tell you over a beer one day. Can we get out of here?"

The Russian did not reply to the American. He turned to Natasha. "Kak u tibya djela? Nam para." he said. *Everything okay? It's time to go.*

Natasha nodded. "Kak u tibya? Spaciba. Ja gotova." *How are you? Thanks. I'm ready.*

The inspector gestured to another policeman to take off Natasha's shackle. The chain slid from the ring and spewed onto the wooden floor.

"Wait a minute," said Sullivan. He moved his chair even though his hands were still chained to the desk. "You're taking me with you, right? You need me."

"*Need you?* Since when did a Russian *need* an American? You must go back to CIA school."

"Igor—"

Ryzhakov silenced him with an index finger to his lips. He whispered, "You can tell me more over beer one day."

"No games, Igor. This is politics, plain and simple. Our people have a deal. Tell them to take these things off me."

"I appreciate your offer. But the English speaker I need is Mr. Jack Steele."

"This is a joint operation. My government will chase your ass down to the end of the earth and back!" Sullivan's face turned red. "WE HAD A DEAL!"

Natasha and Ryzhakov left the room and were about to close the door behind them.

"The American?" asked the inspector.

Ryzhakov made a fist and raised his arm in a gesture of solidarity. "My gift to you. Keep him safe. He may be valuable."

★　　★　　★

Ryzhakov escorted Natasha down the sad corridor toward the main entrance. He wrapped the winter jacket he had brought for her around her shoulders, but his chivalrous gesture meant nothing to her. She did not thank him.

They encountered bewildered glances from local North Korean policemen who had never seen a foreigner inside their building let alone one of each sex. The couple exited and climbed into the Jeep. The engine was running, and Ryzhakov's North Korean military escort sat in the driver's seat.

"Tell me, dearest one," Ryzhakov said to Natasha, "where is our friend, Mr. Steele?" They climbed into the back of the Jeep, and he held Natasha close to him with one arm in a vice-like grip around her delicate shoulder. He spoke inches from her ear, almost whispering.

"He was injured. Maybe he's dead."

"You are lying."

"Igor, I do not know. Believe me." She tensed and began to tremble ever so slightly. How long could she manage to deceive him?

He gripped a handful of Natasha's hair just above the nape of her neck. He began to squeeze. "Dearest one, let me ask you again … Where is Steele?"

"Igor, I promise you this. I don't know."

Ryzhakov cursed as he rammed her face down onto the seat in front. It was cushioned, but Ryzhakov was brutal, as if he was really trying to knock her out. She did not make a sound. Her eyes were open, but the blow dazed her. Still she said nothing. She raised her hand to her nose to stop the flow of blood.

"Why do you protect this man? You are destroying every-thing we have—for *him?* We can have a beautiful life together." Deluded though he was, he searched for acknowledgment in her eyes. "It will be beautiful, I promise."

Natasha sat up straight, brave, fearless, blood streaming down her face from a very bloody nose.

"Please, I beg you. Do not make me do this." He stroked the side of her cheek. Tears welled up in her eyes. One rolled down her cheek, and he carefully wiped it away as if he were tending a sick child. Then he took out his handkerchief to mop up the blood. He took a deep breath trying to keep his temper under control.

The Russian took out his satellite telephone and dialed the one-bedroom apartment in Vladivostok, where he had ordered Natasha's son be held captive. He placed the receiver to his ear and then offered it to Natasha. "For you."

Natasha took the satellite phone and even before she put it to her ear, she heard his voice: "Mama? 'Allo, Mama?" Natasha had wrongly assumed that her son was safe at his grandfather's. Ryzhakov's people were everywhere.

Her stomach flipped. She felt nauseous. She had become somewhat used to the physical and sexual abuse in the seven years she had known him, but Igor had never threatened Bova.

"Mama?" The sound of his voice made her neck and face flush red. Like any parent, she could not bear the thought of her child—her only child—being harmed in any way. But she should have known by now that Ryzhakov would do anything to achieve his goal; he was relentless, determined. Since this mission began, he had become more unpredictable and violent than she had ever known. During the last few years, he had indeed shown much affection for Bova—at one point she thought perhaps he had loved Bova like the son he never had. But now she knew that Igor had lied when he said he would raise Bova "like his own son." *Who is more deluded, Natasha or Igor?*

Natasha held back tears as she tried to muster enough self-control to converse as though all was well. "*Bovinka—*"

Igor snatched the cell phone and slapped it shut. "Pozhalsta," he said. *Please.*

"Drive," she conceded. "I don't know his location exactly. But I can show you where he was injured."

"Good, Natashinka. Very good."

★ ★ ★

Ryzhakov ordered his Korean escort to wait at the police station. He would not be needed for the next phase of the operation—witnesses not welcome.

The driver got out.

Ryzhakov adjusted the driver's seat, clunked the Jeep into first gear, and set off. "Steele will be our impartial observer. He will reveal the truth, and people will believe him."

CHAPTER EIGHTEEN

Yongbuk Region, North Korea

Steele lay on the dusty wooden floorboards listening to the snapping of dry wood on the fire in the next room. Apart from crackling and popping on the hearth, he heard no other signs of life.

He unfolded the delicate piece of paper again—it was the thinnest piece of paper he had ever touched. Again, he read the prayer. He had never thought about his life in these terms. But the message was refreshingly simple: ignorance to wisdom … restlessness to peace … desires to contentment.

He began to judge himself harshly. *He* was more ignorant than wise. How could he end up on the other side of the world, risking his life and away from his wife in her hour of need? He had always obeyed other peoples' rules, regulations, and recommendations, and allowed himself to be influenced by their judgments. *The trouble is, Dicky, as an Army superior once said, "You're not as bright as you think you are."* He had followed his intellect, not his heart. He had always tried to do what other people thought best for him—money, success, fame, family. *Bullshit!* Why had he become a tank commander in the British Army? Was that supposed to make him happy or bring peace and contentment? *To whom?* How could it? What was he thinking? He had joined essentially a killing machine, impressively wrapped and steeped in tradition, history, uniforms, medals, and the latest killing technology and firepower. "Boys with toys," his left-wing friends at Exeter University used to chant to tease him and the other military types. He had been lured by the romantic notion—a century or more out of date—of the cavalry officer and the gentleman's lifestyle. A Renaissance man even? *In retrospect, ludicrous. Or am I just wiser now?*

He read the prayer once more and concluded that *he* was not at peace—certainly not now. In fact, on reflection, he had *never* experienced peace. Short bursts of happiness, contentment, so-called "achievement" and fun perhaps. But never *peace*. How many people knew the real meaning of the word? His priest had once told him during Church of England confirmation classes when he was sixteen that it was necessary to *experience* God, not just read about Him. The same applies to *peace*, the priest had suggested. Finally, two decades later, he was beginning to understand what the priest had meant.

He had always been searching, seeking for something better, never satisfied with the moment. As a teenager, he was always on the move: He chased girls, played the trumpet in the London Schools Symphony Orchestra, went traveling in Europe and beyond. Then it was time to make money, have a career. But, in retrospect, none of those things, of course, had brought *peace*. He possessed a wealth of desires and an equal amount of material possessions, none of which, he began to suspect, would ever result in true contentment.

His door suddenly opened.

Steele started, unexpectedly prized from the cavernous corridors of his thoughts. "Hello?" Scrambling to his knees too quickly and looking up, he felt light-headed. An old man with a mop of white, shoulder-length hair stood in the doorway. He wore a goatee beard not unlike a caricature of a traditional martial arts master.

"How do you feel?" the old man asked in a soft, near-perfect English cadence.

A five-language polyglot himself, Steele was impressed when a foreigner spoke English with an impeccable accent. "Who are you?" he asked.

"My name is Chen."

"Hello, Chen."

"Thank you." Chen nodded, and smiled. "How do you feel?"

"Fine, thanks." His head was throbbing. It hurt to be on all fours, finally using his brain to string just a few words together.

"Calmly," said Chen.

"Where am I?"

"Calmly ..."

"Why am I here?"

"You are free to go at any time. When you are ready. But it was important for your wound to heal."

"*Ready?*" Steele rubbed his face with two hands. "Ready for what? I'm ready. I need to leave."

"Leave when you are ready, my son."

Son? Only London taxicab drivers ever called him *son. Who is this strange old man? Am I dreaming?*

The old man approached and helped him to the edge of a chair. Chen was thin and majestic but deceptively strong—enough to lift Steele. A white lock of hair flopped over to one side as he bent down to help.

"You have an important task—I know this," Chen went on.

"I'm sorry," Steele said. "I have to leave."

"As you wish." Chen bowed his head.

Steele got up and shuffled across the room. He felt weak. He had to reach the town. Lives were at stake. Gaining strength with every step, he picked up his coat and went into Chen's living room. The old man followed. Steele looked out of the window, wondering which way he would go, and how he would get there. He was in the middle of a snowy forest in North Korea.

He lifted the hefty metal latch and opened the door. He looked out, prepared to leave. But something stopped him. Flecks of snow showered from the trees in gentle gusts. But it wasn't just the snow, cold air, and wind that caused him to hesitate.

Wait ... Settle and wait. Patience. You are not finished here.

"This is good," Chen said.

Steele turned. "Sorry?" *He read my mind.*

"Please sit down."

"Sit down?" Steele shivered as he closed the door and replaced the heavy latch. "OK. I'll sit down." *Now what?*

The old man sat down on the floor. His head, face, and torso were still. But his eyes were locked to Steele's. He appeared to be in his sixties or seventies, but his thin, agile body could have been twenty years younger.

Steele liked the old man's moon face. It was kind and attentive. His eyes smiled even when he wasn't speaking. Steele wanted to know more about this man. He wanted to know how Chen could be so still, calm, and peaceful. The old man was a peasant living in the middle of nowhere. But he seemed to be content.

"Where did you learn English?" Steele asked.

"Oxford University, 1966."

Steele's eyes widened. "The year I was born."

"Precisely."

"Precisely?"

"Nothing in life is an accident."

"You think?"

"Yes, Jack. This I believe."

Steele stared at his host. "How did you get here? Where are we? This is insane."

"Except for the time in your country, I have always lived here—this is my home."

Steele swallowed. His mouth was dry. "Why study in England?"

"I was fortunate. I tasted Western culture—good and bad. My government paid for me to travel to Europe and learn about your country."

"You were a spy?" asked Steele, only half joking.

"No. My interests were academic. I spent several years preparing and studying English for my journey. I wanted to appreciate every second." The old man chuckled to himself. "And I did. But I was happy to return home."

"You were born here?"

"Yes, close by." The old man stood up and stretched.

"You came back?"

"I have everything I need here."

Steele gently massaged the dressing on his shin, where the animal trap had devoured his skin. "Thank you for fixing my leg. Feels much better." Steele began to massage his shin nonchalantly, but then he was confused. "I don't feel any pain. That doesn't make sense. What did you do to it? How long have I been here?"

Chen got down on one knee and placed his hand over the bandage for a few seconds. He closed his eyes and took a deep breath. "Your leg is healed, Jack. Take off the bandage." He smiled.

Steele unraveled the dressing. Granted, it didn't hurt, but to expect the thing to have healed was absurd. "I wish it was—"

The dressing fell to the floor. Steele's eyes ballooned. There was no sign of a wound. It had vanished.

"How ...?"

"The all-knowing nature of the universe. The unknown power that guides us all. God, some call it, God."

Steele rubbed his leg, incredulous, searching for signs of the wound. He scratched and pawed at the skin, looking for even a slight abrasion or scar. But he found nothing. His eyes studied the old man as he tried to make sense of what had happened. "Well," he said slowly, wondering if this was a dream. "Thanks."

Steele had nothing else to say. His last recollection was a gaping wound on his leg. Now there was nothing. A miracle was the only word to describe it.

"You are welcome."

"Was that your trap? For animals?"

"No."

Steele switched to reporter mode, looking down stroking his lower calf. "You live on your own?"

"I was married. My wife was beautiful."

"Yes. I saw the photograph."

"No more questions." The old man sat down on the floor and crossed his legs with the ease of a six-year-old. He straightened his spine. "It is time for me to help you—"

"Don't you get lonely here?"

"I am never alone. He is always with me."

"*He?*"

"He. She. It. God." Chen opened his arms and brought his hands together in front of his chest. He closed his eyes for a few seconds.

"God?" asked Steele.

"Some people use that name. But it is just a name. As long as you are talking to 'God,' no harm can come to you."

"Do you have a family?"

"No family."

"Friends?"

"Friends are merely crutches. We lean on them when we are weak."

"Bit depressing?"

"And when we are strong, they lean on us. God is my friend."

"How do you know?"

"One day you will remember these words. Friends distract us from the path to God. You must learn that *every* man is your friend. *He* is the only one we can rely on. He loves you as no other is able."

"God?" Steele smiled inwardly. In some ways, what Chen said made perfect sense. But after all that had happened in the last twenty-four hours, a conversation about God was a stretch to say the least.

"*He* is too powerful, too wonderful. It is not possible to put Him into words."

"Right …" Steele paused. "Sounds as if you have quite—"

"You are troubled. You have many questions. Help me to help you. You are nervous and restless both inside and out. This is why you have been sent to me."

Steele nodded slowly. *This enigmatic old boy was quite some-thing.* "Mr. Chen … I don't know who you are, or how you found me. I wasn't *sent* here. My plane crashed, and I got caught in an animal trap."

"You were sent."

"By who?"

"God."

"*God?*" Again, Steele nodded skeptically. "Why did God send me to *you?*"

"You are looking for five thousand people in a prison camp. I know this camp."

"You do?" Steele felt the adrenaline start pumping through his veins. *How could this old Zen master possibly know …*

"I was there for five years."

Steele searched Chen's eyes for any hint of deception. He found none. "Why?"

"These souls have given their life to God. DPRK does not accept this."

"That's why they're in the camp?"

"Yes. They believe …"

"And you?"

"I practiced with them."

"How did you get out?"

"They made me leave. The guards said unexplainable things happened in my presence."

Steele thought of the wound on his leg, then continued, "You know these people in the camp?"

"Universal friends I shall call them. They have transferred their attention from life's worries to the infinite joy of God real-ization. They have surpassed physical identification with ego and have vowed to search for the soul. They experience total God communion night and day."

"OK. Fascinating …" Steele couldn't quite believe what he was hearing. "They're allowed to pray in the camp?"

"No. But no one can stop them. These five thousand men and women are enlightened souls. They know their purpose."

"To spread the word of God from a prison camp?"

"Not necessary. They are already at one with God. They are the most blissful people on earth. They have stopped searching for meaning. They have no desires."

"That's wonderful, Chen. But we have to get them out of there, or they will die. We only have a few hours."

"They do not want to leave. They will never leave of their own accord."

"They're about to be blown up into little pieces."

"That is not their concern. They do not care what happens to the earthly body. It is immaterial. Like me, they have everything they need: food, shelter, peace. They have no desires, young man, unlike you who have many."

"Chen, you don't get it. They are in grave danger right now."

"I have a gift for you."

Steele sighed. "I don't have time for this."

"I give you the gift of silence." Chen placed his palms together in front of his chest.

"Thank you but I have to leave. Your friends need me more than you do right now."

Chen closed his eyes and took a deep breath. "The world is sick, and the epidemic of delusion is spilling onto the streets. If every man and woman would sit on their own in a room and listen to the silence, our world would be at peace. The violence would end, and the delusion would settle."

"Delusion?"

"Yes, the delusion that our physical world is real."

"I don't follow … Our world's not real?"

"Life is in our mind, not here with you and me." Chen clapped his hands so loudly Steele started.

"Interesting. But it's not that simple."

"It is *precisely* that simple." Chen wagged his bony finger. "Few men can sit in a room, close the door, and enjoy the supreme bliss of silence."

"Maybe you're right …" Steele gnawed the inside of his mouth and glanced at the falling snow through the window.

"Your world is the sum total of your thoughts."

"That makes sense, Chen. But—" Steele paused. "Maybe I'll come back and visit you when this is over. We can talk some more."

Chen smiled as if he had foreseen this reaction.

"Ask me a question, any question, and I will answer."

"I really don't—"

"Ask."

At first Steele thought he would ask an awkward question, just to humor the old man and prove him wrong. But after a few moments, Steele decided there was nothing so important he needed to know, that the exercise was futile. He continued to stare at Chen, thinking that perhaps there was something to ask that would help him with this story. *What would I most like to know in the whole world? I bet the old man can't answer ...*

Steele stared deep into Chen's eyes. The old man's pupils were like drops of black ink. Steele suddenly came to a surprising realization. He had always had questions—he had always wanted to know more and more and more. *I could ask about Peter.* But this time Steele said, "There is nothing to ask."

A warm smile crept over Chen's face.

"Precisely." He seemed to read Steele's mind. "You have all the answers you need. Inside you."

Steele's eyes narrowed as he weighed what the old man had just said. Then he dismissed it. If only that were true—*I have all the answers I need?* Impossible, surely?

"Sit with me," said Chen. "Close your eyes."

Chen closed his eyes. In spite of everything, Steele surrendered and allowed himself to be still. It was as if he couldn't stop himself. Logic and reason told him to leave at once, find Natasha and save those wretched souls in the camp. But for once, Steele followed his heart.

He crossed his legs, placed his hands on the floor in front to stretch, and sat up straight. That much he remembered from the odd yoga class he'd sampled.

"Listen to me, carefully," Chen went on.

"I'm listening."

"Cover your ears and close your eyes." Chen splayed his fingers on both hands to cover his ears. "You will hear a many tiny sounds—creaking, vibrations, perhaps even the sound of your own heart—but you must listen for His vibration."

"Vibration?"

"Like the ocean. You will know when you hear this. It is the sound of God."

Steele was intrigued. He had never thought of there being an actual "sound" of God.

"Concentrate on this sound as if it is the most important sound you have ever heard. A sound you have been waiting to hear your whole life. Focus the sound in the middle of your forehead."

"Third eye?" Steele recalled Sandy telling him about the "third eye," a spot between the eyebrows that was a kind of spiritual focus point when meditating, praying, or doing whatever yogis did.

"Yes, some call it the third eye."

Steele adjusted his position. He thought of Sandy, how she had tried to persuade him to take a yoga class ever since he had known her. "Like this?" he asked, adjusting his position and touching his third eye with his middle finger.

"When you are ready," said the old man.

Steele copied Chen and placed his fingers over his ears to block out any sound, even though the only thing he could hear was the faint crackling of the fireplace. "You're teaching me to meditate?"

"Meditation... prayer. It doesn't matter what you call it. Just *experience* the sound of silence and the mud of delusion will fall away. You will be blessed with the power of soul intuition."

"I can't wait. You make it sound easy."

"Not easy. This depends on your desire to learn. I believe you have a great desire to learn, Jack."

"So, you'll let me go when I hear the ocean?"

"You can go whenever you wish. Whether you are ready is up to you."

Steele raised his arms to allow his fingers to cover his eyes and ears. He did something he had never done before.

Jack Steele sat still and did nothing at all.

★ ★ ★

Steele found staying still difficult at first. Restless. He would try for a few minutes and then leave. His thoughts were scattered, timeless, endless, bombarding shells of a life's recollections and memories from childhood to the present—the pretty nursery school teacher he was smitten with in her blue housecoat, his primary school teacher he pitied because she walked with a crutch, his racist grammar school mathematics teacher who picked on the black kid in his class every day, and the Church of England confirmation classes he wasn't ready for and didn't understand. A thousand thoughts and memories. And they were all still swirling inside his head.

Then he catapulted to the present—the slaughtered babushka and back to Sandy's miscarriage.

After several minutes of the tunnel of thoughts from his past, he gradually entered a new world—a world that he would never be able to describe, the world within a world that was inside him.

He became less aware of time passing. A few more seconds went by. It was a start, but it wasn't meditation in his conventional understanding. He had fleeting moments of silence and thoughtlessness. He felt extreme peace. Several times he caught himself thinking thoughts but managed to return to the exercise. It was as if the external world no longer mattered. The feeling of tranquility was unlike any other sensation he had ever known. Just as he allowed himself to be swathed in the stillness, the front door of Chen's hut smashed open, shattering his silent world.

⭐　⭐　⭐

Ryzhakov and Viktor stormed across the threshold. The old man stood up as if to welcome them, but Ryzhakov struck him on the side of the head with his pistol butt, knocking Chen to the floor. The old man hit his head on the edge of the fireplace and crumpled to the ground.

Steele edged over to Chen and tucked a blanket under his head. "Chen, you told them I was here?" said Steele, mystified.

As he sat upright, he said, "I did not tell them, my son."

"Shut up, old man," Ryzhakov yelled. "I don't need help of an old peasant." He grabbed Steele by the collar and pulled him up. "Mr. BBC, I am very pleased to see you."

The old man put his hands together and closed his eyes.

Hyde Park Corner, London

Sandy's black cab rounded Hyde Park Corner in peak rush-hour traffic. The overwhelming cacophony of horns and engines was eased momentarily as a mounted Metropolitan policeman halted the four lanes of traffic to allow the Queen's Life Guard detachment of twenty black horses to pass into Hyde Park on their morning exercise routine.

She had not given the driver a final destination. All Sandy had said was, "Somewhere near Harrods." She still could not decide where to go. The inside of her head was like a pinball machine gone berserk.

As the soothing clip-clopping of one of London's finest tourist attractions trotted in front of her, she glanced across at the sandy-colored stone of Apsley House and recalled how much Jack loved the Cotswold stone of the same color. She stared fondly at the former residence of the Duke of Wellington and forgot her nightmare for a moment.

In high school, she had once written a paper on the Iron Duke after discovering a book on British military history in the library, and the address—Number One, Piccadilly—had intrigued her.

Anyone with an address like that, she had decided, deserves to have a project written about them.

Apsley House had been at the top of her list of places to visit during her first trip to London after graduation. Danner had fulfilled his ten-year-old promise to pay for the trip. *Who is the real Blake Danner?* What else had he not told her during those formative years?

The Household Cavalry detachment passed proudly under Wellington Arch, and the traffic edged forward ready to flow once again. Only the Queen's Life Guard was permitted to cut across the center of Hyde Park Corner and pass under Wellington Arch itself, Jack had once explained to her. The black Irish thoroughbred horses and their khaki-clad riders were part of the ceremonial unit of Jack Steele's former regiment—the Life Guards, Household Cavalry—and another reminder of him. And now she was beginning to miss him and regret their last conversation. She needed to make contact and tell him what had happened as soon as possible.

"Knightsbridge Barracks," the driver informed Sandy, "they're just down the Carriageway over there—look." He wagged his nicotine-stained finger westward down Rotten Row—the broad dirt track for military and civilian horses that runs the entire circumference of Hyde Park. "IRA blew the whole lot of 'em up a few years back. Sinful that was. Diabolical."

"Yes, terrible," she replied. Just the kind of cheerful info she needed right now.

"Terrible thing it was ..." he continued, "There was I, minding me own business just driving back to Victoria Station—" The cabbie stopped midsentence as another black cab appeared from nowhere and completely cut them off. "Bloody hell, mate! Where d'ya think you're going?"

He slammed on the brakes, then the horn, and Sandy grabbed the side rail to keep from being thrown forward. The other cab had broken the law by cutting across Hyde Park Corner itself. Reaching the other side, the traffic in front of Sandy's taxicab was forced to come to an abrupt halt. A fugue of London car horns complemented the rogue cab's outlandish maneuver.

"Wanker! What's he think he's doing?" exclaimed the driver. "First time in twenty years I've seen someone try that number."

A man jumped out of the cab and ran toward them through the thwarted mess of cars and buses. It was Blake Danner. He reached Sandy's cab, opened the door and jumped in.

"All right! All right, mate! What d'ya think yer doing?" Then the cabby recognized him—"Bloody Nora, it's your old man!"

"Dad! You're *crazy!*"

"Sorry, honey. You'll have to trust me."

"Sure as hell I—"

"You all right, love?" The cabby's eyes were glued to his rearview mirror.

"Yes. I'm fine, thanks." Sandy squirmed into the back corner of the cab. She stared at her father as though he were Franz Kafka's beetle.

"Sandy, listen. You need to come home with me. I've got your old passport. It's still valid."

"Forget it, Dad. I'm staying put."

The taxi's diesel engine finally ticked forward as the traffic started to move again.

"Tell you what, folks," said the driver sympathetically, "I'm going to let you out at Pizza on the Park. All right? You can pop into the Lanesborough. Have a nice cup of tea and sort yourselves out. Know what I mean? This one's on me."

"That won't be necessary," replied Sandy. She looked her father straight in the eye, and with all the momentum she could muster in the restricted confines of a London cab, she threw a punch.

One was enough …

Danner recoiled and slumped into his seat. He was dazed and disoriented.

"BLOODY HELL! STEADY, MISS!" The cab driver had reached his limit. "Right, OUT! Boaf of ya!"

Sandy rummaged inside her father's Harris Tweed jacket and hit the target. She pulled a fist full of pound notes out of his wallet.

Passport? Where's my passport? He said he had her passport. She tried the other side of the jacket. *Yes!* At that moment she knew where she was going.

Danner, still nursing his bloody, possibly broken nose, mumbled something about Sandy's right hook. She turned back to the driver. "This should cover it." Sandy gave the driver two £20 notes for his trouble and a third one for the Lanesborough Hotel. "My dad can get cleaned up at the hotel. Give this to the doorman."

Sandy scuttled from the taxi. A red-faced mounted policeman was standing up in his stirrups, conscientiously trying to get the cars moving again a few yards away in the middle of Knightsbridge. Narrowly avoiding a cycle dispatch rider cutting through the jam and oblivious to the cyclist's stream of obscenities, Sandy made her escape. She was swept up by the hodgepodge of traffic. Sandy hurried around the corner into Grosvenor Crescent and hailed another cab.

"Where to, darling?"

"Heathrow Airport."

"Right you are."

"How long?"

"Takes about forty minutes. That all right?"

"That's fine, thanks."

Sandy took one last look at majestic Apsley House. She recalled this was the exact location Jack had spotted his brother standing next to a Bosnian Serb war criminal's daughter the very day he had been murdered. She clenched her teeth, exhaled, and settled back, wondering if the Duke of Wellington had seen this much action during his days there.

CHAPTER NINETEEN

Yongbuk Region, North Korea

"You're mad," whispered Steele, holding a cup of water to Chen's lips. Igor had allowed him to fetch one from the kitchen once Viktor had searched him and confiscated the Swiss Army knife he had taken from Sullivan. "What exactly do you want from me?" Steele asked Igor.

"You are my eyes and ears," he replied. "Every attack needs eyes and ears for the assault."

"I told you. I'm a journalist."

"You're an important man. When you understand what is happening, you will want to tell the world, I promise."

"What did you do with the UN inspectors? You want to tell the world about them?"

"Natasha is comfortable with you, you know. Don't worry about UN."

Steele ignored the Natasha remark, but he did wonder where she was. "Have you shot them? Buried them alive?" He wasn't sure how far to push it. *How the hell did Igor find me so soon?*

"We are all going to Yongbuk. I have something to show you. You are former *tankist*, you will find it interesting." *Tankist* was the Russian word for tank soldier or commander.

Steele looked down at Chen. He was weak now, his breathing shallow, but his eyes still sparkled wisdom and calm. Chen tried to stand up.

"Sit down, old man!" snapped Ryzhakov.

"Sit down," repeated Steele, softly. "Please."

"It is better, old man," added Viktor, his voice weaker than Steele had remembered. Steele observed that Viktor's voice was a little hoarse. He appeared tired, exhausted even. He had deep bags under his eyes, and his forehead was glistening with beads of sweat in the warmth of Chen's hut where the fire was still burning.

Chen got to his knees. "We must learn to love the silence." He put his hands together again, praying.

Oh Lord, he's going to get himself killed. "He's sick. He needs help."

"Enough!" shouted Ryzhakov.

Still Chen continued to move. He leaned toward the fireplace and picked up a poker.

This is insane. Suicide. "Sit down, Chen!" he warned, trying to pull him back down to a sitting position. "These men are dangerous. It's me they want. Stay out of it. Please."

Chen stretched out his arm to seize the poker. He smiled just as he had smiled when he invited Steele to ask any question and Steele had replied there was nothing to ask. His eyes smiled too. Chen was being irrational, now ignoring Ryzhakov's direct command. He was picking a fight with a killer.

Then Steele understood.

In a split second, he read Chen's expression. The old man was orchestrating an opportunity—for him to escape. He was making a sacrifice, quite possibly the ultimate sacrifice, something Steele had never contemplated except once in Bosnia.

Chen raised his arm, now holding the orange-hot poker from the fire. Ryzhakov pulled out a gun. Viktor stared at the old man, shaking his head.

Ryzhakov raised his pistol, pointing at Chen.

"Nyet!" *No!* Viktor hurled himself at Ryzhakov, clumsy like a bear. Steele saw confusion in the killer's eyes and seized the moment Chen had created for him. *Chen wants me to save those people.*

Viktor slammed Ryzhakov to the floor. He lifted Ryzhakov's

shoulders and thumped his head onto the floorboards to sub-due without serious injury. Ryzhakov fought back. The two men rolled one way then the other, scuffing up dust and dirt from the floor of the primitive hunting shack that made both men cough as they fought.

Steele bolted for the exit. The hinges almost split their sockets as Steele flung the door open. He skidded awkwardly down the short flight of steps from the front door. He managed to stay upright.

A shot rang out inside, deafening, even with the insulation of the snow all around. Seconds later, another shot. Anyone's guess who remained alive inside … Should he go back? He had no weapon, and he was hobbling on his ankle. He would be slaughtered.

Steele recalled the look in the old man's eyes. They had sparkled graciously and given Steele the permission he needed to flee. He ran to the Range Rover Ryzhakov and Viktor had arrived in. He had to get to the prisoners in the camp. *Will I make the ultimate sacrifice if it comes to it? Will I risk my life for these prisoners as Chen just did for me?*

Opening the vehicle door, he caught Natasha's instantly recognizable scent. He saw her sitting in the back seat. She was gagged and bound with tape around her hands and feet.

"Are you OK?" he said, untying the gag, ripping off the tape and glancing over his shoulder toward the hut.

She nodded. "I'm good."

"We need to leave fast. You can show me the way to Yongbuk."

"I'm sorry, Jack."

"Igor did this?" He examined her face delicately with the tips of his fingers—the bruises were ugly but not serious.

"Jack. It's too late."

One more shot rang out inside the hut. Steele jumped into the driver's seat, turned the key, revved the gas pedal, and slammed his foot down.

"We have to try!" he shouted above the roar of the engine.

"Wait, if I come with you, Igor will kill my son. I have to stay."

"Natasha, listen to me. Ryzhakov will not kill your son. He will have to kill me first, do you understand? If you stay here, you'll die anyway."

"You have no children. You don't understand. I must protect Bova."

Steele slammed his foot on the brake. In the rearview mirror, he saw Ryzhakov appear on the porch. "You want to stay?" He leaned over and opened the door. Natasha looked at Steele then turned around. She saw Ryzhakov standing outside the hut, taking aim at the vehicle. A shot rang out, pinging off the roof. Natasha screamed, but the bullet had missed.

Steele ducked. "BASTARD!"

Hunched, keeping low behind the wheel, he kept his foot on the brake for a second and slipped the Range Rover into four-wheel drive. They accelerated away from the next bullet, and the one after that.

His foot flat to the floor, he maneuvered the vehicle along a narrow track with a steep bank on one side and a bottomless pit on the other. He stole a couple of glances in the rearview mirror at the gunfire behind them as he negotiated the treacherous route. Moments later, he looked rearward again, then forward to see the way ahead. Suddenly his eyes widened as the Range Rover skidded and Steele lost control. They were about to crash into a large fir tree.

Moscow

The sleet fell at a forty-five-degree angle. Anderson climbed out of the white Range Rover, which bore British Embassy plates and a CD—*Corps Diplomatique*—metal plate on the rear. He was alone, thankful to enter the North Korean ambassador's Moscow residence without a hiccup even though he was not expected this late. The sleet had made a slushy mess on the forecourt, and Anderson would have hated getting snow on his brown leather Oxford Brogues. *Galoshes was a good move tonight.*

He swallowed hard as he approached the main entrance in the middle of the night. He knew the ambassador didn't sleep much, and now Anderson would demand an explanation after the recent unscheduled and unforeseen press conference and confusing rhetoric coming from Pyongyang. Anderson himself had initiated contact with the North Korean ambassador in the first place. Far too much at stake not to thrash out this latest unacceptable development in person.

Anderson was ushered into an ornate, dimly lit library, where he had enjoyed several constructive meetings with the North Korean ambassador two months ago during conception of Operation Tumen. At times, he had felt as though *he* was the British ambassador. A good feeling. Sir Brian Pendlebury had permitted Anderson to negotiate on his behalf. The British ambassador had clearly wanted to distance himself from the MI6 op. If it went south, he could blame Anderson. Failing that, Anderson knew Pendlebury would be sure to point the finger at the Americans.

Waiting patiently in a large burgundy leather armchair, he circled his finger in one of the many studded buttons indented on the arm.

Finally, the North Korean ambassador entered with his assistant. "Welcome, Mr. Anderson!" He sat down behind his desk and didn't appear at all disgruntled at being disturbed so late. "How can we serve Her Majesty's government?"

"Mr. Ambassador. No games, please."

"Games?" The ambassador said something in Korean to his assistant, who left the room.

"Sir, the press conference?" Anderson cocked his head to one side.

"The press conference?" The ambassador nodded slowly. "Now I understand. Please. Things are not as they appear."

"With respect, sir, I should bloody well hope not—" Anderson stopped, took a deep breath and gently exhaled. He clasped his hands in a gesture of calm. "Mr. Ambassador, sir, after today's theatrics in Pyongyang, to say that we are very concerned would be an understatement."

"It has no meaning. It was, if you please, our insurance." He mirrored the clasping gesture.

"DPRK has made an unequivocal declaration of aggression against the United States and her closest allies. You practically declared war, for God's sake."

"We held press conference. That is all. We took no action. Just words ..."

"What would you have us do? Ignore the threats? We're not playing charades. Mr. Ambassador, you are playing with fire."

"Mr. Anderson. I am man of my word. Your American friends are nervous. This is our insurance."

"Insurance?"

"If your Russian terrorist fails to deliver. If target is not destroyed, we have strategic insurance, like any ... business transaction."

"This is a little more than a business transaction."

"We cannot lose face before our people."

Sweet Jesus Christ, what if we fail? "We will not fail," Anderson parried.

"You have my word not a single shot will be fired in anger unless provoked. That is all we are saying. You have my word, Mr. Anderson."

Anderson grimaced. "Who's in charge? Who's running the show?"

"Don't understand."

"Who's pulling the strings? General Sung? The chief of staff?"

"None of your concern." He smiled coldly. "Every official and citizen knows their station in DPRK."

The leather creaked as Anderson moved uneasily in the

armchair. "Tell me something, why not sabotage the reactor yourself if you have such good command and control over there?"

"This is our business. Not yours." The ambassador's aide entered without knocking and planted a tray of tea on the small walnut table next to Anderson. "You came to me with this idea, and we approved. Nothing has changed."

The aide hovered.

"Tea or coffee?" asked the ambassador, gesturing to the tray.

"If you can't give me a plausible explanation for the press conference, the Russians and the Americans might withdraw." The aide was still waiting to pour. "Tea's fine, thank you. And if the Russians withdraw, Mr. Ambassador, our comrade terrorist would run scared, and we both know that would prove catastrophic."

"Then I suggest you complete the task before that happens. You have my assurances our press conference was theater for the world's gossip mongers." The North Korean diplomat drained his teacup. "You are fully aware of our domestic situation. We must keep certain factions, how to say, away from true picture … They have no knowledge of Operation Tumen. They think they are in control."

The corners of Anderson's mouth turned down. "Hmm, I see." This made sense. Anderson lowered his lips toward the hot, tangy tea and carefully took a sip. "We proceed as planned?"

"Of course."

"Very well …" His tea now cooled, Anderson sipped gingerly, put down his cup, and stood up to leave. "One other thing."

"I listen."

"We have reports of a journalist—a British journalist—sticking his nose into the Tumen Operation. His name is Jack Steele."

"What do you wish us to do?"

"Ryzhakov will take care of him. But if your people come across him first, we request—unofficially of course—that he is permanently removed from the picture—at the earliest opportunity. Best not to take chances."

The ambassador frowned mockingly. "I detest people who try to spoil things for the rest of us." He smiled, showing his square, yellow front teeth. "I will see to it that he does not remain a problem."

"Thank you, Mr. Ambassador."

★   ★   ★

Anderson's Range Rover cruised down Mosfil'movskaya Ulitza toward Novoarbatski Most, one of the main bridges crossing the Moskva River. His vehicle wasn't permitted to use the special fast lane in the middle of the main traffic artery reserved for emergencies and Russian government officials—but at least, thought Anderson, obliging Moscow traffic police had the decency and discretion to wave his CD Range Rover through several red lights.

Arriving back at the embassy, Anderson was pleased to see his night staff—all one of her—settled at her desk, prepared for business as usual, as if it were 8:00 am. She would be prepared, he knew, for the inevitable tasks he was known for demanding day and night. On this occasion, however, he had promised himself to remain calm and to think clearly. The situation demanded it. His first priority was to contact his unidentified superior in London.

Anderson was patched through to MI6 Headquarters and began to relate his conversation with the North Korean ambassador. "I have assurances from the North Korean ambassador there will be no first strikes by DPRK forces," he said, sounding his most convincing, confident, and reassuring.

"What about the troublemakers?" the voice asked. "The hardliners?"

"My man says it was theater. Goading the Americans."

"Didn't sound like it."

"Sir, I have every confidence—"

"Unfortunately, Anderson, you haven't given us much reason to have any confidence in anything you do or say."

Anderson bit a tiny chunk of flesh from the inside of his bottom lip. *Bastard.* He hated this man, this White Hall desk wallah, whoever he was, however senior he was. How dare he just sit there and bark orders. Anderson was doing his damnedest to make the world safe and secure. But having to report to this imbecile riled him to the core.

"Ryzhakov is ready when we are," he said evenly.

"Are you sure?"

"We can strike today." Anderson fingered the embossed gold lettering SDA on his leather ink blotter. *Why would anyone choose David as a middle name? So common.*

"DPRK has threatened to use a force if provoked. Once and for all, are you telling me they're bluffing?"

"Correct."

"What about our *London Standard* fellow? Any word?"

"Jack Steele may have found out more than he should have done. But we'll take care of him."

"Once you find Steele—you have your green light."

"Understood."

"Make sure the body never surfaces. Keep us posted."

"Roger that." *Crystal clear.*

The call ended.

Anderson became ever more determined that Operation Tumen would succeed. *Make sure the body never surfaces. With pleasure.*

Anderson leaned back in his desk recliner. His stomach churned thinking about the cynicism and lack of confidence his superior had shown in him. *Damn the fuckers!* He would show London, Sir Brian, and anyone else who was watching, what kind of a world-class diplomat and genius mastermind he was. North Korea would be the last country Jack Steele ever set foot in alive.

Yongbuk, North Korea

There were so few vehicles in the small near-deserted town of Yongbuk that locals had been gossiping about the presence and back-and-forth movements of an unfamiliar black Range Rover for the last twenty-four hours. Most had only seen a vehicle like this on television and in movies.

Apart from the large dent on the front fender where Steele had smashed into the fir tree (but kept moving), the polished, mud-splattered Western symbol of affluence and power now cruised toward the checkpoint on the outskirts of Yongbuk. The guards waved the SUV straight through. With its tinted windows, no one could even tell its occupants had changed—Jack Steele had replaced Igor Ryzhakov behind the wheel.

"The first plan failed. How soon will he organize Plan B?" Steele asked Natasha.

"The first plan was supposed to fail. The suicide bombers were for you."

"What?" Steele spluttered.

"Make you trust him."

"I'm missing something. How does blowing us to pieces make me trust him?"

"We were rescued, no? They did not shoot us down."

"The whole thing was staged?"

"Not exactly. Sullivan landed in the wrong location. Everything else was real."

"Sullivan? Are you sure?" Steele thought about Chen. "My mashed shin seemed pretty real."

"I don't understand."

"Never mind. Did Igor say anything about his Plan B?"

"Nothing. Except ..."

"What? You have to tell me."

"One thing. One of the Russian sergeants at the airfield ..."

Steele waited, glancing at her.

"I recognized him from an old photograph. He served with my husband in Afghanistan."

"Another pilot?"

"No. *Tankist*."

"Tankist? What was he doing?"

"I noticed him and mentioned this man to Igor. He said I was mistaken."

"But you saw what you saw?"

"Yes."

Steele scanned the built-up area of the town center they had taken five minutes to reach from the checkpoint. The handful of hunched locals they saw on the streets shuffled along zombie-like. Their expressionless faces cried out for a rest from life's struggles, men and women alike.

Strangely, Steele cared about these strangers more than his own friends back in London. These people were helpless, and he wanted to help them. He wondered how many of them had friends or relatives in the prison camp. Chen had said that many of the prisoners' relatives came to live in the town to be near their loved ones.

Steele turned the corner onto a narrow street. Identifying a small café-bar, he pulled over. "I have no idea how to stop your crazy husband, but somehow we have to evacuate this town and the camp."

"How? No one will believe us."

They got out of the Range Rover and entered a small café-bar with a faded sign of a teapot hanging above the door. The only thing to say it was open for business was the muffled sporadic shouting from inside through a door that did not close properly. They could also hear the incessant drone of a television.

As they entered, the man behind the counter welcomed them, bowing, nodding profusely, and gesturing them to sit down at one of the tables covered with a paper table cloth. Presumably the owner, he was about sixty-years-old, bald, with bulging eyes and no hair. He behaved nonchalantly, as if foreigners came into his establishment every day. He shouted something in Korean. An old woman came bustling through the beaded hanging curtain that divided the café from cooking and living quarters. Unlike her husband, the old woman's open mouth could not hide her surprise at seeing foreigners on their premises. She stared, as if trying to work out who they were and what planet they had landed from. Steele guessed she had never seen a foreigner in Yongbuk before.

The woman also bowed her head, handed them a menu, and smiled. Like her husband, she invited them to sit down and told them by gesturing that she would come over to take their order.

Steele took the opportunity to place his hand on Natasha's back and guided her across the room. They sat down at a table with a view of an old black-and-white television set mounted on a metal bracket. No two chairs were the same—different styles and multi-colored coverings. No two tabletops were the same color except for the white disposable paper table coverings on all of them. The television was louder than necessary, but no one seemed to be watching—neither the old men sitting on the other side of the room nor the proprietors themselves. Steele had read that state TV channel was permanently switched on—by law perhaps?

Two old men paused their conversation to stare at Natasha, not so much at Steele, before continuing their game of cards. Steele closely examined his surroundings—the café patrons, the warped, snowstorm television picture, the rich, mysterious aroma of homemade soup wafting from the kitchen, and the gray street outside he could just make out through the grimy window that hadn't been washed for a decade. His world had been transformed, and his reality was blurring at the edges. *How the hell did I get here?* He could not answer. The smell of the soup—chicken perhaps?—made his stomach rumble.

Natasha tucked her rich black hair behind her ears and sat up straight. "Jack, we can never be together. You know this."

Steele raised his eyebrows. "Where did that come from?"

"I see how you look at me."

"Natasha, I ... I'm falling for you. I want you to know."

"Thank you." They both smiled.

It wasn't the answer he had expected, but he had no idea what to expect anyway. He shrugged to acknowledge the absurdity of the romantic encounter.

"I knew this," she said.

"I'm a bit obvious."

"I am not stupid."

"I know."

He smiled. His eyes creased at the edges. Mildly relieved she had read his mind, he was, however, disappointed with her answer. Natasha continued to capture his attention and nurture a desire inside him unlike anything he had ever known. "What do you mean?" he asked innocently. *In another lifetime, I'd kiss you now.*

"We are different. We have spent our lives in different worlds. I have a son. He is my love. He is my life."

"Why didn't you want to tell me about Bova?"

"I am afraid for him. But it is too late now. Igor will take him if he hasn't already."

"Abduct him?"

"Yes."

Steele paused. He looked up. On the television, the comforting-when-travelling CNN logo caught his eye. North Korean State television was showing footage with the CNN International logo in the bottom corner.

He froze.

On the screen a few feet above him, Steele saw a picture of *himself* larger than life! *What the ...! This cannot be happening ... Jesus Christ!* He lowered his gaze.

The North Korean footage was from a recent daily press briefing in Moscow. Steele sat perfectly still, his eyes darting to the owner behind the counter and then to the old men sitting at tables nearby. So far, no one had noticed. *Why would they?* His photograph was up now—the one from his press accreditation ID card. Instinctively, he started to run his fingers through his hair in a feeble attempt to cover his face with his hand.

"What is it?" Natasha asked.

"Look ..."

"What?"

"Wait ..." Steele eyed the TV again, then scanned the owner and the card players ... Another old man was engrossed in what looked like a newspaper crossword puzzle, and the others were still absorbed in their silent card game. Confirmed; no one had put two and two together.

Finally, after what seemed like an eternity but was really only about five seconds, Steele's image disappeared. More images of the press conference followed. He recognized Jeremy Bowen, a colleague from the BBC, in one of the cutaways. Bowen was one of the few Western journalists allowed to work in the North Korean capital. Even he was not allowed to leave the capital without special clearance from the Press and Information officer at the DPRK Defense Ministry. Steele had been streaks ahead of everyone on this story. But now his picture was being paraded across the hemisphere. *Why now?*

He sat up straight, craning, intently listening to the report. He had to figure out what they were saying. Now a stony-faced North Korean general, short with gray hair, was addressing a handful of mostly North Korean journalists. Still not understanding a single word, Steele did his best to monitor, to glean something. He saw archive shots and stock footage of the North-South Korean border and US troops patrolling the border on the south side. He saw a familiar CNN journalist sending a report from the border—a report, which Steele knew for a fact was dated. That journalist was now based in London. But none of this helped. He still couldn't work out what the hell was going on.

Then the female announcer, who looked like an opera singer from Gilbert and Sullivan's *The Mikado*, said something transformational. Suddenly, patrons were tuned to the television. The old men looked up from their cards, and the proprietor behind the counter shouted to his wife, who immediately came scuttling. She torpedoed through the beaded curtains as if she had won Kim Jung Ryul's lottery.

Steele whispered, "Natasha. Can you understand any of this?"

"Wait ..." She studied the TV screen

Steele tried to read the expressions inside the café—fear? Outrage? Hint of emotion in the eyes? But their faces remained blank and expressionless, giving away nothing—*impossible to read*. He just couldn't discern if they were surprised, concerned, horrified, or all of the above.

"I have watched many years of state television. I know the difference between 'routine news' and 'serious news,'" said Natasha. "This is very serious."

Graphics appeared on the broadcast—a checklist of some kind. They were accompanied by small stick-figure illustrations of people in their houses, shutting doors, closing windows, feeding and sheltering animals, and generally taking protective measures in their own homes to secure themselves and their property.

"They are preparing for war," Natasha concluded.

Steele had come to the same conclusion. "I agree."

Then, suddenly, it didn't matter anymore. Everyone in the café-bar suddenly looked at Jack Steele, a moment after his picture appeared again.

"Let's get out of here," he said calmly.

They stood up. He smiled and thanked everyone as they headed for the exit. The Koreans looked back and forth as they saw images on TV of the foreigner who crossed a few feet in from of them.

Once outside, Steele and Natasha broke into a steady trot. Reaching the first street corner, Steele looked back to see if anyone was following.

"It's okay, I don't see anyone," said Natasha.

Steele said, "We're going to the TV studio. We passed it on the way in—it's a few blocks back."

"I saw the mast. But you are crazy. They will arrest us!"

Steele eyed Natasha. "Precisely. If that's what it takes."

"I don't understand."

"We don't have a choice. Trust me. I don't give a damn about the reactor, but I came here to give those prisoners a chance. Chen saved my life. I owe him."

They marched almost in step to the television studio. No one followed. The cold air encouraged a brisk pace, but there was no need to run. The streets were deserted. Where *were* these locals? Didn't they work? Didn't they shop? Buy groceries? *Don't these people eat for crying out loud?* Steele hated not knowing the answers when something didn't make sense. When he was four years old, riding on the top of a red London bus, he remembered asking his mother, *What if there were nothing? What would there be?* The fact that his mother didn't know the answer—Don't be silly, she had said—sent his young mind into a whirlwind of curiosity and unanswered philosophical, metaphysical, and spiritual questions, many of which, if he was honest, still remained a mystery.

Natasha slowed and turned toward him. "You are not worried for your story?"

"Lives are more important." He frowned. "Igor wants to blow this place sky-high? Fine. But let's get the people out of here. It's the least we can do."

"Igor didn't know about the prison camp."

"You think so?"

"I think."

Steele shook his head. "He doesn't give a damn. But whoever's helping him on this side knows about it for sure."

Natasha hesitated. Then she said, "*Your* government also paid him to do this."

"That's ridiculous. They're involved, but they're not *paying* him." They continued walking. "*Are* they?"

"Everyone is involved," Natasha said. "You understand nothing. Stupid Englishman. The UN came here to make things better—for the economy. But this was excuse. These men were spying in Russia, China, and North Korea, gathering the information they needed."

"For what?"

They turned a corner, and as a police Jeep sped past, Steele pulled Natasha into a doorway. Steele was about to continue his line of questioning, but something stopped him. He moved a fraction closer, that delicate line between his desire to kiss her, taste her, and the outright risk of rejection. She was married—to a monster. He knew this was neither the right time, nor place, nor situation, but he stayed close ...

She said, "It's not easy for me. Tell me ..." Natasha stood calmly, inches away from allowing him to put his lips to hers.

"What do you want to know?" He could feel the electricity between his mouth and hers.

Steele leaned in. He kissed Natasha on her perfect lips. At first, she did nothing. Then she kissed him back. It was perhaps the most satisfying kiss Steele had experienced. If it never happened again, Steele would be content. As for Natasha, he couldn't tell.

"Jack ..." Natasha pulled away from their embrace and pointed to a huge satellite dish and a two-hundred-foot-high mast on one of the buildings two blocks away.

He looked up. "That's it—see the dish and radio mast? Mobile phones don't work here, right?"

"No."

"Come on. That must be the TV station." He took Natasha's hand and led her across the desolate street.

★　★　★

Five minutes later, they had entered the TV building and were sitting on a bench at a low table stained with circles of dried coffee. More coffee was being served. Three young North Koreans had introduced themselves as local journalists. One of them, with shoulder-length black hair and a moon-shaped face, spoke workable English. Apparently, he had told them, his polyglot was from listening to the BBC World Service on a shortwave transistor radio his grandfather had given him when he was eight—a crime that could have put his parents behind bars.

"What's your name?" Steele asked.

"Bae Jong-hoon. I am from Yongbuk."

"Bae-Jong-Hoon?" Steele stressed each syllable, trying to nail the correct pronunciation. "My name is Jack Steele. We have come to warn you. Your people are in great danger—all of you, especially those at the camp." He took a sip of the tepid, weak coffee.

"What is this about?" asked Bae Jong-hoon, offering Steele some slightly congealed sugar lumps from a small, cream-colored porcelain bowl.

"I'm good, thanks." He raised a hand. "Your people are in danger … There are lives at risk. *Now.*"

"Who are you talking about?" The journalist spoke faltering English with a BBC accent, but his comprehension, Steele sensed, was dubious.

"You live next to a nuclear reactor. Do you understand?"

"Nuclear reactor. Yes. Americans destroy the world, *Pow!*" He released his closed fist to make an open palm fingers extended.

"No, no. *Yongbuk* has a nuclear reactor. You build nuclear weapons here. Explosion. *Pow!*" Steele mimicked the journalist's MO. He made a fist and imitated the sound of an explosion like a child playing cops and robbers.

The other men stared blankly. Steele began to suspect that far from being journalists, these men were more like technicians, whose job was to maintain and broadcast state TV locally—certainly, he was slowly realizing, not the right people with remotely enough clout to organize a mass evacuation of several thousand from the town, let alone a prison camp they didn't even know about that was guarded by armed guards or even military.

The smaller, fatter journalist from the group returned with a plate of waffle-like cookies, as Sandy would say—more waffle than cookie, thought Steele. *At least they're trying to be hospitable.*

Then a man wearing a police uniform entered the building. He was older than the three journalists who had been hosting them. Armed with a pistol, he began shouting and waving it in Steele's face while showering him with a fine spray of saliva.

Steele did not understand a single word, and no one seemed willing to translate. The man became increasingly more animated. Steele wiped his face, which annoyed the man further, but that gave him the unwarranted excuse he needed to strike Steele in the face with a single blow of his pistol butt.

"This is Ji Chang-wook, our police inspector," the boyish-featured journalist finally offered.

Lying face down, Steele gingerly touched the side of his head to assess the damage. Natasha knelt down to examine the wound.

"Just stay down here," he said. "This guy's vicious."

Natasha obeyed.

"Any suggestions?" asked Steele, smiling.

Ji Chang-wook placed his boot on the back of Steele's neck and pressed down. "It's okay!" said Steele. "Please, it's okay. We want to help you." The weight of the boot lingered then eased, and for a second Steele thought the worst was over.

Then the sole of the inspector's boot crashed down on the back of his head.

Everything went black.

CHAPTER TWENTY

Vladivostok, Russia

The last few days had been the most exhilarating of his entire life. Twelve-year-old Bova Klimova had ridden in police vehicles at high speeds with sirens blaring all over the towns and suburbs of Khabarovsk and Vladivostok. Using his legendary swimming skills, he had helped catch a dangerous foreigner who was a crime suspect to boot. The British man had been a member of a group of sophisticated international thieves who were using false UN and journalist IDs to attack and rob local citizens. Bova Klimova, Igor had declared, was a local hero.

The Amur River had been freezing, but he was used to it. His grandfather had introduced him to ice bathing when he was six years old. Just a quick dip during winter months but enough to get his body used to freezing temperatures for years to come.

After the arrest of the foreigner at the river, Bova could not understand why the Englishman had been released from captivity so soon. But then, as Bova had learned from his grandfather, you can never understand everything adults do or say.

Both his mother, Natasha, and Igor had praised him for his courage and bravery. Igor had told him that he had performed his duty *like a Soviet hero*, and that one day he would make a fine policeman. Bova had already decided, however, that he would never become a policeman—they were not well-paid in his country, and most seemed, to him, uneducated and, in many cases, dense. Furthermore, he did not want to become anything like Igor Ryzhakov. Not his real father, Ryzhakov had married his mother but had not, it seemed to Bova, made her happy. She cried too often because of him. Igor had beaten his mother several times over the years, and Bova would never forgive him for that.

After the swimming episode, Viktor had told Bova he would be rewarded. Bova could not understand why this stranger had then taken him by force and locked him in an empty room in a Vladivostok apartment. Apparently, Igor had sent the man to protect Bova from dangerous foreigners. *Who are you? Where's my mother?* His questions went unanswered. He had been demoted from Vladivostok Kraj *geroi*—hero—to prisoner in one day.

Bova listened through the locked door. He planned to escape as soon as possible. Igor and his mother would expect this. Bova could hear Igor's voice telling him to do it.

This was a small *kommunalni* apartment—a shared apartment, one that several families would normally occupy, except that as far as Bova could make out, he and his captor were alone. The makeshift divisions between rooms had virtually no soundproofing.

His captor in the next room had ignored Bova's cries. He waited a few more minutes and tried again. "Let me out!" he shouted in Russian. "I am Bova! Natasha's son! I will tell Igor! He will toss you in jail! Jackass!"

After a few minutes of the shrill insults, the captor finally responded.

He unlocked the door, entered, and approached the boy, grabbing him by the scruff of the neck. "Malchik! Tixo! Ja tibya ubyou!" *Boy! I'll kill you if you don't shut up!*

Bova began to punch, arms flailing every which way. He knew Igor would come and save him eventually. He had not believed the man's claims that he worked for Igor. Igor would not do this to him, Bova knew for sure. Igor loved his mother—most of the time—and would never want to harm her son.

After the violent outburst, the man shoved Bova across the room, closed the door again, and locked it. Bova sat cross-legged on the floor with his shoulder to the partition wall. He angled his neck to push his ear against the wall and listen to a series of muffled telephone conversations. Still Bova could not make any sense of his imprisonment.

About ten minutes later, the door opened again. The boy's captor walked in with a tray of *blini*—pancakes—and a glass of sour grape juice. Bova had lost his appetite, but he took the glass of juice and guzzled enthusiastically. He would save the pancakes for later.

"When can I see my mother?"

"You'll be lucky if you ever see your mother again." The man's face contorted so that he snorted and laughed at the same time. "Only joking, little one. Learn to behave yourself. If you cross your fingers and legs, and don't wet yourself, you might live to tell your friends about this" The man guffawed.

Bova hated people who laughed at their own jokes. "Igor will kill you if you harm me or my mother."

"Shut it!" The man picked up the tray of food and left the room. "Igor is the one who wants you here, little fool."

"Wait, I want those pancakes."

"Too late."

The door closed.

Bova sat in silence and drained his glass. Surely, Igor could not be responsible for this? The man must be lying, deliberately taunting him.

Bova thought about what his mother had always told him: *Do your best and be kind.* He wasn't sure how he could do his best in this situation, but he decided that he should be brave and not lose hope. He told himself that the man had no reason to hurt him or his family. Perhaps this was even a case of mistaken identity? *Who am I kidding …? Wishful thinking.*

Suddenly Bova heard a groan. Someone else—not his captor—was in pain. Someone was being brought into the *kommunalni.* From the sound of things, someone was being dragged into the apartment. Punches or kicks were being dealt.

The door opened. A disheveled yet distinguished looking man in his fifties with silver hair and wearing a dark-gray suit was shoved through the door and thrown across the room.

"Some advice," said Bova's captor in Russian, "do not try to escape. The boy dies if you try."

The man sat up, frowned, and tried to catch his breath. He appeared not to understand what was being said. Bova scrambled to his feet and approached the man. He didn't look Russian. His suit was dirty and rumpled. The man had deep, dark bags under his eyes and a cut above the right one.

When the man focused on Bova, there was a glint of a smile in his eye. Slumped against the wall, he was too weak to support himself.

"It's OK, Mister." Bova knelt down beside him and used both arms to prevent the man falling to one side. He pulled the sleeve of his thermal sweater down over his hand and wiped a trickle of drying blood from the man's cheek. "My friend will free us. Don't worry." Bova spoke English with a heavy Russian accent.

The man looked at the boy and nodded. "I'm with the UN. My name's Kurt Halsinger. You are Bova?"

Bova didn't understand everything the man was saying, but he recognized his own name. The injured man was a foreigner—another one. He had a kind face, and Bova did not feel threatened. *I have to escape with or without this man.*

Yongbuk Region, North Korea

Ryzhakov found an old motorcycle in the shed next to Chen's dacha. He picked up a piece of rag, unscrewed the cap, and dipped it into the gas tank. The tip of the rag soaked up a small amount of gasoline. "Chort vozmyi," Ryzhakov muttered. *Damn it!* Almost empty, but at least he didn't need much gas to cover the ten kilometers back to Yongbuk town.

He mounted the motorcycle and used the incline leading down from the hut to jump-start it. It roared in to action. *Thank you, Chen.*

Twenty minutes later he was back at the desolate army barracks outside Yongbuk, the town not marked on any official North Korean maps. He collected a new military escort driver without a hitch. Without the escort, things might get complicated at checkpoints.

It was time to launch Plan B.

In the DPRK military Jeep, they headed toward the forming-up point—as it was known in the military—for Operation Tumen. Igor Ryzhakov was used to setbacks. He was an Afghanistan veteran and ran one of the most lucrative black-market operations ever organized in Russia. He was used to turning *problema* into dollar signs.

Three kilometers outside Yongbuk, Ryzhakov's escort nodded to the guard at the entrance to a deserted refueling station. Once inside, seven T72 tanks stood ready, breathing like mechanical dragons, engines running. Commanding this skeleton, elite fighting unit was a retired Russian army tank corps sergeant called Mishka—little Michael. Ryzhakov had personally handpicked him.

The smell of hot engine metal and the powerful rumble of idling tanks twenty times louder than a truck reminded Ryzhakov of his ten years of active service as a tankist during the Soviet Union's occupation of Afghanistan. The occupation had turned into a bitter—and in retrospect most would say futile—conflict, one that the Soviets wished they had never attempted.

Ryzhakov had been promoted to colonel and awarded a secret and for-internal-eyes-only prestigious military honor—the Golden Sickle—for defeating a group of vicious Afghan fighters who had outmaneuvered and taken his squadron by surprise. Were it not for the quick thinking and bravery of one Captain Igor Ryzhakov, the enemy would have destroyed the entire squadron of tanks, officers, and soldiers alike.

Like all good officers, he had kept in touch with some of the soldiers under his command. Many years later, he periodically hired them to commit low-level, cross-border smuggling with North Korea as well as unofficial "law enforcement" operations. Essentially, he had become a law unto himself in the Vladivostok Kraj with a small army of willing volunteers who zealously seized the opportunity to make hard cash in the chaotic lawlessness of the post-perestroika era. In their eyes, Mother Russia owed them big time for the Afghanistan fiasco and their sacrifice therein.

Ryzhakov shook Mishka's hand with a grip that said, *Don't fuck with me or I'll kill you.* "Kak tam? Vsoh normalno?" *How's everything going?*

"Vsoh pod kontrolum, tovarish Polkovnik." *Everything's fine, comrade Colonel.* He used Ryzhakov's military rank and saluted with the traditional Soviet Army karate-style chop across the chest. "Kak u vas djela?" *How are things with you?*

After the brief exchange with his mission commander, Ryzhakov began to inspect the half-squadron of T72 main battle tanks. He picked one at random, climbed up onto the turret, and, lowering himself down to the prone position, dipped his head inside the turret to confirm correct stowage; that ammunition and equipment had been properly secured. He noted the perfect mix of both armor-piercing and the more conventional and tank-busting high explosives he'd specifically ordered for the job.

After more random checks on three other tanks—cleanliness of barrel housings, rear-wheel axle lubrication, hydraulics, and most importantly, gun-laser adjustments and spotless external lenses—Ryzhakov returned to Mishka, who had been patiently waiting.

"Here are the plans," said Ryzhakov.

"Thank you."

"Targets—one to ten, two locations. Five kill-points per target." He pointed to various references on the map. "No infantry support."

"Shouldn't be necessary."

"Precisely. Use high explosive rounds for the prisoners."

"Very good, comrade Colonel."

"Execute swiftly," he concluded, raising his fist in a gesture of solidarity and unity for Mishka and the other soldiers taking part. "No mercy. Mission is czar!"

Then Ryzhakov took a few steps back from the line of tanks and, scanning the line of tanks, nodded slowly, lips puckered. "Ne ploxa," he concluded. *Not bad.* He was impressed with the preparations, satisfied his efficient fighting unit was ready for active duty. If anything, this unit was overkill. Its size and fire-power were capable of executing the mission twice over. But he wanted to be sure. This unit would render the entire Yongbuk complex inactive and inoperative for the foreseeable future. Killing the prisoners, though regrettable, would be even simpler.

"We are at ten minutes notice to move," Mishka said, saluting.

"Excellent. I have faith in your leadership." Igor smiled and then, almost as an afterthought, added nonchalantly, "I will not be joining you for phase one."

Mishka lowered his gaze. "I am disappointed, and I was looking forward to our mission together. You are military legend in the Vladivostok Kraj."

"Once a soldier ... always a comrade. I know you will make me proud."

"As you wish, Igor Pavlovich," he replied.

"I have faith in your abilities and your loyalty. I know you will not disappoint me."

"Very good, comrade Colonel. Until we meet again." Mishka clicked his heels and saluted.

"Of course. I will come and celebrate your success."

"Thank you. We look forward to it."

Ryzhakov climbed into his Jeep. He began to hum *Lucy in the Sky with Diamonds*, his favorite Beatles song. He congratulated himself for negotiating the price and recruiting the detachment of reliable Russian soldiers. It was good to have his *ribyata*—lads—taking part in the foray. He was certain they would not fail.

But now he had to find Jack Steele. The Englishman had caused too many problems.

Kill him straight away? No. He may still prove an asset. Insurance, as per his original plan. But one thing was certain—Steele would not leave North Korea alive. The journalist would prove a useful tool for reporting this event to the international media—showing the world what so-called "civilized" Western governments were capable of. Yes, he needed Steele for that phase of the operation. But he had taken a personal dislike to Mr. BBC, for personal reasons, and once business was taken care of, he would kill Jack Steele.

Ryzhakov climbed into his SUV and requested his North Korean escort to drive back toward Yongbuk. He hoped the North Korean police chief had made progress locating the foreigner. In these parts, where most people had never seen a foreigner, Steele could not remain at large for long.

Pyongyang, North Korea

In Pyongyang, the president's chief of staff clicked the television to mute. He was amused by the sense of foreboding and panic the old-guard general's press conference had caused. The international news media had gone into overdrive, salivating at the prospect of renewed conflict on the Korean Peninsula after so many years of peace. It was news certain to boost viewer ratings.

The telephone rang.

"I am listening," said Colonel Cho Myung-chul.

"Do you know Jack Steele, a British journalist?" The North Korean ambassador in Moscow spoke softly.

"*Steele*? No, Excellency, I have not heard of this man." He sat very still, listening intently. Everything was going according to plan. He hoped this latest call from Moscow would not sabotage his mission.

There was uneasiness in the ambassador's voice. "He must disappear, as though he never existed."

"A journalist? No problem," replied the colonel. "This is good news, Excellency. He can be removed without retaliation from his government. An American?"

"British. His people are also concerned his presence will ruin everything."

"I understand, your Excellency. I will attend to this immediately. Where is he?"

"He is with the Russian in Yongbuk."

"Thank you, Excellency. Please do not concern yourself any further. Consider the matter closed."

The colonel hung up and pressed the red intercom button on his desk.

"At your service, comrade Colonel," came the reply from his military assistant in the next room.

"I wish to speak immediately to the chief of police in Yongbuk. *Immediately.*"

Heathrow Airport, London

Passing successfully through newly installed—post 9/11—security X-ray machines at London Heathrow, Sandy was thankful to put her shoes back on. No holdups or awkward questions. Even the Sikh airport security guard had smiled.

Sandy checked she had retrieved her worldly possessions from the plastic tray and walked across the duty-free hall packed with sparkling designer shops and expensive-smelling boutiques. *I swear I can smell Coach leather!* Sumptuous perfumes wafted from the Harrod's cosmetics counter. She couldn't resist a brief detour for a squirt of the newest Chanel—a ritual and MO she had learned from her mother.

Sandy heard the last call for her flight, and her pace quickened as she trotted toward the gate along the moving walkway. She skipped off the end, and, for the first time in days, she felt free. She was excited to see Jack, even if she had no clue how she was going to find him. Even if she had screwed up big time on her last call with him.

Then came a personal, last-call announcement for Sandy Steele to report immediately to Gate 52. *I'm nearly there. Now what?*

At Gate 52, Sandy saw the last passengers disappear from the departure lounge down the ramp to the aircraft. Sandy looked around to see if anyone was following. *Nothing unusual.* She'd made it. She was going to get out of this godforsaken city and put its bad memories behind her.

"Excuse me. Mrs. Steele?" A man in a navy pinstriped suit with a blue-and-white striped shirt and red paisley silk tie suddenly stood in front of her, blocking her passage.

"I'm late," she said, frowning. "That's my flight." She pointed to the gate, dreading the thought now that this was no accident.

"Ms. Danner? Mrs. Steele?" said the man, insistently.

"Mrs. Steele. I'm married." Sandy could see British Airways ground-staff tidying up the desk next to the gate, ready to close the flight. "What's this about? I have to catch my flight."

"Come with me, please, Mrs. Steele. Just a routine check." Mr. Silk Paisley grinned.

"*Routine check?* Bullshit! I'm gonna miss my flight, damn it!"

"My apologies, Mrs. Steele. This won't take long. We'll have you on the next flight..."

Sandy took a deep breath, exhaled, and said good-bye to BA Flight 35 to Moscow.

CHAPTER TWENTY-ONE

Yongbuk, North Korea

When Steele came around, Inspector Ji Chang-wook had appeared ready to beat him again. But Steele quickly explained that he was ready and willing to confess on camera to spying. What's more, Steele's idea all along was to hold a press conference. He persuaded the inspector that it would be better for him to make a name for himself first and beat Steele later—"You will be the first DPRK police inspector to make international headlines with a Western spy's sworn confession and denunciation of the West on live television."

It would undoubtedly—Steele had belabored the point—lead to a promotion, but more importantly *a move*, to Pyongyang. The inspector's eyes had lit up, and he agreed that it was an excellent idea. *Gullible arsehole. Or perhaps I'm a much better actor than I thought ...*

Becoming a self-confessed spy on local North Korean television, Steele had determined, would spotlight international media attention on the story he was about to break—assuming he could escape and actually break the story before someone silenced him. It was a long shot. But it was the least he could do after Chen had perhaps made the ultimate sacrifice for him.

His idea was simple: give locals advanced warning of the imminent attack on the nuclear reactor and the prison camp on live television.

Steele knew he must quickly and efficiently deliver his

message before the TV journalists translated and realized exactly what he was doing and pulled the plug on him. But if just one local official took his information seriously, it might just be enough to get them to evacuate.

Steele was counting on the fact that North Korean authorities—notoriously suspicious of foreigners—would investigate his information-warning and take urgent measures to thwart the attack.

If, however, his warning failed, he would have to stop a squadron of Russian tanks from destroying a nuclear reactor and five-thousand innocent civilians on his own. His leadership and tactical challenges during active duty service in Operation Desert Storm and Bosnia now paled in significance compared with the enormity of this task.

Sitting on a chair in front of the camera, Steele beckoned to Bae Jong-hoon, the young Korean journalist who had been in the room when they first arrived at the television studio a few hours earlier. Steele liked his face and the way he had listened and observed when Steele had first arrived. He sensed this was a man he could trust. *Anyone who has listened avidly to the BBC World Service since childhood must have learned something!*

"Listen, my friend," Steele began among the hubbub of electrical cable dragging, electronic beeping, and testing going on beside them. "Did you study journalism?"

"No, I did not," replied the earnest young man. "But I listen in secret to BBC every day and also CNN for many years. I start work in Yongbuk and I will go to work in Pyongyang one day."

"You are a journalist at heart? Am I correct? It's in your blood?"

"Yes. I always want to be journalist."

The inspector had disappeared moments before and would probably return soon.

"Look at me. We don't have much time." Steele looked intently into the young man's eyes. "Please look at me. Do you trust me?"

The Korean squinted nervously. The blinding studio lights suddenly lit Steele in preparation for the imminent broadcast. The young Korean glanced over at the police inspector's henchman. Steele could see the journalist was nervous, probably fearful that he might be reprimanded or worse, reported to official channels for fraternizing with foreigners.

The young man said, "You are British spy. I cannot trust you."

This was the general consensus among the television studio journalists, Steele realized. They had grown up believing whatever the North Korean state had brainwashed them with.

Steele whispered slowly, "You know that's not true. What do your instincts tell you?" His eyes narrowed, and he looked the young journalist in the eye. "What if I was just like you? A reporter doing his job …?" Every inch of his body language told the truth. People had to trust your face, your eyes, if you want to be a successful journalist. Steele had learned over the years his most important asset as a journalist was his honest face.

Bae Jong-hoon stopped pretending to plug wires into the desk console next to the microphone and looked at Steele.

"Jong-hoon—What if I was in trouble because I was trying to save someone's life? Not just one person, but five-thousand North Koreans."

The Korean thought for a few moments, analyzing Steele's expression. "Why would you do that?"

"Why wouldn't I? If I knew something you didn't? I'm a man with a heart just like you."

Bae Jong-hoon looked around to see if anyone was observing their conversation. "I would listen and make decision."

"Okay, listen. Your government is making nuclear weapons. The Americans have paid the Russians a lot of money to destroy these weapons. Your government wants to kill the people in the Yongbuk prison camp—I don't know why."

Bae Jong-hoon shook his head. "You are mistaken. There are no prisoners here."

"There are five-thousand prisoners. They will die within hours if you don't help me."

Bae Jong-hoon bent down and pretended to tie his silver fake Adidas shoelace. "People are watching us. You have proof, Mr. Steele? Can you give me proof?"

"No proof. You have my word. That's all. You decide."

Bae Jong-hoon walked away without saying anything. Steele felt sick and empty, as though his insides had been pumped dry. He hadn't eaten properly for a week. He swallowed and sat up straight in his chair ready for his performance. He looked straight into the camera lens, took a few deep breaths, and prepared for his confession.

Inspector Ji Chang-wook ended his call and entered the backstage area of the TV studio. The red ON AIR light started flashing above one of the studio entrances. A gray-haired, bucked-toothed technician stood to one side of Steele and silently counted down—three fingers ... two fingers ... one finger.

Steele was live on North Korean television.

★　　★　　★

The press conference began as Steele had planned. Before Ji Chang-wook had left to take his call, he had been visibly salivating, licking his lips at the thought of his promotion. He had caught a Western spy single-handedly, and the foreigner was about to confess on a live feed that could be accessed across the nation—and for that matter, the world. It was as though the inspector could smell the honor that would be bestowed upon him.

Steele began by looking into the camera and introducing himself. "My name is Jack Steele. I am a British journalist and work for the *London Daily Standard*. I have been involved in a secret Western plot to destroy an important facility in your beautiful and beloved North Korea ..." He had to seize the audience's attention first and then hit them with the warning before they cut him off. *Few more seconds at most.* Steele continued, "Dear citizens of Yongbuk … there is a nuclear reactor here and it will be attacked tonight!" He increased his volume and intensity. "ALL CITIZENS ARE IN DANGER! THE ATTACK IS TONIGHT! You must—"

The live press conference stopped as abruptly as it had begun. The lights went out. The studio lights and sound system fizzled out as the workers froze and stared at each other in surprise.

A faint orange glow from the half-dozen studio arc lights allowed Steele to make out a scuffle that had broken out in the opposite corner of the studio. Some of the participants were agile but two were slammed to the floor in yelps of pain.

A diversion? Before Steele could decide, Bae Jong-hoon approached and gestured for Steele to follow. He was leading Steele away from the pandemonium. *Wait, where's Natasha?* Steele glanced right and managed to reach out for Natasha, who had been standing near the camera tripod in the semidarkness. "It's me. Let's go," he said to her, as he was being pulled away by the journalist.

Bae Jong-hoon gripped Steele's arm and said, "It's OK, Mr. Steele. Come with me."

"Where are we going?"

"We have all heard stories about the reactor and the camp. You are telling the truth. But you need to leave now for your safety."

Steele followed Bae Jong-hoon through a door that led to a dark corridor. "Please don't stop, Mr. Steele. Come with me," the young man urged.

Moments later they reached the back of the building and exited, a heavy fire door slamming behind them.

"Good-bye, Mr. Steele. Good luck." Bae Jong-hoon disappeared back into the studio.

Steele and Natasha reached the end of the block. As they rounded the corner, headlights of a waiting SUV momentarily blinded them. Steele heard a familiar voice—with an American accent.

"Sullivan?" Natasha said. "It's the American."

Mike Sullivan was waiting, window open, in a Jeep with a North Korean policeman. "It's OK," he said with a smirk. "He's one of the good guys. Get in."

"I was wondering how you were," Steele said.

"I somehow doubt that. Wait a second," Sullivan said, scowling at Natasha. "We need to ditch the girl."

"Forget it."

"I said, ditch her."

"Why?"

"My orders are to get *you* out of here. No one cares about the girl."

"Wrong. I care about her. She stays. She's with me. Or I take my chances alone."

"Fine. Get in. Let's hope she doesn't get us all killed."

★　　★　　★

Sullivan genuinely did not want to kill the girl—for a start, she was a beautiful woman. He felt a warped sense of chivalry—one that he knew, however, would not stop him from doing his job. He did not have time to argue with Steele. The inspector's men might charge out of that door at any moment. Even though he had bribed the inspector to stall his superiors, he knew the agreement had not included physically snatching the prize trophy—*Jack Steele.*

With his two new passengers, Sullivan accelerated into the main street and headed south toward the border. He planned to assassinate Steele—and now the girl, which would be a damn shame—near the border. Preferably in no man's land—he hoped that location would be desolate enough and make any search too complicated so that he could make a clean escape back into Russia, and then home.

★　★　★

"Where are we going?" Steele asked.

"Do you care?" replied Sullivan. "I'm getting your ass out of here. Isn't that enough?"

He has a point. "On a good day, yes." *This whole situation makes no sense.*

"I'm here to save your ass."

"I'd rather you didn't bother." Steele leaned forward and grabbed the policeman's pistol sitting in the front seat. "Thanks for the offer, but I'm in charge now. Pull over."

"Stop messing!" shouted Sullivan. "Cut the crap and give him the pistol. I need to get you out of here. Alive!"

"Pull over!" shouted Steele.

Sullivan pulled over.

"Out!" Steele gestured for the policeman to get out, which he appeared to do gladly. "Now drive."

"You've got this all wrong," said Sullivan. "This is a mess."

"Let me explain the mess so you can understand. I am officially a British spy—" Steele placed the pistol barrel on the side of Sullivan's head. "You need to listen to *me.*"

"Put the gun down. We're heading to the border. We'll be safe."

"Bullshit." Steele could feel the blood surging through his body. He might need a surge of adrenaline. "Here's the change of plan. Flexible at all times, remember? Didn't Langley teach you that?"

Sullivan relented, but Steele kept his guard up. Things were starting to make sense. *If the Americans are somehow involved with Igor, Sullivan will blow my brains out if it comes to it.*

Natasha said quietly, "We have to get to the reactor."

Steele nodded.

"OK, OK. What's the plan?" said Sullivan. "I'm listening."

"We—all of us—are going to stop Ryzhakov and his men. Keep driving."

"Where to?" Sullivan protested.

"Three guesses …" Steele took out the map Chen had given him for safekeeping. "The reactor."

Sullivan put his foot on the brake and slowed to make a U-turn. "Go ahead, Steele. You're in command."

"But first, we pick up Chen and Viktor," Natasha said. "You know the way."

"Wait, Chen's alive?" asked Steele, relieved and genuinely happy in this moment of madness.

"Yes, I guess he missed. Igor likes to scare people, but even he has limits."

Steele said, "Not from what I've seen. But that's great news."

Sofiyskaya Embankment, Moscow

Anderson had been leaning back in his chair, "taking a moment," as he liked to say, or waiting to put out the next desk fire, as his colleagues would say. He had been patiently waiting for the latest word on Jack Steele. *Jack fucking Steele.* As soon as the CIA or North Korean authorities found him, he would give Ryzhakov the green light for the main attack on the reactor. Too risky to proceed with Steele on the loose. Things were almost under control.

He glanced up from his desk at the television monitor and did an immediate double take. He grabbed the TV remote and turned up the volume. He edged forward on his chair with such momentum that he almost fell off. "For crying out loud!" he growled. "Now, what the bejesus …?"

CNN International was broadcasting grainy, faded pictures of a North Korean press conference. Steele sat front and center of the camera looking jaded but clearly compos mentis. He was making some kind of announcement. Anderson flipped to UK Sky News Channel … they were showing similar images. The chyron read: *Yongbuk, North Korea.* He clicked back to CNN— this footage of Steele was being broadcast via satellite around the world.

Jack Steele is giving a press conference in Yongbuk, North Korea for Christ's sake!

"What the bloody ..." Anderson spluttered, swallowing hard to stop himself from choking. Unless there was a teleprompter, Steele was speaking extemporaneously. He appeared calm and confident. A simultaneous translation into Korean by a translator with a hoarse voice—Anderson never trusted people with weak voices, especially in translation—covered Steele's words so that Anderson could only hear snippets of his message.

"... and I have no grievances against the Democratic People's Republic of Korea ... regret my actions and hope that my confession in good faith ... people of Yongbuk. I have ... the British government, and I am now cooperating ... my intention ... thank you."

CNN's screen went black. Then Anderson realized, in fact, it looked as though the lights inside the studio had been cut. Dark shadows remained, and panic ensued. Shouts could be heard in the background after the *clump* of Steele's mic dropped to the floor. Then the report stopped abruptly, and Christiane Amanpour returned.

Anderson rubbed the mole on his chin while simultaneously twisting his face.

At first, he had thought Steele was being paraded as a spy. But his manner had seemed too relaxed. Amanpour announced they would replay the tape once the package was ready with subtitles as they were unable to remove the simultaneous interpretation audio. She apologized for the poor technical quality of pictures due to the local TV station satellite feed, adding that if anyone did speak Korean, CNN could not verify the accuracy and therefore offered caution concerning the North Korean Defense Ministry translation of Steele's words.

Anderson continued to massage his stubble cheek, then snatched the satellite phone from his desk. He dialed a number from memory.

The international number rang a couple of times and then switched to voicemail.

"This is Moscow. Jack Steele is at the television studio in Yongbuk. Kill him. Then proceed with Tumen immediately."

CHAPTER TWENTY-TWO

Yongbuk Region

Inside the small military fuel compound a few kilometers from Yongbuk, Igor Ryzhakov could smell success amid the clouds of tank engine exhaust that chugged out into cold night air. Within the next few hours, his men would execute the task—another $5 million in the bank—this portion delivered in person and in cash by a bogus UN messenger, currently under lock and key in Vladivostok.

And that was just one part of the intricate tapestry he was so expertly weaving. *Chort vozmi.* Luck of the devil. *And I'm the Devil!* Everything's under control. He would ignore Anderson's assassination order for the next forty-eight hours. But once he had finished with Steele, and Steele had performed his journalistic duties, Igor would obligingly carry out Anderson's end-ex request to terminate Steele.

First, he had to locate the Englishman and make him report all the facts as accurately as possible. He would show Steele irrefutable evidence of his own dealings with the British Embassy in Moscow as well as involvement from the Americans and the North Korean officials. He would prove to Steele that both East and West were responsible for Operation Tumen—that axis-of-evil East and holier-than-thou West were, in fact, inextricably linked, *adnavo polya jagoda*—one field of berries—or as his Englishman pawn would say, "cut from the same cloth."

Ryzhakov possessed numerous recordings of his telephone

conversations with Simon Anderson, as well as evidence that large amounts of foreign currency had been handed over. He might even allow Steele to talk to the UN "official" in Vladivostok even if he was a spy. Steele would have no choice but to tell the world—his conscience and professionalism would demand it.

Ryzhakov double-checked map coordinates and the route to the nuclear facility and the prison camp. *God only knows why North Koreans want to slaughter five thousand detainees in the camp.* But that was none of his business. It just gave him five thousand reasons to execute his vendetta against the so-called super powers and North Korea as ruthlessly as possible and take their money.

Sitting and observing in his SUV, he felt the ground tremble as the T72 tank convoy left the compound, the heavy metal tracks on each tank grating and grinding into the dirt in spite of the six-inch layer of snow. Tanks were dirty, smelly metal beasts, but *en masse* they exuded an obscene beauty. It sent a shiver down his spine to watch and listen to their black silhouettes rumbling away into the night, and to recall the sweet sound of roaring tanks from operations in Afghanistan all those years ago. He had earned his reputation as a mighty tank warrior. He nodded and smiled, remembering the attack he was most proud of—the one that had made him famous (or infamous depending on which side you were on) and earned him the title of *voyenni geroi*—military hero—and his medal.

He shivered as he looked up at the crisp, cold, cobalt-blue night sky. Not a cloud in sight. Even, he mused, the stars were looking down at the convoy of death far below. And he was its creator.

The stars, however, were safe from Ryzhakov's impending act of madness on earth. He wished he could have commanded the lead tank just like the old days. But his immediate task was equally pressing. He followed the convoy for a mile and turned off at the first crossroads to proceed to his own target—Jack Steele.

Pyongyang, North Korea

The North Korean chief of staff walked briskly as he entered Kim Jung Ryul's majestic presidential suite. It was a short walk across the corridor, but he was relishing every moment. It had been originally his idea to contact Western powers and bait them with this plan. The British had swallowed the idea hook, line, and sinker without blinking. *Fools*—the North Korean people would never negotiate in earnest with Western powers to solve internal domestic issues. But the British diplomat had not needed much persuasion. The ruse had worked so far. He and the president now sat comfortably on the fulcrum of power and might and were in a perfect position to decide how best to play their next diplomatic hand.

"Your Excellency. Phase one is complete," began Colonel Cho Myung-chul.

"Our misguided general has no idea?"

"Nothing, Your Excellency."

"Operation Tumen is underway?"

"Many will die."

"But thousands more will live..." The North Korean president stroked the longhaired gray cat that was settled comfortably on his lap. The cat purred in gratitude.

"You are correct, Excellency."

"We must think of the greater good of our comrades."

"I agree, Excellency."

Kim Jung Ryul uncrossed his legs and took off one of his pink satin slippers that resembled, in fact, one of the ballet slippers of the colonel's daughter, although a slightly brighter shade of pink. The colonel was surprised by the size of Kim's big toe. Bulbous to the point of repulsion—the nail on his big toe had been severed at one time and had never grown back completely. The colonel had heard rumors that the president enjoyed having his big toe sucked. The idea (and image) disgusted him as did the numerous women who came to the presidential apartments on a regular basis for such practices. The colonel was grateful to have a wife and a daughter who he loved, even though he rarely spent time with them. It was a trade-off. He knew they were safe, materially taken care of. He knew his family lived in the lap of luxury compared to the average North Korea citizen. But he wished he could see more of them.

"How many will die?" the Dear Leader asked.

"Several hundred work in the reactor and five thousand in the camp."

"What brutal infidels these Americans are …!"

"Yes, Excellency. To cooperate with our madness."

"For the greater good, Colonel."

"Thank you, Excellency. It is my honor to serve you and our people."

"The plan is ready and secure?"

"Yes."

"No one will ever know who is responsible?" Kim replaced his slipper.

"If anyone, Excellency, the Russians will be blamed."

The president laughed. The cat sprang off his lap.

The colonel nodded and smiled. He walked to the door and turned. "When this is complete, we will be in a position to negotiate UN economic rejuvenation plan. It will very much favor our interests, Excellency."

"That pleases me. Thank you, Colonel Cho. By the way, Colonel, how is your beautiful family?"

"They enjoy life, Excellency."

"Send them my good wishes."

The colonel bowed his head and exited.

Yongbuk Region, North Korea

The bullet had grazed the side of Viktor's neck. It was only a flesh wound, but he had been knocked unconscious for a few moments from falling and hitting his head on the base of the fireplace trying to save Chen.

Viktor woke up and looked around. Ryzhakov had gone. After ten years of working for Ryzhakov, and witnessing countless innocent victims fall prey to his intimidation, bullying, violence, and even murder, something inside Viktor had snapped. Images of his wife and daughter skating across the ice in Vladivostok had flashed through his mind as he lunged at Ryzhakov, aiming to prevent yet another death of an innocent victim—old man Chen.

Viktor had not intended to kill Ryzhakov. He wanted to subdue him, that was all—break the apparently vicious cycle inside Ryzhakov's head that told him to kill every time someone stood in his way or threatened him. Ryzhakov had pointed and fired the gun at Viktor, but missed, perhaps intentionally?

Chen was lying down, confused, holding a blanket to his shoulder and nursing his wound. Viktor filled a basin of water in the kitchen and returned to clean the wound. He had trained as a paramedic in the Soviet Army. His service in Afghanistan—where he had first met Igor Ryzhakov—had given him hands-on experience of treating gunshot wounds and more. Chen's wound was not life threatening.

"How did the Englishman find you?" asked Viktor. They conversed in English.

"It was a sign."

"What did you say, old man?"

"I have a map and the ..." Chen waved his empty hand but could not finish his sentence. His breath was short. He appeared disoriented, discombobulated.

"What can you tell me, old man? Where is Steele? What did you tell him?"

Chen tried again. He took a deep breath. "You are surrounded by evil," he said.

"I know this," Viktor replied, somewhat perplexed by the obviousness of his statement. "My chief is a vicious man. You are correct." Viktor leaned forward and adjusted the coat he had placed behind Chen's head for a pillow.

"I am good. You can leave now."

"Old man, what did you give the foreigner?"

"Yongbuk is a dangerous place."

"I don't understand. Explain, old man?"

Chen was still finding it difficult to talk. His speech was slurred, and he was sweating profusely. Viktor feared that Chen would pass out. Perhaps the shoulder wound was more serious than he had suspected. Apart from dressing the wound, he couldn't do much more without proper medical facilities. "Here. Drink water," Viktor said, holding a cup of water to Chen's lips.

Chen drank enthusiastically. "Go to the drawer. Promise me … you will help," he said.

"What do you need?"

"Go … go there." Chen pointed.

Viktor got up and walked to the chest of drawers. He pulled open the top drawer. It was empty. "There's nothing here."

Chen wagged his finger at the chest of drawers. Viktor bent down and opened the lower drawer. Inside was a pile of papers. Viktor held them up, coughing from the dust his rummaging had disturbed.

"Bring everything," said Chen, beckoning.

Viktor looked under the papers. He found a copy of the King James Bible in English and a souvenir brochure of the Great Wall of China. "Is this what you're looking for?" Viktor was confused.

"Yes. Bring it to me. Bring everything."

Viktor walked across the room with the books and papers, dumping them on the floor next to the old man. Chen opened the brochure, and a folded map fell out.

Viktor picked up the map and opened it. "This map? Is this what you want? Why are you telling me this?"

He was confused. In the back of his mind he was wondering if he would ever see his family again. Instinct had told him to save this old man, but he wasn't sure why. Now he was concerned for his own family's well-being. Ryzhakov may have even already given the order to punish or kill them all.

Chen pointed to the map again. "God people in danger," he said.

"Good people in danger?" repeated Viktor. He looked at the map where Chen was pointing. The location was close to the Yongbuk nuclear reactor.

"*God* people. Many doctors. Go!"

Viktor understood. Somehow Chen wanted Viktor to save the people of Yongbuk. Ryzhakov's squadron of tanks would be launching their attack at any moment. "I need transport. A car?" said Viktor, gently supporting Chen's fragile shoulder. It seemed as though Chen was falling asleep. "Chen, please?"

"No transport," he mumbled.

Viktor hurried outside. Behind the house under a sheet of plastic was a rusty old motorcycle. Viktor prayed it still worked. He did not think to check the gas level. Both tires were completely flat. "*Eto gavno!*" shouted Viktor. Piece of shit.

Then he stopped.

Viktor heard the sound of a car engine in the distance. *Thank God.* He waited patiently.

★   ★   ★

Steele's heart pounded. He was pleased to see Viktor but wasn't sure if that meant Ryzhakov was nearby. He kept the gun pointing at Sullivan's head and told him to pull up alongside Viktor. *And what about Chen?*

Steele opened the rear door. "Viktor, are you alone?"

"Chen is in the hut."

"Is he all right?" Steele asked.

"Flesh wound. Not serious."

"Can he walk?"

"Yes, I think so." Viktor's eyes narrowed. "Why?"

"No time to explain. He comes with us."

Sullivan objected, "You're wasting your time, Steele. I'm telling you, don't do this."

"And I'm telling you to shut it!"

Sullivan cursed under his breath.

Viktor walked back into the hut and helped Chen into the Jeep.

"I have the map," Viktor announced, and proudly handed Steele the map. "The prison is here."

Steele unfolded the map. "Excellent, Viktor. Get in. Chen, are you OK?"

"Yes, I am good."

Viktor climbed in and kissed Natasha on her forehead.

"Steele, this may seem like a dumb question," said Sullivan, now visibly sweating. "You think you and your friends are going to stop a unit of tanks?"

"I'll get back to you on that."

Sullivan sneered.

"And I have one for you," Steele said.

"Go ahead."

"How does this feel?" Steele struck the side of Sullivan's head with the butt of his pistol. "From now on, just drive."

Somewhere above the Baltic Sea

Sandy sat next to the man in the pinstriped suit on BA flight 0872 to Moscow. In less than two hours, they would touch down on the snow-cleared runway at Sheremetyevo Airport on the outskirts of the Russian capital. The temperature would be well below freezing.

She had only known the man in the navy, pinstriped, double-breasted suit for little more than an hour. Though he had no chin, he was obviously important. He had used his authority to delay the British Airways flight for at least fifteen minutes while he questioned her.

Chinless had explained in a cold, arrogant manner that he and the British security services "really did want to help." He knew that Sandy had been abducted and that her husband was in trouble. If she cooperated, he gave her his word that British authorities would do everything within their power to ensure a satisfactory outcome for all parties—whatever that means, Sandy thought. Even though she had purchased a ticket, the man had escorted her to fly as his guest in first class. He also invited her to remain with him *as our guest* in Moscow to help assist British and American authorities investigate Jack Steele's disappearance. Chinless had refused to give further details.

"Disappearance?" Sandy said. "He's not missing. I spoke to him yesterday."

"I'm sure we can work things out once we're in Moscow. Rest assured we'll do our best for all of you."

Sandy held her next thought as the campy flight attendant sporting an absurdly dark tan for the time of year asked if they wanted water or orange juice. His teeth flashed a white, TV-commercial smile, which Sandy wondered how he could afford on flight attendant's salary.

Taking her juice and pretzels from the tray, she asked if she could have an extra glass of water. She always drank lots of fluids on a long flight.

"Who do you work for?" Sandy went on.

"You already asked that, Ms. Steele."

"I know. You didn't answer. Foreign Service? MI6? Military Intelligence?"

"As they say, 'If I told you, I'd have to kill you.'" This was his first attempt at humor.

Pompous chinless ass. Sandy didn't laugh. "Very funny. Don't give up your day job ... *as they say.*"

Chinless sipped the orange juice and sparkling water mix he had specially requested. "All you need to know for now is that I work for the good guys," he continued. He tried to smile, but to Sandy it came across as a sneer. "We're just trying to get your husband out of a spot of bother."

"What's he done?"

"We don't know exactly. That's part of the problem. We'll know more when we arrive."

"I know Jack's in trouble." Sandy decided to share some info in the hope of something in return. "The local police kicked him out of some little town on the other side of Russia. Accused him of stealing or trying to drown someone. Next thing I know, I'm out cold and being stuffed in the back of a car. Turns out my father might have had something to do with it."

"How do you know Mr. Danner was implicated?"

"I saw him. He knew exactly where to find me."

"I see," said Chinless. "But there was no ransom?"

"I don't know. I escaped."

Chinless frowned and pursed his lips. "We believe the people your husband is working with were also responsible for your attempted abduction. As to the extent of your father's involvement, we're not sure about that."

This was all new information. "What do you mean? *Attempted?* It was a done deal. Some thug knocked me out. I escaped."

Sandy's new companion adjusted his navigation screen on the back of the seat in front of him and tapped it with his nail. "Shouldn't be long now," he assured her. "We'll be there in no time. A car will be waiting."

"I can hardly wait. What if I refuse?"

"Trust me, it's better for your husband if you cooperate … and for your father too for that matter."

"Perhaps the next British Lurch will be more forthcoming."

"No need for that tone, Ms. Steele. Just doing my job."

"Sure you are, sorry."

"You're in good hands. Just sit back and enjoy a rest. You've earned it."

"Thanks." Sandy knocked back her water in two more gulps.

She hated the small measures you got on planes. She swirled the ice around in the plastic cup, crunched the ice cubes before swallowing. She tried to sleep, but her mind wouldn't settle.

Sandy couldn't decide if she was trying to find Jack because she loved him or because she was afraid of the alternative, of being alone. Her father had put her life in danger, she reckoned. All these years he had cared more about his wife than his daughter. It was true, Jack was the only person who really cared for her.

Having consumed several cups of juice and water during the flight, Sandy excused herself and got up to go to the bathroom. Most people were sleeping. Alternating a touch with left and right hand, Sandy steadied herself on the seats as she moved down the aisle. She noticed a young woman around her age asleep on her mother's shoulder. Sandy thought about her own mother. Why had her mother abandoned her years ago? Was it the rocky marriage that had sent her away? *Or was it my fault?*

Sandy's mother was English. She had left Danner and returned to London when Sandy was in high school. Sandy had visited her during summer vacations, and her mother had been generous with her time and money. But somehow it was never enough. How *could* it be? How could two weeks, twice a year, make up for all that time growing up without a mother every day? She remembered her fourteenth birthday party, which her best friend's mother had organized because Sandy's mother lived in England. She recalled some of her girlfriends complaining how uncool and embarrassing their mothers were. To Sandy, these complaints were bratty and ungrateful. She would have given anything to be able to participate in the complaining, to bitch about her own mother. But she couldn't. She had only seen her mother once that year and had suddenly realized she didn't know her own mother even well enough to gossip about her.

And now her father had let her down too. Not only for more than a decade had he abandoned her for his work and a string of girlfriends, culminating in the sham marriage to Anna, but now she suspected he was somehow involved with her abduction. *Bastard!* She could never forgive him.

Sandy noticed the occupied light above the aircraft bulkhead near the WC. But she continued toward the back anyway. A large man exited the bathroom on the right, and she decided to wait until the one opposite was free. On airplanes, she always checked out who had been in the bathroom before her. Sandy went past the curtain and bulkhead to the back of the aircraft to ask the bouncy flight attendant for more juice while she waited.

"Certainly, Madam," she chirped.

Sandy peeled back the cover and drank the orange juice in four or five gulps, then glanced up and almost choked. Her eyes widened. Someone had followed her to the back and stood looming next to her.

"Dad!"

★   ★   ★

Danner held up both hands to calm his daughter. He pulled her gently around the corner to the door, so they were out of earshot from the flight attendant, who had been staring to see if everything was all right.

"It's okay. It's my dad. He likes surprises."

They disappeared from view.

"Honey, please listen to me," Danner continued.

Sandy nodded and shut her eyes for a second, taking an exhale.

"Honey, you have to listen." He searched deep into Sandy's eyes. "Hear me out. Please."

Sandy swallowed and nodded. She had promised herself a minute before that she would never forgive him. "How did you get on this flight? What are you doing here?" She immediately became aware of her short, rapid breathing and told herself to exhale.

"Sandy, let me explain."

"You've said it three times. Go ahead, Dad. I'm listening."

"OK—"

"But I want answers. You've got two minutes."

Before he could speak, Danner released his daughter's forearm, grabbed her in a bear hug, and held her as tight as he could. His eyes filled with tears as he held her close. She pulled away slightly and looked up at him. Her eyes watered, but she wasn't crying yet. Perhaps there was still hope, she thought. Perhaps he wanted his daughter after all.

CHAPTER TWENTY-THREE

Sofiyskaya Embankment, Moscow

Anderson took a large gulp of coffee and prepared for a shitstorm. Seconds later, Ambassador Sir Brian Pendlebury stormed into Anderson's office and slammed the door behind him.

Anderson stood up. "Good afternoon, sir."

"There's nothing good about it." Pendlebury was visibly upset as he walked over to the window. He stared out, unable to look Anderson in the face, and began talking as if conversing directly with the giant Kremlin domes across the river. "What on earth have you done, man?"

"Ambassador, everything is under control, sir." Anderson lied. Everything was far from being under control. The world had just seen a British journalist confess to spying in North Korea hours before Operation Tumen was due to launch. The journalist had not spoken under any kind of duress. He wasn't bruised or bloodied. He had volunteered the confession freely. The announcement therefore appeared genuine. Anderson refused to accept defeat. "Sir Brian—"

"Shut up, Simon!" The ambassador sat down and loosened his burgundy and navy-blue striped Guards' tie. He whipped out a navy polka-dot cotton handkerchief and wiped a small white globule of saliva from the corner of his mouth. He spoke slowly and quietly. "Anderson, my dear fellow. Let's not waste time. I acknowledge I was fully aware of your insane scheme, and I should have, of course, scrutinized it more thoroughly. Too late now. Spilt milk. The question is: what are *we* going to do about it?"

"To be frank, sir—" Anderson sensed the ambassador did not have much patience left. "I'm afraid there isn't much we can do."

"Hoo-bloody-ray! Is that the best you can do?" Pendlebury's cheeks became ruddier by the second.

"Sir. *We* made a deal with the Koreans. *We* hired the Russian. *We* paid him, or will have done within hours, if he hasn't already received it. Yongbuk will be unserviceable."

"Destroyed?"

"Rendered useless at least. No one could have foreseen Jack Steele. He came out of nowhere."

"And World War III will kick off shortly thereafter. But that's obviously a minor hiccup in your book."

"With respect, Ambassador, it's not that—"

"Oh, it's not? As soon as so much as an old lady farts on or near the border, the Dear Leader and his military might have threatened a counteroffensive against the South Koreans—insert Americans—and whoever else they decide is not flavor of the month."

"Ambassador, if I can explain? I have assurances from the North Korean ambassador himself that there will be no acts of aggression against US forces. They were taking precautions. That's all."

"And when did you receive these 'assurances'?" asked Pendlebury.

"Lunch time."

"Before the Pyongyang press conference?"

"Just after. I went straight over to see the ambassador."

"I'd love to give you a pat on the back, but I'd probably knock you out cold."

Anderson squirmed in his seat. *I'd love you to try it.* He wanted to tell Pendlebury what he really thought—*utter dimwit, the biggest arsehole I've ever met.* "Sir—"

"You're asking me to take seriously an unofficial conversation you had with the North Korean ambassador, versus an unprecedented public declaration of aggression against our allies for the entire world to hear and enjoy?" Pendlebury wiped the right corner of his mouth. "Not to mention our journalist from a London rag telling everyone he's a bloody spy!"

"Sir Brian, in fact—"

"*Plus* the fact that we're about to witness an apparently deadly attack on their nuclear reactor—doing the New Guard's dirty work for them—which is quite literally about to blow up in our faces!"

Anderson's face twitched involuntarily. He was at a loss for words for the first time in his career. "I have every confidence—" he began slowly.

"Thank heaven for small mercies." Pendlebury stood up, walked toward the giant window and pointed at the Kremlin. "And what on earth do *they* make of all this?"

"I believe they will support whatever action we take."

"What do you suggest I tell the prime minister? I'm speaking to him in ten minutes."

"SIR!" A shrill voice rattled through the intercom speaker on Anderson's desk.

Anderson pressed the talk button. "What is it, Jenkins? Better be urgent."

"We've intercepted reports from the North Koreans—unconfirmed explosions in the Yongbuk area, possibly the reactor. Awaiting satellite confirmation."

"Perfect," said Pendlebury. "Just bloody perfect!"

Yongbuk Region, North Korea

Steele had no idea what he would do if, and, or when he located the tank unit. At Sandhurst, the instructors had called it "initiative." "Anything could happen in the next twenty-four hours, gentlemen!" the Coldstream guards platoon color sergeant used to bark at the Sandhurst officer cadets. "And it probably will, sirs!" Never a truer word spoken, Steele now thought, as they emerged from the dark forest searching for the tank troop kill unit.

The bumpy track through the dense silver-birch forest led to a clearing on low ground. They surveyed the terrain to the front. As the Jeep edged slowly forward onto a ridge, the nuclear reactor and confines suddenly came into view less than half a mile below them.

"Stop," Steele ordered.

With Viktor still pointing the pistol at Sullivan's temple, Steele got out of the Jeep and walked away from the vehicle. He picked his way over some rocks and stared incredulously at the deserted moonscape of dilapidated buildings in the near distance. *That's the reactor?* This characterless group of nondescript gray buildings was the cause of so much fear and potential conflict in the world. *Amazing,* he thought, *in a sad and pathetic way.*

Somewhere in the near distance, he could hear the unmistakable rumble of the approaching column of tanks. The gentle vibration reminded him of the long, endless nights of tank, artillery, and machine gun fire in Sarajevo—artillery and tank shells pounded the sitting-duck citizens in their apartment blocks night after night during his tour as a UN peacekeeper. Technically he was an UNMO—United Nations Military Observer. Tank rounds swept relentlessly across the horizontal plain at night like a lightning storm turned on its side. The piercing *whizz-bang* sound of tank fire interspersed with the staccato *rat-a-tat* of 7.62mm machine guns. With little else to do but watch the show night after night, Steele and local Muslim friends had stood on Sarajevo apartment balconies like sports spectators watching gun battles between Bosnian Muslims and Bosnian Serbs. Some UN peacekeeper *you* are, they had often joked as he stood next to them enjoying humanitarian-aid pizza that was basically a piece of dough from the oven with a dash of salt and whatever herbs grown on a balcony could be found to garnish. After Bosnia, he had hoped he would never witness another tank battle as long as he lived.

"So this is what all the fuss is about," he said under his breath, looking down at the Yongbuk nuclear reactor. In the near distance was a group of huge, windowless concrete buildings, floodlit from the ground up. The area was deserted. Steele saw and heard a couple of guard dogs walking free and barking. He looked closer. One of them trotted up to the fence and started growling in his direction. Even at a distance, the guard dog could sense the stranger.

Then silence. For a moment, Steele thought they had arrived at the wrong location. No more distant sounds of tank movement or rumblings.

Then he saw something totally out of place to the wooded surroundings. The finest beam of red light zapped in front of him and disappeared like magic. He rubbed his eyes. At first, he thought he was seeing things. But then, turning, straining to see in the distance behind him, he saw another flash of red light.

Of course. Laser light. *Laser from a tank.* His worst fear was confirmed.

Behind him, on higher ground and slightly to the right, approximately half a mile away, a line of seven bulky black silhouettes—the tanks—appeared on a distant tree line positioned side by side. They were lined up in fire positions along the edge of the wood they had just exited. They waited silently like evil metal monsters ready to spit poison. Every barrel pointed toward the reactor. Then Steele realized he was standing in direct line of fire between the tanks and the reactor. The laser beams of red light and the adjustments of the tank barrels told him they were about to open fire.

He immediately darted back toward the vehicle. But the show of death had started.

The first *whoosh-bang* of a single tank round cracked like a frenzied whip under Armageddon skies. Its impact against one of the reactor buildings lit up the surrounding area for miles. Steele watched, openmouthed, as the round burst through the thick concrete fortifications of the nuclear reactor as though it was made of eggshell.

In the next few seconds, each tank opened fire. The intensity of the pounding got louder and louder. Tank rounds were passing directly overhead. He kept running as best he could even though his ankle felt weak.

Having survived the first wave of tank rounds, Steele suddenly felt invigorated and even invincible. Far from being terrified, he felt ready to face the supreme, ultimate challenge—escape or possibly even death?

Yet more explosions, fireballs, and now small-arms fire from the machine guns mounted on each tank. The small-arms fire was pointless—there *were* no infantry targets—but Steele knew from experience that tank gunners like to fire off small caliber rounds to fine tune the precision of the tank's main armament strikes. But he also knew that machine gun 7.62mm caliber fire was less accurate and therefore, in his current position out in the open, put him in lethal danger of being hit by small-arms fire—much more so than the tank rounds themselves. In other words, it was likely a stray bullet might fall off its trajectory and pierce Steele's skull any second.

Even if he made it back to the vehicle, and even if the Jeep was still in the same location, they were all in grave danger. Safety was beyond reach now. If Viktor was waiting for him, it was only a matter of seconds before one of the tank commanders or gunners spotted the Jeep and opened fire. Once locked on, it would take less than ten seconds for the commander to issue a fire mission and destroy them.

As he ran, Steele prayed, and yes, prayed again. Breathless, he chanted the same message over and over as he stumbled across the terrain: *Please God, save me, I love you, God!... Please, please God, save me, I love you! ... If you're up there, Peter, help me out!*

Steele's ankle gave way. He tripped and fell against a tree trunk to his right.

A split second later, a volley of machine gun fire made a twelve-inch gash in the same tree. Horrified, he observed the damage to the tree and then saw himself—Jack Steele—in a kind of out-of-body experience he had never known. But he was still alive.

★   ★   ★

Had he not stumbled at that precise moment, Steele would have surely perished. *Thank you, God! Thank you!* Then he realized more than ever before: *I love Sandy Steele.* He wanted to be with her. In the midst of this chaos, he was never more certain of anything in his entire life. He would do anything to see her again, be with her again. He saw them together in their idyllic sandy-colored stone cottage in the Cotswolds. What about the prisoners? If Steele helped them or tried to save them, Ryzhakov would kill Sandy. It was conceivable he might have already.

Steele was close to the Jeep now. It had maneuvered into a gully for protection. Surprisingly, Viktor had waited for him. Every muscle in his body felt primed, full of energy he had never known—not just adrenaline, but something more, something magnificently powerful. He sprinted to the Jeep, pulled the door open, and dove in. "Go, Sullivan!" he shouted, "Drive now! Go!"

"What's the matter, Limey? You scared of the dark?" Sullivan snarled.

"No, I'm scared of getting my brains blown out. *Drive!*"

Sullivan reversed then shot forward, gaining speed and momentum as quickly as possible as he drove into a stretch of low ground that might lead them to safety. As he maneuvered between the tanks on their right and the reactor on their left, he glanced at Viktor, who was still pointing the pistol at his side, and then told Steele, "I would have left you, but your friends felt bad for you."

Tank rounds and small-arms fire traversed the skyline. Vicious streaks of white fireballs and explosions continued to light up the night like frenzied fireworks. The nuclear reactor was being demolished in a matter of minutes. Not completely destroyed, but certainly incapacitated. Sullivan revved his engine, trying to gain traction. The four-wheel drive mode was flagging but kept going through the snow and ice. The tank assault increased in intensity.

"Come on, Sullivan! Get us the fuck out of here!" Steele shouted.

"Don't worry, Limey. I know how to drive." Sullivan grinned. Though at gunpoint, he seemed to be enjoying himself in spite of the shelling and semiautomatic small-arms fire.

Steele was silent, but his eyes lit up like the tank lasers as he glanced left and right, willing the Jeep out of the curtain of fire.

Every few seconds, another shower of shrapnel from the reactor cascaded to the ground in the distance. They might be blown to pieces at any moment. Steele watched the blazing inferno of concrete towers disintegrate to their left, an electric constellation of sparks and debris falling out of the night sky. Buildings began to crumble, toppling like Legos. The destruction was too bright now to even glance at. The smell of cordite filled the vehicle. From the right, relentless pounding, orange bursts and flashes of tank and small-arms rounds hitting the Yongbuk nuclear reactor blinded them. Steele thought his eardrums might burst.

And yet, he refused to admit defeat—*not ready to die.* He had escaped too much in the last three days for it all to end here and now. *No way!* He glanced at Chen, who was still and silent, eyes closed. *Praying?* And as the explosions raged, Steele too was overcome with a feeling of calm and hope. *It's not my turn to die.* He had faith. He somehow knew his prayer would be answered.

A piercing explosion directly above the vehicle ripped open the roof. The cold air lashed Steele's face. The roof had partly disintegrated, evaporated into the night. Miraculously, everyone inside was unharmed. The vehicle kept moving.

Sullivan rammed his foot to the floor. Natasha gripped Steele's arm so hard he thought she must have drawn blood.

Viktor's nostrils widened and his mouth twisted.

Sullivan cursed as the wheels spun helplessly in four-wheel drive as they hit a patch of ice. "Come on! Come on!" he ordered, clamping his teeth and jaw.

Steele, Sullivan, Chen, Viktor, and Natasha. They were all in this together.

Chen opened his eyes and smiled. "Everything is as it should be," he announced as though waking from hibernation.

A smile? "Great, Chen. Very encouraging." Steele steadied himself as the vehicle lurched left and right. "Which way is the camp?" he asked Viktor. "We must get to the camp."

Viktor peered at the map, pointing. "I see now. We follow road—there!"

Chen nodded. Just as he did so, the tanks stopped firing. But for how long?

"Yes!" shouted Sullivan, slamming the steering wheel. "Yes! We made it."

The vehicle had completely cleared the line of fire.

"But you're wasting our time," said Sullivan. "We haven't got a hope of stopping those tanks. We have nothing for Christ's sake."

Steele turned and peered into the distance. Two hundred yards away, he could see the black metal beasts turning, starting to move to their next location. He had to get to the camp first. They had to warn the prisoners, release them ...

What about Sandy? When Ryzhakov finds out ...? What about Bova?

"Viktor, how far?" asked Steele.

"Perhaps three miles?"

"Give me the map and keep driving." Steele reached forward and took the map from Viktor.

"We will help you, Jack," replied Viktor. "We have experience, but Igor's men are much better trained than us."

"Have faith, my friend."

Viktor shook his head. "It is impossible to stop them."

"Never say never ..." Steele was positive, almost smiling. "We have a few secret weapons of our own. According to the map, we are about three miles away. We have an advantage."

"I don't hear tanks anymore," said Natasha. "What advantage?"

"We should have at least ten minutes on them."

"The prisoners are waiting for you," said Chen, his eyes closed again. "They know you are coming."

"Good. Perhaps they'll be lining up at the gate." Steele checked the map. "We want them out of there as soon as we tell them what's going on."

Chen did not respond.

★   ★   ★

Three minutes later, the Jeep clipped the crest of a hill and the camp came into view below. Steele's jaw dropped. *Where's my cameraman when I need him?*

The prison camp below was unlike anything he had ever seen. Yes, it was a camp surrounded by barbed wire, just like you'd see in a 1945 WWII movie; the huts were outdated, made of wood, surrounded by high wire fences; the corrugated roofs were covered with snow. It looked as though it had been constructed fifty years ago.

But there was something else.

Like the reactor, the camp was floodlit. There were hundreds, no thousands of people sitting on the frozen, snow-covered ground—motionless—occupying every inch of space around the wooden huts. *Falun Gong?* The scene reminded him of the Falun Gong meditators he had seen sitting on a New York sidewalk a year earlier.

From the Jeep's vantage point, it looked as though every person was a life-size cardboard cutout. They just didn't look real. From the stillness and intensity of their posture, it looked as though they were in meditation or prayer.

"My bloody video camera," he said out loud.

"Pass the bag," Viktor said to Natasha, pointing to the rear.

She reached into the back and retrieved a blue day sack.

"My camera?" exclaimed Steele.

"Surprise!" Viktor said, grinning.

"How the—"

"I thought it will be useful," Viktor said. "I took it from Igor's driver.

"Fantastic ..." Steele took out his camera and checked the battery strength—at least a third battery full, *and* half a sixty-minute tape left. Perfect. He switched on and began filming. "Crucial ..."

★   ★   ★

Steele could hardly contain himself. He had shot footage that could be used as evidence to this atrocity. Now he just had to free the prisoners, get the footage out to the world, find Sandy, and live happily ever after ... *No one said it was going to be easy, sirs!* Another quote from his Sandhurst instructor came to mind.

"What are they doing?" asked Natasha. "Who are these people?"

"They are sitting for God," replied Chen.

"For God?"

"Their thinking is noble; their choice is simple. God is the only thing they desire."

"But they're prisoners?" said Steele.

"To outsiders, they are prisoners. To the government, they are prisoners. But they are more realized and advanced than you can ever imagine."

"*Realized?* What do you mean?" asked Steele.

"They were ignorant. Now they are wise," Chen said. "They were restless, now they have peace. They had desires, now they are content."

"Just like the prayer." Steele put his hand on his back pocket. He still had the prayer safely tucked away; the one Chen had given him.

"They cultivate friendliness toward the happy, compassion for the unhappy, delight in the virtuous, and disregard for the wicked."

"But why are they sitting in the freezing cold?"

"They do not feel the cold. They are not interested in their 'earthly' shells." Chen smiled.

"Do they have a death wish?" asked Steele.

"Their thoughts are concerned with more important matters."

The vehicle was now a few hundred yards from the camp boundary.

"Jack," Viktor broke in, "We don't have much time. You want to crash gate?"

"Wait." Steele gripped the dash, still pointing the camera, zooming into the sea of calm inside. He spoke in genuine disbelief as he filmed, "This is bloody extraordinary."

Natasha said, "You men are crazy. If we crash gates, guards will shoot us."

"Fair point," chimed Sullivan.

"Shut up, Sullivan! Go down there." Steele pointed to a track, which split off to the left away from the camp. "Stop when I say." His third escape from death in three days had given him a renewed sense of life's purpose and a confidence he had felt only once before—the time he lived to tell the tale of an artillery shell landing thirty feet away from him at a Sarajevo UNHCR humanitarian food aid warehouse.

Steele weighed his options like an army general with ten thousand soldiers at his disposal, except there were four of them, including one traitor. The tanks would arrive at any moment.

"Chen, if we get those gates open, will they leave the camp?" Steele sensed he knew the answer.

"They will not leave," said Chen. "It is the enemy of God who must leave."

"Chen, this is serious, those tanks will blow them to pieces. You have to help us."

"I *know* they will not leave." Chen was adamant. "I will leave you now and wait."

"You're injured?"

Chen held up both hands. "No injuries. It's good. This is *my* story. These people will need me. I know where I must be."

The vehicle pulled over, and Chen climbed out. He bowed his head.

"Don't worry," said Steele. "We will help them."

Chen nodded. "I know."

Steele took a deep breath. He surveyed the several thousand people sitting before him. Puffs of cold air breath floated like cigarette smoke above every one of them.

"The tanks," Steele was thinking out loud, "We have to sabotage them."

"Who?" asked Natasha.

"The tanks."

"Impossible," said Viktor. "They will see us."

"Not necessarily."

Viktor insisted. "They have machine guns mounted on the turret. A single burst will slay us."

Steele opened his window. "You hear that?"

"I hear them," said Natasha. "They are close."

Steele looked around for a tank's optimum fire position on the target. *If I was unit commander, where would I place my fire position? High ground, line of sight, within range ... not too far from the main target.* People sitting on the ground made small targets. *If the tank rounds don't neutralize them, well-aimed machine gun fire will.*

"Up there!" he said finally, pointing to the top of the next ridge.

Sullivan followed Steele's direction and continued to drive the contour of the ridge. Then they descended slightly before rising and approaching a clearing just inside the forest—it boasted the perfect view of the camp.

Steele was certain the assault group would choose this location.

"Pull up and listen carefully," he said forcefully.

★   ★   ★

The distant rumble of engines gradually turned into the heavy squeaking and grating of huge metal tank tracks. The assault group took up their fire positions on a flat ridge three hundred yards from the target. Seven tanks lined up feet apart, their side stowage bins almost touching. Once firm, they owned the terrain for miles, including the prison camp.

Over the radio, Sergeant Mishka gave the order to close down the turret hatches. The commanders pulled their turret hatches tight shut and prepared to load ammunition for the fire mission. Mishka peered through his periscope at the target. He swallowed hard; steadying his grip, he tried to pretend the people sitting before him were not real.

The target was clearly visible. The prisoners were still. Mishka had assumed all the prisoners would be asleep in their huts. He wiped his upper lip and felt sweat trickling down his neck from under his helmet and headset. His gunner sat positioned between Mishka's legs. Mishka kicked him to make sure he was ready.

"*Naxal!*" he shouted. Idiot.

Mishka's sweaty hand gripped the radio yoke around his neck. He switched the toggle button from vehicle to squadron net. He pressed the send button on his handset and gave the next order.

"Hello, all units ... Load HESH and await further instructions, out."

HESH was a type of ammunition with enough high explosive to impact a wide area, perfect for killing this mass of people. Those who did not die immediately could be finished off with a sweep of machine gun fire. *Soft targets.* The commanders and gunners from each tank surveyed the target from left to right and back again. They waited for the order to fire—no heavy armor or concrete to destroy—just wooden huts and human flesh.

★　★　★

In the camp, the prisoners remained calm and in deep prayer, oblivious to the killing machines high on the hillside. The prison guards, hearing and seeing the arrival of the tanks in the distance, hoped and assumed it was some kind of military exercise the authorities had forgotten to warn them about. But they also prepared to defend themselves if the tanks became hostile.

Even with the powerful searchlight on one of the towers, it was hard to see the threat. The guard commander shouted for calm, but someone else shouted: "Open the gates! Open the gates!" This set off a chain of events—whistles, more shouting, loading of rifles, dogs barking—that made every prison guard flee his post and the camp as though his life depended on it, which it did.

The prisoners were alone; they remain seated and did not move.

★　★　★

Commander Mishka glanced at his watch. It was time. He surveyed the target one last time. One target down, resulting in the nuclear reactor being incapacitated. It was never meant to be completely destroyed, and no one wanted a nuclear disaster. One to go, he reassured himself. *Ryzhakov will be full of praise for me.* The last target had been easy—no people visible—this one was more challenging.

Staring intently through the periscope, he was relieved he did not believe in God. He clicked the radio transmission button.

"Attention all call signs, this is Zulu Bravo," he began. "HESH … prisoners … five hundred meters … ON!" As he gave the fire order, he too lasered his target to set a point for his gunner to fire the first round.

Keeping his thumb on the send button, he could hear the reverb of his own breath inside his headset. This was it: seven tanks about to open fire. These moments were what he had lived for all those years as a Soviet tank warrior in Afghanistan. *The adrenaline rush when you order a kill is unlike any other feeling.* The "killing" was easy to forget. But you had to get everything just right—fire position, choice of ammunition, target location, target priority, and of course perfect timing—calm and professional always. Yes, that was it. He was a professional and loved himself for it.

He pressed his transmitter. "FIRE!!!" he bellowed.

"FIRE!!!" shouted the remaining commanders inside their tanks, echoing the frenzy of their commander's voice.

★ ★ ★

Jack Steele had also been a tank commander, serving in the first Gulf War—known as Operation Desert Storm, or Op Granby, depending on whether you were American or British—and Bosnia. A tank commander has to do ten things at once: map read, assimilate orders from higher command, switch back and forth on callsign, troop, and squadron radio nets, command his own tank as well as those under his command, locate the target, issue the fire order, fire, hit the target, report on fire mission, and conserve ammunition. He had passed gunnery school with flying colors, and he had always listened carefully to the British army's old and bold noncommissioned officers—NCOs—and the pearls of wisdom they shared. Always calm under pressure, he loved the multitasking nature of the job.

When Steele saw the tanks lining up on the ridge above him, he suddenly recalled an anecdote told by his gunnery corporal of horse, the Household Cavalry equivalent of a sergeant. The corporal of horse had explained how, as a prank on some Sandhurst officer graduates, he had once prevented an entire squadron of tanks from completing their gunnery shoot. It was simple: he had stuck a tiny piece of gaffa tape over the small laser eye on the outside of each tank—making the laser unserviceable—US—and thus temporarily immobilizing the tank's ability to fire. At Bovington Camp, home of the British Army's Royal Armored Corps gunnery school, no one had taken the anecdote seriously, but right now it was Steele's only hope and the best he could come up with.

Steele lead Viktor across the hillside to the tanks, their hatches closed, meaning none of the commanders would be poking their heads out of the turret for the time being. With Viktor serving as his lookout, he rummaged and found some electrical tape from a stowage bin on the side of the first tank. He crawled onto each tank, around the edge of the turret, careful to remain out of periscope vision, and he placed a small piece of electrical tape over every tank's external laser window.

Steele worked his way along the row of tanks and stuck tape across seven small laser windows. Viktor climbed up to join Steele, who banged on the turret of the end tank. The commander opened immediately. Steele punched the man out cold, and they hoisted him out of his seat onto the turret. Viktor took the commander's pistol from his shoulder holster and rolled the man off the tank onto the snow. He then used the pistol to order the gunner and loader out of the tank, knocking them both unconscious as they emerged.

Finally, Steele ordered the driver to get out and climbed into the driver's compartment.

★　★　★

Commander Mishka completed his fire order and got the biggest shock of his life. Expecting one of the most catastrophic slaughters of his career on his order to open fire, he pressed the main armament trigger …

Nishta. *Nothing.*

He thought he was dreaming. "FIRE!!!" he screamed again for the benefit of his own crew, kicking the gunner in the seat below him. It had never happened before on his T72 main battle tank, but perhaps his trigger had malfunctioned? Then he realized something else … *No other tank has fired. I must be dreaming.*

He repeated the order over the radio. Six fingers belonging to six gunners in six tanks squeezed their main armament triggers again.

Silence.

★   ★   ★

Steele seized his opportunity and jumped into the driver's hatch. He shifted into reverse and maneuvered the beast to the right side of the remaining six, so that he faced the line of tank barrels at a ninety-degree angle.

"POYEXALI!" Viktor shouted as he lowered himself through the hatch into the commander's seat above Steele. *LET'S GO!*

Steele grasped the tank steering levers and accelerated toward the line of 125mm gun barrels. Using his left and right steering levers on each side of the driver's seat, Steele made minor adjustments as he plowed straight for the other tanks' barrels.

Just missing the hull of the first tank, he careened into its barrel.

"TARGET!" he shouted, as he continued to smash through the rest. It took just seconds to make every barrel unserviceable. After the third tank barrel had been demolished, he had to reverse, correct course, then accelerate forward to advance.

Viktor prepared to fire the machine gun mounted on the turret as the tank crews opened their hatches to see what had literally rocked their world. He pulled the trigger and spent a three-foot belt of ammunition in ten seconds. It was enough to injure two of the soldiers and keep the rest inside for the short amount of time it took Steele and Viktor to run back to the Jeep and clear the area.

Every man in Mishka's unit was still alive, but their mission was a failure.

CHAPTER TWENTY-FOUR

Sofiyskaya Embankment, Moscow

"I believe you know each other," said Pendlebury, ushering the tall American into his office. It was 4:30 pm.

Anderson stood up and offered his hand to Edward Warrior, the US ambassador. He had always held him in the highest esteem, more so than his own British superior. Having liaised with the Americans on numerous political and security issues since arriving in Moscow, he had rapidly concluded that, far from being equals in the "special relationship," America was the big brother, over whom the British had virtually no real influence or power. *Fair weather allies* is how he would have described Anglo-American ties. The faithful British puppy sits patiently waiting for the occasional pat on the head and the next bone to be thrown from the US administration. Anderson had decided long ago that the so-called "special relationship" currently had no clear benefit to the British at all. At least not that he could fathom. However, he often found himself wishing that the Brits had the same global and financial political clout as the Americans. They could get things done, even if the proverbial head often had no clue what the tail was doing. The West was in charge, and the world was a mess. But a well-ordered mess, and good old blighty remained satisfactorily well up on the pecking order. The yanks always took care of their allies at least.

"Wonderful to see you again, Ambassador," Anderson said. "How are you?"

"Could be a helluva lot better," replied Warrior. "I thought, mistakenly, we could leave this one in your not-so-capable hands."

"Thank you, Ambassador," Anderson replied sarcastically with an obsequious grin. "I apologize." Anderson flashed another false smile. He made a mental note to review his high opinion of the Americans when this was over.

Pendlebury said, "Gentlemen. Please. We don't have time—"

Warrior frowned. The beaten leather armchair creaked its melody as he sank into its smooth contours. "First question: How in God's name did we ever trust this lunatic, Ryzh ...?"

Pendlebury cleared his throat. "We really need to—"

"*Ry-zha-kov*," Anderson prompted slowly, as if giving traffic directions to a foreigner.

"Ryz-ha-kov." Warrior inserted his index finger behind his top shirt button to loosen his bowtie. Wearing evening dress, he was irritated to be missing the cocktail party reception at the Bolshoi Theater where, post performance, all the pretty ballerinas were invited to join the diplomatic big wigs in costume. He loved the ballet and detested any kind of crisis outside of work hours.

"It's my fault." Anderson was determined to keep a lid on the pot about to explode. "I take full responsibility. I checked his background with my sources—military honors in Afghanistan, professional family history, service to party and country, high-ranking police inspector ... perfect cover, I thought. His father was a top Politburo surgeon—apparently murdered by North Koreans, which is why he was eager to put one over on them. On paper, he was the perfect man for the job."

Warrior uncrossed his legs. "On paper?"

"Unfortunately, he screwed up," Anderson said.

"Only half," Pendlebury added. "He rendered the reactor inoperable, but none of us knew about the prison camp."

Warrior exhaled. "Explain *exactly* what happened?" he asked in a low, calm voice.

Anderson continued, "The last time I spoke to Ryzhakov, he mentioned insurance of some kind. I ignored the comment. I thought he wanted more money. Turns out he was talking about the infamous Jack Steele."

"He's using the journalist to do what exactly?" asked Warrior.

"Be a journalist, report what he saw," replied Anderson. "Literally took him along for the ride to act as his personal reporter."

"He had orders for Christ's sake—to intercept and terminate. Our man missed him?" exclaimed Warrior.

"Yes. And he failed," said Anderson, enjoying the fact that even the Americans make mistakes. "Things don't always go according to plan," he offered.

"And why destroy this prison camp?"

Pendlebury held up both hands. "We don't know yet—doesn't make any sense. North Koreans are a ruthless bunch. But massacring their own?"

"Perhaps it does," countered Anderson, clasping his hands in prayer formation. "What if Ryzhakov uses Steele to reveal his sources as well as the people who hired him to commit all these barbaric acts of terrorism?"

The facial expression of every man in the room froze. Then Pendlebury said, "You mean … *us*. All of us?"

The three men looked at each other uncomfortably, knowing they were all to a greater or lesser extent implicated.

"For God's sake, would anyone believe him?" asked Warrior.

"We can't afford to take the chance," replied Anderson.

"What proof can he have?"

"It's like this, Warrior," continued Pendlebury. "Ryzhakov scored several million dollars from us, and the same again from DPRK. He's loaded, and he's been paid twice for the same job and bound to have covered his arse somehow—taped his phone conversations perhaps? Just in case things went pear-shaped and he was blamed."

"I take your point. Anyway, North Koreans must be as happy as a goddamn *pig in shit*." Warrior slapped his chair in frustration. "Their reactor's gone, their domestic problems are solved for the time being, and they have enough dirt on us to wipe out their 'pariah status' for fifty years."

"*If* ... word gets out." Pendlebury grimaced, trying to be positive.

"That's the part we're still not sure about," Anderson said.

Warrior sat up in the noisy leather armchair. "What do you suggest?"

Anderson said, "We must use all necessary means to ensure Jack Steele does not—How can I put it?—get home in time for supper."

"I hate this. We've kept the peninsula stable for fifty years," said Warrior, massaging his eyebrows with two fingers. "And all this on my goddamn watch! Goddamnit! I thought this was going to be an invisible strike."

"It looks like we have no choice with Steele," said Pendlebury. "We cannot leave ourselves open to blackmail or any more shady deals with our axis of evil friends. If Steele lives, we're totally screwed."

"I don't like it either. But better to get him now, while the whole world thinks he's a spook." Warrior nodded, affirming his own thoughts.

"What about the wife?" Pendlebury asked Anderson. "How's their relationship?"

"Good as far as we can tell. She should prove excellent bait. She's landing at any moment at Sheremetyevo. Apparently, she's even invited her father along ..."

"Two for the price of one perhaps?" said Pendlebury.

"Sandy Danner will become *our* insurance policy," replied Anderson.

"Does she have any idea?" asked Warrior.

"None." Anderson shook his head.

Yongbuk Region, North Korea

Mishka had failed. He had executed only half the mission. As he spoke on his cell phone, Ryzhakov trembled with disappointment. Mishka explained how the tanks had been immobilized, and then had the barrels smashed out of their sockets.

"Nevazmozhno ... nevazmozhno ...!" Ryzhakov repeated over and over. *Impossible... Impossible ...!*

Ryzhakov encouraged his driver to hurry, knowing he was just minutes behind Steele. The vehicle raced in Steele's wake along bleak, dusty tracks that passed for roads in the Yongbuk countryside and beyond.

He was confident Steele could not get far because he had set up a roadblock near the Russian border just before the Tumen River. He took the pistol from his belt and placed it in his lap. He sneered. Steele was an idiot if he thought he could get back to Russia. But it was also true he didn't stand a chance if he stayed in North Korea.

Up ahead, Ryzhakov saw Steele's Jeep slowing down before the checkpoint. Kim Jung Ryul's men certainly had good control over their military on this border. He ordered his driver to slow down so he could observe the scene before they got closer. Steele he could handle, but Sullivan was CIA, a shrewd operator who could not be underestimated. As Ryzhakov pulled up behind Steele, he got out and advanced.

★ ★ ★

They pulled over close to the border checkpoint on the south side of the Tumen River. The border guards manned their posts up ahead. In the semidarkness, Steele watched Ryzhakov approaching on foot in the rearview mirror.

Steele knew anything could happen in the next minute, and no one in the outside world would ever know. Steele's nostrils widened, his face becoming taught, almost grimacing. Every other muscle in his body tightened to full alert.

Ryzhakov stopped next to the Jeep. He acknowledged both soldiers at the checkpoint with a wave—he obviously knew them—and then turned to tap on the window with his pistol.

"Good evening, comrades," he said, waving his pistol back and forth at them.

Natasha said, "Igor, ti suma sashol? Gdyje ti bil?" *Igor, are you crazy? Where have you been?*

Sullivan leaned forward, his hand sliding down his leg toward his ankle holster as he said, "How you doing, Igor?"

"Me?" replied Igor, enthusiastically, "I'm doing great. Where you guys heading?"

"We were just—"

Ryzhakov raised his pistol and shot Sullivan through his right eye. The entry point was neat and tidy, but a six-inch area on the back of his head was blown away. Small fragments of bone and brains showered the rest of them.

Natasha screamed.

Steele froze. He now realized Ryzhakov was capable of anything. Him next? Viktor? Natasha? Ryzhakov had murdered Steele's passport to safety in cold blood. He had been counting on Sullivan to get him back to Moscow.

"He was going to kill you," said Ryzhakov.

"Really?" Steele was skeptical.

"He was going to kill you and my beautiful wife." Ryzhakov paused. "You don't believe me?"

Steele nodded. "Sure, I believe you."

"Come with me, Jack. We must talk. Viktor also."

Steele had no choice. He climbed out of the Jeep, scrutinizing Natasha and Viktor for any small clue about his fate. Was this the plan all along? But why kill him now? For seven years, Natasha had suffered and survived Igor Ryzhakov. It was still impossible to know what kind of a hold he had on her. Her expression gave nothing away.

★ ★ ★

Ryzhakov escorted both men back to his vehicle and invited them to climb in. Ryzhakov mounted and closed the door.

"Jack, you are good man. The reason I invited you here, ..." he began slowly.

Steele looked away, exasperated. Was this some kind of macabre warmth before he shot him in the head too? "You've been busy."

"You too."

"Thanks, Igor. I always knew we'd get along in the end."

Ryzhakov glanced at Natasha, who was still sitting in Steele's Jeep. "She is a good actress, no?"

"Natasha had me fooled, I confess." Steele decided to play along, but he really had no idea how she had him fooled or what Igor was talking about.

"She has everyone fooled. Natasha is a goddess. Do you love her?"

Steele frowned. "Strange question."

"Why?" Igor wagged the pistol now. "If she could choose, I know she would leave me and live with you a happy life in England. Am I correct?"

Steele shook his head. "My wife wouldn't be too happy."

"Natasha has a place in your heart?"

"I don't understand." Steele continued to play schtum. Ryzhakov was perceptive—a madman, but a perceptive one. Or perhaps Viktor had said something about Natasha? Their first night at the safe house near Khabarovsk?

"Never mind, Mr. BBC. We have work to do." Ryzhakov corrected himself. "*You* have work to do."

"Great."

Ryzhakov pulled out a miniature tape recorder from his leather coat and pressed play. Steele heard two male voices— one English and one with a Russian accent that sounded like Ryzhakov.

The recording lasted about thirty seconds.

Steele was baffled.

"You want to listen again?" Ryzhakov asked.

"Who's Anderson? Who is he?"

"He has an important position at your embassy in Moscow. You could say he hired me."

"Interesting. Are you saying he represents the British government?"

"Yes, that is precisely what I am saying."

"Officially?"

"If he does not, someone is playing a very expensive joke on your country."

"And Sullivan?"

"He was going to kill you. This I swear." Ryzhakov cocked his head. "I am Soviet army veteran. I still have honor."

"*My* government hired *you*? They paid you?" asked Steele.

"Yes."

Steele wanted to be sure he understood the relationship. He grimaced. "The British government wanted you to destroy the Yongbuk reactor?" Sullivan was telling the truth after all. And now he was dead.

"Correct. Your government, my government, DPRK. One big fat conspiracy."

"And I got in the way?"

"For them, a little. If not you, then someone else."

"You didn't mention the prison camp?" Steele said, testing, wondering if he was signing his own death warrant by mentioning it. "Wasn't that part of the deal?"

"You are a courageous man. Clever man."

Steele nodded. "Any *tankist* veteran would have done the same."

Ryzhakov also laughed. "I will be sorry if something happens to you."

"Trust me, Igor. Me too."

"But—"

"But if I help you ...?" Steele envisaged his frontpage story becoming a reality after all. "You have your money. I would have my story. Just like you planned?"

"It is not about money. When the North Koreans, or the British or the Americans, find out what you did, how you mess things up for them, they will have no choice ... you know too much."

Steele swallowed, trying not to think about the impossible mess he was in.

"Why were you chosen?" he asked.

Ryzhakov flipped open the cassette flap and turned the miniature tape over. "The question is why *not* use me? Why would they risk getting caught? I am a vicious murderer by reputation." He pressed play.

Steele listened to another short recording. Ryzhakov asked Anderson if he had any objection to the North Korean's demand to destroy a second target—a prison camp—close to the reactor:

Anderson: *"None at all. Be my guest. How many of these religious fogies do they want to get rid of?"*

Ryzhakov: *"A few thousand. I don't know exactly."*

Pause ... Then Anderson: *"Well ... it doesn't sound like we should be involved in that sort of thing, but whatever you need to do. Means justifies the end and all that twaddle."*

"Enough," said Steele. He took a deep breath. Ryzhakov had a point: Once the people behind this understood Steele's level of knowledge and involvement, they would want him dead no question. "You think this tape is enough?" Steele was thinking journalistically big picture. "You think I can use this tape?"

Ryzhakov nodded. "I think it is enough. I also think it is the only way you can stay alive now."

"You want me to say that you were hired by these Western governments?"

"It is the truth."

"How do I know? What if I decide this tape's not enough?"

"I will give you more proof."

"I'm ready. Go ahead."

"Two UN officials recently visited Yongbuk. They were spies. I kept one for you. You will interview him in Vladivostok. You will honor truth. I know this, Mr. BBC."

"You're a confident man, Igor."

"I have my insurance. I have the two women you care about, even if you yourself don't know which one is most important to you. Even I do not know."

Steele snorted lightly. He knew, but at least he had something to keep Igor guessing, which might prove useful.

"So I will kill both of them if you do not execute your task successfully," Ryzhakov added. "I like to keep things simple. Let's go."

CHAPTER TWENTY-FIVE

Sofiyskaya Embankment, Moscow

Inside the British ambassador's ornate, wood-paneled office, the air was stuffy and stale. An air of helplessness and tension lingered—three important men expecting one of the others to come up with a solution.

"We're losing control. I think it's time we paid a visit to the Kremlin," announced Pendlebury. He waited a moment, and then added, "What say you, gentlemen?"

They avoided eye contact. Anderson broke the silence. "You think they'll stick with us? Not drop us right in the shit? Let's be honest, if it were us, we'd wash our hands ..."

"I appreciate your optimism," added Warrior. "Makes me feel warm and fuzzy."

"At least they'll want to distance themselves from Ryzhakov," continued Anderson. "Bloody madman. Bloody Russians."

"You picked the motherfucker! God damn you, Anderson!" Warrior exclaimed.

Pendlebury kept his face expressionless. *Steady ... Think it through, man.* "Gentlemen, the way I see it, we have two perfect scapegoats—Ryzhakov *and* Steele. That should be enough to satisfy our Russian friends. Remember, all that matters now is what can be proved, or rather, what can't be. If we find them first, we'll promise to eliminate both of them."

"Shouldn't be difficult, *if* we get the Kremlin on board," Anderson concluded. "Neither the Brit or our Ruski will want to hang around in North Korea for long."

A knock at the door halted the conversation midflow.

Hugo Jenkins scurried into the office, even more flustered and redfaced than usual. He said, "Sirs, this has just come in." Uncertain who to hand the signal to first, he gave it to Anderson, who was nearest.

Anderson read it, frowned, and passed it to Pendlebury, who also frowned, then gave the bad news to Warrior. "Sorry. Sullivan's dead."

"Perfect timing," said Anderson sarcastically. "Plan A down the shoot."

"We'll send someone else, dammit!" Warrior shook his head and exhaled sharply.

"Unfortunately, we don't know if Steele plans to give any more press conferences, and if so, in which country," continued Anderson. "Jenkins, any more from the ops. desk?"

"I checked," Jenkins replied, exceedingly pleased with himself. "They suspect Steele's left North Korea and gone back to Russia. *With* the Russian."

Pendlebury stood up. "Call the Kremlin, Hugo. Tell them we're on our way. We'll be there in fifteen minutes." He turned to the American ambassador. "Coming, Edward?"

"I'll pass. Need to call New York and explain this shit show. We made a small loan to some friends at the UN. I'm curious to see what happened to it. I'll stay in touch."

"Roger that."

Vladivostok, Russia

Bova Klimova woke up in darkness. Where was his mother? Where was Igor? Why hadn't they come for him?

The gray-haired foreigner was still asleep in the corner. Bova had made him as comfortable as possible. At least, he had tried.

It was late. The smell of fried *blini* wafted from the kitchen. He could also smell the dankness of this communal apartment. He guessed he had not slept long. Forcing himself to stay awake, he had tried to eavesdrop on every telephone conversation in the next room over the last twelve hours in case his mother or Igor had called the man.

He made up his mind to escape but had not yet formulated his plan.

Bova rummaged for the flashlight he'd found in a dusty drawer. He heard a clanking sound—utensils being placed on a tray—coming from the kitchen. Then footsteps. The door opened, and the large-framed, bald-headed man in his late forties entered with the *blinis*—Russian pancakes. He held eye contact with Bova, not taking any chances, as he bent down to set the tray on the floor. He left quickly, slamming the door.

"Spaciba!" shouted Bova. *Thanks!*

The boy surveyed the platter. Inedible. His captor, the "bald eagle," obviously had no clue how to make pancakes. But he was hungry, so he picked up the fork and wolfed down the whole plate in less than a minute. Hopefully, the man would bring more for the foreigner.

★   ★   ★

The Russian captor in the *kommunalni* apartment was pissed off. This job was the last thing he wanted to be doing right now— guarding some brat and an old man he couldn't understand. But, like a lot of other people in this town, he owed Igor Ryzhakov.

Suddenly, muffled screams and a rasping sound came from the locked room. The Russian quickly approached Bova's door and listened carefully. The cries were getting louder. He still wasn't sure, however, if they were genuine. Planting his foot a couple of inches from the door, he unlocked it. So far so good. He looked through the crack in the door and saw Bova on the other side of the room writhing on the floor clutching his stomach.

★   ★   ★

"Ahhhhhhhhhhhhhhhh! Pomogi! Pomogi mnye, pozhalsta!" screamed Bova. *Help me! Please, help me!*

Bova wasn't sure how much time he had left before something disastrous happened to him, or when his window of opportunity might come. So he decided to create his own.

This first round of screams would be a test. From the man's speech and behavior, Bova could tell he was a blockhead. He would make mistakes under pressure.

As soon as he saw Bova writhing on the floor, the man ran back into the kitchen. He returned seconds later with his cell phone. He approached Bova and dialed a number on his mobile phone at the same time, all the while careful to keep his distance.

"OK, OK, boy," he said. "Calm yourself. I'll help you."

Bova squinted at the man, careful to keep his eyes closed "in pain." The Russian edged closer, phone in one hand, the other arm outstretched. Bova screamed again. His voice was straining so much that he began coughing for real, then choking a little. He took full advantage of the coughing fit to enhance his performance.

The man finally crouched down next to the boy.

Lying on his side with both knees drawn up to his chest, Bova rolled onto his back and let both feet rip into the man's face. At the same time, Bova snatched the fork lying on the tray next to him—made of plastic but enough to do harm. Bova jabbed it into the man's face, not caring where it struck. It snapped on impact but drew blood. Lots of it.

This time it was the man's turn to scream—but in genuine agony. The prongs of the plastic fork had pierced the man's eyeball. Blood gushed. The Russian was spitting with fire and fury. He collapsed to his knees, both hands sealed over his right eye. Seeing him up close, Bova imagined the man might have been attacked with clubs or knives, but probably never a plastic fork. Bald Eagle lunged at Bova's ankle but missed by a mile.

Bova bolted through the apartment to the front door. As he grappled with the lock, he felt a grip around his ankle but kicked out with his heel and freed himself, using his momentum to keep going. He almost tripped but regained his balance, and then, just to be safe, he turned and stamped his heel into the side of the man's head.

Exiting the apartment, he turned to see that the key had been left in the door! He slammed it shut and smiled as he turned the key. Bald Eagle was definitely a fool, as he had suspected all along. As he descended the stairs two and three steps at a time, he jabbed his fist in the air in a private moment of jubilation. "Poko!" *See you!*

He was free.

There was only one problem. He had no idea where he was or where to go next.

Bova just wanted to go home. He wanted to call the police. Igor would come and arrest the man, throw him in jail, and set the foreigner free. His mother would be proud. He had used his initiative to defeat the criminal. Perhaps they would write about him in the local newspaper or interview him on television? He might get another ride in a Vladivostok police Jeep.

Reaching the ground floor, he bumped into an older babushka, causing her to drop her shopping bag. He looked back and yelled, "Izvinitye pozhalsta!" over his shoulder. *I'm sorry!*

"Molodoi chelovyek! Pochemu ti bez shapka?" the babushka replied. *Young man! Where are you going out without a hat?*

Back to his world. This was a familiar cry of Russian babushkas. They were always acutely concerned about children catching cold. As Bova ran into the street, he stumbled. Faltering, he managed to glance back toward the babushka to acknowledge and thank her for the concern.

"Doma. Eta doma!" *It's at home!*

The last word was cut off by a deafening screech of brakes.

A truck appeared from nowhere. The driver had switched off his lights—common practice in these parts to prolong the life of the headlamp bulbs in short supply.

No headlights! I'm going to—

Bova did not finish this thought. The last thing he saw was a huge black shadow hurtling toward him, followed by a deafening thud—the sound of his own body hitting the front grill of the truck.

★   ★   ★

Two hours later, Ryzhakov's party, including Steele and Natasha, had cleared the border without a hitch and arrived at the Hotel Stalingrad in Vladivostok. Ryzhakov's men escorted Steele up to the hotel suite on the third floor.

Viktor had given his word to Igor that he would follow orders. Afraid not so much for his life but for what Igor might do to his family, Viktor promised to remain loyal to the man who had once saved him from a stiff prison sentence. He had driven Natasha back to her apartment a few blocks from the hotel where Igor had promised she would be reunited with her son.

Steele had survived the most treacherous two days of his life. Even Ryzhakov's suite in the Hotel Stalingrad felt comforting and safe for the time being. It was a miracle he had returned in one piece, but he was still in grave danger. The North Koreans, the British, and the Americans, and possibly Igor Ryzhakov himself, all had reasons for wanting him dead. *No one said it was going to be easy, sirs! No way out, east or west …*

He sat down and scraped his fingers through his mud-caked hair. It was only now he noticed patches of tank oil on the sleeves of his jacket. Ryzhakov had moved to stand over him, arms crossed, like a teacher waiting for his brightest pupil to finish a test. Steele took out his miniature leather Filofax from his money belt—safely wrapped in a plastic bag.

"Okay, Igor," he said, "You want to tell the world? Give me the telephone and I'll see if anyone's interested …"

"Here." Ryzhakov handed it to him. "International."

"Thanks." Steele flicked through his Filofax and made a short list of his most cherished media contacts around the globe. Mainly Europe, but USA too. His editor was obviously the place to start, but Steele wasn't even sure if anyone at all would believe him let alone save his life.

Minutes later, there was a knock at the door. Viktor had returned. He entered nervously and his boss shot him a look that Steele interpreted as, *I'll kill you if you screw with me again.*

"Bova was in an accident," Viktor announced.

★   ★   ★

"You've seen him?" asked Ryzhakov, knowing he had ordered a trusted associate to take the boy captive along with the UN spy until further notice.

"I went with Natasha to the hospital," said Viktor. "He's fine."

"Natasha stayed at the hospital?" asked Ryzhakov.

"She went home to fetch some of his clothes."

"What happened?" asked Steele.

"He was hit by a truck," replied Viktor.

"He'll be okay," said Ryzhakov, not caring either way.

"Ti znal ob etom?" asked Viktor. *You knew about it?*

"Ja vsoh znayu," Igor replied. *I know everything.*

★   ★   ★

Steele started to dial one of his media contacts, then changed his mind. "Viktor, we need the videotape. I left it in the car. In my backpack." He had planned to keep the video a secret but realized now he had little choice with Ryzhakov demanding he break the story from Vladivostok. The audio tapes of Anderson were good. But the video tape of the prison camp were even better.

"What tape?" asked Ryzhakov.

Viktor said quickly, "Natasha has the tape."

"There's a tape with footage of the tank assault on the reactor and the prison camp," Steele lied, trying to buy time—no one had shot footage of the reactor being destroyed. "It doesn't prove anything, but it might help."

"How did you get this?" asked Ryzhakov.

"The video camera in my backpack," said Steele. "You took it for safekeeping, remember?"

"Only spies carry cameras."

"And journalists." Steele smiled.

"Pencil is not sufficient?"

"Video camera saved my life once."

Igor raised his brow. "How?" He seemed genuinely curious.

"I got caught up with the Bosnian Serbs in Sarajevo a few years ago. I was having a liaison with Radovanović's daughter."

"Dr. Radovanović? Leader of Bosnian Serbs?"

"Yes. The only way to get out alive was to hand over the tape I'd shot with footage of SAS soldiers abducting her. Serbs wanted to hand copies out to every journalist in Sarajevo. I never got the credit, of course, but it saved my life." Steele glanced at Viktor and back to Igor. "We need the video tape, Igor. I want this story as much as you do. Pictures paint a thousand words, video ten thousand ..."

"We will broadcast these pictures on VTV. I will fetch this tape from Natasha. Viktor will bring you to VTV when I have it."

"Igor, when did the UN arrive in Vladivostok?" *I need the complete picture for crying out loud ...*

"One month ago."

"Did you know they were coming?"

"One of my assistants received a fax from Moscow, from UN liaison office, telling us to expect three officials."

"How do you know the men who arrived were from the UN?"

Ryzhakov paused. "I don't know this. Natasha spoke with them, and I became suspicious. I told her never to speak with them again."

"Why suspicious?"

"Natasha said they were asking questions—unrelated to our region and our local economy. They wanted to know if the police could maintain law and order. I trust no one."

"Igor, what if those guys weren't UN officials? What if they were working for someone else?"

"Who?"

"British or American security services?"

"Why?"

"To watch you. Their government spent money hiring you. They wanted to check you out."

"Moscow recommended me to them. Introduced me."

"Precisely. You were Moscow's man. I'm guessing you have a very dubious record on top of all your other achievements?"

"Dubious? I am Afghan veteran."

"Afterward."

"Perhaps."

"Perfect for Western authorities. What better profile for the attack on North Korea?"

"I don't understand."

"If you succeed, great! If you fail, then no one cares about you? You're a terrorist thug and corrupt official who deserves to die."

"Maybe."

"You were used, Igor. That's all I'm saying."

"Perhaps. I hate US. I hate interference. I hate hypocrisy. I hate them acting like world police. They pick their way around the world's poorest nations based on greed and self-interest— like candy in a store."

"I agree," said Steele.

Ryzhakov turned and took out his pistol from inside his coat pocket. He pointed it at Steele, who looked down the barrel of the pistol with confidence. He knew Ryzhakov needed him.

"You are learning, Jack," said Ryzhakov, grinning. He lowered the pistol. "I will get this tape, and we will show the world. Viktor will stay here with you."

"No problem," said Viktor.

"Do not disappoint me this time." He pointed the weapon jokingly at Viktor.

Then he left.

CHAPTER TWENTY-SIX

Kremlin, Moscow

The Kremlin internal security guards saluted and stepped aside as the CD-plated Range Rover rumbled across the cobblestones under the majestic redbrick Kremlin portico. Anderson observed how the buildings inside the Kremlin were surprisingly modern, more so than one might expect from the historically fortified exterior walls. The large windows reminded him of the Royal Festival Hall in London. Once inside, huge chandeliers dominated every room. Off-white sheers hung floor to ceiling—they need a dry-cleaning, he thought, as they were escorted down a seemingly endless red-carpeted corridor.

The British diplomats entered a large, spacious office with a desk dwarfed by the size of the room. The walls were plain white with gold crown moldings and decorative, fake-Corinthian plaster pillars. The mostly wood furniture was finished in several coats of high gloss lacquer too slick and shiny to possess any charm or character. Not quite Buckingham Palace, Anderson mused, wishing he was back in London attending a Buck House garden party or investiture.

This was the office of Foreign Affairs Chief Liaison Officer Sergei Leontyev. He had been Anderson's official contact in the Kremlin for Operation Tumen, even though, officially, the name did not exist.

Leontyev rushed into the office as though he was late for Lenin's funeral. He shook hands aggressively with his guests and gestured for them to sit. Leontyev took his place behind the tiny bare desk on top of which sat a solitary, faded pea-green telephone with no dial.

"I don't recall if you gentlemen know each other. This is Sir Brian Pendlebury, British ambassador," Anderson began.

"Leontyev, Sergei Mikhailovich. Ochin priyatno," the Russian bureaucrat replied. *Nice to meet you.* His tone said otherwise.

"It seems we have a bit of a problem," said Pendlebury.

"Always problems," grinned the Russian. "This would not be Russian Wonderland without problems. Even my wife cannot live without *problema.*" He chuckled.

Anderson continued, "Mr. Leontyev, if we might get straight to the point. We have an extremely urgent but delicate situation. What is your position vis-à-vis the Russian authorities and Igor Ryzhakov?"

Leontyev gave a foxy scowl only Russians are capable of. "It is … classified."

"Sir, we appreciate your position, but Ryzhakov is a key element in Operation Tumen. Furthermore, if you are unable or unwilling to help us, there is grave danger of hostilities on the Korean Peninsula by tomorrow morning. Our little project is about to become global news unless we—all of us—take immediate action."

"Ryzhakov has left North Korea," Leontyev disclosed. "He returned to Vladivostok. The mission is over, as far as we are concerned."

Pendlebury cleared his throat. "Mr. Leontyev, with respect, our mission has only just begun. DPRK could lob a shell into South Korea at any moment in retaliation for what we have done. Thanks to Ryzhakov, they have a bombsite to show the world and a British journalist who has by all accounts witnessed the entire episode. We have no control over him, and we have enough damage control on our hands to last a lifetime."

Leontyev cleared his throat and said, "If Ryzhakov talks, this will cause immense embarrassment to all our governments."

"Precisely." He glanced over to Pendlebury. Progress, he thought.

"How much does the journalist know?" Leontyev asked.

"He probably knows most of it," said Anderson. "And we have no idea where he is. He may still be with Ryzhakov. We've lost one of Ambassador Warrior's men, who was to eliminate Steele. We need to get to Steele before he tries another media stunt."

Leontyev nodded in agreement. "We will find him."

"And Igor?"

"Yes."

"Thank you," said Anderson. "If you can get to Steele, please take him out, or whatever you feel most appropriate to silence him."

Pendlebury shifted uncomfortably and remained stone-faced. "Sergei Mikhailovich, every media outlet around the world is studying Steele's North Korean press conference. The BBC is demanding answers from the FCO and a dozen other Whitehall departments. We don't have much time to manage our response. If Steele has a scrap of evidence, all our governments are completely scuppered, and that's putting it mildly."

"And we need proof of death," added Anderson. "Just to be sure. Photo's fine."

"Normalna. Xarasho," the Russian agreed. *Fine. OK.* "We will make arrangements. Don't worry. Proof of death. No problem."

"Excellent," said Anderson, releasing an audible grunt of relief. "Then we have an understanding. Thank you, Mr. Leontyev. We are exceedingly grateful, and I can assure you this cooperation will pay dividends for Anglo-Russian relations."

"Blah, blah, blah … I understand, Mr. Anderson."

Nods of approval all round ignored the *blah, blah, blah* utterance. Anderson stood up to leave. For the first time in forty-eight hours, he began to think his career might be salvageable.

The paneled door of the liaison office burst open. The short, rotund assistant wearing a cheap suit and garish purple tie hurried in and settled at Leontyev's shoulder. He leaned down to whisper to his superior. Leontyev nodded, his face showing no expression. "Please, gentlemen," said the Russian. "Before you leave, I have something important to share with you."

Now what? Anderson glanced at Pendlebury, tension stretching across his face.

"North Korean military have fired shots—small arms—at an observation post in South Korea. One soldier was killed. South Korean security forces have returned fire. Satellite imagery tells us North Korean heavy armor has moved from depth positions to take up offensive or defensive positions along the border—we are not sure which."

"Hostilities between north and south would shatter fifty years of peace on the peninsula," said Pendlebury.

Leontyev replied, "I understand, believe me. North Korea is our neighbor."

"Please make Steele your top priority," added Anderson.

"Comrade Steele will rest in peace within twenty-four hours. You have my word."

Vladivostok, Russia

Viktor went to the refrigerator in Ryzhakov's hotel suite, pulled out a bottle of vodka, and poured himself a drink. "Do you understand what has happened?" He did not offer any to Steele.

"I think so. The North Koreans are butchers, and we have all been supporting them."

"Jack, you must leave here immediately. You must escape."

"Escape? Where do you want me to go? I need that tape. Igor and I have the same goal—at least in the short term. I hate to say it, but we need each other." Steele shrugged. "At least he can't shoot me ... yet."

Viktor popped a piece of cured sausage he'd found in the fridge into his mouth and began chewing. "You think he won't shoot you as soon as you give him what he needs?"

"You're probably right."

"Why do you think I hid tape?"

Steele's eyes lit up. "Where is it? With Natasha?"

"Natasha does not have tape." Viktor's tone became urgent. "You must take next tram. From the balcony."

"What!?"

"Climb onto the balcony and jump onto the tram. You must do this. Igor's men are outside."

"Are you insane? I'm not a bloody stuntman, Viktor."

"When you land, keep your head down, and stay down until you reach the next stop—*Okeanskiy*. Go to the back of the tram and climb down the ladder."

"You're insane."

"You have no choice."

"Then what?"

"Regional Children's Clinic No.1 is one block down from Okeanskiy on Prospekt Ostryakova. Bova is on the second floor of hospital. Room 232. He has the tape. It's up to you now."

"What about you?"

"I'll meet Igor when he comes back. You must take the tape to studio. Vesti Primorye news station is ten minutes by taxi. Tell them my name, and they will know what to do. Ask for Sergei."

"Can they get us an international feed?" asked Steele.

"Yes. Sergei expects you."

"Ryzhakov will kill you when he finds out."

"This is my problem. For now, I have advantage." Viktor smiled, showing his gold teeth. He held his arms out. "Hit me."

"What?"

"Punch me … in the face. You must knock me unconscious."

"I can't."

"You must. You will have more time. Less suspicious."

"Hit you?"

"Then get the tape. Broadcast."

"Why are you doing this?" asked Steele.

"I must. It has taken me too long to understand this."

"What about Natasha?"

"Natasha is courageous. She will take care of herself. Don't worry."

His story wasn't dead yet. *All I need is the tape. Every editor in the world will run those pictures. But on my terms.*

From inside the hotel room, Steele heard the crackling of electricity on the overhead tramline cables signaling the next tram's approach. He had no choice. "What's that?" he said, pointing to the door.

Viktor turned, but there was no one there. Steele packed a huge blow to his chin, sending him across the floor. He was out cold. *Not bad.*

Then he shook his hand in pain, walked to the window, and climbed onto the balcony. He looked back at Viktor. Thankfully, none of the guards had heard anything.

★　　★　　★

The tram stopped below the window outside Igor's suite, just as Viktor had said. The street was deserted, so no one would see him jump. Mentally, Steele negotiated his trajectory through the electric cables and jumped from the balcony …

Perfect landing. Ankle no worse for wear.

The tram doors opened, then closed almost immediately. No passengers getting on or off. A mixture of snow and icy slush had settled on the roof. The tram moved off. Steele lay flat on the roof, gripping tightly to the ventilator with every muscle in his body.

Regional Children's Clinic No.1, Vladivostok

Bova felt energized after dozing for an hour. It was dark outside the Children's Hospital No.1 in downtown Vladivostok. Bova knew where he was, but for a few seconds had forgotten *why* he was there.

Then he remembered.

As he tried to turn onto his side, he felt the pain shooting to other parts of his body. The image of the truck bearing down on him made him scrunch his eyes shut. He shuddered at the thought.

Then he smiled recalling his dream. He had dreamed that his mother had been to visit him lying in the hospital. She had told him he would be on television, that he was a hero for the second time in a week, and that he was going to receive a medal. She had given him the medal to guard.

His door was ajar. Recognizing the dozing policeman sitting outside his room in the corridor, he felt comforted. It was the one who had given him a ride in the patrol Jeep when Igor had left. But why were they guarding him? Or was he a prisoner again? He took a few more moments to think. He had to get up and out. He had to find his mother; only she would tell him the truth. *Where is my mother?* He would leave the hospital and find her … without the police.

Bova heaved himself out of bed and crossed to the cupboard on the far wall. A small plastic object dropped to the floor, but the guard outside didn't stir. Bova looked down and saw a plastic bag. He did not have time to examine its contents, but it looked like a miniature Hi8 tape in a case. Bova silently closed the door. The policeman was still dozing …

Bova felt stiff. He was in pain, but he was able to walk at least. His clothes had been neatly folded and placed on the middle shelf. He quickly got dressed. As he was pulling on the second boot, he heard a conversation outside his door. The policeman had woken up and was talking to someone. The voices came toward his room, and he jumped back into bed, pulling the sheet up to his neck.

The door opened, and a doctor with gray hair and black bushy eyebrows entered. Bova pretended to be asleep. The doctor glanced at the file hanging at the end of his bed, made a couple of notes, and left the room.

Coast clear. Bova threw off the sheets and went to the window. He opened it slowly and quietly climbed out onto the fire escape.

Then he remembered—the bag with the tape. He had put it back under the bedclothes. He had to get it. If his mother had left it for him and it wasn't a dream after all, it must be important, and he should take it with him. As he reached the bed, again he heard voices and footsteps just outside his door. He snatched the bag and stuffed it down his pants.

The door opened.

"Malchik!" the doctor boomed, seeing his patient was fully dressed. *Boy!* "Shto takoi?" *What are you doing?*

"*Ahhhhhh!*" Head flipped backward, perching on the edge of his bed, Bova screamed at the top of his voice as though in excruciating pain. His trick had worked before. Rolling away from the doctor's view, he stuck two fingers down his throat to make himself sick. Sputum dribbled down his face. He had never tried this before. But he had seen Igor do this many times in the bathroom after drinking too much vodka at his mother's apartment—he had said it made him feel better. Bova turned to face the doctor, who was calling for a nurse.

The policeman entered. "Why is the boy dressed?"

The doctor was asking himself the same question. "He was already—"

Before the doctor could finish his sentence, Bova leapt off the bed and ran. He kept low, negotiating the two pairs of legs standing near the door. His speed took both men by surprise as they tried in vain to intercept.

The heavy ache in his right side grew worse by the second. But he was Natasha's son, and he maintained his momentum toward the stairs. He had to escape, and his mother was counting on him.

The policeman launched after the boy, shouting orders into his handheld radio. But he was too late. Bova had scurried down the flight of stairs like a mouse. He turned right down a corridor leading to the rear of the building and exited the hospital's rear entrance.

★ ★ ★

It was market day. A handful of traders had already begun to set up their stalls.

The narrow alleyway behind the hospital was less than fifty yards from the market square. At least two-dozen people, mostly old women, were unpacking and laying out fresh fruit and veg.

Bova used his small stature to disappear into the crowd as the traders were selling. Among the cries of "blini," "kvas," and "igrushki"—*pancakes, kvas,* and *toys*—Bova looked back every few seconds to see if he had lost the tail. *So far so good.*

He reached the far side of the market place and paused to catch his breath. Suddenly, he felt a strong hand grip his arm from behind. Someone was pulling him into a storeroom. It was dark and damp. All of Bova's kicking and wriggling could not weaken the iron grip of his assailant.

The metal door slammed shut, leaving Bova in the darkness. He was a prisoner once again.

★ ★ ★

Two hundred yards down Okeanskiy Prospect, the tram stopped at the next stop. Steele crawled along the top of the tram and climbed down the utility ladder at the back of the tram car. He looked around; all clear. The streets were dimly lit and deserted.

He ran down the side road, as per Viktor's instructions, to the Central Regional Children's Hospital No.1. As he walked up to the entrance, an ambulance was pulling up. The rear doors opened, and a little girl with black hair was carried out on a stretcher into the hospital. Steele went up to the stretcher and held the child's hand. He smiled at the attendant and greeted the child.

"Everything's going to be just fine, God bless you, little one," he said warmly in Russian.

"You know her?" asked the paramedic.

"She's my neighbor's daughter," replied Steele with a smile. "I promised to meet her here, make sure everything's OK. Her mother's on her way from work." Steele gripped the side of the stretcher as it was wheeled into the emergency room and past a policeman smoking a cigarette on duty.

"Don't worry, comrade … she'll be fine," replied the paramedic. "You are not from here?"

"Riga," Steele replied. "I'm from Riga." This was the best answer to get around his not-quite-perfect accent.

Inside the hospital, Steele ascended two stairs at a time to the second floor. Room 232 was to the right. He kept going and reached Bova's room. *Strange … easier than I thought.* He saw no trace of security or police. Viktor had warned it might be difficult to get access to Bova's room.

He pushed the half-open door and entered Room 232. He saw no sign of a patient, let alone that Bova had ever been there. The bed was newly made. *Ready for the next patient?* The smell of fresh cleaning fluids lingered. Bova, if he had been here, had already gone.

"Excuse me," a nurse said in Russian. "Can I help you?"

Steele turned. "Oh … no. Thank you." He hesitated. "I'm fine."

The nurse frowned. "Are you looking for someone?"

"No. I mean, yes. Perhaps you can help me. My name is … I'm a British journalist. My name is Jack Steele. I'm looking for Bova Klimova. I was told he was here."

"He left. Thirty minutes ago. He was under police protection, you understand. You should speak to the doctor. Perhaps—"

"No, that's okay. Thank you." Steele smiled. "Can you tell me where he went?"

"No. The policeman said he wouldn't get far."

"I don't understand."

"He ran away. Escaped. But they said they'd have him back in no time."

"What were his injuries?"

"I can't discuss that. Speak to the doctor. Wait here." She left the room.

The nurse's shoes squeaked as she walked down the corridor. It wouldn't be long before Miss Squeaky Shoes returned. Steele took one cursory glance around the bed area. *Nothing.* He opened the cupboard. *Empty.* Then he walked back to the staircase, trying not to draw attention to himself.

As he reached the half landing going down, a voice boomed out from above.

"Excuse me! Can we help?" The doctor's voice echoed down the stairwell in Steele's wake. "Wait, sir! One moment, please."

Steele pretended not to hear and kept going.

He reached the penultimate landing near ground level and glanced up to see a silhouette two floors above—*a policeman perhaps?* Whoever it was had a pistol drawn and was pointing straight at him. "Jack!"

Igor!

Steele launched himself, bounding down another half flight. Too fast. He tripped awkwardly at the bottom and rolled onto his side. As he tried to get up, he saw Ryzhakov athletically descending the stairs a few flights above. *I have to lose him.*

"Skolko let, skolko zim!" Ryzhakov shouted as he pounded down the stairs. *Long time no see!* Two henchmen were on his heels. "Jack, you have nowhere to run."

★　　★　　★

Ryzhakov reached the ground floor and collided with a hospital porter wheeling a stretcher. He picked himself up, with no apology to the porter. "Hey! Did you see a foreigner? He's dangerous. Did you see which way he went?"

"Yes, comrade Ryzhakov," the porter replied, recognizing

the chief of police. "He ran to the main entrance." The porter pointed in the opposite direction.

Ryzhakov stopped in his tracks, turned 360 degrees, and hurtled toward the main entrance. He reached the street, but Jack Steele was nowhere to be seen.

CHAPTER TWENTY-SEVEN

Sofiyskaya Embankment, Moscow

"The Secretary General of the United Nations demands an immediate cease-fire."

Pendlebury read aloud from a communiqué marked URGENT. His face reddened, but he continued impatiently, "Shots have been fired in anger. This situation cannot be allowed to escalate."

Anderson was relieved the relevant parties had agreed to come to the embassy at such short notice. The British Empire had at least one drop of clout left.

Both North and South Korean ambassadors had arrived at the British embassy together and on time.

"Gentlemen. Thank you for coming," Anderson had greeted them.

Pendlebury began talking as soon as the men entered his office. He did not wait for them to take a seat.

"Will you people comply, for crying out loud?" Pendlebury began. Anderson knew both he and the ambassador took their duty to Queen and country very seriously. He knew Pendlebury would deal with him later. The immediate priority, London had apparently said, was to "contain" the situation. Pendlebury was ultimately to blame for not keeping a tighter rein on Anderson, and Anderson knew it.

The room fell silent.

The North and South Korean ambassadors sat a few feet from one another. Ridiculous, thought Anderson, these people have been arguing for fifty years—can't they just forgive and forget—have a gin and tonic, play some cricket or croquet, and let bygones be bygones. Sitting side by side, the Korean officials could be blood brothers. The men looked identical except that the South Korean ambassador's suit was more expensive.

Warrior, the US ambassador, loosened his tie and slid off his jacket as he entered the mini summit. He had hurried from the US Embassy where he had been trying to organize the Sullivan replacement. "I should warn you that the Russian president has invited us to remain here until an agreement has been reached."

"In other words, no one's leaving until we've sorted this bloody mess out," added Anderson, bluntly.

Vladivostok, Russia

As Steele exited the back of the hospital, the ambulance driver was closing the rear doors in preparation for driving away. It was the same driver attending the little girl on the stretcher Steele had spoken to on the way in.

"Poyexali!" Steele shouted, pleading. *Let's go!* "Someone is trying to kill me."

Nothing so dramatic had ever happened to the driver in all his years at the Vladivostok hospital. He had heard on his radio that Ryzhakov was in the hospital searching for a foreigner. Like many of the hospital staff, he hated Igor Ryzhakov, so-called police chief of Vladivostok Kraj, but as far as he and his circle of friends were concerned, the man was a gangster.

No question. Anyone in trouble with Ryzhakov was a friend of his. The ambulance driver shifted quickly through his gears, excited by the drama and apparent danger.

"Davai! Davai! Ladno!" he shouted. *OK! Let's go! Let's go!* The ambulance skidded around the first bend, speeding away from the rear entrance of the hospital.

★　　★　　★

Thank God for the help. Steele gripped the handle above his head.

A volley of shots rang out behind them. Presumably at them, but nothing hit the ambulance.

Steele and the driver eyed their prospective wing mirrors to assess the threat. Ryzhakov and his men were running toward their vehicles in the distance. The police fired several rounds at the ambulance, but they were out of range, too far away to do any damage.

"It's okay," the driver shouted in Russian. "They can't shoot straight."

"Thank God!" Steele was comforted. *Thank heaven for small mercies.*

"And I am the best driver in Vladivostok Kraj!"

"Delighted to hear that." Steele couldn't help smiling.

"Don't worry," continued the driver. "I am no friend of Ryzhakov! He has ruined our town … our lives …"

"What do you mean?"

"This man is murdering bastard."

"I've noticed."

"Everyone knows this. He is Devil-God of Vladivostok Kraj. Worship him or you die." The driver checked his mirror. "We are clear now. Which way?"

"*Vesti*—VTV." Steele knew he would need help from the television studio to find Bova and Natasha. He would enlist Sergei—Viktor's contact—for help. He also reckoned Bova might have found his mother by now anyway. They could try her apartment later. It was crucial for him to make contact with Sergei before others realized he was the British fugitive Igor was hunting.

Steele asked, "What's your name?"

"Rajko."

"Nice to meet you, Rajko."

"Me too."

"And thank you."

"Not Russian?"

"It's long story."

The driver laughed. "And you are not from Riga? Am I correct?"

"My name's Jack Steele." He extended his hand, never more grateful to make a new friend.

"There was rumor at the hospital that Ryzhakov was holding someone, a child. This man has no limits. He will silence anyone—even a child."

The ambulance skidded as the driver pressed too hard on the brakes to negotiate the next turn. Steele was pleased to get as much distance as possible between him and Ryzhakov's police militia.

"Latvian. My father was Latvian," Rajko went on.

"I see."

"My mother is Russian."

"I thought this was a closed town?"

"My father used to work for Ryzhakov. Import-export."

"Used to?"

"He's dead. Six months ago—officially, he committed suicide."

"I'm sorry… You think Igor was responsible?"

"Igor *was* responsible. My father refused to continue to work for him."

Steele had found an ally, and he was sitting right next to him.

"Rajko, I need your help. It's very urgent. Do you know a boy called Bova Klimova?"

"Of course. He goes to school with my daughter."

"Ryzhakov was holding Bova in the hospital. He escaped."

"You need to find Bova?"

"Yes. It could save my life and, frankly, yours now, too."

"It's okay. I am not afraid of Ryzhakov. I can help you."

"Do you know where Bova lives? His mother is Natasha."

"Yes, but if you are right about Ryzhakov the boy will not go home."

Rajko made another turn and eased off the gas. "When he escape from hospital?"

"Not long ago … within the last hour."

"Look at the market place. I will try other places too," Rajko suggested.

"The market place?"

"Children like it there. It's near clinic. They sell toys."

"This early in the morning?"

"The traders arrive early. The children steal food. Good hiding places for games, too."

Rajko's idea made sense. Steele had no alternative, and he had to start somewhere to locate Bova and hopefully the tape.

The ambulance cruised through the cobbled side streets of Vladivostok town center, skidding and bumping across slippery metal tram rails. Fortunately, at least two dozen ambulances were in service that day, and the inept local police would take time to locate and search all of them.

Steele scanned the pavements hoping, praying, to see a lone Bova walking along.

"Rajko, drop me at the television station," Steele said suddenly. "You try the market place. There's something I need to do urgently."

"As you want. No problem."

"Keep searching. Don't stop until you find him."

"Sure. I find him."

"Our lives depend on it."

"I understand."

"Bring him to VTV. Ask for Sergei."

"Okay. I got it. BBC rules the waves!" Rajko punched a fist of solidarity in the air while making the witty reference to the patriotic song "Rule, Britannia!" and BBC World Service in the same quip.

They pulled up outside the television studio, and Steele got out.

"Good luck," Steele said. *Not sure who needs it more.* "And thanks!"

Steele entered VTV and approached the front desk. "I am looking for Sergei," he said to the receptionist.

"Your name?"

Steele paused. "Tell him a friend of Viktor is here."

"One moment." The girl got up and walked into a room behind the desk.

He glanced up at one of the television screens in the front lobby. He could not believe his eyes. Playing simultaneously on five monitors around the front lobby was Steele's taped "confession" from North Korean television. From now, every single person in Vladivostok and God knows where else would recognize him.

Sofiyskaya Embankment, Moscow

Pendlebury smiled weakly, looking more uncomfortable than ever. Anderson was subtly trying to take charge. "Please, gentlemen, we really do need an answer," he said, addressing everyone in the room.

"We have already complied with the secretary-general's request," replied the North Korean ambassador. "We guarantee no more shots fired." He glanced at his South Korean counterpart. "We see no reason why events of last two days cannot remain inside this room. On one condition."

Pendlebury shot Anderson a look that said, *Don't worry, I've got this* ... "Greater Tumen Initiative?" Pendlebury asked tentatively.

"Yes, GTI." The North Korean ambassador nodded. "This matter is very important for my country."

"Understood," Pendlebury continued. "I have some good news for all of us. I have assurances—obtained directly by me—from the permanent British representative to the United

Nations that GTI will commence in two weeks. Your country … and yours,"—he looked at both North and South Korean representatives—"will receive an immediate UN aid package of fifty million dollars—in phase one. Russia and China will receive similar amounts once they agree to UN observers tracking all economic and financial aid."

At once, smiles and handshakes filled the room as well as some stretching and sighs of relief.

"Glad to see we've all relaxed," Anderson commented. The men now resembled a group of CEOs who had just survived a vicious take-over bid, he thought. "The Greater Tumen Initiative is—in principle—born. No one ever need know about Operation Tumen. As far as we are all concerned, it was unknown terrorists who incapacitated the nuclear testing facility."

"Precisely," said the North Korean ambassador. "In any case, we will smother this information."

Anderson continued, "North and South Korea were on the verge of hostilities, but no one can prove any of it."

"What about Steele?" Warrior asked, as the ambassadors prepared to leave.

"No word on Steele. It's only been an hour," said Anderson. "We're working on it with the Russians. No need to worry. We'll find him."

Pendlebury's telephone rang.

Jenkins stepped forward to answer. He listened for a few seconds and then put his hand over the telephone speaker. "It's the front desk, Sir Brian. Blake Danner and his daughter have just arrived …?"

"Thank you, Jenkins. Go and bring them up."

Pendlebury and Anderson performed a synchronized quarter turn to the Korean diplomats who stood up, bowed, and exited.

Jenkins ushered the Korean ambassadors out of the office.

Pendlebury and Anderson looked at one another and smiled.

"They swallowed it!" said Anderson sotto voce. "They're as gullible as we thought they were."

"Your best idea to date. I'll give you that."

★　　★　　★

Blake Danner and Sandy Steele entered the British ambassador's office and were greeted by Anderson's sweaty palm. He smiled his warmest fake smile.

"Thank you so much for coming all this way," he said. *How much do they know? And when was the last time they watched international news?*

"Bullshit!" Sandy hit back. "We didn't exactly have a choice. What's with the personal escort, Mr. Magoo, over here?"

"Forgive the inconvenience ... intrusion, but we felt you'd be safest under our watchful eye," Anderson said in his best reassuring voice.

"Is that right?" she replied. Anderson could tell she was not buying it.

"What the hell is going on here?" chimed in Danner. "We demand an explanation."

"Your husband ... your son-in-law ... is in trouble. We thought you would want to help."

"Why do you think I'm here?" Sandy asked sarcastically. "To see the Bolshoi? What's happened to my husband?"

"Jack has, shall we say, upset a lot of people," said Anderson.

"It's very serious, I'm afraid," continued the ambassador.

Sandy turned to her father. "Dad, we don't have to listen to this BS."

"Let's hear them out." He eyed Anderson. "Tell me what's happened to my son-in-law, or I'll go to the nearest goddamn US news bureau and ask them to find him."

"Did you know you husband has confessed to spying in North Korea?"

"Bullshit." Sandy's face was flushed.

"On live television." Anderson spoke calmly.

"My husband is not a goddamn spy," she said. "Believe me, I'd know."

"Unfortunately, that's not how this appears to the rest of the world," added Sir Brian.

"Just tell me what you've done with him?" she said. "Where is he?"

"I'm pleased to inform you that Mr. Steele is fit and well, and on his way back to Moscow. You'll see him tomorrow," Anderson lied.

Danner put his arm around Sandy. "We're pleased to hear that."

"The main thing is that the situation has been contained—for the most part."

"What *situation?*" Sandy shook off her father's arm.

"We suspect that your husband is trying to sabotage a UN sponsored plan to inject millions of dollars of economic aid into the tri-state Tumen region. It's known as the Greater Tumen Initiative. You'll read all about it in the newspapers soon enough."

"That's insane. Why would he do that?"

"That's what we'd like to know. We understand you've been having financial difficulties?"

"What the hell are you talking about? First, that's totally BS. Second, our finances are none of your business anyway. Jack had an interview on the Amur River, Monday. He called me from Khabarovsk, at least on the train out of there, and told me they'd arrested him on some dumb pretext and released him. That's all I know."

Anderson stood up. "Mr. Danner, it would be best if you take your daughter back to your hotel. Stay there for now ... Our driver will deliver you safely."

"Is that an order or a request?"

"Neither." Anderson ignored Danner's aggressive tone. "We'll leave one of our people there in case you have any questions."

"Questions?"

"Problems. Once Mr. Steele arrives back tomorrow, I'm sure we'll have a much clearer picture."

"Fine with me," Danner said.

"Dad? We don't have to do this …" Sandy objected.

"Like I said. That's fine with me. Sandy, it's time to go."

★ ★ ★

A few moments after father and daughter had left, Anderson turned to the British ambassador and said, "We may have to organize something for them too. I don't trust Danner senior. And the girl is far too curious … and capable."

"Jesus, man! We're not eliminating anyone else. Is that clear?"

"You're not keeping up, sir. Steele, and Danner, and his daughter, are the only people who can screw things up for all of us. If New York cancels GTI—and they will if Steele or his family have anything to do with it—we're all completely fucked … permanently."

Pendlebury frowned. "Perhaps. You might be right."

"I'm glad we agree. GTI doesn't pass go if Op. Tumen sees the light of day."

Vladivostok, Russia

In the reception area of VTV, Steele watched thankfully as the images of himself on television disappeared after a few seconds. The quality of the footage was poor. Hopefully, he could remain anonymous a while longer.

Steele exhaled, realizing that anyone in the reception area might notice he was the man on the television screen. *Calmly active, actively calm … It's not over until it's over … Got to keep going.*

He picked up a magazine and pretended to flick through its tattered pages. *Come on, Sergei, where are you?*

Seconds later, the door behind the reception desk opened.

A short, thickset man with thinning black hair, large spectacles and a shiny face entered with a sense of purpose. He locked eyes with Steele and appeared to recognize him. "Mr. Steele?" he asked. A security guard with a Kalashnikov rifle followed close behind him.

Steele's stomach flipped ... *Why the armed guard?* "Yes," he said finally.

"Mr. Steele. I was expecting you. Follow me, please."

Jack stuck out his hand. "Jack Steele. Nice to meet you."

"Lebedev, Sergei Viktorovich," he said, leading the way. "People who want something from me call me Serge." He chuckled and took off to the rear of the building with Steele following cautiously.

"Wait, Sergei Viktorovich?" Steele asked after a few moments.

"Yes, Viktor is my father. He speaks highly of you." Sergei smiled warmly. "Your story sounds very interesting, Mr. Steele. Please, we don't have much time."

Bolshoi Kamenny Bridge, Moscow

Under a cloudless winter sky, the Kremlin domes sparkled like gigantic Aladdin's cave treasures. The British embassy Range Rover drove Sandy and Blake Danner up Tverskaya Street, formerly known as Gorky Street, toward the hotel.

"You think they're telling the truth?" Sandy whispered so that Chinless, sitting next to the Russian driver, wouldn't hear.

"I don't know what to believe. Something's up," Danner replied.

"You're hiding something." Sandy frowned.

"I'm not. I just need to think. Where did you say Jack was working?"

"Khabarovsk, near Vladivostok."

Danner took Sandy's hand and leaned close to her. "Here's what you need to do."

He whispered into her ear for a few seconds. Then he squeezed her hands while looking deep into her eyes, and then wrapped both arms around her for a hug.

The driver glanced periodically into his rearview mirror, but, like Chinless, could not hear the conversation.

Sandy leaned into her father's arms, and for a few moments nothing else mattered to her. She looked up. "Now what? How am I supposed—"

"You'll know when the time comes."

The Range Rover slowed and stopped at a red light on Tverskaja and Gazetny Pereulok. Danner flipped the handle to open the door and hopped out into the street like a robber in the night. Phase one complete.

★　　★　　★

"Hey!" shouted the British agent. "Bloody hell!" Danner threw off his seatbelt and scrambled out of the car, narrowly avoiding a tram hurtling past. The hazard gave Danner—now on the other side of the tram—a few seconds to make his escape. Despite his age, he ran away and disappeared into the crowd of late evening shoppers bundled up against the cold. Chinless descended but decided pursuit would be futile.

Way to go, Dad. She had reconnected with her father. He hadn't hugged her in years. *Perhaps things have finally changed?*

She had no money, no phone, no husband, and now no dad. It felt lonely, but it was her turn. Staring into the driver's rearview mirror, she saw him scrutinizing her and sensed he was trying to read her next move. She returned a *don't-mess-with-me-asshole* look.

"*Bugger!*" shouted the chinless wonder from outside the car. He was already on his cell phone. Over the noise of the traffic, Sandy could just make out what he was saying: "*I lost him. Yes, I know … I know … Do I stay with the girl?*"

The driver got out. He gestured nervously toward Sandy,

but Chinless was too busy on his phone to pay attention. Sandy slowly edged forward, hugging the leather seats in preparation.

The Russian driver again looked nervously in her direction.

Suddenly, she jumped into the driver's seat, planting her foot on the brake and throwing the car into gear—an automatic. The *clunk* of the Range Rover made both men turn.

But it was too late. Sandy hit the gas pedal. The stolen vehicle screeched off down Ulitza Tverskaja, immediately careening into the VIP traffic lane to avoid the Muscovites and their cars. As she narrowly avoided a traffic policeman standing on a small podium in the middle of the wide boulevard, she heard him blow his whistle at her as if it would make a scrap of difference.

Thirty seconds later, she turned into a side street, stopped, and dumped the car. She heard sirens not far away. Hurrying toward Ulitza Tverskaya, Sandy was trying to figure out how to contact the CNN bureau. Now. Luckily, she also had the driver's cell phone, which he had left on the front passenger seat.

She pressed one of the keys, but the phone was locked. She needed directory inquiries ... *in the middle of Ulitza Tverskaya?*

CHAPTER TWENTY-EIGHT

Vladivostok, Russia

Outdated Hollywood movie posters decorated the narrow corridors of VTV. Steele felt like screaming. He never imagined his job as a journalist would mean him trying to save the world, or at least a small part of it. He wasn't even sure if he could save *himself* now. He felt painfully weary, his brain was rattled, and he no longer knew the good guys from the bad—if there was even any difference anymore. He turned to look at the armed guard following them. Even if he wanted to leave, he couldn't ... *Please God, don't let Viktor double cross me ...*

"Serge," he said, "I met a man called Rajko. He drives an ambulance—"

"I know Rajko. He's good guy."

"Great. He's coming here. You have to let him in. He'll have a boy with him. It's very important."

"Bova?"

"Yes?"

"That won't be necessary," Sergei replied confidently.

"What won't be necessary?"

"We already have what you are looking for." Sergei turned and gave Steele a pat on the shoulder.

Steele recoiled, and his eyes widened. "Wait, you found Bova? The tape?"

"Both are here."

"How?" A wave of relief washed through Steele's body, mind, and soul. "Where? How?"

"Follow me." Sergei continued walking.

They entered a small room with a threadbare couch and faded pink plastic garden chairs. There was also a small coffee table with an ashtray of cigarette butts. Bare and grubby, it resembled a factory worker's lunch room. On one side of the room was a large glass window, though not to the outside world. It was difficult to see through, a partition of some kind. Steele could make out the metal arm of a boom microphone glinting in the darkness. A sound studio, he concluded.

Sergei knocked on the window, and the lights came up in the next room. Steele peered through the window and saw a young boy.

Bova?

"You found him!" exclaimed Steele.

"So what is your connection to this boy?"

"Your father told me to find Bova. He has the tape."

Sergei motioned to his guard to unlock the door. "Bova wants to go on TV. Says he is local hero. No one knows he is here."

"If he has the tape, he will be a hero. Trust me," said Steele.

"Have you watched it?"

"I filmed it." Steele shrugged. "It shows terrorists trying to destroy the Yongbuk nuclear reactor in North Korea …"

Sergei raised an eyebrow, looking skeptical.

"Serge, could we just play the tape? I need to check it."

"I have looked at this tape," Sergei said bluntly.

"And?"

"There is nothing on tape."

Steele turned pale. He broke a sweat. "That's not possible! There's video from North Korea on that tape. I was there."

"The tape is blank. It has never been used." Sergei held up the tape, pointing to the small red safety tab still intact.

Steele shook his head, refusing to believe. "Let me talk to the boy."

They entered VTV studio A.

Moscow, Russia

Shivering, Sandy strode down Ulitza Tverskaya, nervously glancing over her shoulder every few seconds to see if she was being followed. She mumbled quietly to herself, "Where are you, Jack Steele? Where the heck are you, Jack?"

She entered one side of a large department store selling women's clothing. The store covered an entire block. She walked through the store to the other side, stopping to try on a couple of fur hats. She looked around her. Still no one, as far as she could tell.

Sandy picked out a rabbit-fur winter *shapka* from one of the stands when no one was looking. From another rack she swiped a fur coat. No one saw her. She exited the store as quickly as she had entered, twisting her blonde, shoulder-length hair and tucking it under the fur hat.

Sure as she could be that no one was tailing her, Sandy stopped an old man walking in the opposite direction. "Excuse me," she said, "do you speak English?"

The white-haired man with a red bulbous nose and ruddy cheeks smiled. "Yes, I do, my dear."

"Great. Please, what's the number for directory enquiries here in Moscow?"

"Nine-one-nine, young woman."

"Thank you, sir. Thank you so much."

"Anything else?" The old man chuckled. Sandy could smell alcohol on his breath. He looked at her flirtatiously.

She shook her head. "No, thank you."

"American?"

"Yes."

"Have a nice day, as you say! God bless George Bush!"

"Same to you. Thank you."

The old man saluted as Sandy continued.

She jogged down the busy sidewalk, sidestepping the evening shoppers on their way home. Then she entered a stationary shop in search of a telephone. Immediately, she spotted a tele-phone next to the cash register and pointed. "Please?"

The expressionless cashier nodded. Sandy dialed nine-one-nine and asked for the CNN Bureau, Moscow. Then she hung up and immediately redialed.

One ring and a young female voice with only a trace of Rus-sian accent said, "CNN, Moscow."

"Good evening, this is Sandy Danner." Sandy wasn't sure what to say next. "I'm ... I'm an American. I need to speak to a reporter. It's urgent."

"One moment. I connect you to news desk."

A couple of clicks later, a male voice—intelligent, no non-sense—answered. "Brad Pitock."

Sandy's chest tightened. She was excited. The voice was calm and professional, somehow seasoned. *But will he believe me?* "Hi Brad, this is Sandy Steele," she began. "My husband is Jack Steele. He's a British journalist. Have you heard of him?"

"No, ma'am."

"He's—"

"Wait a second," Pitock snapped. "Did you say British?"

"Yes. He's a journalist. He went to Vladivostok on assignment—"

Pitock cut her off. "Jack Steele? He was on television today?"

"No, no," she explained, "he's not a TV reporter, he works for the *London Daily Standard*."

"Ma'am, if it's the same Jack Steele, he gave a press confer-ence in North Korea this morning. He told the world he was a spy."

Sandy shook her head. "There must be some mistake," she said, recalling what Anderson had told her but refusing to accept there was any truth to it. "You must be confusing him with someone else."

Pitock scoffed. "Ma'am, how many Jack Steeles can there be seven times zones away on the other side of Russia right now?

North Korea's right across the border … Did he say why he was going there?"

"NO, HE DID NOT! ENOUGH ALREADY!" she shouted. Then added quietly, "You don't understand."

She had to deny the ridiculous accusation, but this was the second person in one day who was telling her Jack was a spy. *Is that even remotely conceivable? No way.* Jack had been unusually distant since this whole Russia thing began. Maybe that was why she didn't feel close to him anymore? Perhaps that's why she had pushed him away? Did her father know? Is that why he was trying to help her? Why had her father insisted that she flee the British authorities in the middle of Moscow?

"Ms. Steele? Are you there?"

"Yes, I'm here," Sandy replied, quietly, her brain reeling.

"Can you come to the bureau. I'll send a car for you. Where are you?"

"I can't. I'm being followed …" Sandy was reeling through the events of the past few days. She desperately wanted to make sense of it all. *I need to speak to Jack, Goddamnit! I need help!* "Meet me in Red Square," she said forcefully. "Bring your cameras."

"Ms. Steele … wait—"

"I said fifteen minutes. Be there or you'll regret it!"

Sandy pressed the END CALL button.

Then she grabbed some white card and a marker, threw down a ten-pound note, and left.

VTV, Vladivostok, Russia

Inside VTV studio A, Bova jumped up to greet Jack Steele. "Mister Jeck! How are you?" Bova smiled, throwing his arms around Steele's waist with a hug. "I am pleased to see you again, Jack. Where is my mother?"

Steele ignored the question. "I didn't know you spoke such good English—"

"They told me my mother was with you. And Viktor. Where is Viktor?"

"Bova, are you OK?"

"Yes, thank you. I'm good. Sergei found me near the hospital. He saved me."

"How did he find you?" Steele turned to Sergei.

"My father sent me to hospital. I arrive and see boy running down the street."

Steele continued. "Bova, listen to me carefully. What happened to the tape? Viktor said he gave you a tape."

"Viktor? I don't know. I was in the hospital. I was dreaming my mother came to visit me. She told me to keep my hero's medal safe. But when I woke up, I find two tapes, one without a case …" He thrust his hand down the front of his pants, producing the plastic bag with one Hi8 DVD tape still inside. "I give the first one to him." Bova eyed Sergei. "But this one has your name on it. Here!" He opened the case and handed Steele the second tape.

Steele read the label. It said: FOR JACK STEELE.

"Have you spoken to your mother?" *Would Viktor find her before Igor?*

Steele was grateful. "Thanks, Bova," he continued. "This is great. Well done!" He handed the tape to Serge. "Play the tape. Bova, wait outside for us, please?"

Sergei locked the ultrathick soundproof door. "Just in case," he said.

Steele nodded.

Sergei inserted the tape into a mini DV video camera he had taken from a shelf. He plugged a cable into the camera from his desk console, switched on a bank of monitors, and stepped back.

Steele crossed his arms and nibbled the inside of his cheek, waiting to see if the footage was usable. He half expected to see Chen magically giving him the interview Steele wished he could have taped. If it weren't for Chen, there would be no footage in the first place.

They watched and waited. After a few seconds, everything became clear. Unbeknown to Steele, Viktor had filmed the entire attack on the nuclear reactor. He had shot everything from the vehicle—Steele could even make himself out in the far distance of the footage they were viewing. The DPRK, the British, the Americans, the Russians—none of these bastards—could ever deny that Operation Tumen took place.

"Amazing!" exclaimed Steele. "This is *perfect*. Yes, we can use this."

"Who shot this?" asked Sergei.

"Me and your dad. But I think your dad's a better cameraman than me."

"Yolki-palki, bozhe moi!" Sergei exclaimed, his eyes glued to the footage. *My God, fir trees 'n sticks.* "He should have been journalist. I swear CNN's gonna love this."

The screen went black.

"Listen, Serge—"

"Wait." Sergei held up his hand. "There's more. Audio track. Listen."

A British man's voice could be heard on speaker talking to Igor Ryzhakov about *final preparations for Operation Tumen*. Steele asked, "Who is that?"

"Igor is talking to someone called Anderson."

"Anderson must be one of the British goons behind all this. Igor recorded him for insurance."

Steele's neck veins bulged as he tried to control his rage. If he hadn't been there, Operation Tumen would have sentenced thousands of innocent prisoners to death—on the orders of London and Washington, not to mention UN involvement. He felt sick, betrayed by the countries whose integrity he had trusted and for whom he had worked for all these years. *Bastards.* "We don't have much time," he said. "A lot of different players are mixed up in this. I need your help, Serge."

"No problem. Whatever you want."

Steele's narrow escapes from death over the last few days

now seemed unimportant. He was beginning to understand what all the lies, murder, destruction, and killing were about. Ryzhakov was the executioner. But Steele's own government was one of the commanders-in-chief. Furthermore, once British, American, and Russian authorities understood that Steele had been present during the attack and had footage to prove it, they were sure to kill him.

He could feel himself breaking out into a cold sweat. He was more terrified now than he had been over the last few days. Somehow the adrenaline would keep him moving. The next few moments would dictate whether he lived or died. They had to get these pictures on air. Yes, he would tell comrade Ryzhakov's story, but not how the Russian had intended. He would tell CNN or the BBC or Sky, or whomever he could find, what kind of a devious, evil maniac the West was proud to sponsor and hire for hard cash.

"Ryzhakov will arrive any minute—" said Sergei, his voice quivering.

"I know."

Steele swallowed hard, thinking, biting the inside of his mouth so hard he could taste blood. "We have to get this tape on air." A voice inside him told him not to proceed because Sandy might be killed or injured if he did. It was one thing to risk his own life, but how on earth could he even contemplate endangering Sandy? *And what about Natasha? Do I risk her life for the greater good?* It was all horrendous; he couldn't even begin to contemplate these choices.

The telephone on the console rang in sound studio one.

Sergei picked up. *"Allo?"* He listened, then frowned. "Shto? Xorosho, ja ponyal." *What? OK. Understood.* Sergei hung up and said, "Ryzhakov's men have arrived. They are at the front. They want to speak with you."

"You cannot let them in. Promise me?"

Sergei nodded. "I know this, Jack. Believe me." Sergei pressed the intercom button and ordered his security guard to keep the outer door to studio A shut for as long as possible. He didn't mention who was coming. "Bistra!" he said to them through the intercom. *Quick!* "And hide the boy. We have intruders—not long before they get here."

Sergei secured the bolt on the six-inch-thick studio door.

Steele wondered if Bova should stay with them but decided it would be safer for him outside with security.

"They'll shoot the windows," Steele said.

"No. They can't."

"They can't?"

"Bulletproof. A legacy from Comrade Stalin."

"Stalin?"

"All television and radio stations were constructed with heavy fortification—just in case … Stalin was a paranoid! He wanted his media men to tell lies in safety."

"God bless Stalin."

Steele observed the harried expression of the guards through the thick glass partition as someone on the other side of their door tried to break in. "Can we get a live feed?" Steele asked, eyes glued to any movement on the outer door.

"I'm trying. We are VTV, not BBC Bush House. Satellite costs more than one thousand dollars a minute. The host must sponsor us."

Sergei pulled open a drawer next to him. "I have an idea," he said.

He took out a laptop computer, picked up the digital video camera, inserted the mini DV tape, and closed the tape compartment. "Call CNN, Moscow. Number is in here." Sergei passed a black file to Steele. "Page 1. Tell them everything. Davai! Davai!"

Steele opened the file and found a direct line to CNN under International News Bureaus: CNN was at the top. He dialed.

Sergei was rewinding the videotape inside the camera. "Even if they agree, it will take too long to wait for satellite time. This is quicker." Sergei queued up the tape.

"What's quicker?"

"Get them on the telephone. Americans love British accent." Sergei continued typing commands, and then fed wires into his computer from the video camera and back into the monitors.

"Send it to them via dial-up?"

"Yes."

"No answer."

"Try again. You made mistake."

Steele dialed again. "How long?"

"Leave it to me," reassured Sergei, who continued checking his video was ready to send.

A loud thud from the studio waiting room made them look up.

Two policemen entered. They had finally shot the lock off the outer door.

Bova? Where is Bova?

An awkward scuffle broke out between the VTV security guards and the two policemen. The four men separated, walking backward to each corner, boxers in the ring—pistols and AK-47 rifles drawn, each man pointing at their opposite number.

Ryzhakov appeared briefly in the doorway. He drew his weapon, then disappeared from view.

"Come on! Come on!" Steele pressed the receiver to his ear. He wasn't as confident as Sergei about the bulletproof glass.

"Shit! I forgot," said Sergei.

"What?"

"I was wrong about the bulletproof glass."

"But you said—" Steele's eyes were blazing.

"I don't remember exactly. It's true what I said. They remodeled this studio a year ago. Money ran out and bulletproof glass too expensive."

"Shit!" Steele froze, his heart racing. *I have moments to live.* The he heard a distant voice on the other end of the telephone— the CNN bureau receptionist. *Surrender, or finish what I started?*

He took a deep breath. "This is Jack Steele from the *London Daily Standard*," he said, hairs standing up on the back of his neck. *Now or never.* "Put me through to your bureau chief. This is an emergency! I repeat, an emergency!"

A few seconds felt like minutes.

"Jed Butler."

Thank God. Steele could not believe his luck. CNN's ubiquitous correspondent in Moscow was on the line. This guy lived and would probably die for "breaking news." Now he'd have buckets full.

"I have sensational footage—a massacre in North Korea ..."

"Is this a joke?" replied Butler.

"No joke. The attack was organized by a secret Western alliance."

"Really? Nice one. They're all sons of bitches, right?" Butler's tone dripped acute cynicism verging on derision.

He doesn't believe a word. "You have to listen to me. I have proof." Steele spoke quicker now, more urgent. "This is Jack Steele from the *London Daily Standard.* I repeat ... US, Britain, and Russia are responsible for this terrorist attack."

"Wait a second ..." Butler suddenly remembered the name. "Jack Steele?" he exclaimed. "Where are you calling from?"

"Vladivostok. View the footage. I'll stay on the line. But you have to do the interview right now."

"I'll set the feed up. Don't go away."

"No! There's no time for a feed." Steele looked at Sergei, wanting an update.

"What do you suggest?" asked Butler.

Sergei double-clicked on his mouse several times, then smiled.

Steele turned to Sergei, his eyes begging for a *yes.*

"Ready," said Sergei. "His email?"

Steele beamed. He never dreamed an email might one day save his life. "Jed—your email address? Quick."

Butler recited and Steele repeated, carefully writing down each letter as he spoke: "j e d @ c n n m o s c o w b u r e a u d o t c o m ... All one word, no caps," he said quickly.

Out of the corner of his eye, Steele observed movement on the other side of the glass. He heard the muffled sound of gunfire. *Shit!* "They're coming in …"

One of the TV guards was squirming on the floor clutching his chest, blood seeping through his puffy, white fingers. The second TV guard squatted against the wall, trembling for his life. It didn't matter who fired first, but the intruders were armed and ready to fight.

Looking at his men, Sergei said. "God bless them! Loyal comrades …"

Both policemen pointed their weapons at the glass partition. "Sergei!"

"What's going on?" Butler asked. "Do we have breaking news or not?"

"It's coming," replied Steele. "Sergei!"

"One second … downloading."

The policemen opened fire directly at the partition window with their semiautomatic rifles.

But the sound of a dozen bullets hitting the glass was no louder than Sergei pounding his laptop. Steele and Sergei smiled. *Nine lives?* The glass was bulletproof after all.

Steele looked at Sergei and cursed.

"I was wrong," Sergei said. "Must have been studio B!"

Steele took a deep breath and blew out. "Studio B? You're a journalist. Get your facts right next time."

"Sorry." Sergei was glued to the screen. "We have a glitch."

"What now?"

"Windows won't open this attachment. I don't understand."

The policemen tried again—they fired another volley of shots. Steele shivered involuntarily as he saw the muzzle flash from both weapons less than ten feet from him but still not penetrating the glass. Thank God the sound was still barely audible. The glass really was bulletproof.

"Try RealPlayer," Steele suggested.

"What?"

"See if your laptop has RealPlayer. Sometimes it's faster." Steele scrambled across behind the console and sat down at the laptop. "Here, let me try."

Crack! Crack! Crack! Bullets. A small split appeared in the glass.

"Not good!" exclaimed Sergei, breathing heavily. "Stalin was a cheapskate. Bulletproof glass Russian style."

Ryzhakov shouted orders at the two policemen, who had paused to reload with fresh magazines.

Steele prayed. He thought of Chen, who was smiling at him in his mind's eye.

"Steele? You there? Is that gunfire?" Butler was panicking. "What's happening? I didn't receive a damn thing!"

Steele pressed the receiver to his ear, his eyes glued to the screen. "I'm here, Jed. Technical hitch rectified. I'm sending you the video attachment. Open it with RealPlayer. Got it?" Steele lifted his finger to press send.

"Bozhe moi!" Sergei jabbed Steele on the shoulder. *My God!* Steele's brain automatically aborted the finger-on-mouse command for a moment. "Jack!"

Steele looked up. The first policeman was banging on the glass with his rifle butt, pointing at Ryzhakov, who stood in the doorway pointing a gun at Bova's head.

"He'll shoot!" Sergei insisted.

"No, he won't." Steele studied Ryzhakov's face. He knew this man. He'd seen him operate at close quarters. He read uncertainty on Ryzhakov's face. Steele was sure. He had to follow his gut.

What if my gut's wrong?

Damn it. Steele woke the electronic mouse again and raised his index finger to send.

Ryzhakov screamed at Steele through the glass—violent, threatening aggression as he pointed his gun to Bova's head. If he pulled the trigger, Steele would never forgive himself. He thought of Chen.

Chen? The old man's voice somewhere inside him told him Bova would live.

"He'll shoot," Serge repeated. "I know this man."

"No. He will not." Steele broke eye contact with Ryzhakov, looked down at the screen and clicked on the mouse. "It's done," he said quietly.

Steele saw movement behind Ryzhakov. A single muffled shot from the corridor. Ryzhakov fell to the floor. Bova froze, locking eyes with Steele, not daring to look down. Slowly, the boy turned toward the open door and corridor behind him as Steele and Sergei watched from the studio.

Bova saw his mother. He smiled.

At that moment, Steele saw Natasha too as she came into view outside the studio's green room. She was holding a pistol.

He had a sense of what would happen next, but he was powerless to stop it. It felt as though his insides were about to implode. It was the most helpless feeling of his life. It was over in seconds.

"*NYET!!! MAMA!!!*" Even through the glass, Steele and Sergei could hear Bova's muffled scream. Ryzhakov's bodyguard turned and fired at Natasha point-blank.

Steele started for the door, but Sergei blocked him with a bear hug. "It's too late. If you die too, no one can ever explain this."

Natasha, resigned to her fate, did nothing except smile at her son as the bullet pierced her chest and she was slammed to the wall behind her. As she slid to the floor, she smiled at Bova, managing to extend her hand toward him.

Steele read her lips as she said to her son, "Moy malchik … Ja tibya lyublyu." *I love you, my boy.*

Steele's eyes welled up.

One of the policemen grabbed Bova by the scruff of the neck and picked him up under one arm. He pointed his pistol at Bova's head and started shouting again at Steele to force him to open the door. But Steele knew he would not pull the trigger. With his boss now lying dead on the floor, it would be life in prison or even a death sentence if he harmed the child.

★   ★   ★

The video attachment opened on Jed Butler's laptop in Moscow.

"Got 'eem!" shouted Jed. Silence. "Jeez!"

"Good," Steele replied. "I'm still here." The footage was finally in the hands of CNN International. It would take less than a minute for "Breaking News" to hit world screens.

But something was off. Jed Butler had stopped talking.

"Jed?"

"Oh … my … God," Butler said slowly.

"What's wrong?" Steele glanced at Sergei, nostrils flaring, confused.

"Jack, can you see our broadcast from your location?"

"Serge, do we have CNN?"

Sergei hit a red button on the console desk in front of him. The bank of ten monitors in front of them revealed CNN International's live feed.

"Do you see this?" asked Butler.

Steele could hear commotion and some laughter in the background of the CNN bureau. Then he saw why.

"Yes," he said slowly, "I see her."

What he was seeing now was more shocking for Steele than the images from Yongbuk. He squinted and looked again to make sure he wasn't seeing things. Steele saw Sandy as he—and the entire world—had never seen her.

He stared at the screen. A large crowd of people gathered around the spectacle, some laughing and sniggering, some just staring with poker faces. Apart from her fur hat and coat and Nike sneakers, Sandy Danner stood naked on Red Square.

Red Square, Moscow

Orchestrating the outrageous media stunt had come to Sandy after the encounter with the old man on Tverskaya Street. He had flirted with her. She could tell he'd been drinking. It dawned on her that she needed to do something so outrageous and crazy if anyone was to pay attention to her. One of her strengths was her beauty and, frankly, her body. *Use what you've got!* After her father's warning in the Range Rover that Jack's life was in danger and his instruction to get to the CNN bureau, she knew she had to get Jack into the media spotlight immediately, before the Brits and whoever else was involved made him disappear forever.

Sandy had nothing to lose. She had always been proud of her body—her blonde, silky hair and her perfectly proportioned curves had turned heads since she was fourteen years old. On Red Square, Sandy stood almost naked in front of the CNN cameras. Passersby were stunned and amused. They had never seen anything like this on Krasnaya Ploshadz.

She shed her last layer of clothing, the fur coat. Stark naked, Sandy shivered in a wave of goose bumps covering the surface of her body. *Damn, I wish I'd thought this through. I'm fucking freezing ...* She wondered what her privileged Mainline friends in Philadelphia would say if they could see her now.

Around Sandy and the camera crew that included Brad Pitock, the crowd gathered and grew larger by the minute. Sandy was putting on a show for them, and she knew it. And that was the plan. A show that people would not forget, that would draw attention to her one and only cause—Jack Steele. *I only have one shot.*

Muscovites were pointing and gesticulating. Perhaps they saw it as a post-perestroika bonus? President Putin's so-called new age of democracy?

"Krasavitza!" cheered a man in his fifties with gold teeth. *What a beauty!*

"Get dressed, young woman! You should be ashamed!" shouted one babushka, her expression at first registering sheer surprise, then shock and disgust, then mild amusement, all in the space of a few seconds.

"Bravo!" shouted a young man in a white fur hat and coat. "Claudia Schiffer!"

Sandy raised a placard overhead, revealing her perfectly formed breasts. A cheer went up in the rapidly multiplying crowd. Some clapped. Others were now running across Red Square, having seem the furor on television screens in shop windows.

Wondering how long before she would be arrested, Sandy prayed Jack could see her wherever he was and whatever kind of trouble he was in. She hoped it was worth it. She prayed it would work.

"Let's do this," she said to Pitock.

"You have everyone's attention."

He told his cameraman to start recording. "Turnover."

"Sound speed."

If her insane publicity stunt failed, at least he would know she loved him. Deep down, she knew Jack wasn't a spy. This was her way of making up for the lie about the miscarriage. She thought about the last time they were together, and the danger Jack was facing. *For you, Jack.*

Vladivostok, Russia

Steele stood watching the screens. *What is going on?* The camera zoomed in to show the message Sandy was carrying on a piece of white card. It read:

> JACK STEELE IS INNOCENT.
> I LOVE YOU JACK.

A feeling of exhilaration flooded his veins. It was a mixture of pride, joy, relief, and love, not to mention amusement. Sandy was truly one of a kind. But this was no time for sentimentality. Sandy, amazingly, was trying to help him, but immediate life-and-death concerns before him meant there was no time to decipher her efforts.

Still under the firm grip of the policeman's arm, Bova needed help. Steele saw the boy's terrified expression through the thick glass as he opened the bolts on the sound studio door.

Steele opened the door, and the policeman was already lowering his pistol. Distracted by two dead bodies—Igor and Natasha—within feet of him, the bizarre and unexpected CNN images of a beautiful naked woman on the monitor on the wall above him appeared to cause the policeman further confusion, and his attention flicked between the two spectacles.

Natasha was dead, but Bova would live. She had saved her son.

A loud *thwack* came out of nowhere.

Steele and Sergei flinched, but both immediately realized the shot had come from the bank of television screens. The live camera shot on Sandy tipped one way and then the other. The cameraman had lifted his camera off its tripod and was taking shelter. After another piercing *crack* of gunfire, the viewers around the world saw the camera crashing to the ground as if the cameraman himself had been shot.

The camera settled motionless on the ground—half the viewfinder was filled with the cobblestones of Red Square. But the top quarter of the camera's viewfinder was far more disturbing.

Sandy was lying naked on the ground with a mass of comrades in fur coats crowded around her as the world watching CNN was left hanging. Steele stopped breathing for a moment. All he could do was pray. *Tell me she's going to live, Chen. Tell me she's going to live ...*

The screen went black for a few seconds. Then the CNN broadcast returned to the stern face of the CNN anchor in the London studio. "... and ... we will try to return to the unfolding events from Red Square as soon as possible ..." The anchor took a deep breath, visibly shaken by what he'd seen. Nervously, he touched his earpiece, looking off camera to his producers for guidance. Next story?

He continued, "Moving on to today's other top stories …"

Steele dropped the telephone receiver. He stood motionless, his jaw open.

Sergei said, "Don't worry, Jack. You are safe now."

What the bloody hell! "That woman is my wife." Steele slumped to the floor head in hands. "That's my wife, Sandy."

CHAPTER TWENTY-NINE

Red Square, Moscow

The last thing she'd expected was gunfire.

Crack!

Two guards, Kremlin soldiers, came running, shouting orders into the crowd. A Kremlin official, who had been watching the scene unfold from his office overlooking Red Square, had alerted the Kremlin Internal Security guards. The guards had reacted immediately to the events taking place on Red Square. Outraged that someone would dare pose naked yards from Lenin's tomb, the official had barked down the telephone that the guard commander had five minutes to remove the naked woman if he wanted to keep his job *and* his pension *and* not be thrown in jail.

The guards on patrol around the exterior Kremlin walls grasped the urgency of the situation and immediately took off. They had been ordered to arrest the woman by force if necessary.

But the crowd was enjoying the enigmatic spectacle of the beautiful woman, clearly a foreigner. They began to jostle and obstruct the guards as they fought their way through the crowd.

"Leave her be!" a man shouted.

"Bully!" cried a young woman.

An older babushka deliberately stuck her foot out to trip one of the soldiers and shouted, "Russian Federation stinks! Freedom to women!"

It worked.

The soldier crashed to the ground, pistol in hand. Redfaced and humiliated before the large crowd, and only two months serving his unit, he decided to take control more forcefully. He held his pistol in the air and fired a warning shot, causing even the courageous older babushka to panic.

"Idiot!" screamed the soldier's staff sergeant who was ten years his senior. He slapped his subordinate on the head, knocking his hat off, then pulled him away from the crowd to reprimand him, much to the amusement of the ever-growing crowds of locals and tourists. They cheered and jeered at the same time.

Instinctively, Sandy had dropped flat to the ground, and soon reached for her thick fur coat. Most people around her simply crouched down, but Jack had often recounted war stories from Bosnia to his wife about the importance of taking effective cover from small-arms fire—the flatter you were to the ground, the more chance you stood of avoiding the bullets. That's why Sandy lay on the cold snow with her fur coat wrapped around her as best as she could manage. Then she lay perfectly still.

★　★　★

Brad Pitock couldn't believe his luck as the drama played out in front of him. This was a journalist's dream, especially for one who had never managed to be in the right place at the right time in ten years of searching for the limelight of TV news. He had a reputation for covering "breaking news," but the inside joke in the newsroom was that for poor old Brad, it always turned out to be breaking non-news. The inside joke had gained momentum over the years, and Pitock was determined to reverse it.

At first, he thought his cameraman had been shot. But having confirmed Andy to be alive and well, Pitock helped him up off the ground and manically positioned him to set up the Sandy Steele shot. His senses now on full alert, he weighed his options for how best to make use of these extraordinary pictures of Sandy Steele and the story that connected her to a British spy.

By this time, onlookers had helped her up and done up her fur coat.

"Are we rolling?" he asked. It was more of an order than a question.

Pitock held the shotgun mic toward Sandy.

"Speed!" the cameraman confirmed.

Pitock pointed to the portable satellite equipment. "Everything good?"

Andy the cameraman nodded. "Waiting for the feed."

"Ms. Steele? Sandy? Are you all right?"

Sandy looked up. "I wasn't expecting—"

"False alarm," he assured her. "Crazy Russian guards weren't expecting your crazy stunt."

"I wasn't taking any chances. I only had one shot at this."

"Sandy, believe me, we are taking you seriously. The whole world was watching. Camera's rolling. A few more questions before the police arrest all of us?"

"Sure. Go ahead."

He delicately positioned Sandy two feet to her right so her back was toward St. Basil's Cathedral. *News is pictures.* His portable satellite phone buzzed. It was Jed Butler calling from the CNN bureau. Pitock begged him to keep the live feed open. "Yes, everything's fine. We have her. We're ready ..." He handed the satellite phone to his assistant. "Ms. Steele, what can you tell us about your husband's whereabouts? Are you aware of reports that he is a self-declared spy?"

Sandy buttoned her coat and stood tall. She felt empowered now that she had the attention of the international media. She dropped her white card on the ground, and the cameraman panned down to get a close up of the words. Andy panned up as she pulled up both sides of the fur collar around her neck and adjusted her long blonde hair from inside the coat so that it lay like embroidered gold on the rabbit fur.

"My husband works for the *London Daily Standard,* and I'm afraid for his life. I believe his current assignment is the reason

Western authorities want to harm him." She spoke off the cuff—but eloquent, strong, and resolute.

"And you think this is connected to your husband's confession on North Korean TV that he was involved in some kind of espionage?"

"I don't know. I know that's he's in trouble with the British, the Russians, and maybe others. But he's not a spy. I can promise you that."

"What's your reaction to his confession? Do you think it was genuine or made under duress?"

"I didn't see it. But I'm certain it wasn't genuine. I know my husband. I've known him for years. He's kind, loyal, and hard-working. I trust him with my life, and I'm certain he'd never betray his country or mine. He believes in reporting the truth, the power of the free press, and justice for everyone."

"But how can you be so sure he wasn't working for Western authorities? Journalists make great spies."

"He was being threatened … maybe blackmailed? I was abducted three days ago in London. I escaped. That's why I'm here. I have a lot of unanswered questions myself—"

"Brad!" The CNN AP handed Pitock the satellite phone in the middle of the interview. "It's important."

He listened intently for a few moments.

Pitock circled his hand for Andy to keep filming. "They're cutting back to the studio, but they want us to keep rolling." His eyes widened and his head jerked forward. "Jack Steele's on the line … from Vladivostok!"

Vladivostok, Russia

In Vladivostok, Steele was still reeling from the images of Sandy on the television.

Sandy's alive! Unharmed! Thank the Christ.

Still, he was surprised by the realization that images of his naked wife had been broadcast all over the world. He was filled with an unexpected sense of pride. That was a stunning performance. She did that for *him*?

Sergei handed him the landline.

Red Square, Moscow

"Ms. Danner. It's for you." Pitock handed Sandy the satellite phone. The crowd settled, sensing the importance of the phone call, wanting to hear every word even if they didn't understand English.

Sandy frowned. She was confused. *Now what?* She took the cell phone.

Jack said, "Sandy?"

"Jack?" Sandy took a step back. "I don't know whether to laugh or cry."

"I saw the whole thing. I saw you."

"Crazy, right? And you? Are you safe?"

"Yes, I'm safe. At least for now."

Onlookers continued to watch, some riveted to the spot.

"Thank you, my darling!"

"You're welcome." Her relief was unmistakable. Tears rolled down her cheek.

Seeing Sandy's joy, some in the crowd instinctively clapped.

The AP took the phone from Sandy and handed it to Pitock, who raised his brow, nodded to the cameraman, and launched into his piece-to-camera interview: "We've met Sandy Steele, but who exactly is her husband, Jack Steele? To find out, we are live to Vladivostok." He pressed his finger against his earpiece. "Mr. Steele? Sir, can you hear me?"

"Yes, I'm, here."

"First off, I'm glad we could get you together with your wife, Sandy Steele. She was worried about you. What was it like to speak to her?"

"Wonderful, thank you. I'm very grateful."

"Jack, we are looking at extraordinary pictures you sent us

of some kind of attack, apparently in North Korea. Can you explain what we are seeing?"

Steele took a deep breath. This was it, the moment he had waited for, wished for, prayed for, and risked his life for. "These images show a terror attack on the North Korean nuclear reactor in Yongbuk. I was there, and I witnessed the entire thing. A unit of Russian tanks carried out the attack."

"But you are telling us it was a *terror* attack?"

"The terrorist responsible was Russian. He forced me to witness his attack. That's the short version."

"You said, *was* Russian?"

"He was shot ten minutes ago."

"Did you see what happened?"

"Yes, he deserved what he got. It's a complicated story."

"But you're safe?"

"Yes, I am."

"Uh … right …" Pitock looked down at his six-inch monitor. "And now we are seeing footage of what looks like people praying? Lots of them. Thousands? Am I correct?"

"Yes. That's right."

"Who are they?"

"They are innocent people, imprisoned for their spiritual beliefs. The terrorist was going to slaughter these people."

"How many?"

"Several thousand."

"You say you know who is responsible?"

"Yes …" Steele paused. He took another deep breath.

Having yearned for this moment for years, Steele took a few moments to reflect. He thought about Sandy. He thought about Chen and weighed the consequences of sharing *everything* he knew, including the taped conversations with Anderson and Ryzhakov.

Silence.

"Mr. Steele, can you hear me?"

In a split second, Jack Steele changed his mind about the

direction of the interview and the information he was willing to share.

"A man called Igor Ryzhakov was responsible," he continued. "He was chief of the Vladivostok police."

Steele decided God would forgive him for not telling the whole truth and nothing but the truth. Western governments, the Russians, and North Koreans would deny any involvement. He would never be able to work as an international journalist in any meaningful way ever again. Much more importantly, he concluded, the Tumen region—Russians, North Koreans, and Chinese—would never get their economic aid package. Natasha's dream of a rejuvenated Tumen region would be dead along with her. If anything, he should do this for her.

His knowledge of Operation Tumen, together with the audiotape evidence he had deliberately *not* downloaded to CNN, was his passport out of Russia and to safety. In some ways, his knowledge might achieve more left on the back burner than if he revealed it to the world here and now.

"The UN has developed a plan called the Greater Tumen Initiative, or GTI—to inject millions of dollars into the region … This is an economic rejuvenation plan. The plan will benefit the tri-state region known as the Tumen Triangle—Russia, North Korea, and China. It will bring hope and potentially prosperity to the millions of people living in unacceptable poverty. But through blackmail and subterfuge, Igor Ryzhakov was trying to sabotage the initiative."

"Mr. Steele," said Pitock, looking at Sandy, "Are you spying for British authorities?"

"No, I am not a spy."

"But you're a British journalist. Why didn't you run this story with your own newspaper?"

"Fair question. Honest answer. CNN's quicker, it's that simple. Sorry, London."

"Can you tell us more?"

"The world needs to know what I know sooner rather than later."

"You don't trust the *London Daily Standard?*"

"I didn't say that. When the attacks occurred, there was a lot of confusion and panic. There was probably danger of all-out hostilities breaking out on the Korean Peninsula."

"What was your reaction when you saw your wife naked on Red Square?"

Steele smiled. "Probably the same as yours—she must be bloody freezing, but I'm glad she's wearing a fur hat."

"Did you know she was going to do this?"

"The last time I spoke to my wife, she was in trouble. Now she's safe, and that's what counts. I'm relieved and ecstatic she's OK." Steele paused. "Sandy, I love you, my darling.

★   ★   ★

One mile away on the first floor of the British Embassy, Pendlebury loosened the red paisley silk tie—standard British diplomat issue—that had remained tightly knotted far too long. "Clever bastard. Astonishing!" His cheeks were flushed. "Is there anything we can do?"

"It's too late," replied Anderson. "Glenlivit?" He cursed himself and the entire world.

"What about a media blackout? At least in the UK?"

"It won't buy us much time. More trouble than it's worth. Too suspicious."

Pendlebury shook his head and said, "These images will crucify us if, or rather when, he links them to us—end of fair play Britain. It'll completely screw up our foreign policy goals for a decade. The British public will never forgive us. It's over."

Pendlebury walked to the window. He looked out and watched a small tourist boat taking an evening cruise down the Moskva River. The passengers sat peacefully, looking at the floodlit Kremlin scenery. For the first time in his career,

Pendlebury liked the thought of early retirement. For the first time in his career, he thought he might have to resign. He had given Anderson *carte blanche* to liaise with the North Koreans. The plan had backfired. He could only blame himself. He had completely lost control.

Anderson remained seated. "Steele can't connect the dots. He knows what happened. But he can't prove it."

"Or he doesn't want to … yet. He's not stupid. He's going to wait for the right moment. How do you know your calls weren't taped?"

Anderson shrugged. "We could have him arrested? No point in killing him now. He's bound to have set a trap if anything untoward happens to him. He'll tell his wife everything as soon as they meet, not to mention Danner. God knows who else already knows."

Pendlebury said, "Every news organization in the world will be on us if we so much as sneeze on him."

"There's only one option as we already know. And I suspect Steele knows it too."

"Aid package?"

"GTI." He shook his head in awe. "Clever bastard!"

"Time for diplomacy. I'll call New York."

CHAPTER THIRTY

Vladivostok, Russia

Steele could hardly contain himself. He was dying to see Sandy again. She had proved beyond any doubt that she wanted to see him too, but he would have to tie up loose ends with the world's media from Vladivostok first, then Moscow and London. And with Sergei's help, he would have more control and privacy at VTV than in Moscow. Sergei had promised to keep the media hounds at bay for as long as possible—at least filter them as best he could with his more-than-passable English.

Natasha's funeral was tomorrow. That would be tough for him as he and Natasha had become close. More than close. He would of course attend and do his best to comfort the boy. *Bova needs me.*

Hotel Rossiya, Moscow

Sandy Steele and Blake Danner sat in the lobby of the Hotel Rossiya. International business people and tourists oblivious to the events on Red Square checked in and out while Sandy and her father found a quiet corner to take stock. They drank at least two cups of espresso each as they discussed the past twenty-four hours. At first, she feared she would be recognized—*in retrospect, the entire episode was embarrassing.* But with her clothes on, no one seemed to recognize her or even glance in their direction. Sandy drew no more extra attention than usual.

She had no appetite. Too many questions she wanted to ask her father. She summoned a waiter, who took another order for coffee.

"And some *blini*," added Danner.

Not sure where to begin, she pulled her legs up to her chest and leaned back in the deep leather arm chair. "Thanks for the diversion, Dad."

"I didn't want to leave you. Divide and conquer. I knew it was your best option."

"It worked."

"You did great. But the shock value? Works every time."

"True. How did you know that Jack was in serious danger?"

Danner said, "The whole situation was out of control."

"That obnoxious little bastard, Anderson ..."

"You were right about him," continued Danner. "He's not just an asshole, he's a dangerous and vindictive asshole. Plus, their whole schtick didn't add up."

"I thought he was telling the truth at first."

"That accent can fool anyone."

She nodded. "Yeah."

"I'm so sorry, honey. I'm sorry you had to go through that."

"It's OK. It's over, I think. I hope they'll leave us alone now. At least you know Anna wasn't involved in my abduction."

"I know I said she was crazy, but kidnapping seemed way off the charts."

"Do you still love her?"

"In my own way." Danner avoided making eye contact.

"There you go again, Dad. I hate that excuse."

Danner smiled and held up his hands. "Won't happen again."

Sandy nursed her cup of coffee. "Why don't you like Jack?"

"Sweetheart, that was before I finally understood how much you really love him. It doesn't matter now what I thought. I'll get to know him better. Jack's quite a guy."

"What about me?" She gave him a nudge.

"He's lucky to have you!"

"I agree."

They laughed.

Danner sighed, searching for the right words. "You know, it's nothing to do with you or Jack. It's about me. You see, I understand now, that I never loved anyone. Apart from you, that is."

"You're crazy."

"I'm serious. At my age, it's not the kind of thing you wanna admit—especially to your daughter."

"What do you mean?"

"It's easier to love your child than your partner. With all that you've been through to help him ..." He smiled. "That's true love."

She punched him playfully in the chest. "I still think you can find love."

He shrugged. "I don't know."

"I'll prove you wrong once and for all. Leave it with me."

The waiter set down the steaming plate of *blinis*. As they both began to eat, Sandy realized she was starving.

Vladivostok, Russia

Jack Steele had broken a blockbuster news story on CNN with unprecedented, never-before-seen video. He was relishing the fact that the world's media wanted to talk to *him*. All of them. Under Sergei's enthusiastic, efficient, and technical orchestration, Steele spent the next twenty-four hours at VTV giving interviews to international print and radio news organizations as well as television outlets if satellite time was available. *My journalistic baptism by fire.*

He spoke about his wife's abduction in London, being blackmailed into witnessing clandestine terrorist operations in North Korea, his humanitarian efforts that saved several thousand lives, and being miraculously healed by a mysterious North Korean enigma. He talked about the attempted massacre in

Yongbuk and possible motives without giving away everything he knew. He coveted the information and therefore leverage that would ensure GTI became a reality.

Natasha was watching from above, and Peter, too. He would make them both proud. Chen was now safe. Thank God he and Sandy were both miraculously alive and in one piece.

Steele had Sergei made copies of the secret audiotapes. He also sent audio files as attachments to a variety of trusted contacts. He included, of course, detailed instructions about their contents and what to do with them if anything happened to him.

VTV studio A, scene of carnage the day before, became Steele's global operations center. Steele drained his glass of vodka as Serge entered with a fresh tray of food and snacks. "You did an amazing job with all this, Serge. Thank you."

"You are welcome, Jeck."

"There's only one thing, Serge. When are you going to learn how to pronounce my name? It's *Jack.*"

"I know this, Jeck. *Jeck?*"

"Nevermind. Forget I said anything." He smiled.

"It's OK, Jeck."

"Hey, now everyone knows VTV. Isn't that great?" Steele threw a high-five, a tradition Sandy had insisted he adopt on appropriate occasions. *Now was one.*

Sergei set down the tray. In the middle of it was a smooth, frosted bottle of vodka and a fresh pot of coffee. "Reinforcements," he announced.

"Tools of the trade, comrade ..."

Sergei suddenly looked serious. "Will my country agree to GTI? It would mean a lot for our future."

Steele twisted the vodka open. "Russia is under pressure to allow UN inspectors access to the entire Tumen region. Pyongyang and Beijing have already agreed. It's looking good."

"How do you know this already?"

"I've been chatting with a new friend of mine—a British

diplomat in Moscow. He's very keen to do anything he can to facilitate the initiative."

"Why you are not telling everything in interviews? Who is really responsible ..."

"Wouldn't achieve as much as you think, Serge. Denials all round, bursts of outrage here and there, perhaps a public inquiry or two in UK and the USA. But GTI would die. Your economic future would be back in the dark ages."

"We are not so behind as you think."

"I know that ... of course not. But now at least you'll be in the race."

"When will you release the audiotape? You said this was your proof?"

"Did I say that?" Steele smiled. "I don't recall ..."

Steele poured two shots of vodka. They clinked glasses, looking each other in the eye as they toasted VTV's future.

"So you think we will get economic aid?" asked Sergei.

"I know you will," Steele replied. "I spoke to the British embassy this morning. My 'friend' and I have an understanding. My British council diplomat is remarkably forthcoming."

"He was the man on the tape?"

"Not your concern, my friend. Doesn't matter now anyway."

"So North Koreans are not so bad?"

"I wouldn't go that far. My hunch is that this was exactly what DPRK planned all along. Can't prove it. If I'm right, they played the West like a Stradivarius ... Our buddy, Kim, is a master statesman. Our boys might learn from his playbook."

"Why did they want to kill the prisoners?"

"Who knows? Spiritual dissenters ... Spirituality complicates things in a country full of heathens."

"But they lost their nuclear reactor?"

"Precisely. One less obstacle to international negotiations."

"They don't need nuclear power if they have UN resources?"

"Something like that. Let's face it, they lost *one* nuclear reactor. Who knows what else they have hidden in the most secretive country in the world." Steele shook his head. "God bless the Dear Leader."

The telephone rang for the thousandth time. Sergei signaled for Steele to answer.

Steele picked up ready for another interview. "Hello, VTV, this is Jack Steele."

"Jack, it's Sandy."

"Hello, my darling! Thank God you're OK!"

★   ★   ★

Having slept for twelve hours in Viktor's flat after a long conversation with Sandy, Steele got up, showered, and did his best to look presentable for the funeral. He borrowed one of Viktor's ties. He felt an even greater sense of loss that Natasha was dead than the day before now that events had sunk in. He reflected on the fact that he had been falling for her. *My secret. No need for anyone to ever know.* But Viktor was also close to Natasha. Perhaps he had suspected something as well? Apart from Viktor, no other living soul needed to know.

The line of funeral cars pulled up along the section of the Amurskiy Zaliv inlet near the Vladivostok Fortress Museum. Viktor knew that this was Natasha's favorite spot to go walking and fishing with Bova in Vladivostok. She had left instructions that in the event of her death she was to be cremated with her ashes to be scattered across the water.

Steele, Viktor, Bova, and a handful of friends and distant relatives of Natasha got out of the cars and made their way down to the frozen inlet. An icy wind ripped across the frozen tundra as the mourners stood in silence for the short, informal ceremony.

Viktor said a prayer. Bova gently shook the nondescript black urn to allow his mother's remains to fly away across the snow and ice.

Steele's lips tightened and he placed a hand on Bova's shoulder. "It's OK, Bova," he whispered. "Everything's going to be alright. I promise." *I shouldn't make promises I can't keep.*

Afterward, the funeral party arrived at Viktor's apartment—the Vladivostok safe house. Sergei welcomed the guests, who were all relieved to get out of the cold. They soon warmed up with vodka, *Samogon*—Russian moonshine—and *zakuski*. Hors d'oeuvres.

Viktor sank into the sofa making himself comfortable. Steele and Bova sat down beside him.

"You prefer Russian Samogon or vodka?" asked Bova in English.

"Which do you recommend?"

Bova frowned as if he'd done something wrong. Viktor chuckled.

Steele said, "I'm pulling your leg."

"My leg?"

"Shutka!" replied Steele. *Joke!*

A grin crept across Bova's face that reminded Steele of Natasha.

Steele threw back a shot of vodka with Viktor, and they demolished a salmon cracker *zakuski* each. Steele smacked his lips and exhaled fire from the gulp of freezing Samogon brew. "Bova, your mother was a remarkable woman. You know that? I'm really sorry."

"I know." Bova scrunched his face, trying not to cry in front of the adults. He wiped his eyes with the back of his sleeve. "Why do they say my mother is a hero? How is she a hero if she is dead?"

"She loved her country. And she loved you. That's why she's a hero."

"I know this."

"Don't worry, we'll work it out. People are excited about the future of your town. It's going to change for the better."

"How?"

"Money, Bova. This is a very rich area. Rich in natural resources."

"I understand. Our teachers say this at school. They say we must work with North Korea and China."

"Exactly. If you work together, your future will be richer."

"What about me? What will happen to me now?" Bova frowned.

"Viktor has agreed to take care of you. Until ..." Steele paused. He thought about Sandy, about Natasha, about England and Chen. He suddenly knew how he would honor Natasha.

"Until what?" asked Bova.

Steele looked into the boy's dark brown eyes. He saw a bright, alert, and intelligent young man. "Do you like the idea of visiting me and my wife in England?"

Bova smiled for the first time since his mother was murdered. "With you?"

"I need to speak to my wife. I'm sure she wouldn't mind."

Bova waited, eyes widening. "I can teach her."

"You'll teach her Russian?"

"Bez problema! Yolki-palki!" *No problem! Fur trees 'n sticks!*

Steele laughed. His favorite Russian saying—Bova's too, apparently.

"Excuse me, Jack ... Do you have children?"

"Not yet." Steele ruffled the boy's hair. But my wife is pregnant. Ssshhh, it's a secret."

Apart from shedding her clothes on Red Square, Sandy had dropped another bombshell during their last conversation. She had apologized for the stories, doubts, and lies, and revealed that she had not had a miscarriage after all. Sandy Steele was in fact pregnant.

"What work will you do? This job has finished now. Money?" Bova asked.

"You sound like my father-in-law."

Bova did not quite grasp Steele's thought. He said, "You need lots of money to live in the West."

"I know that, Bova. It's a good question, but you don't have to worry about that. There will always be news stories that need to be told. This was just one of them." Steele poked Bova gently in the ribs. "Yasna, tibyeh?" *Okay?*

"Yasna!" Bova agreed. "Jack, you know what?"

"What?"

"I have surprise for you." He nodded to Viktor as if something was planned.

Steele looked nonplussed. "For me?"

"Follow me. Davai, Jeck." *Come on, Jack.*

Steele got up and followed Bova past some guests raising a toast in Natasha's memory. They walked down the corridor past the Guns N' Roses poster to the bedroom where Steele had slept the night before the convoy. He remembered there was an international telephone in the bedroom and wanted to call Sandy again. "Wait a second, Bova," he said, picking up the receiver.

Bova looked out the window and knocked on the glass. He turned toward Steele and beckoned. "Want to see something? Come on!" Bova waved his arm excitedly. "Davai, Jeck!"

Steele wondered if there were more snow angels to see in the street. He replaced the receiver. "Coming."

He reached the window and looked down at the dustbins. A much bigger snow angel stood next to them this time. She had blonde hair and was dressed in a fur coat and *shapka*, and was gazing up at the window.

"How?!" said Steele surprised.

Sandy waved and smiled. With airplane arms, she allowed herself to fall back into the pile of snow, her hat falling over her face as she landed. She laughed.

Steele and Bova laughed too. "Yes!" Steele waved at Sandy through the window and pointed at Bova with another smile. He picked up Bova and gave him a hug.

ACKNOWLEDGMENTS

Karen Ross for keeping me going during the first few drafts and beyond! Christopher Dawson for his love and kindness. Margaret Bramford for showing me how it's done. Beverly Swerling for mentoring, patience, and believing. Frank Freudberg for fun, frivolity, and facts. Sophie Jenkins for inspiration. Marvlus Mav (thanks, Dad!) for always picking up the phone. Candace Johnson, the most fun, thorough, and talented editor an author could wish for!

ABOUT THE AUTHOR

Richard Lyntton was born (Richard Bramford) in Highgate, London. He is of English descent. He attended William Ellis School, Exeter University, Moscow State Linguistic University (formerly Maurice Thorez Moscow State Pedagogical Institute of Foreign Languages), and Sandhurst. Richard served as a Captain and tank commander in the British Army in the first Gulf War; European Community Task Force Humanitarian Liaison in Russia; UNHCR Liaison Officer, and United Nations Military Observer (during heavy shelling and NATO airstrikes) in Sarajevo, Bosnia; and was a United Nations Television producer in former Yugoslavia. He was called to testify at the International War Crimes Tribunal in the Hague after witnessing and filming human rights atrocities and abuses in Bosnia. His films are archived at the Imperial War Museum, London.

When he's not writing, Richard is a professional actor. He lives in Philadelphia with his wife, interior designer Michelle Wenitsky, and their two sons.

Thank you for reading

NORTH KOREA DECEPTION

The audio book is also available:

**https://www.audible.com/pd/
North-Korea-Deception-Audiobook/B08WDWVFZQ**

✪ ✪ ✪

Get your FREE chapters of

HYDE PARK DECEPTION

BOOK 2 IN THE DECEPTION SERIES

Available NOW! CLICK on this BookFunnel link:

https://dl.bookfunnel.com/jjhh5hgelt

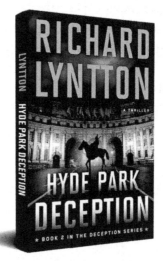

Visit http://richardlynttonbooks.com

Made in the USA
Las Vegas, NV
02 May 2022